THE OTHER

Shari Low

About *The Other Wives Club*

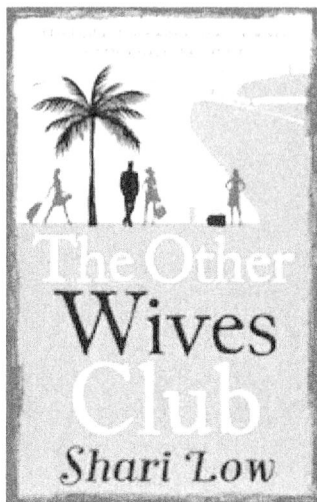

Three women thrown together on a surprise Mediterranean cruise to celebrate a milestone birthday of the man they all once loved. What could possibly go wrong?

Tess Gold – the current wife
When Tess married Drew Gold, she knew his two ex-wives were still in his life. Now Drew has planned a luxury cruise to celebrate his birthday… and the former Mrs Golds are all coming too.

Mona Gold – the second wife
When it comes to style, fashion editor, Mona, never puts a Louboutin wrong. Now it's time to reclaim the only man she ever really loved… if she can tempt Drew away from his new wife for a second time.

Sarah Gold – the first wife, the original

When Drew left her for Mona, Sarah's emotions went into hibernation. Now she's decided to shave those legs and start living again…

To John, Callan & Brad

Everything. Always.

The Marriages of Drew Gold

```
                                                               ┌──────── Lavinia
                                             ┌──── John ──── Penny ──┤
                                             │     b 1984             └──────── Lawrence
                      ┌──── Sarah ───────────┤
                      │ m. 1982   b 1962     │
                      │                      └──── Eliza
                      │                            b 1994
                      │
                      │                                      (stepson)
 Drew Gold ───────────┤      Mona ────── Piers Delaney ────── Max Delaney
  b 1961              │ m. 1999   b 1974   m. 2005              b 1976
                      │ div. 2004
                      │
                      │
                      └──── Tess
                        m. 2006   b 1983
```

1.

All Booked Up

Tess Gold

Tess put her coffee cup down with a sigh. 'Mum, I have to go – an email has just popped into my inbox that I have to reply to.'

'OK, lovely, I'll call you tomorrow or the next day. And if I can find a hotspot I'll scoop you.'

'Skype, Mum. It's Skype.'

'That's what I meant. Stupid name. Anyway, hasta la vista baby, as they say here.'

Tess smiled. 'They don't say that anywhere, Mum.'

'Well, your dad does. Every time I leave the van. He thinks he's hilarious.'

Tess suddenly pictured her mother's slightly sunburned nose wrinkling with affection as she said that and felt a distinct tug on her heartstrings. Retirement had been an adventure for Evelyn and Alan Campbell. A former nurse and policeman, they'd quit at fifty-five, jetted off to Brazil and were currently travelling around the nations of South America in a camper van. Tess tried not to think about it. It went against the natural order of things. Her parents should be fretting over their twenty-eight-year-old daughter having wild adventures, not the other way around. The only thing that was likely to catapult her into mortal peril in Anderson & McWilliam Marketing were the rock cakes that Beryl the cleaner insisted on inflicting on them every Friday.

'Bye, Mum. And give Dad a hug from me. Miss you.'

'We miss you too, sweetheart. Love to Drew.'

As Tess put the phone down and reread the email, she was overcome with an urge to head straight to Glasgow airport and catch the first flight out to join her parents.

It was sure to be more enjoyable the current plan. Ten days on a cruise with her husband, celebrating his fiftieth birthday. So far, so fabulous. Add in two adult children by one of his previous marriages. Could potentially be a little uncomfortable, but still bearable. Add one ex-wife, and the dread factor started to rise. Add in another ex-wife, her husband and step-kid and the shivers ran all the way to her toes.

Suddenly, taking on gangs of brutal drugs smugglers in the hills above Bogota seemed like the preferable option.

"Civilized" Drew called it. Modern. Functional. "We're all grown-ups," was his favourite saying, as he surveyed his multi-generational extended family at birthdays, Christmases and assorted special occasions. He was proud of the fact that he still worked with Mona, ex-wife number two, and took Sarah, ex-wife number one, out for lunch on the anniversary of their divorce every year.

Tess would be lying if she denied that it had taken a while to get used to. But then, she'd known what she was in for. Marrying Drew Gold, a newspaper editor, a man almost twenty-two years her senior, was always going to come with a set of unique baggage.

And now it had come to this.

For his fiftieth birthday, she'd envisaged a romantic week in Venice. Or perhaps a gorgeous, intimate weekend in Rome. But no, Drew had ambushed her – yes, ambushed was the right word – with a two-week Mediterranean cruise with both his previous families, and no matter how much she tried to persuade herself that she should be grateful she was going on such a luxurious break, she was still anticipating the trip with all the excitement of, say, ten days with chickenpox scabs.

'You're thinking about it again, aren't you?' Cameron put a fresh coffee in front of her and sat down on the corner of her desk, squashing the artwork for the Doggie Doo Bags campaign. She'd slaved over a concept for the print ads, but the truth was that if she just put Cameron in a shot, surrounded him with cute puppies and wrote the name of the product along the bottom, every female in the country would be lining up to buy them whether they had a pet pooch or not.

If genetic scientists found a way to combine the DNA of Orlando Bloom and Channing Tatum, the prototype would look something like Cameron. Razor-sharp cheekbones, a thoroughly masculine jawline and dark eyes so intense that only the fact that he was always laughing kept him from looking like a brooding yet undeniably attractive serial killer.

'I am,' she admitted. 'It'll be fine though. Great. Sun, sea, and apparently the ship is gorgeous. I know I'm really lucky to be going.' There was a tone of conviction that didn't necessarily reflect how she was feeling.

'Wow, that's amazing.' Cameron whistled. 'You managed to say all that while chewing your bottom lip.'

'Oh no, was I doing it again?' She delved into her drawer for Vaseline and smeared it on. 'I swear to God, every nerve-wracking event I've ever been to started with me showing up with lips that look like they've spent ten minutes in a blender. At my wedding my gob rivalled Angelina Jolie's. And not in a good way.'

Right on cue Cameron laughed. Again. This level of jolly positivity was not normal in humanity. He was a little slice of levity, sent down by the gods to make the office a happier place. Or perhaps he was just secretly drinking from a bottle of something strong under his desk. If it was the latter, she could be doing with a quick slug herself right about now.

Of course, she could put her foot down and flatly refuse to go along with the group excursion idea, but how petulant would that look? It was Drew's birthday, the big five-oh, and he wanted all his family around him. Wasn't his attitude to his responsibilities one of the things that had attracted her to him in the first place?

For the sake of cheering herself up, she mentally went along with this notion and disregarded the truth – what had actually attracted her to him in the first place was that he was the most charismatic man she had ever encountered, so sure of himself and sharp and witty. Five years ago, he'd been a guest lecturer in her final year at college and he'd given a talk on the future of the newspaper industry. Despite his candid revelation that it was a declining media sector, being superseded by the Internet and twenty-four-hour news channels, by the time he'd stepped off the stage that day there were two hundred students contemplating changing their course from marketing to journalism. It wasn't the brown hair with the grey flecks that gave him an air of rugged handsomeness. Or the gym-built wide shoulders, or the crinkly green eyes that shot mischief across the room. Drew Gold had a presence. A confidence. And a memory for faces that swept her off her feet when they bumped into each other at a charity event a couple of years later. He'd overlooked her waitress outfit and spoke to her like she was the only woman in the room. Later she'd discover that was a talent he'd cultivated through years of doorstep interviews, networking, and later, mingling with the good and the great while keeping a newsroom of jaded, disgruntled hacks on his side. After chatting to him for half an hour that night she knew he was special. The age difference didn't matter. Nor did the job that was paying a fiver an hour that she needed to supplement the internship she had just landed at one of Glasgow's swankiest marketing companies. He asked her to leave with him and she dropped her tray at the door an hour before her shift officially ended. They spent the next eight hours in an all-night coffee shop and married six weeks later.

The extended family was a slightly unwanted gift that came with the ceremony. Didn't every bride get a bread maker, a set of salad tongs, two ex-wives and an instant family?

'So what are you going to do?' Cameron asked, taking a large bite out of an apple Danish he'd liberated from a brown paper bag.

Tess gently prised a portrait of a spaniel from under his right buttock as she contemplated the question. Sometimes she wondered what it would be like to have a normal relationship. Girl meets boy without two ex-wives. They court. Get engaged. Get married. Have children. *Ouch, sore subject.*

Well-practised in the art of the swift rebound, she grinned and injected some much-needed frivolity into the situation. 'I don't know. What would your six-foot Amazonian, very smart lawyer girlfriend do in my shoes? Apart from moan about the fact that the shoes were too small, obviously.'

'She dumped me.'

Cameron made a 'What can you do?' gesture.

'No!'

'Sadly, yes. Said I wasn't focussed enough. She needed someone to "get on board" and "stay on message" and "develop a strategy for moving forward".'

'Tell me you'd have finished with her anyway for overuse of psychobabble lingo.'

4

'I would.' Pause. 'Who am I kidding; I'd never have finished it. She was the most gorgeous thing I'd ever seen and I'm both male and incredibly shallow.'

She snatched the Danish from his hand and gulped the last bite, not caring that this sent a confetti of pastry flakes across her suit, his jeans and a cartoon spaniel.

'You are officially pathetic.'

He feigned outrage at her faux-disgust. 'Hey, I'm not the one going on holiday with her husband's entire Christmas card list.'

'True. We're both pathetic. Want to go drown our sorrows over our clear lack of personal integrity and backbone? Drew's working late and we're not meeting until nine thirty for dinner. You can help me plot ways to delay the others so the ship sails without them.'

'Sure, I'll…'

A loud jangle cut him off and Tess instinctively dug her hand into her handbag and, without even looking, managed to immediately retrieve her iPhone.

'How do you do that? I need a satnav to find anything in a woman's bag.'

'It's a talent.' She cut him off as she checked the screen. *Drew Gold.*

Deep breath. Smile. 'Hey, honey.' He'd never have known she had a care in the world.

'Yep, I just got it. Sounds great. Of course I'm looking forward to it – it'll be good to see everyone again. What's happened? Oh, lord, that's incredible. Of course I understand. No, it's fine – I'm going to go for a drink with a crowd of guys from the office anyway.'

In front of her, Cameron glanced around searchingly, obviously mocking her exaggeration in using the term 'crowd'. She picked up the Danish paper bag and hit him with it.

'OK, honey, won't wait up then. Hope it's not too tedious. Love you.'

As she put the phone down, there was no stopping the sigh. Sometimes she felt she didn't have much say in what went on in their lives. Another Friday night dinner cancelled, this time because of some political crisis that was brewing. Apparently there was a rumour that the French Prime Minister was having an affair with a married supermodel twenty years younger and twelve inches taller, and the world's media was holding the presses for confirmation.

Cameron stood up and brushed the food flakes off his jeans. 'Me and the rest of the "crowd" want to know what's so "incredible".'

'Oh. You'll have to swear not to tell anyone …'

'Promise on my Amazonian ex-girlfriend's life. Don't like her any more anyway.'

'Reports that the French prime minister was caught shagging that model, Elan, in a changing room at Chanel. Drew won't make dinner.'

Cameron reached over and pulled his jacket off the back of his chair. 'Then you're just going to have to put up with me. I'm hereby volunteering once again to be your husband's stunt double.'

It was a long-running joke. How many times had Drew cancelled at the last minute? Or had to leave before their main course was served at dinner? Cameron came to her rescue so often she spent more time with him than she did with her husband.

But there was no point complaining about any of it. She loved Drew Gold and that meant accepting the limitations and constraints that came with being married to him. And the football-team-sized extended family, too. It was worth it, no contest. She never doubted it for a minute. Never.

'And Tess…'

A dash of red lippy gave her a brightness that didn't come from the inside. 'What?'

'If I'm being Drew's stand-in – do I get to sleep with you? Just want to know whether to bring my emergency toothbrush.'

'You know the power of the press can destroy careers, and render, say, a successful marketing guy homeless and penniless, trash his life and leave him on the streets, a gnarled-out junkie fighting every night to survive?'

Cameron nodded thoughtfully. 'I'll just leave the toothbrush in my desk.'

Mona Gold

'There. Right there. Oh, lord, that's it. Yes, baby. Yes...'

Adrian's hand clamped down firmly on Mona's mouth and she rewarded him by biting his ring finger. Hard. It was a testimony to the hours of self-inflicted pain during his daily martial arts session that he barely flinched. If he were a torture victim in a *Bond* movie he'd last for hours before divulging MI6 secrets. 'Ssssh, baby, these walls are paper thin,' he whispered.

Mona wasn't listening. Wave upon wave of gorgeous bliss was flooding from her Revlon Red toes to the tips of her twenty-two inch long copper hair extensions. The low, sexy growl she emitted as she came sent him from noise concern to deep, thrusting climax.

As soon as he was still, Mona pushed back off his rapidly receding cock, unstraddled him and strutted across the office, tantalizingly aware that her back view looked great in just her Louboutin heels and a layer of chestnut St. Tropez. And so it should. She'd worked for that view – one hour of Pilates every morning, three weight-training sessions every week, and at least an hour of cardio at lunch. And the bonus of this energetic session with Adrian was that it burned off the same amount of calories as half an hour on the treadmill. She might even let him do it again and then she could skip sixty minutes in the basement gym later.

The display on her Longines platinum dial told her differently. No time for a replay. Shit, she was late. She couldn't even indulge in her beloved post-coital menthol cigarette. Somehow it made it even more exciting that her nicotine fix was banned by both her personal trainer and the building's health and safety department. And she was pretty sure at least three of the acts she'd performed in the last half hour would have health and safety fanning their clipboards in horror.

'I have to love you and leave you,' she said nonchalantly, as she clipped the front-fastening of her bra, then pulled on her white silk blouse. Together with the forties-style calf-length pencil skirt, it was her standard workwear. She had no time for the jeans and the grunge of some of the young reporters these days. In her early days as a journo out on the street, chasing a story to prevent her editor firing her before that day's deadline, she'd quickly realized that if she dressed for success there was more chance of finding it. The exhausted A&E doctor, the young junior lawyer in a prestigious firm and the cop with the loose tongue always responded better to a mini-skirt and matching jacket, complete with wild hair and luscious red lips. Well, it had been the nineties.

Now, two decades later, she was fashion editor of a national tabloid and style just came naturally to her. It was what had attracted her husbands – the first one and the second one. It was what made her the envy of all those overbearing ladies' charity lunches. It was what kept her in a job despite a closet full of heirs apparent snapping at the heels of her Gucci mules.

And it was what allowed her the regular indulgence of sex on her office sofa with a finely toned specimen who wouldn't be out of place on the pages of *GQ*. Outside that office, over a hundred newspaper employees sat eating quarter-pounders and chicken pesto wraps out of cheap plastic wrappings while inside she indulged in something far more appetizing. She was sure some of them guessed what was going on, but she really didn't give a damn.

Adrian reached over and pulled his Armani boxer shorts off the back of the sofa, then placed them across his crotch.

'Bit late for modesty,' she teased, as she clipped on her huge pearl earrings. She hated that pearls were back in this season. For her they were never out, but now the Saturday night streets were teeming with chunky girls in ridiculously skimpy tart dresses, dripping with strands of pearls they bought for three quid each out of an accessory shop wedged between a dry cleaners and a kebab shop on the high street. It devalued the look, but she still wasn't prepared to let it go. Forties-style fashion was her trademark and she wasn't ready to change it, even if the jewellery had been hijacked by a squad of hen-night slappers with streaky fake tan.

Adrian's broom-length eyelashes swept up as he levelled his gaze at her and let out a playful groan. 'Man, that was amazing. We should do this more often.'

Mona's senses tingled. Why was it always the best-looking ones that were the most needy? You'd have thought that the very fact they could get any girl they wanted would make them cool and cavalier, but she'd found the opposite to be true; Adrian being a case in point. It was no secret that he'd slept with half of the female fashion scene in Glasgow, yet he'd been giving her those puppy-dog eyes for months. Photo shoot after photo shoot, she poured him into everything from country casual tweed to rock-star leather, teamed him up with everyone from pop stars, to gorgeous models, to a large basset hound called Bert, and still he'd watched her every move. She'd sensed it. Ignored it. Enjoyed it. But had done nothing about it until today, when he'd appeared for a meeting in a tight white T-shirt, jeans and boots. It was the boots that had sealed the deal. Sometimes a bit of a rough edge was just what a woman needed after a morning spent with the finance people picking over every detail of her department's budget. Bloody parasites. This paper wouldn't have a fashion section if it wasn't for her. Didn't they know she was already working miracles with the pittance they gave her?

'So, listen…' Adrian said, as he pulled his boxers back on and then stood up to retrieve his jeans from the top of her mini-fridge. 'How about dinner tonight? Or maybe this weekend?'

A little piece of Mona died inside. This wasn't how it worked. A lunchtime quickie was not the preamble to a long and lasting relationship. Sometimes she longed for the era when a guy spent all of the first date trying to get into your knickers and then disappeared when he succeeded because his inbred double standards now classed you as cheap. Ah, the good old days.

This little dalliance, enjoyable as it was, wasn't something she was going to pursue. Adrian: male model. Twenty-three. Mona: fashion editor. Thirty-seven. Afternoon quickie: yes. Relationship: no.

There were many things she aspired to being, but a cougar wasn't one of them.

Fully dressed now, she sat on the clear Perspex chair behind her high-gloss black desk and clasped her hands in front of her like a stern headmistress about to give out detention. Her fingers were itching to get to her keyboard and check the events of the last hour. If the rumour about Elan was true, it would move her fashion input and byline to the front pages. Playtime over. The ability to compartmentalize her life was one of her biggest strengths and today's sex compartment had just slammed shut. Time to get back to work.

'Adrian, this was great.' Always start by pointing out the positives. 'But I'm afraid…' Her attention was caught by a flickering icon on her screen and she momentarily turned away from the sight of him buttoning up his Levi's.

A couple of clicks later, her interest piqued by the latest email in her inbox, she returned her focus to him and took up where she'd left off. 'Look, I'm really sorry, but I'm afraid I'll have to hurry you. Something's just come up and I have to sort it out.'

'Problem? Can I help?'

It was a sweet offer but somehow she didn't think that the fine art of diplomacy and tough problem-solving would be his strong point. However, if she ever had an issue that could be solved by an expert making a three-point turn at the end of a catwalk, he'd be the first person she'd call.

She sighed, her whole focus now back on the screen in front of her.

'Nope…' she said, more to herself than him. 'Not unless you want to help me figure out a way to break it to my current husband that we're going on holiday with my last one.'

Sarah Gold

Sarah ran her finger around the edge of the mixing bowl then rewarded herself for a morning of hard endeavour with a large dollop of sponge mix. The dog would be taken round the park twice today in the vain hope of burning the calories that had just settled on her hips.

Who was she kidding?

The dog would get the usual half-hour walk and then good intentions would be cast aside in favour of a quick coffee at Tickle Your Fancy in the village high street. Several members of the community council still turned a shade of outraged puce every time they passed the cafe with the titillating moniker. Sarah loved that Susie and Jo, the lovely owners, didn't give a flying fig roll about the disapproval.

Turning the CD player up, she started to sing along without even realizing it. Tim McGraw was singing about what happened to a guy who found out he didn't have long to live. Something about love deeper, give forgiveness to enemies and ride a bull called Fu Manchu. It was the kind of cheery stuff that got her through the day. Her affection for country music – whether the sad "I've just been dumped" or the upbeat "yeehah" stuff that made her shake her pants in the privacy of her kitchen - invoked much hilarity among her family and friends, but she remained defiant. If Dolly Parton was wrong, Sarah didn't want to be right.

She popped two perfectly symmetrical, round baking tins in the oven, then checked the temperature again. Twenty-five minutes, two hundred degrees. She'd have to pop out later to get the cherries that were essential to the design, before starting on the intricate carving and icing that would be necessary for the finished product – a cake in the style of a 34DD bra, complete with voluptuous pert breasts and indelicately prominent nipples. It had been ordered by the friends of a recently divorced woman, about to turn fifty, who had just flown to

Poland for a spectacularly successful breast uplift to mark the start of her new single life. It was always a relief when the cake mimicked the new boobs rather than the old – required less icing.

It only took a few minutes for the kitchen to be infused with the intoxicating aroma of baking. It was her favourite smell in the world – better than any expensive perfumes or lotions. She still found it difficult to believe that a hobby taken up to keep her mind off her divorce from Drew over fifteen years ago had turned into a successful business due to nothing more than word of mouth, good fortune and a knack with an icing bag. It had started off small. A birthday cake for the neighbour's little boy in the shape of a football. A tennis court sponge for the caretaker at the park's retirement party. A marzipan beach scene for friends destined for faraway shores. And tits. Lots of tits, for everything from hen nights to the current boob job-unveiling ceremony.

Her eyes flicked to the clock. Twenty minutes to go. She could nip for a quick shower. Phone her girlfriend Patsy for a gab. Or read the next few chapters of the Jackie Collins bonkbuster that was shouting out to her from the kitchen worktop. Jackie. Definitely. She'd just sat down when the slamming of the door derailed her appointment with a tall, dark, beautifully formed billionaire shipping heir called Bobby.

'Hi, Mum, how's it hanging?'

Sometimes her daughter asked her questions to which there was just no answer. She stuck to a fairly predictable, 'I'm good, sweetheart. What are you doing home? Didn't you have double maths this afternoon?'

Eliza dropped her bag – a Mulberry Mitzi she'd received from her father last Christmas - at the doorway and flounced across the kitchen, all long limbs, huge blue eyes and flowing, shaggy blonde hair that – to Sarah's amusement – required an hour of work every morning to look tousled and au natural. Her Amazonian-slash-surfing-chick child flicked off the CD player with a disapproving, anti-country grunt, then zeroed in on the oven and peered in the door. 'Eeeew, gross. I can't believe you make cakes like that. It's, like, *mortifying*.'

Sarah nodded in agreement. 'I know. I'll be getting a job in a lap dancing bar next. So, maths? You didn't answer my question.'

'Skipped it. It was, like, so tedious and I need to go shopping. Chantelle is going to meet me and we're going to head into town. Dad gave me his credit card at the weekend and said I could spend two hundred pounds. An early birthday treat.'

Sarah tried not to let her feelings show in her face. What were they? Disappointment? Irritation? Blind bloody fury? How many times had she asked Drew not to fork out cash like it didn't matter? It was a losing battle. Eliza had him wrapped around her manicured little finger (courtesy of last month's little 'treat' – a day at a city centre spa). Oh, to be sixteen-almost-seventeen with the world at your buffed and pedicured feet and unlimited funds from the Bank of Dad.

Psychologists would say that guilt was at the heart of Drew's extravagance when it came to his youngest child.

Sarah would lay down her life for her daughter, but she wasn't blind to her faults. Eliza was spoiled. She was high maintenance. And she had a very distant relationship with the value of money.

Being the youngest in the family, she was indulged. By Drew. By her older brother, John. And, yes, there was no denying that Sarah wasn't always as strict as she should be with her little pre-divorce baby. The psychologists would probably have something to say about that, too. John was ten when Eliza came along – and looking back Sarah could see that having another baby was a last-ditch attempt to salvage a marriage that was on a slippery slope of complacency and growing incompatibility. The divorce papers had thumped on the mat on Eliza's first birthday. Sarah had taken Eliza to a coffee shop, cried into a carrot cake, and then went shopping and spent a large chunk of her monthly maintenance payment in the most gorgeous little baby boutique in the mall. Six months later she'd gained forty pounds, but her daughter had a wardrobe to die for. By the time Eliza was toddling, Sarah realized that the indulgence had to stop, but it was a lesson that Drew had yet to learn.

'Do you want to come with us, Mum? I could, you know, style you. Bring you into this decade.'

The cheeky grin and light banter in Eliza's voice took the sting out of her words. It was an ongoing joke that Sarah's standard uniform of calf-length denim skirts, mum-jeans and fleece tops would come back into fashion one day. But what was the point of being a slave to fashion when she was too busy being a slave to a teenage daughter, a grown-up son, a daughter-in-law, two grandchildren and a burgeoning industry in tit cakes? Pursing her lips, she gave her daughter the 'don't go there' stare. Which was pretty similar to the 'behave yourself' stare and the 'if you've borrowed my gold chain, you'd better get it back in my jewellery box before I notice' stare.

'Mu-u-u-m,' Eliza chided. It was obvious what was coming next. The other subject that frequently arose. 'You have to get back out there. How are you ever going to meet anyone sitting in your kitchen wearing a purple fleece?'

'I could meet someone,' Sarah insisted with mock petulance. 'Delivery guys. The postman. The gardener. The old guy who collects for Help The Aged. He's very sprightly for an eighty-two-year-old.'

For the second time since she arrived, Eliza adopted her 'grossed out' face.

'That's, like, so wrong.' She thought for a moment. 'What about Chantelle's dad? He's single again. The French au pair got homesick and left him.'

On her feet now, Sarah simultaneously checked the bosoms in the oven while rolling her eyes. 'He drives a red Ferrari, has blonde highlights and he's had liposuction twice this year. I could be leaping to rash conclusions, but I don't think I could have a relationship with someone when the only thing we have in common is a shade of Nice'n Easy.'

Her daughter giggled.

'Look, I'm fine the way I am. I'm happy. I keep telling you, the last thing I need is another man. I like having my own space.'

How many times had she trotted that old chestnut out? So many times that she just accepted it was true. Her chum, Patsy had heard it a million times. Her son could recite it backwards. She might even have told the old guy who collected for Help The Aged.

And she supposed it was true. She was contented with her life. The thought of getting out there and meeting someone new and starting all over again at the beginning of a relationship made her both terrified and weary. She liked routine. Peace. Calm. No drama. And anyway, one marriage and one devastating divorce was enough for one lifetime.

'Your laptop is flashing.' Eliza idly crunched into an apple as she tapped away the screen saver. 'You've got an email. Oooh, it's from Jorja, Dad's PA.'

It was amazing how such innocuous words could cause Sarah's stomach to launch into a full-scale spasm. On the surface of it, she and Drew had always kept things amicable and pleasant. What other option did she have? They had two children and two grandchildren together. He'd given her the house and supported John and Eliza over the years. They'd always celebrated family birthdays and Christmas together – apart from the years he was with Mona and they jetted off to exotic locations and spent their free time mingling at swanky parties. Urgh, that woman was vile. But of course, Sarah had always been too polite to say that. No drama. Peace. Calm.

'She's confirming the details for Dad's birthday cruise,' Eliza shrieked as she jumped up and down on the spot. 'It's happening! It's definitely going ahead. That's, like, so amazing!'

Oh. Dear. God. Sarah surreptitiously clung on to the kitchen worktop for support. Of course, Drew had mentioned the idea in passing, but she'd been in total denial. She was so sure that either Mona or Tess would scupper the idea that she'd chosen to block it out of her head. But no. As Eliza would say, it was, like, definitely on. This called for yet another Oh. Dear. God.

She couldn't help but look downwards. She was a woman in a calf-length skirt and purple fleece and she was going on an up market, luxury, oh-so-chic cruise. Was it too late to claim agoraphobia? A contagious disease? Nits?

But of course, that would never happen because divorced or not, Drew always got his way.

As her 34DDs turned a slightly charred shade of sponge, Sarah had a horrible feeling that peace and calm would be the last things she would find at sea.

2.

Pack Up Your Troubles

Tess

Tess snapped the lock shut on the suitcase and watched as the other side bulged open. Bugger. The underwire on her too-tight bra dug into her side as she pressed down with all her might on the open side. No good. Not even close. There was nothing else for it. She lay down flat on the case, and let out a grunt of exertion as she pushed again. The gap reduced to about three inches and refused to budge any further. Where was Drew when she needed him?

There were many things that his commitment to his job made impossible. They never spent weekends at the cottage in the Lake District. They didn't go shopping together. They didn't go on long invigorating cycle rides. They'd never taken salsa lessons. Actually she had no desire whatsoever to learn salsa, given that she had two left feet, but that wasn't the point. Why did she always have to do everything alone? Getting a suitcase shut was definitely a job for a two-man team, but – yet again – she was flying, or rather lying, solo. Argh. She had a good mind to 'forget' to put in any boxer shorts for him. Perhaps ten days of going commando might focus his mind on teamwork.

There was only one thing for it. Cameron picked up after two rings. 'Yes, your majesty?'

Tess exploded with laughter. 'If only that were true. Then I could balance ten corgis on this bloody suitcase to get it shut.'

Tess heard a glugging noise down the line. Must have caught him having a beer. Add that to the list of things she and Drew didn't do – chill out with a beer and talk over their day. A wave of exasperation swept over her – she really needed to stop this nitpicking. There was absolutely no point to it. Drew's schedule was an occupational hazard. Anyway, he had promised that he would be home by eight o'clock tonight and they were going out for their own private birthday celebration. Dinner at the Rogano, her very favourite restaurant, followed by drinks and dancing at the Corinthian. They would finally get a chance to talk and get a refresher course on what it was like to be together. She might have to share him for the next ten days but tonight she would have him all to herself and she couldn't wait. A shimmery black dress was hanging on the front of the wardrobe. Her hair was in rollers. All relevant bits had been exfoliated, shaved and moisturized. Her fingernails and toenails were a matching shade of vampish purple and, if you didn't look too closely at the streaky bits around her neck and armpits, the home fake tanning session had been a roaring success. She just needed to get this bloody case shut and she was set to go.

'One is not amused by this packing lark and one wonders if there's any chance you fancy a couple of hours round here today. I'll ply you with food and drink, and the only catch is that you have to sit on my suitcase.'

'Tell me that's a metaphor.'

'Nope.'

His exasperated groan set off her giggles again.

'You realize you're tearing me away from two hours of watching men in large shoulder pads chase each other to steal a ball?'

'I'll make your favourite chilli and there's a dozen Peroni in the fridge.'

'I'll be there in half an hour.'

It was only twenty-five minutes later when the doorbell rang and he wandered in, announcing his arrival with a cheery, 'Husband Stunt Double Service to the rescue. Suitcase-shutting a speciality.'

Within the hour the clasps were shut and locked, and Tess and Cameron were sitting in their usual positions on either side of the island in the middle of the kitchen. He looked perfectly at home, his black jeans and T-shirt colour-even co-ordinating perfectly with the room.

The first time she walked into this kitchen she'd been blown away by how gorgeous it was. The glossy white units formed a square around the room that was only interrupted by a mammoth black American fridge-freezer. The centre island was like the ones she used to see on American soap operas when she was a kid. The floor was the same sparkly black granite as the worktops and the walls were coated in a textured pearl paper. All this kitchen needed was a willowy blonde pretending to whip up a Caesar salad and you'd have a scene from an architectural magazine. Instead there was a five-foot-five, size twelve to fourteen brunette, with huge brown eyes, a streaky décolletage and a messy bob that would be slightly reminiscent of Rachel in *Friends* if it wasn't being stretched into submission by eight large pink sponge rollers.

Cameron popped the top off another Peroni and dipped a Dorito into the pot of chilli in front of him.

'So, what's the plan then?'

Tess interrupted the task of fishing the kidney beans out of her bowl to answer him. Kidney beans revolted her but at least once a week she made a huge pot of chilli, and put the beans in because Drew loved them. Invariably, half of it got thrown away because he'd picked up dinner at the office. 'We're having a night out, just the two of us, tonight…'

'Oooohhhhh,' he said with a grin.

'You are so immature,' she replied with an amused shake of the head. 'Anyway, dinner tonight, then we fly to Barcelona tomorrow morning and head straight for the boat. It sets sail at six o'clock tomorrow evening, and the fun begins.' It took every ounce of joviality she possessed to leave the sarcasm out of the end of that sentence. It would be great. It would. She would have a chance to get to know Mona and Sarah better. They'd only met a few times at family occasions, so they'd only managed to establish a superficial acquaintance. She could also spend quality bonding time with the slightly demanding Eliza, and build a relationship with John and Penny, Drew's son and his wife. It would be great. Definitely.

'Still trying to convince yourself that you'll have a great time?'

Bloody hell, it was like he could read her mind.

She nodded a little guiltily and for once the jovial grin dropped from Cameron's face. Her first thought was that she'd messed up the chilli. Too much tomato puree? Not enough spice?

'You know, sometimes he doesn't treat you the way you

should be treated.' His words were soft, almost sad, and when his eyes eventually made contact, his expression was so earnest it caught her breath.

'What... what... what do you mean?' The surprise was affecting her fluency of speech. This wasn't like Cameron. He didn't do deep and meaningful incisive analysis of anyone's relationships. He did best friends. And beer and chilli. With beans.

'Come on, Tess. Look, I've never said anything before because, to be honest, it's none of my business. But you deserve better than this. Shit, I've turned into cliché-man.' He ran his fingers through his shoulder-length blonde hair. Tess had spent the last year talking him out of getting it cut because she thought it made him look like Chris Hemsworth in Thor.

Despite the fact that her mouth was open, no words would come, allowing him to carry on speaking.

'Drew's a good guy, but you spend your whole life waiting around for him. It's like he's more important than you in this relationship and that's not right.'

His rant ran out of steam and he put his head down.

'Wow.' It was all she could muster under the circumstance. And was it just her or was it getting really warm in here? She could feel little bursts of perspiration pop up under her rollers. Classy.

After a few moments of awkward, crackling tension, a burst of defensiveness kicked in. 'That's not true,' she blurted, a little unconvincingly because, let's face it, she'd had similar thoughts many times over the last few months. But somehow, admitting it out loud seemed like a betrayal of her husband and her marriage. 'Our marriage is great. And it's not Drew's fault he has a crazy job. I knew what he did and what I was getting into when I married him.'

Which was true. Almost. But it did feel that he was here even less than usual over the last year. And yes, sometimes it felt like he was less committed to spending time together than ever before. But that wasn't his fault. It was the nature of the changes in the newspaper world. It had become even more demanding as papers merged, folded and fought for survival in a declining market, battling against the 24/7 media coverage of TV and the internet.

Cameron was staring at her now, his brown eyes taking in

every detail of her expression. 'And how's that working out for you?'

Ouch. What was this? Tonight was supposed to be about suitcase-shutting and flippant banter, not a marital therapy session that made a stab at her heart.

That's when the tears ambushed her. Not flowing down the face, poignant, movie star tears – just the welled-up, appearance-of-hay-fever ones. But still, that never happened to her. The only time she ever cried was in the case of tragedy, acute pain and Meryl Streep movies.

'I… don't… know.' Sniff. Then a tidal wave of disjointed, contradictory thoughts. 'It's just that I keep hoping things will change. And I don't mind, not really. Well, I do. But I thought that I'd get used to it. Then he invited everyone on this cruise and I think he doesn't even want to be with me when we're on holiday. I mean, who invites their ex-wives? But I don't mind. Well, I do. I just think sometimes that maybe I'm not enough for him. Perhaps he's bored. He must be. I bloody am. Oh my God, I can't believe I just said that out loud. I don't mean it…'

'Maybe you do,' Cameron answered softly.

There it was. Maybe she did. Maybe it was time to start facing reality and getting honest with herself.

'Are you happy with him?' Cameron continued to probe.

'Yes!' So much for honesty. Her rueful grimace conceded that might not be strictly true. 'At least, when we're together I am, but the rest of the time it feels like we're…' She thought about it for a moment. 'Going through the motions.'

Where the hell had that come from? Going through the motions? The motions of what? Two people who'd lost something somewhere along the path of their marriage?

How had this happened? How had the inability to shut a suitcase turned into a devastating realization about her life? One fat tear rolled down her cheek and plopped down onto a pile of kidney beans.

Cameron's eyes were still on her, his expression one that she didn't recognize. He was probably wishing he'd stayed on the couch watching American football instead of being landed with a bawling woman in rollers.

'I think I could make you happier.' It wasn't said in the tone of a grand gesture of gushy emotion. He said it gently. Almost matter-of-fact. And totally unexpected and confusing. She grasped for a bit of clarity.

'Wh… what?'

'It's time I told you. Should have done it ages ago. I was going to, and then you met Drew and married him so quickly…'

'Wait a minute – how long have you felt like this?'

'Since we first met.'

'So all this time I thought we were best friends and you were just hanging around because you fancied me?' Even as she was saying it she knew she was being harsh and unfair, but this felt like an ambush and the shock was making her shoot her way out of Dodge.

He looked understandably hurt. 'No! I mean yes. Both! I didn't want to cause problems in your life or risk ruining what we already have. But it makes so much sense. We're great together, Tess. Nothing even comes close to the friendship we have. And I fancy you like crazy…'

'You fancy every woman with a pulse like crazy.' It was an old, standing joke between them, but it fell flat given the present circumstances.

He carried on. 'And I want children, and so do you…'

'Don't even go there.' The flash of anger in her eyes stopped him. It was the one taboo subject, the one thing she would never discuss.

'OK, I'm sorry, but… I could make you happy, Tess,' he repeated. 'And stop chewing your lip,' he added with a grin.

The ringing of the kitchen phone made them both jump. When she didn't answer it, it switched to her voice telling the caller to leave a message.

'Hey, babe,' Drew's baritone thundered down the line and she immediately felt guilty, despite having done absolutely nothing wrong. Cameron's gaze still held hers in an almost defiant stand-off.

See? She was married! How dare he come into her kitchen and lay all this stuff on her. This was just another one of his stupid phases, like skinny jeans or when he insisted on travelling to work every day on a Segway. Drew was calling her right now and didn't that prove that things between them were fine?

Or not.

'Listen, I'm really sorry, but I'm going to have to miss

21

dinner tonight. I had Jorja call and cancel the reservation. Big story breaking – premiership player shagging another player's missus. Sorry, love, but I'll make it up to you tomorrow. Why don't you phone Cameron and go for a drink? See you when I get home. Love you.'

The award for completely ironic bloody timing goes to Drew Gold.

It was difficult to come back after that, but she gave it her best shot.

'Cameron, I'm sorry. But I can't be having this conversation. Drew is my husband.'

There was a toe-curling scraping noise as he dismounted off the bar stool and pushed it back from the island. He was leaving? He was just going to say all that stuff and then leave?

'Not from where I'm standing.'

She stood frozen to the spot while he smiled sadly, turned and left. A million thoughts collided in her mind and she was so frazzled she could only settle on one: Drew Gold was about to find out how it felt to go commando.

Mona

The Steakhouse at The Blythswood Club was a chaotic throng of Glasgow's glitterati. Since it opened, the private member's club had been the bustling epicentre of Glasgow's more upmarket social scene and Mona Gold had been a member since day one. By the time she made her way from the reception downstairs to the upstairs bar, her favourite Kir Royal was waiting for her. So was her husband. Piers Delaney was holding court to half a dozen younger men, all impeccably dressed and clearly hanging on his every word. It was a familiar sight. His national chain of sports shops had made him a very, very rich man indeed. Dressing the nation's disaffected in tracksuits and trainers had put the man behind the company in Savile Row suits. There was even a rumour that he was up for an honour in the Queen's New Year list. Just a few years into his sixth decade, he was well-respected, successful, intelligent and generous – and shagging his twenty-two-year-old secretary. Of course, he had no idea Mona knew, but those early pre-fashion years as an investigative journalist had left traits that prevented any chance of being cuckolded by an arrogant entrepreneur. That business trip to New York last year? Three nights in the Mandarin Oriental with Emily the Typing Frump. Mona wasn't sure if she was more insulted by the betrayal or by the fact that the woman he was screwing behind her back bought her shoes from Clarks. She thought about confronting him but decided against it. Actions like that required thought, plans, an exit strategy, and she hadn't yet decided on the latter. The only thing she knew for sure was that if he could indulge in illicit fun, then so could she. Barely a week had passed since then without incredible sex, and it was rarely with her husband.

'Hello, darling,' she whispered breathlessly, as she gave him a fleeting kiss on the cheek.

At least half of the men he was talking to appraised her from head to foot. It always gave her a buzz to know that she hadn't lost it. In fact, she truly felt like she was coming into her prime. Her early twenties had been about building her career, her late twenties had been about being married to Drew, and now that she was in her early thirties – OK, her late thirties – life was about enjoying everything she'd achieved while maintaining the looks and figure of a twenty-five-year-old. Going by the expressions on these guys' faces it was working.

Piers didn't even notice their reactions. Fool.

'I think our table is ready, darling, so we can go on through.'

The bartender must have been reading her lips because he immediately appeared at her side with a tray, took her drink and whisked it through the restaurant to their table.

It was always the same one. A booth at the window, furthest away from the entrance, with Mona seated on the left so that she could keep an eye on who was coming and going.

She stopped to air-kiss at least ten people on the way. Everyone knew her and she knew everyone – Glasgow might be a large city, but she worked hard to make sure she was a big fish in the socialite pond.

'It's exhausting coming out with you, do you know that?' The smile on her husband's face said that it was supposed to be a joke, but Mona knew that it masked a very real feeling of irritation. It was difficult to remember the time when his jokes made her want to laugh and his touch made her want to get naked really quickly. Sometimes she wondered if the whole relationship had been some kind of messed-up competition in her head. A great big 'fuck you' to Drew after he ended their marriage. After all, what could be more satisfying than marrying fabulously successful businessman Piers Delaney just weeks after the decree nisi for her divorce from Drew Gold hit the doormat?

Mona just smiled in reply to his jibe, flashing the gleaming white pearlies that came courtesy of regular whitening treatments at the Visage Lifestyle Clinic. It was practically her second home. Botox. Fillers. Laser treatments. Teeth whitening. Massage. Acupuncture. She was probably their best client, but it was testimony to their expertise that it didn't show. There wasn't an over-plumped lip or an over-raised, frozen eyebrow on Mona's face. It took a whole lot of work to look that natural.

Piers leaned back as the waiter filled his glass with beer. It infuriated her that he could afford the best champagne, yet he happily settled for a beer with dinner. 'So… what's happening in the handbag world this week, then?'

The hairs on the back of her neck flicked to the upright position. Demeaning bastard. This was a guy who made a fortune from track suits. Not exactly haute bloody couture. However, tonight wasn't a night to take him to task. Time to play nice for the sake of the bigger picture. Or luxury cruise. It had been torture persuading him to go on this trip and she just knew he was looking for an excuse to cancel. In the end she'd used every piece of leverage she had to get Piers to agree to embark on a voyage with her ex-husband, his former wife and family as well as his latest wife. She reminded him that having a good relationship with the editor of Scotland's national newspaper was crucial for his companies. She'd had sex with him for twelve, Viagra-fuelled hours. Finally, her last ace card had been to invite his son, Max. The relationship between father and son was distant, both in emotion and geography. Max's mother had taken him to live in London when he was a baby and his childhood had been punctuated by weekend and holiday visits. Now that Max was in his thirties, the two men got together when their schedules allowed. That masterstroke had sealed the deal – Piers agreed to go and Mona got what she wanted. Not that she'd ever doubted she would, but she had no intention of blowing it now and having to endure the whole 12 hour Viagra persuasion session all over again.

Only after a large gulp of Kir Royal did she trust herself to speak without antagonism. What was his question again? It took her a moment to recall what he'd asked, shrug off a new wave of irritation, and put together a non-confrontational answer.

'No, nothing in the handbag world worth getting excited about. Enough about work – are you looking forward to seeing Max? How long has it been?'

Piers narrowed his eyebrows as he pondered the question. 'At least a couple of months. Don't know where my time goes.'

To a hotel. In New York. With a woman in sensible shoes.

'He sounded pretty excited about it,' she lied. It had taken three phone calls, a glossy brochure and much pleading to make him come. Sometimes Max wasn't the most pliable of characters. 'He's really looking forward to seeing you.' Another lie. As far as she could recall, Max's exact words were a light-hearted, 'Don't you think I'm a little old to be taken on holiday by my dad?' That little titbit wasn't for sharing with the man sitting across the table. Instead, she subtly applied another layer of SPF factor fifty manipulation. 'I'm sure it will be lovely. And it means a lot to Drew that you're coming. You know how he loves the whole "big gathering" thing.' That was true. How ironic that it suited her purposes now, yet it had driven her bloody mad when they were married.

'I just don't understand why he wants his ex-wife there.'

Mona laughed. 'Because we're friends. The fact that we were married has nothing to do with it. I'm his confidante and he enjoys our company.' It wasn't strictly true, but it would do for now. The truth might just put Piers off his steak.

All that mattered was that they were going and right now that was all she cared about. Where better to work on that exit strategy than in the sunny bliss of the Mediterranean?

Sarah

'I want to leave,' Sarah announced.

'No.'

'Right now.'

'No.'

'I swear to God, I'll scream. Or set off a fire alarm. Or phone the police.'

Patsy got a fit of the giggles, then grasped Sarah by the shoulders. 'Pull yourself together!' she laughed, while aping the actions of the leading hero in a disaster flick, trying to calm down a hysterical hostage as the bad guys pondered over who to shoot next.

The young girl with the gothic hair and nose piecing behind the till in River Island eyed them suspiciously. There was no way those two were shoplifters – far too conspicuous. They did look a bit deranged, though. The taller one had pink hair sticking out from underneath her beanie hat, and was wearing a white and pink tie-dyed maxi dress. The other one had on a denim skirt and a... eew, a fleece. They were, like, so ten years ago. On top of all that the women were totally ancient. At least forty-five.

'I do not believe I'm here,' Sarah said wearily. 'Buying clothes is my idea of hell.'

Patsy was low on sympathy. 'I do not believe that you left it until today to shop for this trip. Just be grateful that Eliza isn't here. I had to bribe her with twenty quid not to show up and drag you into the size 8, teenage nirvana of Topshop. Right, let's get organized. I've got a list.'

Sarah watched, open-mouthed, as Patsy pulled one side of a cornflakes box from her bag, turned it over, and proceeded to rhyme off what was written on the back of it.

'Ten pairs of knickers, four of them sexy with matching bras.'

Sarah's face turned the same shade as Patsy's hair and

mortification robbed her of the power of speech.

'Four one-piece swimsuits with matching sarongs.' Patsy looked up. 'Don't take offence but those abs haven't seen a gym in, well, ever. And I say that from a place of love.'

Dear God, this was like spending the day with Gok Wan's evil, non-identical, hippy-chic twin. And she was still going.

'Ten cruise-casual outfits, fully accessorized. Ten evening cocktail dresses, various styles. Three evening dresses. Three sets of nightwear, one raunchy in case you get lucky.'

Where was that fire alarm?

'One wrap for chilly evenings – preferably pashmina. I've heard that's all the fashion these days. One light cardigan. One pair of jeans…'

'I have jeans!' Sarah managed to blurt.

Patsy countered her objection with, 'That were manufactured *after* 1984. Oh, and shoes. Two flip-flops, two wedges – one day and one night – one pair of comfortable yet chic walking shoes, three pairs of drop-dead-gorgeous heels.'

Sarah groaned in despair and Patsy replied with an arched eyebrow. 'What? Count yourself lucky – I had a pair of furry mules on there as well, but I took them off when I scored out the erotic negligee. Didn't want you embarrassed if you get stopped at customs.'

Sarah sighed. 'I'm welling up with gratitude.'

Patsy ignored the sarcasm and ploughed on with a breezy, 'So you should be. Right. Let's get to it.'

In less than fifteen minutes Patsy had accumulated an armful of garments and was prodding Sarah in the direction of the changing room.

'Six items maximum,' a cheery, WAG-in-waiting told them at the entrance.

Patsy did a quick count. 'That's fine – there are twelve here so that's six each.' Before the WAG-in-waiting could compute this logic, Patsy was already past her.

They headed into the largest cubicle: double-sized and perfect for those requiring a second opinion, whether they wanted it or – in this case - not. Patsy held up the first outfit as Sarah stripped to her underwear.

'It's a good thing that we're heading to Markie's underwear department next. Fishing boats could catch tuna with those knickers.'

Sarah looked down at the offending undergarments in question. White, large, and yes, they'd probably seen better days. And no, they didn't match the nude, bland, slightly stretched bra, either. She'd got dressed in a hurry this morning and since her knickers hadn't been viewed by another living person anytime this decade, she hadn't given underwear a second thought.

'You're supposed to be my non-judgemental friend.'

'You're right. Now put this on and cover them up before I'm forced to call the gusset police.'

That started it. The giggles came and wouldn't stop until the tears were running down her face. Two almost-fifty-year-old women, in a changing room, one of them practically naked, and both doubled up with laughter. Sarah didn't even want to contemplate what people in the other changing rooms were thinking. But for once she didn't care.

'Oh, Patsy, I feel like we're sixteen again and you're dragging me into C&A for a frock for the school dance. Remember? That was the first night I kissed Drew. And I already had a boyfriend. What a tart I was! I'd fancied him for years, though, and he knew it.'

'You're right. I should have kept you home that night. Your whole life would have been different. Maybe you'd have stayed single and been Sarah Armit forever. Or perhaps you'd have married Phil Kenny.'

'Oh my God, Phil Kenny! Whatever happened to him?'

'Found dead in a brothel in Thailand.'

'You're kidding!'

'Nope.'

'On balance, I think I was better off with Drew then, don't you?'

'Nope. You'd have got Phil's insurance money.'

That set them off again, with Sarah sending up apologies to the heavens in case the dearly departed Phil Kenny was listening.

When she finally pulled on the first dress, she stood back to survey the reflection of a gorgeous but simple white calico maxi that skimmed her ankles while revealing an inch of nude bra at the top. Patsy stood beside her so that they were both appraising the vision in the mirror.

'A decent bra would be a start, but the rest of it looks great.

Or at least, it will when you've got a bit of colour.'

Sarah wasn't so sure. Was it a bit bridal? A bit… well… noticeable? These days she preferred to blend into the background and this dress was definitely not wallflower material. She stared at the mirror again and realized that she didn't look tragically bad. The kids wouldn't cross the road when they saw her coming. Well, Eliza probably would, but that was just standard teenage behaviour. The boobs looked a bit droopy, but as Patsy so helpfully – or brutally – pointed out, a new bra would sort that out. Her arms were still tight and toned, courtesy of all that cake-mixing. The fabric seemed to glide over the areas she disliked most (hips, bum – thanks to all that cake tasting) and the long length had a slimming effect that was rather… well, flattering. Maybe this one would be fine. The price tag caught her eye. Or maybe not. A hundred quid! That was three tit cakes! And she'd probably never wear it again after this trip.

'Right, that one's a yes,' Patsy informed her.

'I really don't think…'

'Stop!' Patsy put her hand up and went into full-scale bossy mode. 'I'm here for thinking, you're here for obedient, but life-enhancing action. Just take that off and get this next one on.'

Sarah prided herself in knowing when to pick her battles and this wasn't the time to go to war.

The next four hours were like being caught in a tumble dryer of clothes racks and changing rooms. An hour before the shopping centre was due to close, they staggered into Starbucks, laden down with bags, most of which Sarah had already decided would be going back, unworn, as soon as she got back from the cruise. What a complete waste of money. She didn't need all these clothes. On the rare occasion that she left her kitchen, she didn't go any further than the high street, the park, or – when she was really pushing the boat out – the local pub with Patsy. A leopard-print maxi dress with matching shawl was going to look more than a little out of place at the Dog and Sausage.

They both ordered large lattes and lemon muffins and plonked themselves down at the first free table. Sarah eased off the Converse trainers that were now digging into her swollen feet. Eliza would kill her when she found out Sarah had borrowed them, but she'd known she'd be on her feet all day and the only comfy shoes she had were the Crocs she wore all day around the house, Uggs in both black and brown, and her wellies with the repeating ducks pattern. Somehow she didn't think Patsy would appreciate any of those choices, so she'd panicked and raided Eliza's wardrobe for something flat but not friendship-threatening.

'You know, there's no point starting the diet today.' Sarah reflected, justifying the large slice of sponge she was about to consume. 'But… actually you look like you've lost a bit of weight.'

Patsy suddenly went bright red and involuntarily adopted a coy expression. Sarah paused, muffin in mid-air and surveyed her pal. Patsy hadn't been coy since she snogged her first boyfriend sometime around 1976, so… oh no.

'Are you sick?' Sarah asked, holding her breath.

'No, you daft cow, I'm not sick. I've met someone.'

'You're kidding!' It took Sarah a few seconds to realize that could be taken in an insulting manner, so she blustered out a clarification. 'Not that you shouldn't meet someone! But it's just that… well, you said after Dick you'd never do it again. I seem to remember a comment about resealing a part of your anatomy.'

'That might have been a tad rash.'

There was a stunned silence as Sarah absorbed the newsflash. This was great news. Amazing. It had taken years for Patsy to get over losing Dick to a dinner lady from Wales that he met on the Internet. For more nights than she cared to – or could – remember, they'd sat with a bottle of wine while Patsy broke her heart and they made insulting generalizations about the male species and the things they'd like to do to them with a bargepole. Despite Drew's betrayal, Sarah never actually meant any of it, but for the sake of moral support and unconditional devotion, she went along with every one of Patsy's declarations as to why the only thing that would make her feel better was hiring a hitman. In the end, Sarah had talked her out of cashing in her endowment policy and typing 'killer for hire' into Google.

'Pats, I'm so pleased for you, I really am. So who is he? And how did you meet him? And will this require coffee refills? And should I get them now so we don't have to interrupt the juicy bits?'

Patsy laughed and nodded, sending Sarah haring up to the

counter, to return five minutes later with another caffeine fix for two.

'He's a policeman. He was the one who came when my car got stolen from the driveway and then I bumped into him again in Superdrug the following week and…'

'Am I allowed to make immature jokes about "further investigations" and "taking down your particulars"?'

'No.'

'OK.'

'His name's Don, and it's three weeks now and we've been out a dozen times and we seem to talk every day. He's nice, Sarah. Really nice. I'm just taking it a day at a time, but I haven't felt this good in years.'

Sarah felt her heartstrings ping as she glowed with happiness for her friend. Patsy so deserved every single moment of this new romance. Sarah spontaneously leaned over and squeezed her tightly, then grinned when another thought occurred to her.

'Patsy, I've just realized that your timing just couldn't have been better.'

'Why?'

'Because you've got a new man, and…' she gestured to the pile of clothes bags stacked around her, 'I'll give you all this lot when I get back and he can take down the particulars of the best dating wardrobe in town.'

Tess

It was after midnight when Drew got home, and Tess was sitting in bed waiting for him. There had been no further calls or texts. The cool touch of the crisp white Egyptian cotton sheets did nothing to calm her.

In the last few hours she'd picked up the phone to call Cameron a dozen times but never got further than the seventh digit. Her lips were chewed raw and her stomach was churning.

Drew hung up his jacket on the door of the wardrobe. 'Sorry I'm so late, babe. What a night.'

'That's OK.' But it wasn't. It really, really wasn't.

'Turns out our tip was correct. In fact, not only was he shagging one of his teammate's wives, but he was also up to no good with his wife's twin sister. These guys are unbelievable.'

Normally she'd agree and they'd chat about the situation, but somehow tonight the words wouldn't come. At this moment, nothing was more unbelievable to her than the acceptance that there were problems in her marriage and the shock of her best friend in the world declaring that his feelings for her were more than platonic.

How had she not seen this? And how was she supposed to feel about it? She didn't have the answer to either question.

He slid his trousers off and hung them on the trouser press. He was neat that way. Methodical. Disciplined. Standing in front of her now, giving her all the gory details about the scoop, she zoned out and tried, for the first time in way too long, to appraise him objectively. He still looked great. He might not have had the time to go to dinner or pack his own suitcase, but he always made a window in his day to work out. Yep, that was yet another thing that was more important than spending time with her. Usually, he popped down to the gym in the basement of the office, but sometimes, on the rare occasions when Glasgow weather permitted, he'd cycle for an hour. He might have been only a few days away from fifty but his body was stuck at two decades earlier.

His physical shape might not have changed, but now, looking clearly, Tess could see that other things had definitely shifted. When they were first together he would look at her when he spoke, engage her in conversation, listen to what she had to say. Now he just imparted news. It was a one-way conversation. In fact, she could dispense with eighty per cent of their current relationship by just reading his newspaper every day.

The sparkle had definitely dimmed. The only consolation was that she knew he loved her and she loved him. Didn't all marriages go through periods like this? Whenever a magazine ran a story on a couple that had been married for fifty years, they always said they'd had 'ups and downs'. Perhaps this was just a five-year dip and the cruise would nudge them back on to an upwards phase again…

The cruise on which he'd invited his whole family.

'Drew, can I ask you something?' He was so deep into the story about the football player with the wandering balls, that her interruption surprised him. 'Why did you invite everyone to go with us on this trip?'

He stopped with his boxer shorts at half mast. It wasn't an image that made for serious conversation. 'Because I thought the company would be fun,' he said dismissively, before stepping out of the underwear and turning to reveal a perfect arse. Perfect. This was so off-putting.

'But you never asked me what I thought before you did it. Maybe I'd have preferred it to be just us.'

There was an uncustomary edge of challenge in her voice but Drew clearly didn't recognize it. He slipped into bed and threw his arm across her stomach.

'Honey, I did it for you, too. I know you miss your mum and dad, and have no other family around, so I thought it would be good for you to get closer to Mona, Sarah and the kids. They're your family, too. It'll be great.'

There was an edge of finality in his voice that told her the conversation was over and soon his breathing slowed as he began to slip into sleep. No 'How was your day, darling?' Or 'Sorry again about ruining our plans.' Or even a 'Did your best friend try to persuade you to leave me today?'

In his defence, though, his explanation made sense. She did

miss her parents, so perhaps it was a lovely gesture if you looked at it that way. He'd been thinking about her, wanting her life to be better.

'I love you, honey,' he murmured, his voice thick with sleep. He loved her. And he'd been thinking about her when he'd planned this. Perhaps things weren't in such a 'down' cycle after all. Maybe she was over-reacting. Misunderstanding his intentions. Taking everything too personally.

She slid down in the bed and he automatically spooned her so that she could feel his soft, sleepy breath on the back of her neck.

Hours later, as the sun began to rise, she gave up on the sleep that refused to come.

Mona

Mona brushed her teeth and flossed for the second time in an hour. She'd been hoping that Piers would be so tired that he'd settle for an early night. Perhaps he'd even had a lunchtime quickie with Emily the Frump. Apparently not. As soon as they got home, she headed to her dressing room, brushed her teeth at the vanity unit and there he was behind her like a predatory mate. She used to find his assertiveness and self-confidence appealing. Not now.

His hand slipped around and fondled her breast as he watched her in the mirror. He got off on that. She used to like it too. The ultimate narcissistic encounter. Now it was easier to close her eyes and pretend it was Lance from the tennis club or Adrian the hot model.

In her imagination tonight it was Drake, an up-and-coming photographer who had kept her steamy hot on a skiwear photoshoot in Verbier. This encounter with Piers wasn't quite as rewarding or enduring. Without the staying power of his chemical enhancers it was over in ten minutes, leaving him breathless and Mona verging somewhere between dissatisfaction and relief.

This couldn't go on.

After a quick shower, and another brush of her teeth, she padded across the mahogany floor and dropped her satin wrap on the gold chaise longue at the end of the bed. Piers was already snoring when she joined him under the black silk sheets. They were such a cliché, but he loved them.

Half an hour later, she couldn't listen to his snoring any longer so she got up and went into the guest room. This was more her style. She'd designed it in her favourite Cape Cod vibe, with a distressed white finish on the four-poster bed that blended perfectly with the soft vanilla cream linens and the upholstery on the overstuffed sofa under the window. The only splash of colour came from a pale blue silk-spun rug on the floor and a huge vase of red roses on each of the bedside tables. It was stark, stunning but charming, and she loved it.

For the second time that night she slid under covers with a sigh and realized that if it wasn't for the indomitable powers of Botox, her face would be in a permanent frown.

Hours later, as the sun began to rise, she gave up on the sleep that refused to come.

Sarah

Sarah took her purchases straight from the shopping bags and transferred them directly into her suitcase. The labels were left on deliberately so that anything she didn't wear could either go to Patsy or back to the shops on her return. She just hoped that the case didn't go missing because if she was asked to identify it by the contents, she wouldn't have a clue.

Packing done, she popped into Eliza's room to make sure her daughter was organized. The first thing she saw was a tower of three huge suitcases, and the second thing was a sixteen-year-old with a skin colour that closely resembled radioactive material. 'Eliza! What happened to you?'

'Double Fake Bake at the salon then an overlay of gold shimmer. What do you think? Isn't it, like, so cool?'

Sarah bit her tongue. What was the point? Eliza was clearly thrilled with her metallic hue. Would anything be gained from arguing that it was actually, like, so extra-terrestrial? She must glow in the dark. It was a small comfort that if there was a night-time disaster on the ship, Eliza could be put on deck to guide in the emergency helicopter. Sixteen years of bringing up a girl had taught her when her opinion should be left unsaid.

'Yes, love, it's, erm, cool. Are you all packed?' She had to be. Given the pile of cases, there couldn't possibly be anything left in her room.

'Ready to go, Mum. And I've looked up the ship online. It's amazing. There are nine bars!'

'You're sixteen.'

Eliza rolled her eyes, clearly rejecting this biological fact, and went back to crimping her hair to the shape of a large herbaceous shrub. "But I look, like, much older. I'm sure dad would let me have like a spritzer."

"I highly doubt that but good luck trying, darling."

Sarah decided that she'd leave the alcohol battle for Drew to fight. It was about time he learned to say no to his daughter.

Back in her bedroom, she texted her son to remind him that she'd meet up with him in Barcelona. John and his wife, Penny, had flown out a day early to get their babies, Lawrence and Lavinia, acclimatized to the heat. She was thrilled she would soon see them all. Since her grandchildren had been born three years ago she'd had them at least a couple of days a week to give Penny a break and she loved every moment of it.

The phone beeped almost immediately with a message from John confirming the plans. Great. She was glad they would all be going aboard together. Safety in numbers. A lot of water had passed under the bridge between her and Mona and they'd come to the point where they could rub along together in relative harmony, but that didn't mean she welcomed spending time with her. They had absolutely nothing in common except several years spent sleeping with the same man, at least one of them over-lapping.

As for Tess, she always seemed quite sweet. Harmless. Although given the age difference, Sarah did occasionally feel like she slipped into a maternal role. How the wives of those polygamists in America did it, she'd never know.

Kicking off her slippers, she climbed into bed and grabbed her Jackie Collins bonkbuster from the bedside table. It would usually totally consume her as she slipped into the pure escapism of the decadent glamour and scandal, but tonight a recurring thought kept niggling at her: Tess would be going on this trip with Drew; Mona would be with Piers; Patsy had now met someone to share the fun things in life; and she was alone.

It had been the case for a long time and it had never occurred to her to mind, but for some reason tonight she was bothered by it.

Maybe Patsy was right. Maybe it was time that she got back out there and opened her mind to a new relationship.

She realized that the thought excited and terrified her in equal measure. Actually, if she was being honest, it was probably eighty: twenty in favour of terror. But what was the alternative? A lifetime of wearing bad knickers because no-one ever got close enough to notice? Another ten years at the coalface of novelty cakes? There had to be more to life. The book slid back on to the nightstand as she snuggled down under the duvet. No more thinking tonight. She'd worry about it tomorrow.

Hours later, as the sun began to rise, she gave up on the sleep that refused to come.

3.

All Aboard

Tess

'No, Mum, not yet. We're in the taxi on the way to the ship now. It's blistering hot here.'

Tess had to shout to be heard over the noise of the taxi and her phone felt like it was melting in her hand. The Spanish driver took the hint and opened the windows just as the first rivulets of sweat ran down her back. Sweat marks were going to be a great look for embarking on a swanky cruise. She returned her focus to the conversation just as her mum said… no, her mother did not say that!

'Mum, can you repeat that please?'

As she listened, she realized with a sinking feeling that yes, her first take on the conversation had been the correct one.

'No, Mum, I do not need tassels for my…' She stopped there, suddenly aware that the driver might possess more than a smattering of English. 'I don't care if all the girls wear them at carnival time. No, I don't need to know you have them too.' Until that moment, Drew had also been chatting on his iPhone to the office, but he paused and was now staring at her with obvious curiosity. The combination of his puzzled expression, the sweat, the apprehension about the trip, the anxiety of the last few days and the absurdity of the conversation caused a complete descent into hilarity. 'Oh, Mum…' There were no words. At least, none that she could get out. The driver was looking in his rear-view mirror now at the crazy Scottish lady who was laughing uncontrollably.

Tears streaming down her face, she eventually managed to say goodbye and ask her mum to pass on her love to her dad.

Although by the sounds of the conversation, her dad was getting quite enough loving these days.

For the millionth time she thought to herself how much she missed them. Other than an auntie in Kirkcaldy, they were the total extent of her family. Sometimes she thought how great it would be to have sisters and brothers and to have big chaotic family dinners. The expression 'be careful what you wish for' came to mind, as it now looked like she was about to find out. Drew finally finished his call – the sixth one he'd taken in the twenty minutes since they'd left Barcelona airport – and turned to face her as she struggled to compose herself despite recurring waves of borderline hysteria.

'Are you OK?' he asked, bemused at her behaviour. And no wonder. Weren't fits of the giggles supposed to end with puberty? It was amazing how one call from her mum could lift her mood and completely distract her from the stresses and worries.

'My mum's nuts.' The laughter started again, but this time she got it under control after a few moments. 'Honestly, Drew, if I'm like that in thirty years' time you have my permission to ground me. Or make a reality show about my exploits.'

Was it just her imagination or did a weird look flicker across his face when she said that? No, she was being paranoid. Urgh, she had to shake this off and get herself into her usual positive, happy state of mind. Only optimism and a sense of humour were going to get her through the next week, so she might as well start now.

'The sheep,' the driver said suddenly. Tess immediately looked out of the window expecting to see gambolling lambs and woolly ewes, but instead she realized they were about to go over a long bridge to… There it was. The ship. Or to be more accurate, several ships: huge cruise liners all lined up in a row to her right-hand side. The bridge dipped down and to the right as they merged onto the pier at Port Vell, and drove past one magnificent spectacle of engineering after another. She read the names of them as she passed. *Norwegian Epic, Voyager of the Seas, Ruby Princess, Allure of the Seas, Carnival Magic, Thomson Destiny*, and finally, right at the end, *Vistatoria*.

Wow, it was grand. Tess had already checked it out online and knew that it had fifteen decks and carried three thousand passengers at full capacity, but to actually see it was breathtaking. And they were going to circle the Med in it! She tried to remember the itinerary off the top of her head. Barcelona. Palma. A day at sea. Sardinia. Messina. Naples. Rome. It took her a moment before the others dropped in. Livorno. Genoa. Monaco. Barcelona.

For the first time, she felt a little bubble of excitement, and she automatically turned to her husband to gauge his reaction, only to realize that he was dialling another number on his phone. Irritation replaced excitement. If she was a betting woman she wouldn't put her last tenner on his iPhone making it to the ship. A carefully orchestrated nudge and it would be condemned to forever swim with the fishes.

He'd promised that as soon as they boarded he was officially off duty. If she so much as caught him asking for the Wifi password she was going to be furious. Come on! Didn't he realize she was struggling here? Of course he didn't. He thought everything was just wonderful. It crossed her mind if she was a premiership footballer or a reality TV star, then he might be a bit more observant about the state of her marriage.

Conveniently, he only hung up when the taxi drew to a halt at the port. She tried not to be irked that there was no time for last minute whispers or kisses before they met the others.

The embarkation process was surprisingly swift, much more efficient than an airport. A porter took their bags from the car, and after showing the boarding passes that were in the ever-efficient Jorja's itinerary pack, they were ushered through security, issued with ship passes, had their photographs taken, and then made their way across the gangway.

Stepping into the foyer was like entering a different world. The atrium stretched up from their level and burst through the top of the ship, only a domed glass ceiling between them and the blue of the sky. The walls on every side were punctuated by gold and glass bullet-shaped lifts shooting from top to bottom.

Tess could do nothing but gaze around in wonder. Perhaps ten days on here wouldn't be so bad after all, even in the company of two ex-wives.

'Good morning, sir, can I help direct you?' A happy soul in a smart blue jacket and white trousers, who was, according to his shiny gold name tag, 'Arnie, Nigeria', welcomed them.

'Good morning,' Drew replied with a charming smile. 'Are the rooms ready?'

'They'll be free in about an hour, sir. Can I just check your Sea Pass?'

Drew held out the credit-card-like pass that was to be used for opening doors and charging goods to the room account.

Arnie, Nigeria's smile widened even further. 'Actually sir, you're in the Destiny suite and those rooms are already open. If you'd like to make your way to deck twelve, someone will greet you there.'

Ooooh, the Destiny suite. Tess liked the sound of that.

On level twelve, the ping to signal the opening of the doors had barely subsided when 'Colita, Brazil' greeted them with yet another beaming grin. Forget Disneyland. This was clearly the happiest place on earth and it was beginning to rub off on her

'Ah, Mr and Mrs Gold, welcome to the *Vistatoria*. Your suite is ready, if you'd just like to come this way.'

Tess tried to absorb every detail so she could relay it all to her mother next time they spoke... if she could get the whole nipple tassel scenario out of her head. Carpets. Stare at the carpets. The thick, navy pile with the gold 'V's embroidered in a regal pattern. She glanced upwards. The pale cream walls with subtle antique gold band running along at waist-height. The stunning artwork on the walls. It was like the poshest hotel she'd ever been in.

'This is so beautiful,' she whispered to Drew. He squeezed her hand and she realized that his iPhone was out of sight. Good to start the cruise on a miracle.

Colita, Brazil opened a mahogany door and led them inside. 'Here we are. The porters will bring your luggage up shortly and in the meantime there is a magnum of champagne cooling on top of the bar.' She gestured to the silver ice bucket on a black marble semicircle in the corner of the room. 'I will leave you to get settled, but if I can be of any assistance at all, please press six on your telephone.'

With a smile, she was off, gently closing the door behind her. Tess waited until she was sure she was out of earshot before whistling, 'Oh. My. God. This is the most beautiful room I've ever seen.'

The carpet looked like it was made of shimmering copper and contrasted beautifully with the pale cream silk paper on three of the walls. It was almost like the designer kept the decor elegant but simple because he or she knew that it could never compete with the most stunning feature of all – a whole wall of glass overlooking the glistening blue of the ocean. The suite was at the front of the ship so they could see for miles. Plopping her bag down on the exquisite chrome and glass dining table, she spun around. The mirrored dressing table, with matching bedside units, were the perfect accessory to the overstuffed pale blue sofa. Facing the sofa, next to the bar, was a giant flat-screen TV. In the opposite corner, a glass staircase rose up to a glass-balconied mezzanine floor with a huge king-sized bed.

Her experience of luxury holidays was limited. When she was growing up, Evelyn and Alan's idea of upgrading meant packing away the tent and going for a caravan instead. Not that she minded. Her whole childhood was bursting with memories of fantastic times spent rock-pooling and dancing at holiday park discos. She'd only experienced luxury travel after she met Drew. On their honeymoon they'd stayed in a beautiful hotel in Venice that oozed old-school class but, if she was completely honest, it felt a bit intimidating. Much to her husband's amusement, she had never been able to get out of the habit of cleaning up before the cleaner came.

Other than a couple of long weekends in New York, that was the only holiday they'd had until now. They'd booked several times only to have to cancel it because of one breaking story or another.

But now they were here. And this was truly spectacular. If only Cameron could see… She froze.

'What's wrong?' Drew asked, as he handed her a flute of champagne. 'You look really serious.'

'Nothing at all,' she shrugged. 'Just blown away by this. I'm not going to ask, but I bet it cost more than I earn in six months.'

Drew leaned down and, for the first time in ages, spontaneously kissed her. 'You're worth it.'

'Ah, that would be really impressive, if L'Oréal hadn't got there first,' she said teasingly, sliding her free hand around his neck and kissing him slowly. His hands circled around her face and she felt the heat of his body as his hips pressed against her. A surge of bliss swept over her. Their sex life had definitely cooled off in the last year or so, and lately it had become, well, a little mechanical. Functional. But this deep, lingering kiss and his gentle touch felt the way it used to do when they were still in the honeymoon period. Now, he could lift her up and carry her upstairs and…

He broke off and looked at his watch. 'Bugger! I said we'd meet the others down in the main bar at two o'clock.'

He didn't even have the consideration to react to her stunned expression. 'Can't they wait? They won't notice. They'll be having a great time. And anyway…' she moved in to kiss him again with a smile, 'we don't have to be too long.'

It was just as well her eyes weren't closed or she'd have ended up kissing thin air because he ducked – DUCKED!!! – out of the way, then said, 'Come on, honey I'll make it up to you later.'

His words had all the emotional depth of a Doggie Doo bag. He leaned down and kissed her on the nose. The nose. Not what she had in mind, but there was no point saying anything because he was already heading to the bathroom with a jaunty, 'Let me just go and wash my hands and we can head down.'

She slumped down onto the edge of the sofa, conflicting thoughts threatening to bring on a migraine. It was the first day. He was just being a genial host. He was excited to see his children. *Don't read too much into it. As he relaxes, things will get back to the way they used to be. Don't freak out. Do. Not. Freak. Out. It will be fine. Great.*

A noise at the door caught her attention and she watched as a white envelope appeared on the carpet. Probably a note to say the rest of the family were looking for them.

Checking the front, she saw that it was addressed to her. Strange. Mona was prone to pretending she didn't exist and Sarah wasn't the pushy type, so it must be from one of the others.

She slid her finger along the seal, and pulled out a sheet of paper with the Vistatoria's heading at the top, and a couple of lines of type underneath.

> Tess, I'm sorry about that conversation but I meant every word I said. Require future discussion. I hope you agree. Am owed some time off so have decided to take a break. Checked the ship's itinerary and have an idea. Meet me in Monaco on the day you dock there. I'll be in the square at noon. Cx

The lock on the bathroom door clicked and Tess quickly stuffed the paper into her bra, hoping that her purple kaftan concealed the bulge. What was Cameron thinking? Was he nuts? Drew could have easily been the one to spot the note first? She couldn't even work out how she felt about it because her heart was beating so hard it was drowning out rational thought.

'Ready?' he asked breezily.

Shoulders back. Big grin. Act normal. 'Ready.'

He held open the door and she grabbed her bag and passed him by. In the old days, he'd have put a hand on her back as they walked. Or even felt her up a little.

Her heart escalated to 'hammer' setting when she realized that Colita, Brazil was standing in the lift area, obviously waiting for her next arrivals. Would Colita mention the letter? Check they'd received it?

Like a Formula One driver heading for a brick wall, diversion mode kicked in and Tess practically ambushed the poor girl. 'Hi, Colita, the room is great, and the view is spectacular. Isn't it spectacular? Thank you so much. We must go now, big rush, family waiting.' And without another word of gibberish, she grabbed Drew's hand and as the doors pinged open, she pulled him into the lift. Now, he was definitely looking at her strangely, and no wonder.

As the elevator rose, the irony of the situation dawned. The nipple tassels, Drew's knock-back, the incredible ship, the major wobbly caused by that outrageous note... The one person she'd usually want to call and share all this craziness with was Cameron.

Mona

Mona stepped out on to the balcony and inhaled the sea air with a sense of achievement. They were here. Right up until the last minute she'd expected Piers to pull out, to claim some kind of work crisis and head back to sportswear HQ. He'd surprised her. Not only was he here, but he was getting into the spirit of things, having already changed into olive Bermuda shorts and a white Hugo Boss polo shirt. He was actually quite handsome. Or at least Emily the Frump would probably have thought so.

She wondered if he had any intention of confessing to the affair. Doubtful. If there was one thing that Piers loved more than himself it was money, and there was no way he'd choose to divorce again. His first wife took him for plenty and he'd partially learned his lesson. On the day before their wedding, his lawyer had appeared with a prenup and Mona had happily signed it. That's what love did to you... Made you stupid. However, even with the prenup, her settlement would be significant. Not that she'd take a penny of his money. Piers wouldn't risk it, though. Unless this fling escalated to something serious he wouldn't make a move that would dent his bank balance.

Anyway, there was no chance of his clichéd little affair escalating to anything permanent. Mona knew her husband. He was all about image and class. Emily might be an amusing distraction, but she wasn't the kind of girl that Piers would marry. The thought should have cheered her, but it didn't.

She took a sip of champagne and watched as a majestic liner left its moorings, passed them and headed out to sea, a crowd on the top deck cheering, laughing and dancing as they went. They looked so ecstatic and carefree that for a moment she wished she was with them instead of here, with a husband she could no longer stand, in a marriage that obviously wasn't enough for either of them. In the early days, Piers had struggled to accept that she refused to take his name, preferring to keep the Gold surname. She'd argued that it was the professional name by which everyone knew her. Now it seemed that refusing to take Piers' name was more of a premonition than an image choice.

'What are you thinking out here?' Piers moved in behind her and put his arm around her waist. She had to fight the physical urge to slap it away. Instead, after a moment's breather she turned to face him, leaning back on the balcony rail for support. 'Nothing at all. Just watching the world go by.'

'How long have we got before we have to meet up with the others?' he asked, and Mona groaned inside. He had his sex voice on. *Bloody hell.* She'd popped in for a quick blow-dry on the way to the airport this morning, and then spent half an hour expertly reapplying her make-up as soon as she got here. If he wanted sex he was going to have to do it standing up and without any activity that would ruin her gleaming mane of 40s style, wavy black hair or smudge her mascara. Did Vivien Leigh ever look like she'd just been energetically hot and sweaty? Nope.

Of course, she could always say no, but that would set the alarm bells off. Piers might criticize many things about her, but she was never one of the 'headache' brigade when it came to the conjugal schedule. Sex was one of her favourite things in life when they married and that remained the case. Just not necessarily with her husband.

She cast a glance over her shoulder and realized that another ship was passing by them. Sex in public was all very well and thrilling, but she had a hunch this would be less than smart given that she had no inclination to inspect the inside of a Barcelona police station.

'Let's go inside,' she murmured, taking his hand. Best get it over with. And she'd go on top. Preserve the make-up.

They crossed the suite to the circular bed in the middle of the room. It was going to be heaven to wake up every morning and see the ocean only feet away. A sharp nudge sent Piers sprawling back on to the white cotton sheets and he reached up to her with a seductive grin.

'Christening the room, are we?' he murmured, like a cat that got lucky and found a bowl of double-whipped, extra rich, organic, truffle-infused cream.

'Well, it would be a shame not to,' she teased, when all she really wanted to say was, 'yes, make it quick, and if you mess up my hair I may turn homicidal.'

Straddling him, she flicked open the button at the top of his shorts, and felt around for the zipper. Got it. She was just about to pull when she was quite literally saved by the bell.

Yes, there was a God.

'Ignore it,' Piers ordered, his hand sliding under her white shift dress and probing for the elastic of her thong.

Too late. With the agility of an Olympic gymnast, she vaulted off him, headed for the door and swung it open.

'Stepmother,' Max grinned, loving the automatic effect that word always had on her expression – straight from 'welcome' to 'irritation'.

Her prodigal stepson leaned down and kissed her on the cheek. 'I'm kidding.' That mollified her. 'And you look beautiful.' She checked out of 'irritation' and headed straight for 'happiness.' The power of the compliment was considerable, especially when coming from a thirty-five-year-old, six-foot-two-inch tall man who – while perhaps more Matt Damon than Brad Pitt – was charming, fit, and had just saved her from having to do some serious repair work on her make-up.

'Hey, how was your flight?' she asked, lingering just a little bit longer than usual on the hug. He deserved it.

'Yeah, fine. And the room is really great. Although,' he whistled as he scanned the suite, 'it's nothing on this.'

'Your father upgraded us. He heard that Drew had booked a suite and of course had to do the same. Apparently this one has five square feet more than the birthday boy, so he's a happy man.'

'Still feels the need to prove he's the richest guy in the room?' It was said with amusement rather than malice.

Mona smiled knowingly. How true that was. As a newspaper editor Drew was paid well, but he wasn't even close to Piers' league, yet somehow, Piers felt the need to wear his wealth on his bespoke-tailored sleeve.

Piers strode into the room from the bathroom, his hand out to greet his son. Mona checked that he'd readjusted himself and there were no tell-tale bulges in the groin area.

Coast clear. And escape from conjugal obligations complete.

'Good to see you, son.' He greeted Max effusively, pulling the younger man from a handshake into a hug. 'How are you?'

'I'm good, Dad. Although not as good as you, clearly. Tell me that tan isn't fake.'

Mona clamped her teeth shut. Now wasn't the time to raise the subject of last week's alleged business trip to Tenerife. Or to bring up his little jolly to New York. Or to enquire as to who exactly was in the party for a golfing break to Palma last summer.

The right time to introduce a few truths into this marriage would come soon.

But only when she was absolutely ready to rock the boat.

Sarah

'Is the cabin to your liking, Mrs Gold?'

'It's absolutely wonderful.' Sarah wondered if she should tip the nice young man who had gone out of his way to show her where to go, but then she remembered that John had told her that the tips were paid up front at the time of the booking so that you didn't have to carry cash on board.

'Thank you,' she told the cabin steward. He was wearing a badge, but without her specs on she couldn't read it. However, she could make out that the very nice young man was smiling an extra-friendly smile at Eliza. Not that Eliza noticed – she was too busy reapplying her lip gloss at the dressing-table mirror.

With a sinking feeling, Sarah realized that she was going to have to keep a surreptitious eye on her daughter this whole trip. Eliza might only be sixteen, but with the hair of a sun-kissed beach babe who'd just stepped off a surfboard, and legs that went on for ever, she looked at least nineteen. When you threw in the fact that she thought she was twenty-five, there was a sure-fire recipe for disaster.

Sometimes it was difficult to believe she'd actually given birth to this glorious creature. Her side of the family didn't do Amazonian beach babe. They did petite and cuddly with a predilection to matronly. She subconsciously ran her fingers through her short, light-brown hair. Patsy had made her get it cut and asked the hairdresser to put some highlights through it, but Sarah wasn't sure it was really her. At least the sprinkling of grey was gone, though. This was going to be a tough enough week without lining up next to the glamorous Mona and the decades-younger Tess with her silver roots showing.

'Mum, come look out here.'

She was momentarily confused. It was definitely John's voice, she just wasn't sure where it was coming from.

'Mum, the balcony!'

If she squinted she could just see the top of John's head, in the corner of the floor-to-ceiling glass door.

They had two rooms, next to each other, on the port side of the ship, deck nine. Apparently they were 'superior ocean-view balcony rooms', but she wouldn't have minded if they were 'bog-standard next-to-the-engine rooms'. Hadn't she and Drew taken John to a caravan at Berwick every year for ten years?

They'd come a long way. Separately, of course.

She weaved through the space between the two single beds and stepped through the open doorway, immediately feeling the heat of the sun and inhaling the smell of the sea. Outside she realized that John must be standing on a chair, as his head was popping over a six-foot partition.

'Would you like me to open the balcony door between the two staterooms?' the steward asked from the doorway. He was so unobtrusive; Sarah had almost forgotten he was there. She looked up at John for the answer to the question.

John nodded. 'Definitely. I wouldn't fancy trying this after a few beers.'

'Are you sure? I mean, I'll understand if you want your privacy…' she quickly added, very aware that this was the first holiday that John and Penny had been on since the kids were born. In fact, she was pretty sure that was the only reason she'd been invited – chief babysitter. Drew knew that Penny wasn't keen to leave the kids with strangers, so he'd come up with a way to make sure he got to spend some chill-out time with his son. That suited her perfectly. It would be good to see John and Penny get a break, too. They deserved it. If she got to sit on this balcony all day, and alternate between a great book and taking care of her two favourite grandchildren, she'd be perfectly happy.

The cabin steward carried out the request. 'Can I help you with anything else, madam?'

'No, thank you.'

'Very good.' With that, he left, carrying the partition, leaving her slightly incredulous. Was this how it happened on the seas? There was always someone there to get you whatever your wanted? You just asked for something and it was carried out immediately? After fifteen years of living on her own, doing everything for herself, that was definitely something she could get used to.

John climbed down from the chair, casually slung an arm

around her and gave her a hug. 'It's a long way from a caravan in Berwick, isn't it, Mum?' he said with a wink.

'I was just thinking exactly the same thing. And you look exactly like your dad did when we used to take you there.'

'Handsome and debonair?' he joked.

'Nope, scruffy and in need of a good haircut.'

A piercing shriek came from inside John's cabin. 'Bet you're regretting getting that barrier removed now,' he laughed as he headed inside to investigate the latest crisis.

At three, the twins were beautiful, cuddly and LOUD. Very, very loud.

Penny appeared two minutes later. 'Oh, Sarah, Lavinia just threw up all over the bed. Can you take Lawrence until I get her showered and changed? John is away to track down some cleaning stuff.'

Sarah nodded immediately. It was only the afternoon and already Penny looked exhausted. Bringing up two babies while working nights as a nurse in the A&E department of one of Glasgow's busiest hospitals was taking its toll. Sarah's heart went out to her. 'Of course I can. I'd be delighted to take them anytime, you know that.'

Stepping into their cabin, she revised that decision slightly. She'd be happy to take care of her grandchildren as long as they weren't projectile vomiting. Poor Lavinia was a grim shade of grey. Sarah gave her a huge hug and then reversed to a safe distance.

'Come on, Lawrence – how about we go up to the top of the ship and watch the other boats?'

There was no doubt whatsoever that her grandson was a Gold. He was the double of his father at that age, and already she could see there was a resemblance to his grandad, too. Thankfully, it was only his looks John had inherited from his father and not his ruthless self-centredness or infidelity gene

'Thanks, Sarah – I really appreciate it. And don't worry, we won't be asking you to babysit all the time.'

'Penny, I don't mind in the least. I love looking after the twins.'

Penny nodded. 'I know you do. But Drew has lined up a ship's nanny for us and he was very explicit about the fact that this is your holiday, too, and you're not here to look after everyone else.'

Puzzlement descended. So if she hadn't been invited to look after her family and provide babysitting backup, then what exactly was she doing here?

4.

Holiday Home Sweet Home

Tess

How did Drew not hear that? Her heart was banging out a tune that could drown out the steel band playing on the top deck, yet Drew remained oblivious. Tess took a deep breath. Then another. And another.

'You OK?' Drew asked, his face a picture of concern.

'Fine,' she smiled and added a wink for effect. Too much? She never winked. Now he would definitely know something was wrong. It was safe to say that if MI6 were in need of a new spy to add to their ranks, they'd best look elsewhere. Subterfuge obviously wasn't her thing.

'Just something in my eye,' she blurted, in the hope that it would explain her anxiety and the wink of a crazy woman.

'Here, let me see.'

Drew gently cupped her face, then prised her eyelid up a little. 'Look up. Look down. Look left. Look right. Nope, can't see anything in there.'

'Must have blinked it out.'

He took her hand and they continued to walk along the sun deck. The highest level on the ship, it was a great vantage point for checking out the views and it was filled with fellow shipmates of all ages, most of them leaning over the railings to watch as yet another huge liner left its mooring and passed them en route to open waters. The captain announced over the ship's tannoy that they'd be leaving next and a cheer went up among the crowd.

Drew must have studied the ship's layout because he seemed to know exactly where to go. That didn't surprise her. That was why he was so good at his job. He planned. He prepared. He delved into the details.

Hopefully he wouldn't delve into her bra and find a letter from her best pal demanding an illicit rendezvous. What the hell was Cameron thinking? How bloody reckless!

His hand slid around her waist as he held open a glass door that led into a bar. A neon sign informed her that it was the Ocean View Lounge, a completely round structure that had windows halfway down to the floor, giving a three-hundred-and-sixty-degree view.

In the bar, he immediately took charge. 'A San Miguel, please. What would you like, my love?'

My love. He hadn't called her that in a long time. Oh, crap, the guilt just nudged a little further up the scale. She needed to process what Cameron had done. Needed space to think it through. If ever there was a time when she actually needed Drew to be distant and neglectful for a few hours, it was now.

'Erm, a white wine please.'

'Pinot Grigio?' asked a very happy Chad, USA.

'That would be lovely, thank you.'

At which point Chad, USA – who had, she noticed, the most perfectly straight, blinding white teeth she'd ever seen in her life – threw a glass up in the air, caught it by the stem, pulled a wine bottle out of a bar-top fridge, popped the cork and poured. Drew's beer was almost an anticlimax after that.

'Are you sure you're OK?' he asked again.

No, she was not OK. Extremely not OK. She'd realized in the last few days that something was going wrong in her marriage. She was on holiday with her husband's entire family. She was about to spend ten days with his two ex-wives. And her best friend had declared his love for her and wanted to meet her in bloody Monaco. She was definitely not OK.

'I'm fine,' she reassured him. Maybe there was a chance for her in the spy business after all.

He sighed softly. 'Look, is it because Mona is about to arrive? I know you find her difficult…'

'I don't. What makes you think that?' she argued, deploying an expression of surprise.

'Because you chew your lip every time you see her coming.'

Right, then. So he did still notice some things. Right now, that wasn't a reassuring thought.

'It's not that I find her difficult…'

Drew laughed. 'But you do.'

'OK, I do. I don't dislike her though. I just find her… cold. A bit brittle.'

Drew nodded. She wasn't saying anything he didn't know already. Not for the first time, she wondered why they'd actually split up. On the face of it they had so much in common. Both in the same industry. Even worked in the same office. Both driven. Ambitious. A little ruthless. With a real thirst and excitement for what they did. And both a little inconsiderate of other people. Or a lot, actually.

The disloyalty in that last thought caused yet another chew of the bottom lip. Many times she'd asked Drew why they'd parted ways and he stuck to the same story that they'd just grown apart. Tess had taken it at face value and didn't take it personally that Mona had never been overly friendly. There were no harsh words, no arguments and no disputes – as Drew always said, they were all grown-ups. Even if one of the grown-ups was always irritatingly perfectly turned out and just a smidgen on the smug side.

'You know she doesn't mean any offence. It's just her way. There's a nice person underneath there, though.' She was sure the parents of serial killers and third world dictators thought the same thing.

'You honestly never find it difficult having your ex-wife working for you?' She'd asked this when they first met and she didn't expect his reply to have changed. Tess had found it irksome at first, but she'd come to accept it as a fact of life she couldn't change, just like his workaholic ways.

Drew took a long gulp of his San Miguel and shrugged. 'Not at all. She's brilliant at her job.'

His reply set off another wave of panic. Forget Mona's job, what about hers? How could she work at Anderson & McWilliam with Cameron after this? A whole new stream of catastrophizing took flight. She would lose the job she loved because Cameron would announce that he couldn't work with her anymore and he was higher up the company ladder than she was. Then Drew would find out about Cameron's feelings for her and suspect her of reciprocation. He'd then realize that their marriage wasn't working and divorce her. And in the space of about three seconds, she was unemployed, homeless and living in a camper van with two hippy parents, one of them wearing nipple tassels. Oh crap, her life was over.

'Well, look who it is.'

The voice came from behind Tess and immediately sent the hairs on the back of her neck up. Maybe Mona did actually annoy her more than a little. She steeled herself and prepared to launch Operation Pretend You're Happy To Be On Holiday With The Husband's Ex-Wives. Was it just her, or did that sound like the title of one of those crazy American talk shows where they did paternity tests and everyone was related to their cousin? Cameron loved those. *Aaaargh, stop thinking about him!*

If anyone was watching them they'd think they were a group of close friends, as much air-kissing, hand-pumping and hugging ensued. Piers was his normal over-the-top ebullient self. Tess actually quite liked him. In the beginning she'd felt a little intimidated in his presence and recoiled slightly from his flash, brash manner. What did a super-wealthy businessman have in common with a marketing executive who spent all day doing vitally important work like dreaming about new ways to bring Doggie Doo Bags to the world? Over the few times she'd met him, though, she'd come to realize that inside he was really just a working-class guy who'd made good and wasn't shy about showing his wealth. In fact, if she was being completely honest with herself, she preferred his loud, charismatic company to spending time with Mona. Oh bugger, more evil thoughts. *Make an effort. Make an effort,* she told herself. *Mona is nice. She is harmless. This is all going to be fine.*

'You look… lovely,' Mona told her with a wide smile. She mentally retracted the 'fine' prediction. The men didn't notice the patronizing undertone, but it was definitely there. She suddenly wished she'd made more of an effort with her appearance. The simple pair of cropped, straight jeans, white wedge sandals and a white T-shirt, with a chunky silver chain and bracelet set that Drew had bought her for her last birthday, had all seemed like presentable enough travelling clothes, but now she felt decidedly underdressed. And overweight. Why hadn't she stuck to the diet and shifted the ten pounds her arse could live without? She was chronically under-groomed, too. All she'd bothered with that morning was a quick coat of mascara and a slick of lip gloss that she'd long ago chewed off.

Mona definitely left her in the shade, in a stunning white crepe, sleeveless shift dress that stopped just above her knees and was accessorized with navy fifties-style kitten heels and a necklace of large navy and white marbles. With her jet-black, Dita Von Teese hair and ruby red lips, she looked like an exotic creature from an old movie. Tess was more suited to being an extra in *Friends*.

'And you are gorgeous as ever, Mona. I bet you're the most glamorous woman on the boat.' And the most bitchy. For reasons of diplomacy, the second comment wasn't said aloud.

Mona accepted the compliment gracefully and offered no objection. Job done, Tess switched her attention to Piers, who was ordering up a couple of cocktails, giving Chad, USA a thrilling opportunity to show off his bartending acrobatics, then back to Piers.

'Did Drew tell me you were bringing your son, too, Piers?'

As she was saying it, out of the corner of her eye she noticed a tall, dark-haired guy enter the bar and come striding over to them.

'There you are. Just in time,' Piers boomed. 'This is my son, Max.'

The newcomer shook hands all round, before adding another beer to Chad, USA's order.

'I'm glad you could come,' Drew told the younger man. 'Mona said that you'd always wanted to cruise the Med.'

Tess caught the hint of confusion that crossed Max's face, before Mona swept into the conversation, pushing her arm through Max's and turning her smile to megawatt. Something odd had just happened but before Tess could work out what it was, Mona interjected.

'It will be great for you too, darling,' she remarked pointedly to Tess. 'Won't it be nice for you to have someone your own age around?'

Mona

Bitch. Bloody bitch. It was the first thing that had crossed Mona's mind when she entered the bar and saw Tess standing there looking carefree, and naturally gorgeous and YOUNG. By her reckoning her replacement must be twenty-eight, but she could be at least five years younger. She didn't have a scrap of make-up on and yet she was irresistibly pretty. Pouring her curvaceous body into a plain T-shirt and jeans just made her look even sweeter. *Bitch.* To keep this figure, Mona hadn't eaten a carbohydrate since somewhere around 1998, and yet here was this *girl*, obviously no stranger to a bacon roll yet managing to pull off voluptuous and gorgeous.

Mona's inner hungry bitch seethed with the injustice of it, but she was smart enough to know that making it obvious wouldn't do her any favours. Drew had always hated her more caustic side and Piers would be furious with her if she was rude. This was only day one – no time to cause issues. Not when there was so much at stake.

She watched Drew effortlessly charm Max and get into a friendly banter with Piers over football – the standard class-bridging, non-ageist, all-consuming topic of the Scottish male.

She wasn't desperate enough to get involved, so instead she turned her attention to Tess. On closer inspection, the younger woman did seem a little tense across the eyes. It was never too young to begin having Botox. Purely as a preventative measure, of course.

She decided to make an effort. 'So, how are things in the marketing world, then?' she asked Tess sweetly.

'They're good. Busy.'

If Mona was a little less ladylike she might have snorted with derision. *Busy?* She had worked twelve-hour days, six days a week for twenty years. *That* was bloody *busy.* Tess probably thought she was rushed off her feet if she didn't have time to pop into Starbucks twice a day.

'Great,' she replied, acting as if she was totally engaged in the conversation. 'What are you working on at the moment?'

She noticed that the tension in Tess's eyes ramped up a little as she answered. 'Oh, just a new dog product. It's a… actually, I won't bore you with it. It's not very exciting.'

For the love of God. Drew Gold was married to a woman who was plugging dog products. How had that ever happened?

It took her a moment to realize that Tess was returning the question. 'And how are things with you, Mona? I saw your double-spread on the resurgence of the military vibe last week. The clothes were beautiful. But then, everything looks fabulous on the models, doesn't it?'

Was this child trying to taunt her? The dress Mona was wearing right now had been from that spread, albeit it had then been paired with a short navy jacket with gold buttons, and braiding on the epaulettes.

She shrugged her shoulders. 'Sometimes. But then, some of those young girls have the IQ of an Ugg boot, so it's just as well they're beautiful.'

Direct hit. Score one-nil to Mona. It was just too easy.

Tess's stunned silence caused a lull in the conversation.

OK, bored. She didn't come here to make small talk and indulge in petty point-scoring with Tess. In fact… She glanced at her stepson and a genius thought slipped into her mind. Her earlier comment about Max and Tess being good company for each other because they were the same age echoed in her mind. Many a true word spoken in jest. Max and Tess. Not a romance, of course, Tess wouldn't have the balls nor, she was sure, the inclination to stray. But perhaps Max could keep Tess just busy enough to put some building blocks for her Piers Delaney exit plan into place.

Sarah

'Come on, Lawrence, let's see what's along here, shall we?' Sarah wandered along the busy deck, gently guiding her grandson with one hand and holding a chocolate ice cream with the other. It had come from the ice cream parlour in the main public area on deck five, which was possibly the most amazing thing she'd ever seen – an actual street in the middle of the ship, with bars, restaurants and shops along either side. She'd already located the ice cream parlour, the pizzeria, the Irish-themed pub and a cake and candy shop that sold the most mouth-watering range of treats, with not a tit cake in sight.

After giving into the temptation of her mint chocolate chip treat (she couldn't bear to wonder how many Weight Watchers points were in it), she stopped to study one of the ship plans that she'd noticed were on the wall beside every elevator. Every deck except the top two were heavily populated with cabins, but some also had other outlets or activities. The main dining rooms at either end of the ship had three layers, spanning decks two, three and four. Deck five was taken up mostly with The Main Street and guest services. Deck six had the Internet cafe, the library and the conference room. Deck seven was home to the ice rink and cinema. The two-storey theatre was at the front of decks eight and nine. The casino and casual restaurant, Waterfalls, were on deck ten, right below the spa, gym and several speciality restaurants. Deck twelve had the kids' clubs, a basketball court and the first of the swimming pools. There was no deck thirteen – a superstitious thing. On the next level there was a wave pool with surfing simulator, an obstacle course, a jogging track, an 'adults only' area and a church. She might pop in there to pray that no one would ever force her to go on the obstacle course. And finally, the very top deck had a bar called The Ocean View and an observation deck with telescopes. Telescopes! Lawrence would love that.

'Come on, my lovely, let's go look at the birds and the boats through the telescopes, shall we?'

Lawrence followed her, toddling along quite happily. He was by far the most placid of the twins, obviously having absorbed all the 'laid-back and content' genes in the womb, leaving 'loves excitement and easily bored' for Lavinia. Not too dissimilar to her own children's splash in the genetic pool.

For a moment, she wished that Patsy were here. They'd probably be in a cocktail bar by now, half-tipsy on pina coladas, and they'd already be fully studied in the entire stock range of every shop on the ship. She'd thought about suggesting she bring her pal when Drew had invited her, but didn't want it to seem like she was taking advantage. Her and Drew weren't exactly BFFs, but she was happy that an easy friendship had arisen from the devastation of their divorce.

She wasn't paying much attention to the gent who held open the lift for them to enter.

'Cute little guy. Is this your son?'

Sarah felt a minor flush of pink in her cheeks as she laughed. 'My grandson. But that question might just have made my day,' she joked. 'And I don't suppose you're Tim McGraw?'

'No, ma'am, but that question might just have made my day, so I guess that makes us even.' Not that Sarah was particularly up on her US dialects, but that definitely sounded like a Texan twang. The white T-shirt, blue jeans, big silver buckle on the belt and cowboy boots added weight to her theory. Oh, bloody hell, a cowboy who looked like a slightly chunkier, slightly older, but ruggedly attractive version of country legend Tim McGraw. On a ship. In the Med. Wait till she told Patsy about this.

Perhaps he was with a tribute act? Or maybe there was a C&W-themed bar on the ship and he worked there.

'What floor ma'am?'

Ma'am. She liked that.

'Top deck, please. We're going to look at the boats, aren't we, Lawrence?'

Lawrence nodded, his gaze transfixed by the silver toecaps of Tim McGraw's cowboy boots.

'That's where I'm headed, too.' His eyes crinkled when he smiled. Sarah tried not to notice. She also tried not to notice his broad shoulders, his flat stomach and his buttocks. *DO NOT GET CAUGHT LOOKING AT HIS ARSE. DO NOT.* This was ridiculous. First day out of her kitchen and she was in a lift with a cowboy with incredibly tight buttocks. Yes, she looked at his arse.

As the lift shot upwards she made a mental note to get a grip of herself. And no, much as she was dying to know, asking him if he had a horse wouldn't be a good idea. *Just keep quiet. And dignified.* If he had a horse called Tonto that was his own business.

'Nate McKenzie,' he drawled, holding out his hand.

Oh bollocks, so much for keeping quiet. 'Sarah Gold. And this is Lawrence.'

After shaking Sarah's hand, he leant down and shook Lawrence's too. So cute. A cute cowboy. Who may or may not have a horse called Tonto. Patsy was going to laugh her arse off.

The doors pinged open and as they both turned right, Sarah wittered, 'Apparently there's a viewing tower along here with telescopes, so that's where I'm taking Lawrence.'

'That's where I'm headed, too,' Nate replied. 'My grandsons are along there, they're a might older than this little guy, and I'm going to track them down.' Sarah tried not to show her surprise. He didn't look old enough to be a grandfather to older kids. She'd have put him at around the same age as her, so somewhere around the forty-eight-to-fifty mark. Still, hadn't she read somewhere that they had children really young in the South?

'I'm here with my daughter and her sons,' he explained. 'I promised her since she was a little girl that I'd bring her to Europe and I'm just gettin' to it now. Sure hope it lives up to expectations.' There was a warmth in his voice that made Sarah smile. Or maybe it was just because somewhere in her head she was still pretending he was Tim McGraw. How weird. Yesterday she was dreading this whole trip and today here she was, wandering along in the sunshine and thoroughly enjoying chatting to a stranger.

They weaved in and out of the crowd as they walked the length of the deck in companionable silence.

'I think it must be round behind that bar there,' Sarah said, pointing to the circular glass structure right in front of them.

'Sarah!' When she was a little girl she hated the sound of nails scratching down a blackboard. She'd just discovered the adult version. Mona's voice rang out clear and grating. Several more familiar faces emerged from the bar.

'Mona! Good to see you. And Drew. Tess. Piers. And…'

'Max,' Mona replied. 'My stepson.'

Sarah knew her cheeks were the colour of Mona's ruby red lips.

'Hey, buddy.' Drew greeted Lawrence, scooping him up and squeezing him, to Lawrence's obvious delight. 'We were just coming to find you,' Drew told her, giving her a quick peck on the cheek. 'We thought we were all meeting in this bar.'

'Oh. I didn't know.'

'Didn't Eliza tell you? I texted her this morning to suggest it.'

'Unless a text involves an eighteen-year-old boy or shopping, she just ignores it.'

'Ah, sorry. That probably explains why she's not here yet either. I should have checked with you, too.'

'No, it's fine. I was just taking Lawrence along to the viewing tower, but we could join you later.'

'Yes, give you a chance to freshen up,' Mona said with a sweet smile that Sarah instinctively knew concealed a caustic barb. *Here we go*, she thought. *Ding. Ding. Round one.* 'Because I think you've, erm, spilled something on your top.'

Sarah automatically looked down, then groaned in horror. 'It's mint chocolate chip ice cream.' Mortified didn't even begin to cover it, made even more toe-curling by the sure knowledge that Mona would be loving this. Her gaze was drawn to another suspicious stain on the other side of her white top, and despite a firm command from her brain to her gob to stop talking immediately, embarrassment kept her chatter going. 'And that one is…' she racked her brain and eventually came to the point of even more embarrassment. 'Actually, you don't want to know.'

'Oh, we do.' Mona giggled.

What would be the penalty for tossing a seven-and-a-half stone woman overboard? Sarah rapidly came to the conclusion that she would do the time.

'Oh, it was just… well, Lavinia was sick and I cuddled her and… OK, I told you that you wouldn't want to know.'

In her subconscious, she heard the splash as Mona and her smug grin hit the water. Thankfully, Tess spoke up with a kindly, 'Not to worry. I bet Penny appreciated your help. Shall we arrange to meet later?' Tess didn't wait for an answer, before her gaze moved sideward. 'Sorry, we're being incredibly rude. I'm Tess Gold.'

It took Sarah a second to realize that Nate had been standing beside her the whole time and had witnessed every word of the exchange. Poor guy was clearly too polite to run for the hills.

'Nate McKenzie. Please to meet you ma'am.'

His voice was like warm, smooth barbeque sauce being poured on a rack of ribs. Dolly should write a song about it.

Drew wasn't looking particularly cheery, but nevertheless he shook Nate's hand and introduced himself. The others followed suit.

'So, Sarah Gold, Mona Gold and Tess Gold – are you three lovely ladies sisters?' Nate asked.

Oh bollocks, Sarah groaned inside. Could they perhaps go back to talking about the vomit on her top?

'No, actually,' Mona replied, her expression alive with mischief. 'We're all Drew's wives.'

To his credit, Nate barely blinked, just gave a small nod and said, 'Well, it was good to meet you folks. You all have a great trip.'

As she watched his back disappear into the crowd, Sarah decided that if that encounter had been the equivalent of riding one of those bar-room bucking broncos, she'd just been bucked off and landed on her bum with a very loud splat.

5.

Anchors Away

Mona

It had taken a bit of deft manipulation, but Mona succeeded in securing the seating arrangement she'd been looking for at dinner: Drew on one side, Eliza on the other. Penny hadn't made it, preferring to stay in the cabin with the still poorly Lavinia, so their table of nine consisted of her and Drew, Tess, Piers, Max, Sarah, Eliza, John and little Lawrence. The dining room had two official sittings, at six thirty and eight thirty, but Drew had booked them on an 'anytime dining' ticket, which meant they could eat whenever they wanted.

Sarah, who had miraculously managed to appear at a gathering without body fluid stains on her clothes, was down at the other end of the table with her son John and Piers, while Tess was between Max and Lawrence and seemed to get on well with both.

Mona cast a critical eye around the room, but it was difficult to find fault with the decor. It was very much in the tradition of the old-school grand voyages. You could almost imagine forties movie stars gliding down the glorious curved walnut and brass staircase. There wouldn't be change out of a hundred thousand for the main chandelier. The tables were made of thick, glossy mahogany, with matching Queen Anne chairs upholstered in antique gold. The overall aesthetic was one of luxury and class. Mona felt right at home.

Piers' booming laugh cut through her thoughts. He just couldn't resist the opportunity to show off and be centre of attention. He'd already ordered two bottles of champagne and was making a big performance about uncorking the bottles.

Why hadn't that annoyed her before they got married? Or perhaps it had and she'd just chosen to block it out? She decided that was the best policy now too and turned to her former husband instead.

'So how does it feel to be fifty?' she asked Drew.

'Old,' he joked. 'Especially when a girl who looks like this is your daughter.'

Eliza had laughed and punched her dad on the arm.

'Where did you get that dress?' he asked, feigning disapproval. 'Isn't it a bit too... sophisticated for you?'

Eliza really did look utterly beautiful, which was just as well because Tess and Sarah were letting the side down with their plain clothes and lack of accessories. Sarah's black maxi dress was unremarkable in every way and Tess was wearing a black gypsy top and trousers. It was difficult to distinguish whether they were dressing for dinner or a death in the family.

'Actually, Mona got it for me. I love it.' Eliza beamed, purring loudly enough for the whole party to hear. At the other end of the table, Sarah almost choked on her gin and tonic. Mona chose to ignore her, struggling to conceal how much she was enjoying Sarah's shocked reaction.

'It was one of the samples from the Antigua shoot last month. Eliza often comes by my office when she's waiting for you and we've found her some great clothes, haven't we, sweetheart?'

The irony wasn't lost on her. When she and Drew were married, Eliza was the subject of many a heated discussion. Why should she give up her weekend in Paris to take a six-year-old to a Barbie birthday party? Why was her attendance mandatory at the end of term dancing display? And why must a large portion of her hard-earned cash – OK, *their* hard-earned cash – go to support a child who clearly had more than she could ever want already? How many bloody pony lessons could one kid need?

Now, their revised relationship was built on very different foundations. Eliza loved Mona because she was chic and stylish, introduced her to cute male models and got her amazing clothes for free. Mona loved Eliza (actually 'loved' was definitely stretching the point, but she happily tolerated her) because she was a direct link to Drew and gave her an opportunity to come off as the really cool, caring, former stepmother. It was a win/win situation. At the other end of the table, she could see Sarah's face of thunder. Another bonus! It seemed her relationship with Eliza infuriated Drew's other ex-wife. Win/win/win.

Eliza agreed, then picked up her iPhone and was soon lost in text world with her friends. It amazed Mona that they were in the middle of the ocean, yet they still had a WiFi signal. If she had time tomorrow she might go online and check out some of the best places for shopping before they disembarked in Naples. She much preferred targeted consumerism to random browsing.

'Missing the office?' she asked Drew, with heavy irony. 'I'm surprised you haven't been checking in.'

'I have, but don't tell Tess. She's threatened to toss my iPhone overboard.'

Mona had struggled not to laugh. As if Tess would have the bottle to pull a stunt like that. Look at her, sitting there chatting to Max, probably about reality TV or something equally inane.

It did give her an idea, though. She leant closer to Drew. 'Well, we can't have an unhappy wife, can we? How about if I check in for you, then bring you up to date with anything you need to know. Filter out the rubbish, but keep you abreast of the important stuff.'

His shoulders actually relaxed a little as she said it. If there was one thing she knew about Drew, it was how committed he was and how he couldn't bear to be cut off from the news. It was one of many things she used to – and still did – love about him.

In fact, she suspected that his desire to give his all to his job was the reason behind this whole big family voyage in the first place. He was getting all his demands as a father, a husband and a grandfather satisfied at the one time. He could return from here, satisfied that he'd been a family guy for a couple of weeks and go straight back to living round the clock at his desk. Either that or he was bored rigid with Little Miss Gypsy Top and couldn't stand being stuck on a ship for ten days with only her company.

He was clearly unhappy. She could see it. He wasn't fulfilled. He wasn't satisfied. And no wonder. What did Tess have to keep a man like him interested? Sure, at the beginning it was probably a novelty for a forty-five-year-old man to have a twenty-four-year-old hanging on his every word, but by the looks of things that had definitely worn off. Poor girl. Mona almost felt sorry for her.

Almost.

She tried not to show her irritation when John announced it was time to get Lawrence off to bed and immediately voices around the table jumped to concur, with clichés like 'long day', 'up early tomorrow', and 'get an early night'. That one came from Piers and it was loaded with such a thick layer of innuendo that everyone laughed.

Mona joined in, even though she was clenching her jaws so tight she almost burst her veneers.

She had to keep her cool. There would be a time to act, but it wasn't now. Hadn't the last few years shown that she was nothing if not patient?

Sarah

It had taken every ounce of self-control Sarah had, not to take the bread roll from the plate on her left and launch it across the table like a scud missile, aimed squarely at the over-painted, smug, vicious, conniving tart sitting next to Drew.

How fucking dare she? And oh my God, she'd just thought the F-word for the first time in years. That was what that fucking woman did to her.

This was so bizarre. In the last fifteen years her relationship with Mona had gone through many stages. There was the pure hatred stage, when she first found out about Drew's affair, and the only reason Mona was still alive was because Sarah didn't know where to buy arsenic. Then there was acceptance, when Mona graduated from mistress to wife, and Sarah knew that for the sake of the kids she had to suck up her own feelings and present a pleasant face to the world. Next, admittedly, came a little snippet of smugness when their marriage ended. Since then, on the few occasions when they'd been together, Sarah tolerated her and kept things civil. She understood that even though Mona and Drew were no longer married, she was still one of his closest friends and would therefore be in attendance at all significant social gatherings.

But the conniving, devious witch had boasted about how she'd given that dress to Eliza! The very dress that Sarah had told her daughter was completely inappropriate to wear to dinner in a room that looked like it could have gone down with the bloody Titanic. In fact, it was too short, too low-cut and too obscenely tight to wear anywhere – which was why Sarah had told Eliza to leave it at home. Not only had her daughter ignored her as usual, but now it turned out that Mona was complicit in the whole debacle.

In a burst of fury-induced comfort eating, Sarah had resorted to eating the bread roll instead of using it in a violent act. It didn't make her feel any better. Now she was just bloody furious with a tighter waistband.

The only thing that had kept her going throughout dinner was Piers Delaney and his endless chatter of funny anecdotes and really bad jokes. Maybe it was her imagination, but Mona didn't seem to give her husband a second glance all night. Not that surprising, she supposed. Mona and Drew had always been impossible to distract once they got talking about work.

Somehow Sarah had managed to get to the absolutely magnificent strawberry cheesecake without resorting to a serious breach of the peace, and it was a blessed relief when John announced he was taking Lawrence to bed and she jumped on the bandwagon. 'I think I'll call it a night, too,' she announced, then – to her surprise – almost everyone else concurred. Were they all, with the exception of Piers, fighting the urge to kill Mona, too?

Back in the cabin, she peeled off the black maxi-dress picked out by Patsy as she chatted to Eliza. She wouldn't be able to return it now, but she'd felt nice in it so it was worth it. Besides, it would come in handy for a show of mourning after she surreptitiously topped Mona.

'So what do you think of the ship then, love?' Eliza didn't even glance up from her iPad. Another one of Drew's 'little treats'.

'Yeah, great.'

'And how was your dinner?'

'Yeah, fine.'

'Do you think you'll have plenty to keep you occupied for ten days?'

'Dunno.'

All those years at school studying the English language were clearly paying off. It would be tempting to get into the whole dress thing with her daughter, but she resisted the urge. It was the first night of the holiday, she didn't want a stroppy teenager for the next ten days, and anyway, she wasn't convinced that the bulk of the blame didn't lie with Mona. What was she thinking, giving a sixteen-year-old a dress like that?

Sarah sighed as she pulled on comfy black velour trousers and a plain black T-shirt (it had been a pyjama compromise with Patsy, who had finally agreed to no lacy baby-dolls or deep-cut cleavages, as long as Sarah chose nothing with spots, stripes or cuddly animals of any species).

'Are you going to be on that thing for a while?'

'I'm on Facebook, Mum,' Eliza replied, with an overtone of 'D'uh'.

'OK, I'm going out for a walk, then. You know, that thing that people do. Sometimes people even walk with friends that they actually meet face-to-face, instead of just sitting at home talking to six hundred and fifty people that they barely know.'

'Mum, you sound so lame.'

Lame. Oh for the days when that meant there was something wrong with your foot. And she got the irony that thinking that made her, in Eliza's eyes, even lamer.

She grabbed a sweatshirt, pushed her feet into a pair of black trainers and headed to the lift. A couple who were fairly obviously on their honeymoon got in at the same time. The tall, blonde girl was wearing a stunning ankle-length silver silk gown and the guy was in a sharp suit with an open-neck shirt. The rings on the girl's wedding finger sparkled in the light and the pair seemed to find it difficult to keep their hands off each other. Sarah felt a surge of happiness for them. It was hard to believe she'd felt like that once. How long ago was that? She did a quick calculation. She'd married Drew almost thirty years ago. Bloody hell, that was a long time to go without the frisson of excitement that came with a new love. There had been a few dates, a few casual relationships, even a low-key romance with a plumber who'd come to fix a burst pipe, but love had never entered the frame again.

Love's Young Dream got off at level ten and Sarah carried on up to level fourteen.

One deck below The Ocean View lounge, deck fourteen had a walking and jogging track that stretched right around the whole ship. A brisk walk – OK, a casual stroll – was just what she felt like after the huge meal and side order of concealed rage.

When she stepped outside, she was glad that she'd brought the sweatshirt. The night air was cool, but the breeze caused by the fact that they were soaring through the seas was bordering on chilly.

Turning left as she came out of the lift area, she peered over the railings on the inside of the track to see dozens of loungers, still laid out in circles around the pool. On at least a dozen of them were couples, some looking up at the stars, some talking intimately, some sleeping, and in the case of a rather large couple who had taken a lounger each, some eating chips. They were even doing that in a romantic manner. This place had turned into the love boat.

Sarah carried on walking, facing into the breeze and loving the way it felt like it was blowing away her stresses. Not that she had many. Life was good, she reminded herself. It was just that, lately, she was beginning to think it might be even better if she had someone to share it with. Bugger, was this going to lead to her devouring Mills and Boon novels, prowling Match.com and never going out without a pair of those magic knickers?

'Hey, what's making you smile?'

Her shriek got carried off in the breeze. 'Bloody hell, Drew, you scared me. And at my age that's not a good thing,' she joked. 'What are you doing up here?'

She immediately clocked his attire and realized it was a stupid question.

'I was in the gym working out, and thought I'd cool down up here with a run.' He slowed down to her pace and seemed quite happy to walk with her.

She couldn't resist having a gentle dig. 'So. First night on a cruise. Your big holiday of the year. With your lovely wife. And you're working out at midnight. I don't know whether to admire your discipline or have you committed.'

'It's an age thing,' he admitted, clearly enjoying her cheek. 'Got to keep the bones moving in case they grind to a halt.'

Sarah laughed and bowed. 'OK, you win. I'm in awe of your motivation.'

It had been a while since they had chatted like this, on their own and free to have a bit of teasing banter. He was still so handsome, she acknowledged. Even now she could see in him the young seventeen-year-old boy who had kissed her at the school dance. He'd taken good care of himself and his eyes still crinkled up at the sides when he smiled. That used to be enough to make her stomach flip with adoration.

'I'm glad you came, Sarah.' A little more serious now.

'I am, too.' For the first time, she realized that she actually meant it.

There was a pause when neither of them seemed to know exactly what to say.

After a few moments, he made the first move to go. 'See you

tomorrow, Sarah. Goodnight. Sleep tight.'

'You, too,' she replied, and then watched as he broke into a jog again and took off.

It was only as he disappeared into the night that she realized she'd missed the perfect opportunity to ask him why he'd invited her along in the first place.

Tess

Tess lay in bed, eyes open, the wall of black outside blowing in a soft salty breeze. Drew had decided to go to the gym for a late-night workout and she was trying not to care that she was spending the first night at sea sitting in bed alone.

She told herself that after the drama of the morning and then the slightly awkward dinner they'd all had together, it was quite nice to switch off and relax for a little while. The conversation had been a little forced at dinner, but thankfully Piers was as gregarious as ever and kept things going. The two bottles of champagne he insisted on buying helped, too. His son, Max, had turned out to be amusing company. He did something to do with computers and was full of funny anecdotes about the office he worked in, and seemed genuinely interested in her job, too. She'd omitted the bit about the work colleague who was currently trying to split up her marriage. Probably not the best topic of conversation for the first night at sea. Or any night until the end of time.

Mona had shone in her usual spectacular way, wearing a pale blue figure-hugging tea dress and silver strappy sandals, her hair pulled back into a severe but stunning chignon. Sarah's gorgeous but simple black maxi-dress and Tess's black trousers and gypsy top had seemed utterly underdressed by comparison.

She reached down to the floor for her handbag and pulled it on to the bed, an action that gave her a pang of homesickness – not for her and Drew's home, but for her mum and dad. Evelyn always slept with her bag next to bed and it was a habit that Tess had developed as soon as she got her first Take That backpack. She felt for the inside zip pocket, slid it open, pulled out Cameron's note and reread it. At least twenty times.

With each reading her heart thumped even faster as she swayed between sadness, annoyance, missing him, irritation, hurt, affection, disbelief and longing to see him walk through the door right now so that they could talk, laugh about this, dismiss it all as a joke and go back to being extremely platonic best friends.

Right on cue the door swung open… and Drew came in, still in a black vest and shorts, with a towel around his neck and a gleam of sweat on his face.

'Hey, honey, still awake?'

Cameron's note was hastily slipped under the duvet, thankfully giving her no time to concentrate on analysing whether Drew's comment had an overtone of disappointment. Of course it didn't. Bloody Cameron was making her question everything.

'I'm just going to grab a quick shower.'

'No problem, babe,' she replied, with a cheerfulness that was definitely skin deep.

As soon as she heard the water turn on she stuffed the note back into her bag and slid it back under her side of the bed. She'd worry about it tomorrow. In fact she wouldn't. It was ridiculous that she was risking spoiling a whole holiday because Cameron was having some kind of confused, mid-life crisis. Time to draw a line under this and refuse to give it a second thought for the rest of the trip.

Resolution made, she pressed play on the iPod on the bedside table and slipped further down into the bed as the sound of Adele's 21 filled the room. She loved this album. It always made her mellow out. The strings of the guitar plucked out the introduction to 'Don't You Remember' and she immediately felt her stress levels slide down a notch.

By the time Drew climbed into bed she was close to being relaxed for the first time in days. The heat of his body warmed her, as he raised himself up on one elbow and reached over to stroke her face.

'Feels like ages since we were together and neither of us needed to get up at the crack of dawn.'

His tenderness made her blurt out the question that had been on her mind for months.

'Drew, are we OK?'

'What do you mean?' he looked genuinely puzzled. Surely that was a good thing.

'It's just that…' How to put this. 'We seem to have slipped into a bit of a rut where there's no time for each other anymore.' There. No accusatory tone. Making a legitimate point without focussing on the fact that it was only him who had no time for her.

He thought for a moment before slowly nodding. 'You're right. I'm sorry, honey. Work has been really tough lately and sometimes, I know, I forget when to switch off and call it a day. And I always think of you as being so independent and just getting on with your life…'

'But sometimes it would be nice to spend that life with my husband.' She hated the way that sounded, like she was rebuking him or taking a fast train to Needy Central. She wasn't. She was just opening a discussion. She watched his face for a flicker of irritation but didn't see one. More relief.

'You're right and I'm sorry. Anyway, isn't Cameron my stunt double for you these days?'

Of course it was a joke, but she suffered such a knee-jerk reaction that he came close to spending the rest of the trip with blue balls. She resorted to skipping right past the moment of truth. 'Cameron's services only extend so far,' she replied when she'd recovered enough to speak, hoping the cheeky grin covered up the panic.

It seemed to work. 'Sounds like I've got some making up to you to do,' he teased.

He leaned down and kissed her, softly at first then a little more insistent, his hand now gently stroking a line down the side of her face, across her neck, to her shoulder, where he peeled down the shoestring strap of her vest. He continued to undress her, his lips never leaving hers, his movements slow and tender. For the first time in many weeks, she felt connected to him, felt the emotion of their relationship take over and block out everything else.

It was only later, as his breath deepened into soft snores, that she realized that from the moment he kissed her until he slipped into sleep, he hadn't used her name even once.

6.

Wake Up In Palma

Tess

It was only 7 a.m. and already the sun was breaking through the morning hue and promising a beautiful day as Tess stood at the railing on her balcony, watching as they manoeuvred into dock at Palma de Mallorca. Just as the ship dropped anchor, Drew sauntered out behind her, carrying two coffees from the table that room service had pushed into the room at the requested time of six forty-five. It was an obscenely early rise for a holiday, but she'd been keen to see Palma from the ocean. And after the wonderful end to the night, she wanted to get the day started and make the most of every minute of their time together.

He kissed her briefly as he handed over a large mug. 'Morning, honey.'

'Good morning. And thank you. I could get used to this.' She took the coffee from his hand and gestured to the view in front of them. 'Not exactly the view I'd been expecting. I was hoping for a glorious, Mediterranean bay.'

'What's wrong with container ships and the smell of fuel?' he asked with a smile.

'You're right. It's completely unreasonable of me to be so demanding.'

When she'd first peeked out and seen where they were mooring she'd checked the *Daily Vista*, the two-page magazine that Colita had left on the desk last night, and realized that they were in an industrial dock a few miles from the city centre. Apparently, it was only about ten euros to get to the more salubrious parts of Palma. 'Have you been here before?' she asked him.

Curious that they'd been married for five years and she had very little idea as to what countries her husband had visited in his life. That's what long working hours and a twenty-one-year age difference did.

'A couple of times. Not since the nineties, though. What about you?' Drew asked her.

She nodded. 'Once. On a school trip when I was fifteen. I snogged Gary Burton on the steps of the cathedral. I may be banned from the city, for all I know.'

When he didn't reply, she turned around to see that he'd already sat down at the balcony table and opened his laptop. She bit her bottom lip, fighting an urge to... she wasn't sure what. Cry? Rage? Yep, rage. Rage was good. She accepted that at home he was a busy man who had to be on top of everything from world events to local news, but she wasn't prepared to play second fiddle to the rest of the world today, or any day on the first proper holiday they'd had since their honeymoon. Hadn't they agreed he wouldn't work onboard? That included catching up with news and browsing global affairs.

Rather than launch the laptop into the Port of Palma, she decided to go for the light-hearted and low pressure route. Maybe he was just out of the habit of relaxing. Perhaps he just needed a gentle reminder. She moved round behind him, snaked her arms around his shoulders and leant in to nuzzle his neck. Was it her imagination or did he just flinch?

'Drew, it's the first day of our holiday. Put the laptop down and back away slowly,' she said, injecting as much humour into her voice as she could muster. 'Come on, there are much better things to be looking at.'

She moved around in front of him and sat on his knees, then leant in for a proper kiss. After an initial split second when she suspected he tried to peer around her to see what was on the screen, he relented to her kiss, sliding his hands up the front of her vest and cupping her breasts. Ah, this was more like it. How long had it been since they had sex in the morning? She was going to make this happen. In fact, she was going to take charge of the whole day. It was time for a new, assertive Tess to emerge from the lip-chewing doormat that she'd somehow become. And Cameron would be hearing about it, too. As soon as she got back she was going to sit down with him, sort it out, make her position clear, and then they'd put all this nonsense behind them. She suddenly experienced a surge of determination of a level she didn't know she possessed. Maybe she'd inhaled a dangerous amount of those diesel fumes.

'So, I was just thinking. Since we've both been to Palma, we could perhaps amuse ourselves here in the cabin for a while, then head into the city for lunch and a wander around the cathedral. I might even relive my youth and snog you on the steps, too.'

'Really?' he murmured, fully concentrating on her now. He'd slipped her vest upwards and was zeroing in for lip-to-nipple contact when…

Brrrrrrrrrrrr.

Tess jumped. What the hell was that?

Drew pushed her back, swept his head around her and went to press a button on his laptop. 'Erm, you might want to put your top back on because this is a Skype call. There's a video option.'

Don't do this. Don't. Didn't he realize their relationship was much more important than taking a call? This was a snapshot of their lives together and she definitely didn't like the way the picture was developing. Anxiety got a hold of her stomach and began to squeeze, and suddenly she wanted to know: what was more important, her or the call?

'Don't take the call. Ignore it.'

He looked at her pleadingly. 'Tess, I can't. It must be important. Everyone is under strict instructions only to call me if it's a matter of life or death.'

So now she knew. There was no competing with this. With a sinking heart, she pulled her vest back on and disentangled herself from him. She was barely decent when he pressed the button to take the call.

Mona's face immediately filled the screen. Tess seethed. Not only did she have to put up with the family party from Weirdsville on the ship, but now one of his ex-wives had actually found a way to get into their stateroom.

'Good morning, Drew, morning Tess,' Mona chirped. There was a hint of smugness there that left Tess in no doubt that she was loving the fact that she could interrupt them whenever she pleased.

Tess moved out of view of the camera and answered with a V

sign. Highly immature and very out of character, but it did make her feel better.

'Tess, did you just... no, must have been a trick of the light.' Mona said.

Oops. Obviously wasn't out of view of the camera after all. She ducked back into full shot and gave Mona a big cheesy grin and a wave. 'Morning, Mona, so lovely to see you there,' she said, in a ridiculously over-the-top sing-song that countered the small yet satisfying act of defiance.

Fuming, she picked up her coffee cup and headed back inside, had a quick shower, then wrapped a towel around her and padded back into the bedroom area. Through the windows, she could see that Drew was still hunched over his laptop, deep in conversation. Urgh. It was bad enough that he was working, without the added irritation of his smug ex-wife. She was never going to survive ten days of this.

Sliding open the wardrobe doors, she realized that she didn't have a clue what to put on because she didn't know what they were doing today. Wasn't this the story of her bloody life these days? Why was she always waiting on Drew, unable to even choose what to wear until he deigned to fill her in on his plans?

Bugger it, wasn't going to sit around waiting for him. She pulled out a pair of cropped white jeans and a pale green jersey batwing top, then threw a few silver chains around her neck and slipped on a pair of silver flip-flops to give the look a boho edge.

Right. Ten more seconds and she was going out there and she was going to slam that bloody laptop shut. She was!

Nine.

Eight.

Her pulse began to quicken.

Seven.

Six.

She yelped as her teeth dug into her bottom lip.

Five.

Four.

Three.

Take-off was two seconds away when a noise at the door made her jump. Three apologetic knocks.

If that was Mona, Tess wouldn't be responsible for her actions.

Full of pent-up fury, she swung the door open, and was

rapidly deflated when Colita, Brazil gave her a sunny smile. 'Good morning Mrs Gold, I have an email for you. It came in to the business centre this morning.'

Tess quickly peered over her shoulder and saw to her relief that Drew was still otherwise engaged.

'Thank you, Colita.' A thought struck her. 'Oh, and Colita, if there are any more of these notes could you just keep them for me and I'll come check in with you when I'm free?'

Colita, Brazil beamed as she nodded gracefully. 'Of course, Mrs Gold. Have a good day.'

The door was barely shut when Tess dived into the bathroom and, with trembling hands, opened the letter. Please make it be from her mum. Or her boss. Or a long-lost relative. Anyone but…

> Tess, I'm sorry to do this but I had to write again in case you thought I'd sent yesterday's note when I was confused. Or pished. I hope that you've had time to think about what I said. Meet me when you dock in Monaco. I'll be in the square at noon. Cx

Leaning forward, she pressed her head against the cool of the tiles in the hope that it would counteract her racing pulse and the beads of sweat that were popping out all over her. What was he thinking? And more to the point, what was she thinking? She had absolutely no idea how to handle this.

Eventually, when she felt her shaking legs could take her weight, she stood up and shoved the letter down the front of her trousers, in the hope of concealing it until she could secretly shred it. After Drew's performance this morning, she didn't think it was at risk of discovery.

Opening the bathroom door, she almost yelped when she saw her husband standing right outside it.

'Are you OK?' he looked so genuinely concerned it triggered another wave of guilt.

'I'm fine. Great,' she blustered.

'Honey…' Term of endearment – more guilt. This was torture. Right, time to get over herself, stop being furious, and revert to plan A – make her marriage better. What they needed was to get out of here, go into town, have a long, leisurely romantic lunch and then come back and finish what they'd started this morning. Yes, that's exactly what they needed. Time. Together.

Drew was still talking. 'Listen, I'm really sorry and please don't freak out...' This didn't sound like it was going to concur with her plan in any way whatsoever.

'But I have to work today. Big story. Huge. And the paper is right at the front of it, so I have to be involved. I'll make it up to you, I promise, I swear. Love you.' He kissed her on the cheek – the cheek again! – and then turned and headed back to his laptop.

Stunned, it was all Tess could do to pick up her bag and head for the door. Drew was so engrossed in his bloody work that he didn't even notice that her knickers rustled as she walked.

Mona

The next time Mona happened upon Dweezil McClinchy, the Bermudan star striker whose position in the Scotland team was granted thanks to a merchant seaman grandad from Dundee, she made a promise to herself to buy him a drink. Or ten. She might even let him lick them from her naked body.

Oooh, that thought just gave her a tremor. Dweezil was six-foot-two-inches of physical perfection… but she couldn't see herself calling out that name in a moment of orgasmic ecstasy. His parents must have seriously disliked him. However, right at this moment, Mona loved him. They'd broken the story last week of Dweezil's affair with his teammate's wife, and a well-placed hack had then discovered that he was also shagging his wife's sister. And now, this morning, they'd been handed a tip that he was also having it off with – she could hardly believe this – the wife of their local Member of Parliament.

Colin Trenchant, the Right Honourable Member for the Greater Glasgow area, had absolutely no idea that there were photographs in existence of his wife Cindy sucking the face off Dweezil in a city centre nightclub, then heading to a budget hotel. Not even a Hilton or a Hyatt!

Mona felt an uncharacteristic giggle take hold. This was bloody brilliant. No other newspaper even had wind of this one yet. It was one of their in-house photographers who had been in the right place at the right time and taken the pictures of them entering together, groping each other in the lobby, then leaving the next morning. This story was going to be big. Huge. The government spin machine would go into supersonic kill mode and all the other nationals would jump on it, so they had to be meticulously careful how they handled it.

Mona had been out of hard news for ten years, but it still gave her a rush like nothing else. The timing couldn't be better. As self-appointed liaison for Drew, it was the perfect opportunity to spend time with him and step back into the delectable rush of a breaking scandal.

She dressed carefully, a white scoop-neck T-shirt, charcoal Capri trousers and black patent leather sling-back wedges, then checked her reflection. Almost there. Large pearl stud earrings finished the look to perfection.

Piers wandered out of the shower with a towel around his waist. He'd had a six-pack when she met him, courtesy of a Japanese martial arts master he had on the payroll. Master Yen had long ago departed back to his native country and now Piers had a rotund stomach, courtesy of too many steak dinners and red wines. There was no denying that he was still attractive, but he was… she struggled to find a definitive answer. She got it! He was too old for her now. That was it. Sure, he was only a couple of years older than Drew, but somehow he'd slipped into late middle age. The lack of exercise. The affair with the secretary. The boring stories. He didn't have a single thing to say that interested her any more. Drew, on the other hand, still had plenty to say that she wanted to hear.

But first, there was some groundwork to lay. She filled Piers in on the story and the need for her to work with Drew on it. 'Seriously? You're seriously going to work today? Who gives a flying fuck if some football player is porking an MP's wife?'

'It's a huge story and of course people care. We're a shallow, materialistic, gossiping society that is addicted to the modern-day cult of fame. It's what makes us special,' she added, with a supercilious grin. Time to play the trump card. 'Anyway, I thought you would want to have some time with Max today. You know, father and son bonding stuff. You wouldn't want me along for that. Go have fun. Or are you worried that he'll wear you out?'

Lesson 101 in the *Dealing With The Alpha Male Handbook* – when all else fails, go for the ego.

He dropped his towel while he searched in the wardrobe, and Mona realized she had averted her eyes. There were many things she could live without seeing this morning and Piers' tackle was on the list.

'Suit yourself, then,' he shrugged. 'I've got a few calls to return, then I'll see what Max is up to. Last time I was in Majorca was at that pro-am golf tournament last summer. Had one too many and bought a jet ski in the auction. Don't even know what happened to the bloody thing.'

Mona remembered the trip well. Not that she was on it, of course. But she had found the receipts for the Presidential Suite with two English breakfasts every morning to be particularly enlightening. She just hoped Emily the Frump had remembered to pack the factor fifty because the midday sun would be hazardous to her washed-out complexion.

Stretching up on her tiptoes, Mona kissed Piers on the cheek, keeping her hips a safe distance from his swaying genitals. Her trousers were crepe and dry-clean only.

'Good idea, darling,' she agreed. 'Why don't I meet you back here for a pre-dinner cocktail? About six-ish? I think we sail at 8 p.m. tonight.'

His grunt said 'clearly displeased, but too macho to appear needy'.

There was a smile on her face all the way along the corridor to Drew's room.

He answered the door as soon as she knocked – great, no sign of Tess - his intense expression a complete contrast to his laid-back khaki T-shirt, cream chino shorts and bare feet. With the chiselled jaw and the wide shoulders, he looked like he'd just stepped out of an M&S advert for summer-wear for the mature man.

'Un-fucking-believable!' Exasperation oozed out of every syllable. 'I'm out of the office for less than forty-eight hours and the biggest story of the year breaks.'

'Do you want me to make arrangements for you to travel home?' She was counting on him saying no. It was one thing her helping him on this while they were thousands of miles away from the office, but there would be no legitimate reason for her to travel back with him. Not even a four-page spread on Cindy Trenchant's past fashion blunders would cut it.

To her horror, he stretched back in his chair, hands behind his head, and closed his eyes, giving her suggestion serious thought. *Say no. Say no. Say no.*

'I can't,' he conceded eventually. 'I've brought everyone here and I can't just bugger off. Besides, how would that look to the guys in the office? I've got to show that I trust them to deal with this. They're good guys, you know that. I just want to make a few phone calls, put in a couple of politically strategic calls to smooth the way. I'll steer the big decisions and preview the copy from here.'

Yes! God, decisive action, power and control were such a turn on. Taking a coffee and a croissant from the room service tray, Mona pulled out a chair and slid into it, then opened her laptop and smiled. 'I agree completely. It's not going to win us a Pulitzer but if we get this right, we'll blow everyone else out of the water. . Now, let's look at the story from all angles. We'll need a four-page spread on Cindy Trenchant's fashion blunders.'

Sarah

'Are you sure you don't want to come with me? Palma has some great shops.' Sarah threw in her best shot, but still Eliza was refusing to bite.

'I'll pass.' Eliza groaned, barely able to open her eyes. Apparently her daughter had an appointment with her bed until at least lunchtime, and then planned to levitate her horizontal self to a sunlounger by the poolside.

Sarah could see her point. When she was that age she'd gone to Butlins with Patsy and they'd spent a week lying by the pool, wearing huge sunglasses so that they could unobtrusively stare at a gorgeous, mullet-haired lifeguard from Skegness. Patsy had even entered the talent show to get him to notice her. Tina Turner's 'Proud Mary' had been murdered in the process.

The memory made her smile and the knock at the balcony door made her jump. John was standing there clutching a very cute Lavinia. Sarah slid the door open and immediately took her granddaughter for a cuddle.

'Well, you're looking so much better, my honey.'

'She definitely is. Was obviously just something she'd eaten. We've just been down to the ship's doctor and he agrees that she's absolutely fine now.'

Sarah blew a raspberry on her shrieking granddaughter's belly.

'I was thinking of heading into Palma for the day, but I can stay and look after the kids if you and Penny want to go wander around by yourselves. I really don't mind, it would be lovely to have them.'

'Thanks, Mum, but the nanny Dad arranged is taking them to the kids' club today and they're enrolled in all sorts of activities. They've got swimming, yoga, painting and music before lunch. I'm guessing it'll probably be Mandarin, the harp and advanced physics in the afternoon.'

Sarah laughed. There was an old saying that a girl was a

daughter for life, but that a boy was only a son until he found a wife. Thankfully that hadn't transpired in John's case – they were still as close as they'd ever been and he never failed to cheer her up. "So we're just going to stay on the boat and chill."

Granddaughter safely returned to her dad, Eliza safely returned to sleep, she scooped up her white leather beach bag – big enough for shopping, cheap enough not to mind if it got stained by sun cream spillage. "Will you check on Sleeping Beauty every couple of hours? When she wakes up she's going to go lie by one of the pools."

"No probs, mum. You go enjoy yourself."

She had every intention of it. Kissing him goodbye, she headed for the gangplank on level three. There were streams of people going in the same direction, so she just followed the crowd, glad that she'd opted for another of Patsy The Bullying Personal Shopper's maxi dresses, this time a zebra-print one that disguised all the rogue lumps and bumps.

It was impossible not to feel excited at the prospect of wandering around all Palma's little back streets and just being a free, independent grown-up for a day. She wasn't wearing fleece and she wasn't in her kitchen, so this was thrillingly close to a grand adventure.

Passport and Cruise Pass in hand, she was in one of the lines waiting to disembark when she noticed that Tess was twenty feet away in another queue. Where was Drew? She had a sudden flashback to many similar scenes from her distant past. Surely… No. She shrugged off the thought. There was no way Drew would have got caught up in a work thing, leaving Tess to spend the day alone. When they were married she lost count of the times that people asked her if she was single, because she showed up to every parents' night, school show, birthday party, wedding, even funeral, without anyone by her side, because Drew was working.

Unable to stop herself, she cut out of her line and across to Tess.

'Good morning!' she greeted her warmly. Tess's head went up with a start and Sarah could see that her eyes were red-rimmed and her smile forced.

'Hi, Sarah. Gorgeous day isn't it?'

Bless her, she was trying to seem cheery and normal. With the benefit of shared experience, Sarah could see right through it. 'Are you OK?' she asked softly.

'Fine. Absolutely fine!' Tess was many things, but fine was not one of them. Sarah knew she should probably drop this, but the younger woman looked so wretched and so deeply sad that she couldn't just walk away.

'And Drew?'

She noticed Tess began to chew on her bottom lip, before admitting, 'He has to work today.' With that Tess's eyes filled up and she quickly put her head down so that no one would notice. Sarah's heart went out to her. *Bloody Drew.* Some things just never changed.

'Look, I'm going to wander around Palma – nothing too exciting, just a bit of shopping and lunch. Why don't you come with me? I'd like the company.'

It wasn't strictly true. She'd been looking forward to wandering around at her own pace, but maybe having someone to chat to would be fine. Besides, she liked Tess and it might be nice to spend time with her.

'Oh, I couldn't impose on you like…' Tess was midway through a firm refusal when her eyes filled up again and she did a U-turn. 'You know what, that would be great. If you don't mind, that is.' Her voice almost built up to firm resolve. 'Thank you, Sarah,' she added softly.

Before she realized what she was doing, Sarah gave her a quick squeeze. She'd always rubbed along fine with Tess and now – to a mixture of horror and surprise – she couldn't help coming over all maternal towards her.

Tess's shoulders went back and she visibly brightened as they made their way through security and off the ship into chaos. There were taxi touts everywhere, shouting, gesticulating, thrusting pamphlets into passing hands.

'Shall we just jump in one of the taxis and hope for the best?' Sarah suggested.

'Where are you two gorgeous girls off to then?' There was no mistaking the booming voice behind them. They turned to see Piers with his son Max, both of them dressed in light chinos and polo shirts.

Sarah gave him an affectionate smile. 'Shopping. Lunch. Bakeries. And if we get really daring, there may be activities involving a sombrero.'

Piers roared with laughter.

'But first we're going to risk life and limb in one of those taxis,' Sarah continued.

'Indeed you're not. There's no telling where you'd end up.' Piers jested. 'Tell you what, I've rented a car for the day to take us up to a golf course about twenty minutes from here. We'll drop you off on the way.'

Sarah looked at Tess, who replied with a 'why not?' nod.

Two minutes later the four of them were in the cool, air-conditioned interior of a limousine, heading away from the docks.

'You know what?' Piers chuckled, cracking open a beer from the mini-fridge. 'I've got another idea. Anyone fancy a bit of an adventure?'

7.

Mad Dogs And Scotsmen

Tess

It wasn't how she'd planned to spend her first day in the sun, but if you were going to get rejected by your husband, dumped on your own, embarrassingly rescued by your husband's ex-wife and ambushed by your husband's second ex-wife's husband and stepson – god it was even complicated to think about – who were in possession of a limousine, then this was the way to do it – a glass of wine in one hand, while snaking up a Majorcan hillside in the glorious sunshine. Today was definitely taking a surprising turn for the better.

'Are you sure you don't mind us tagging along?' Tess asked Piers.

'Of course not – I insist!' He grinned. 'Can't bloody believe Drew and Mona pulled that crap, but since we've both been stood up, I reckon the least we can do is get filthy drunk and enjoy ourselves.'

It was all so wrong, but at that moment it seemed so right.

The original plan to drop the ladies at the cathedral had been scrapped when Piers persuaded them to join him and Max for brunch at some golf club he regularly frequented on the island. Then, while Piers and Max spent the afternoon golfing, the driver would take them to the best shopping areas and then return them to the ship. Sarah had seemed quite happy to go along with it, so Tess felt she couldn't say no. Now she was glad. Piers was great company, keeping them going with tales of his last – by all accounts riotous – visit here.

They reached the stunning landscaped grounds of the golf club, to be greeted by a uniformed concierge. 'Mr Delaney, good to see you again.'

'All right, Camilo? How have you been?'

'Good, Mr Delaney. Very good.'

Tess noticed euros passing hands and wasn't in the least bit surprised by Piers' generosity. In the short time they'd been on this trip, the dynamic between Piers and Mona had been puzzling her more and more. Piers treated everyone exactly the same, whether it was a fellow passenger or a bell boy in a Majorcan golf club. Mona made it quite clear she had no time at all for... well, anyone really. Other than Drew, she seemed resoundingly unimpressed with everyone else she met. The phrase 'opposites attract' had never been more evident.

They were shown to a table on the terrace, shaded from the burning sun by a thick cream awning. The only other guests in sight were a large table of Italian gents. They waved a greeting.

'Just coffee for me, please,' she told the waiter who arrived to take their drinks order. The wine in the car was already making her a little light-headed and it was barely ten o'clock. If she had a couple more her face would be in her brunch.

'Tell you what, let's have both. A bottle of your house rosé and a large pot of coffee, please. And Spanish omelettes all round?' Piers looked quizzically at the others for their agreement.

'Done. Four Spanish omelettes and a selection of pastries, please.'

Beside her, Max just shook his head and laughed. 'Isn't it supposed to be the kids that act recklessly?'

'Has he always been like this?' Tess asked conspiratorially.

'Yep, always. It's only in recent years that I've been able to handle the embarrassment,' he replied with very obvious affection, causing a huge wave of longing for her parents to come crashing over her. What she wouldn't give for Evelyn and Alan to walk in here right now. Of course, the management would probably request that they park the beat-up camper van behind the dumpsters out of sight of their more illustrious members.

Piers and Sarah fell into easy conversation about their favourite holiday destinations, leaving Max and Tess in a comfortable silence. He was an easy guy to be with.

'Are you OK?'

The question snapped her to the present. 'Yes! I mean...

sorry, I was just thinking about my mum and dad and how much I miss them.'

His face clouded over. 'I'm sorry,' he said gently. It took her a second to click.

'No! They're not dead!' Several of the Italians at the other table turned to stare. 'They're travelling around South America in a camper van. You think your dad's off the wall? Last time I spoke to my mother, she asked me if I needed nipple tassels.' A couple of the Italian gentlemen were now actually leaning in their direction, while Piers and Sarah had ceased conversing and were both staring at her open-mouthed.

'Sometimes I forget I shouldn't say things out loud.'

'I think you should have another drink and tell us more,' Piers said, pouring some sparkling rosé into her glass. She shouldn't. She really shouldn't. And she could see that Sarah was hesitating over drinking hers, too. Weren't they going shopping this afternoon? They'd be a mess if they had too much wine now.

Sarah caught her eyes and immediately they both realized they were thinking the same thing. It was Sarah who made the decision. She held up her glass in Tess's direction. 'Cheers – may a day that started out badly get much, much better, thanks to the man with the limo.'

They all drank to that.

As Tess put her glass down she felt her shoulders relax and her mood improve hugely. *Bugger it. Bugger everything. Drew. Cameron. Bugger it all.* This was her holiday and she was damn well going to enjoy it.

'So, we want to hear about these parents that are even more mortifying than mine,' Max reminded her.

Two hours later she was still regaling them with stories, with Max matching every one with an even more bizarre one about Piers, who was clearly loving the ribbing. There was the time he showed up at Max's school with four actors dressed as Power Rangers. The hot-air balloon trip that crash-landed in a bush. Bursting in on Max's first date. Falling in the fountain at Max's wedding.

Hang on, back up.

'You're married?" Tess asked. "I can't believe you've left your poor wife at home.'

'It's complicated. A long story.'

'Cow,' Piers muttered.

'Dad, you cannot call my wife a cow,' Max said, his light-hearted tone coming with an edge of warning.

'Trust me, the alternative is worse,' Piers muttered. There was a couple of seconds' stand-off between the two men, before Tess intervened.

'Well, my parents have never fallen in a fountain. But my mum did once flood Tesco's. Any good?'

The four of them collapsed with laughter and the awkward moment was forgotten.

A small, sharply dressed man approached their table and Tess watched as he put one hand on Piers' shoulder.

'Mr Delaney, welcome back to Palma Vida!'

'Juan, my friend! I've told you before, stop bloody calling me Mr Delaney.'

The other man shook his head. 'So demanding! I always get the guests who are so demanding.'

Piers stood up and they did an affectionate handshake/man hug thing.

'This is Juan Abidos. He's the manager of this five-star golf course in the sun, God help him. Must be hell. Juan, this is my son Max, and our friends Sarah and Tess.'

Juan shook their hands and they complimented him on the wonderful surroundings and food.

'Just a shame about the company, no?' Juan joked, mocking Piers. 'Piers, you know, I should be charging you rental.'

'For what?'

'You have a jet ski in my storeroom. From the auction last year. You could have bought Minorca for what you paid for that pile of tin.'

'Too much wine, no one sitting on my hands – it happens.' Piers accompanied the admission with a sheepish grin. 'Tell me it was for a good charity. I can't remember.'

'The donkey sanctuary in the next village. I do believe that thanks to your kind gesture, all the donkeys are now living in the Hilton.'

Their shrieks of hilarity could be heard on the fourth hole.

God, this was fun. Tess couldn't remember when she'd last laughed this hard or for this long. She was almost sorry that it was time for the men to golf and for her and Sarah to head for the shops.

'I've got an idea,' Piers announced. 'Juan, can you get that jet ski down to the beach for me?'

'Sure, I'll have Camilo drive it down on our trailer.'

'Fantastic! Girls, what do you say we take this party down to the beach?'

Perhaps the fun wasn't going to be over anytime soon.

Mona

'Noooooo! I said the photograph with the pink fucking Uggs. The one where she's wearing the Juicy Couture tracksuit and she looks like a WAG on crack. It was 2010. September. No, maybe October.'

As she said that, she saw Drew's eyes flicker to her and he gave her a knowing smile. Her encyclopaedic knowledge was legendary. Ask her what any celebrity was wearing to any function in the last ten years and she could recount the outfit down to the last detail. She often thought it was a gift Anna Wintour would kill for.

It had been a good morning so far. The story had leaked, but they were the only paper geared up and ready with the details and the pictures for tomorrow's edition. The assistant editors back at the offices were blocking all furious calls to Drew, using the holiday as an excuse. The only one he'd taken was from Jeff McLean, a member of the shadow cabinet and a fellow Scot, whom Drew had known since they both played youth football in the seventies.

'The story is running, Jeff. Trust me, it's better if we get it out there first. The right-wing nationals will milk it to death.'

Jeff rang off with a request that if any further damaging details came to light, Drew would give him a heads-up – Drew agreed, recognizing that a spot of mutual back-scratching with those in power was never a bad thing.

Watching Drew as he negotiated his position and listening to him call the shots was a bigger aphrodisiac than ten buckets of oysters and a crate of champagne. It was all the confirmation Mona needed. The thoughts that had been flying around in her head, the resolve to change her life, the determination to make things right, could all be summed up right there, right then, with one obvious, undeniable fact: she wanted Drew back.

There. She'd admitted it to herself. She didn't want to be with Piers any longer – his loud, uninteresting, adulterous behaviour revolted her. Nor did she want to be single. It was only a few years until her fortieth, and she might be a stunning woman who looked a decade younger, but if she continued to screw twenty-three-year-olds in her office at lunchtime she knew she was only a few rumours away from being a laughing stock.

No, she didn't want to be on her own. She belonged in a couple. The only problem was that she was currently in the *wrong* couple.

Drew was her exit strategy. All she needed now was for him to be on the same page. Sure, there were a couple of slight complications, namely Piers and Tess. Mona almost snorted at the thought. It didn't take a genius to see that Drew and Tess's marriage had cooled. There was no touching, no intimacy, no secret smiles. It seemed… habitual. Monopolising him this morning had almost seemed too easy. He should never have married her, the old fool. A fling with someone half his age was one thing, but marriage? Drew wasn't that guy. He didn't go for vacuous looks and the macho kudos of bagging a hot young thing. He liked intelligence. Stimulation. Debate. Common ground. Nostalgia. History. He was hardly getting those things from a woman who couldn't remember the eighties. No, what Drew needed was Mona.

'I'm going to order lunch. A BLT and a side salad?' The telephone was already in her hand, so it was more of a statement than a question.

Drew stretched back, swinging on his chair, his arms behind his head. 'You must be psychic.'

'Nope, just smart,' she quipped. This had to be played right. With some guys she could strip down to nothing but her Manolo Blahniks and the deal would be done, but not Drew. He wasn't perfect, but he had a level of decency, and he wasn't stupid – probably borne out of spending decades watching celebrities and politicians getting caught with their pants around their ankles. Other than their own affair before they married, he'd never stepped a foot over the adulterous line. No, sex wasn't the way to go here. He had to realize that – no matter what happened in the past – they were meant to be together.

Room service answered with a cheery greeting and Mona quickly rattled off the order before kicking off her shoes and going back to the table.

Drew was talking via Skype to Guy Bennet, his deputy at the office, a gruff Aberdonian with a dry sense of humour.

'So it's front-page splash, details and photographs on pages two and three, back story on four and Mona's contribution on five. The piece on the wife's fashion history and social cock-ups is evil genius, Mona – remind me never to get on your bad side.'

'Good idea,' Mona replied dryly, 'because you should see the dirt I have on you, Guy. Seriously twisted.'

The fuzzy quality of the transmission couldn't hide the fact that Guy paled slightly.

Drew cut off their banter and signed out, promising to check back in again after lunch. He got up and went inside to the minibar, returning with a bottle of water for each of them.

'You don't actually have anything on Guy, do you?' he asked.

'Other than the fact that he has the worst dress sense in the free world? No. But sometimes it doesn't hurt to keep him on his toes and remind him that I'm indispensable and not afraid of resorting to blackmail.'

His moral code made him shake his head, his appreciation of her balls made him smile.

'We make a good team,' she said.

'We always did,' he replied.

There it was. The hint of nostalgia and sadness made her want to punch the air. He felt it too, she realized. Of course he did. He'd be a damn fool if he didn't. When they were together, nothing could touch them. They'd still be together if it wasn't for that one fucking mistake.

At the sound of the doorbell he automatically jumped to his feet and she realized her heart was beating way faster than normal. While he attended to the room service, she made a couple of minor adjustments. First the Capri pants came off, revealing a tiny pair of black bikini bottoms. Chanel. Not that he'd know that, but there was nothing like Chanel briefs to boost a girl's confidence. Then she released her hair from its clasps and tousled it so that it fell in raven waves around her shoulders.

Going the physical attraction, flirtatious sex route wouldn't win Drew over, but it certainly wouldn't harm her chances. She didn't do sixteen hours of exercise a week to keep this arse covered up.

'Hope you don't mind – it's way too hot and those trousers were getting uncomfortable.'

He stopped in the doorway, holding a large tray with their lunches, a BLT for him and a green salad for her. 'Not at all. Would you rather go inside? The air con is on.'

'No, it's fine. This sun is great for the vitamin-D levels.' It was disappointing that his stare didn't linger on her finely toned thighs, but then that wasn't Drew's style. Hopefully he'd give them a few furtive stares when she wasn't looking. She stretched back to allow him to put her lunch in front of her, before he sat down with his own. Manners. Chivalry. She missed that. Piers was attentive, but he was just as likely to tell her to get her own bloody dinner as he was to serve it up to her.

They ate in silence for a few moments before Mona spoke, faux concern oozing from her words.

'So… are you disappointed you missed a day with Tess today? I'm guessing she wouldn't have been thrilled.'

He waited until he'd stopped chewing and swallowed, then nodded. 'Yeah, it would have been great to go explore.'

If there was a prize for lack of conviction he just became the front runner.

'But…?' she probed.

He shrugged again. 'But there's nothing like the adrenalin rush of breaking a new story. We killed it today. That's the kind of high that no amount of walking around Palma could ever deliver.'

'Not even with a beautiful young wife?' She kept her voice light because she was veering into dangerous territory and she knew it. No matter what happened, he would never trash Tess because disloyalty was another of Drew's pet peeves. Hadn't she once been thankful for that?

'Not even with a beautiful young wife,' he answered truthfully. Staring into the distance, he suddenly seemed to be deep in thought. Perhaps that admission had struck a chord with him. Maybe that was the first time that realization had crossed his mind. The important thing was that the face in front of her wasn't the face of a contented man who was utterly besotted with his wife.

It was obvious that the chink in his marital armour was there. Now all Mona needed was a tin-opener and the smarts to pick her moment.

Sarah

'Come on, climb on, love. Jesus Christ, have you never heard of Weight Watchers?'

Sarah couldn't suppress the laughter as she grabbed Pier's ear and twisted. Cheeky bugger. It was rare that a guy could walk the line between charm and cheek, but Piers did it perfectly.

'You're hardly the poster boy for Slimming World yourself,' she replied tartly, then grunted as he hauled her out of the water and on to the jet ski. Yes, a jet ski. Patsy would be so proud.

They'd been at the beach for an hour and Sarah and Tess had been quite happy to recline on the sunloungersand leave the action stuff to the men. Not that Piers bore any relation whatsoever to Daniel Craig or Jason Statham.

'Are you holding on?' he shouted. Piers Delaney. International business icon and man of substance, wearing a collection of chickens on his buttocks. None of them had beachwear with them, so they'd stopped at a little gift shop and bought out their entire beachwear collection of two large swimsuits and two pairs of swimming shorts. Sadly all four seemed to have been designed sometime in the eighties by someone with a chemical substance problem and a love of barnyard animals. Tess's costume was dotted with flying pigs. Max's was a bovine tribute to all things that went moo. And Sarah had thirteen ponies galloping from her hips to her oxters. The dated swimsuit design was the least of her worries.

'I can't believe I'm wearing this in public,' she'd told Tess, as she struggled to cover the worst of her bulges by strategically draping her maxi dress over her legs. 'I'm a breeding ground for cellulite and it's been so long since anything below the neck saw the sun, my entire body is a pale shade of blue.'

'Are you kidding?' Tess had gasped. 'Sarah, you look great. All curvy and voluptuous. And anyway, I reckon we're exactly the same size, so if you won't be self-conscious then neither will I.'

'Yeah, but your boobs still point upwards.' Sarah had given the straps another tug in a northerly direction.

'Sarah, Piers is wearing chickens. I'm wearing sheep. And your cossie looks like race day at Newmarket. There's no dignity in this. Let's just go with it, make sure there's no photographic evidence and promise never to speak of it again.' It was great to see Tess smiling. The girl in front of her was a vast improvement from the distraught woman she'd met this morning. And if Tess could shake off her woes and make the most of the day, then Sarah could, too.

She, Sarah Gold, had thrown off the maxi dress, embraced her cellulite and her ponies, and decided not to give a damn what anyone thought. Which was why she was now on the back of a jet ski, holding on to Piers for dear life. From now on, she was going to be carefree and up for new experiences. At least until she got home and became Mrs Suburban Cake Making Granny again.

They whizzed three times around the bay, with Piers managing to stall the machine twice and narrowly missing colliding with the kind of yacht that celebrities lie on in photoshoots. At one point she caught herself screaming like she hadn't done since a Bay City Rollers concert in 1976. What a rush! She was almost sorry when he slowed down and turned the machine around to face in the direction of the beach.

'Ready to go in?' Piers asked her.

'Sure, let's give the others a turn. I need a large vodka after that.'

'My kinda woman.' He chuckled as he threw the machine into gear and then approached the shore at a snail's pace, careful to stay well away from the snorkelers and swimmers.

Tess and Max were waiting on the beach, ready to take over, and Piers slapped his son on the back as they swapped. 'Now don't crash it. I've still never forgiven you for the Audi Quattro.'

Max looked heavenwards. 'Dear God, I was seventeen. When is he going to let it go?'

'Never. I'm your father. It's my job to remind you of your fuck-ups.'

Back at the sunbeds, Sarah wrapped a towel around her waist and flopped down just as a waiter arrived with cocktails.

'How do you do that?' she asked Piers.

'What?'

'Have drinks delivered without even ordering them?'

'I asked Max to do it before I left. Figured if I managed not to kill us on that bloody thing then we'd definitely need a drink after it. It's a champagne cocktail – is that OK?'

Sarah turned her nose up and feigned outrage. 'Of course not. Some of us have standards. I have a policy only to drink wine with a screw top that costs less than three quid a bottle.'

Laughing, they lay side by side for a few moments, letting their heartbeats return to something resembling normal.

'Mona has really missed out today.' Sarah didn't actually realize she'd said that out loud until Piers shook his head.

'Nah, she hates this kinda thing. Doesn't like anything that messes up her hair. I once bought an Aston Martin convertible and she refused to travel in it unless the top was up. Traded it in for a Range Rover. Driving about in it on my own made me look like a bit of a sad prick.'

Sarah almost choked on her bubbly. Piers certainly had a way of just telling it straight and sparing no blushes.

'In fact, seems like we don't have much in common at all, these days,' he went on, staring into the distance, almost as if he were speaking to himself.

Sensing that this wasn't something to be commenting on, Sarah kept her mouth shut. She hadn't read the page in the social etiquette bible that dealt with interfering with your ex-husband's ex-wife's current husband airing his concerns about their marriage.

'I know you don't like her much…'

'I don't,' Sarah admitted frankly. 'But in fairness to me, she was complicit in wrecking my marriage, was delighted when she took my husband, has a general air of smugness and she's a size eight. I can't possibly be friends with anyone who is a stranger to a carrot cake. But other than all that, I'm sure she's a very nice person.'

Immediately, she worried that she'd gone too far. Piers was Mona's husband and there was bound to be a loyalty there. Hopefully he wouldn't say anything to her. Bugger, what if he did? She'd have to stay indoors for the rest of the cruise in case Mona accidentally-on-purpose sent her overboard for an unexpected swim.

Next to her, Piers sighed and for the first time that day his jolly demeanour slipped. 'You know, sometimes she really is. At least, she used to be. Now I'm not so sure.'

What to do? Should she speak? Let him talk and just listen? Try to cajole him back to happy, effervescent Piers? In the end she went for a midway point between sincerity and optimism.

'You know, Drew and I went through some crappy times in our marriage, too. I mean, before he took off, left me desolate and doomed to end up an old lady with only cats for company. Maybe it's just a low point and things will get better.'

That seemed to rally him. 'Nah, don't think so,' he said very definitely, as he jumped up and fished his mobile phone out of the pocket of the shorts that were folded under the sunlounger. 'If you'll excuse me, I just need to go give my secretary a call. Just make sure that all is OK back there.'

Sarah watched him wander down to the waves and then paddle in the shallow waters with his phone glued to his ear. Surprised at both his words and actions, she couldn't help think that there were some serious undercurrents on this holiday... and they were nothing to do with the seas.

8.

All At Sea

Tess

The pain was the first thing Tess felt when she woke up; a deep, searing pain right across her forehead. It was difficult to say if that's what caused her stomach to spasm or if her abdominal muscles were performing that little trick all by themselves.

Unsurprisingly, groaning out loud didn't make her feel any better and neither did attempting to stand up, but she gave it her best shot, wobbled, then fell back down to a seated position on the bed.

Do not throw up. Do not throw up.

She managed to get one eye open and realized, to her relief that she was in her cabin. That was a plus. The rewind button in her brain refused to co-operate with the events leading up to her getting here.

The beach. Piers. Tess. Max. Jet skis. Cocktails. Lots of cocktails. Laughs. Sun. Driving back to the ship. Heading for cabin. Stop at piano bar on way. One drink. Two. Three. … nope, that was it. That was all she could remember. And why was the theme tune for *The A-Team* stuck in her head?

God, it hurt. It was like torture by Mr T.

Taking a deep breath, she pushed herself upright again, got one eye open and turned to face in the general direction of the balcony. Daylight. She could see it was morning. How had that happened? If she squinted – shit, that hurt too – she realized there was a person… Drew. Yep, Drew was out on the balcony, sitting at a table, hunched over his laptop.

Had she imagined all that other stuff? Was this still Palma and she'd had a weird dream about a highly unlikely group of them getting together and going from a golf course to a beach, donning animal print swimming costumes and whizzing around on jet skis? It did sound completely bizarre.

Summoning every ounce of physical strength, she descended the steps from the mezzanine, crossed the room and pushed open the balcony door, wincing as a combination of heat and sun assaulted her.

'Hey,' he said, with a tight smile. 'How's the head?'

'Erm, tender? I can't believe I'm about to say this, but what happened last night? I've no recollection whatsoever of coming back here and I feel like I've been hit by a bus.'

'Well, if you were, then Piers was driving it.' She realized it was meant to be a joke but he sounded more disapproving than comical. Oh crap, she'd upset him. Second day of the holiday and she'd managed to piss off her husband. Great. Yes, she'd been pissed off with him but that was no excuse for going AWOL and getting wrecked on his birthday trip.

There was a pause that was so pregnant it could have delivered twins. Wow, this was worse than being a teenager in trouble with her parents. Actually, her parents would never have behaved like this. The only time she'd really crossed the line with them was when she said she was going to a sleepover and instead headed off to a new nightclub in town. Her mother somehow found out and decided that the best means of punishment would be to show up in a mini dress and black wig and dance beside her. It was the talk of her sixteen-year-old horrified school pals for months.

But the bottom line was she hadn't behaved particularly well so she should really give him a kiss and apologize. However, the thought of any movement made her want to lie in a dark room. 'Hey, we're moving.'

He glanced back up from his laptop. 'You've just noticed?'

'Sorry. I'm on a delay this morning.' Why did her mouth taste like it had been sanded by a Black and Decker power tool?

'It's a sea day today. Sardinia tomorrow.'

Oh dear. A whole day at sea, with Drew, feeling like this. This wasn't good. This was her chance to spend quality time with him and she was like the last of the living zombies.

'How did the story end up? Were you happy with it?'

For the first time he smiled. 'It was sensational. All the majors have run with it today, we made a killing on the photos and readership spiked to the second highest level this year. Only Wills and Kate's wedding topped it.'

'Fantastic.' Three-syllable word. That made her temples hurt. 'Well, I tell you what. Why don't I brush my teeth, have a quick shower and we can pull up a couple of sunloungers and just lie out here today? A chill-out day. How does that sound?' She couldn't think of a single thing that would be better than a nice, easy day, with no stress, lots of privacy and at least four paracetamol.

'Actually, I have to work again today. I've got conference calls lined up all afternoon. This is huge, Tess, and we've got to stay on top of it. I'm not letting anyone else come in and hijack it.'

'Conference calls. All afternoon,' she repeated in a deadpan voice, before realising that, surprisingly, she wasn't feeling the usual twinge of disappointment.

Oh well. Gift horse. Mouth.

If he was going to be tied up all day then she could climb into bed with some hot tea and the new Harlan Coben novel. She'd been dying to get time to read it for weeks.

Trying not to groan at the crushing pain in her temples, she pushed herself up and was immediately thrown off balance by a dizzy turn. She had questions, lots of them (how did she get home last night, who put her to bed, what must the others think of the fact that she got legless and did she totally embarrass herself?), but she had a feeling it would be better to wait until she could handle the answers before asking.

Shower. Teeth brushed. Clean vest and knickers. Back into bed. Hot date with Harlan. The ultimate recipe for a hangover cure.

'OK, well much as I'd love to blame the rocking of the boat and seasickness for my current state, I'm going to give in to the fact that it's a raging hangover. I'm just going to get cleaned up and go back to bed. Shout me if you need anything…' Inside her head was a little voice saying 'please don't shout. Please don't.' '…And feel free to join me later if you fancy snuggling up.' *Just don't make a noise or any sudden movement because I can't guarantee my reaction*, she added silently.

'Didn't you get the note that was left on the table?'

Her legs turned to jelly and she had to hang on to the back of a chair. This time she couldn't blame the hangover. *Note? Oh fuck. Fuck. Fuck. Fuck.* Hadn't she asked Colita to make sure no more notes were delivered?

Oh God, Drew knew. That's why he was acting so cool. He knew about Cameron and he was furious. Drew didn't do temper or irrational fury, he did cool, calm, deadly seething and that was what was going on now. Well she was just going to have to face it. She hadn't done anything wrong. She'd just tell him the truth. Come clean. Maybe it would even help. Right, she was going to go for it. *Please don't be sick.* This was no time for body fluids.

'Oh. So you know?'

He looked at her quizzically. 'Of course I know. She mentioned it yesterday.'

Mentioned what? Colita told him that she'd been asked to hold back the notes? Now it would seem like she was hiding something and— She sighed wearily – this was all too much. Where was Harlan Coben when she needed him?

'What did she say?' she asked, resigning herself to her fate.

'That she thought you guys deserved a treat so she'd arranged for you all to meet at ten o'clock.'

Wha… wha… what? She didn't understand.

'Hang on a minute.' Slowly, gingerly, she made her way back inside and spotted the white envelope on the table. Heart hammering, she pulled out the handwritten note from inside.

> *Spa day booked. Let's meet at the Divine Bliss*
> *reception at ten o'clock. See you then. Mona x*

Her first reaction was 'Yesssssss!' A serious marital blip had just been averted. This was quickly followed by a second reaction of 'Nooooooo!' A whole day in a public place. With Mona. And a hangover. She preferred it when she was being tortured by Mr T. And she still had no idea what the A-Team theme tune thing was all about.

She inhaled deeply, then exhaled. She could handle this. She could. After all, they were all grown-ups, weren't they?

Mona

On the scale of people Mona wanted to spend the day with, Tess and Sarah ranked somewhere below the founder of Dunkin' Donuts and that bloke who just got life in prison for eating his parents.

It was a necessary evil. This was a tactical game and she wanted to get as much insider info as possible. Plus, her gesture of friendship impressed Drew and that wouldn't hurt her plans, either.

What she really wanted to do today was spend the next eight hours with Drew, working on the Cindy Trenchant story, but there was little more she could contribute and it would look suspicious if she lingered.

No, her time was better spent with Sarah and Tess, finding out how the land lay and getting beautified at the same time.

Not that she needed much work. She'd had her Botox and fillers topped up before she came. Nothing obvious – no startled eyebrows or chipmunk cheeks. She'd had her hair cut, conditioned and coloured, and every hair on her body had been lasered into submission. She'd come rather late to the Brazilian, but she loved it now. A shiver ran up her back as she contemplated what Drew would think of it. *No, don't go there. Not yet.* Plenty of time to fantasize about that when it was closer to becoming a reality.

The sooner the better.

At dawn that morning, she'd given up trying to sleep and did a 10k run around the jogging track, because Piers' snoring could be heard on any ship within a twenty-mile radius. He sounded like a volcano on the brink of eruption.

Alas, that didn't even come close to being the most revolting thing about him. The smell. By the time she got out of bed the suite smelled like a pub floor. He must have been seriously pissed last night when he got home. She hadn't been there to meet him. She had only left Drew's room when Max had appeared back with Tess, and by the time she got back to her own cabin, Piers was lying fully clothed, spreadeagled on the bed, snoring like a hog.

So while a day in the Divine Bliss had the drawback of keeping her away from Drew, the fact that it meant she could avoid Piers was a definite bonus.

As she entered the spa she checked her reflection in the corridor mirrors. All good. No bags under her eyes, despite the fact that she'd had barely any sleep. She deserved a bloody medal for putting up with that man.

The deep mahogany door swept back to let her enter. She had nipped in and checked the place out yesterday and even as a connoisseur of spas, she'd been impressed. They offered a comprehensive list of treatments and the decor was absolutely stunning – gold marble floors, white walls, deep woods in a Balinese style that was complemented by intoxicating aromas of jasmine and coconut emanating from strategically placed oil burners.

A beautiful oriental girl at reception smiled in greeting. 'Good morning, Mrs Gold. Welcome to The Divine Bliss Spa. One of your guests is already in the relaxation room. Would you like to begin your treatments or wait until your other guest arrives?'

'I'll wait. Is there tea or coffee in the other room?'

'Of course, Mrs Gold, and there's also a selection of waters and fruit juices in the chill unit.'

Mona nodded her thanks and headed in the direction of the other room. She'd bet her last salary cheque that it was Sarah who was here already. The older woman was always punctual, mostly, Mona suspected, from anxiety. She didn't want to stand out, be centre of attention or cause controversy by keeping anyone waiting. Poor Sarah. She'd always been a bit of a wallflower. The woman had no idea how to assert herself at all.

'Tess!' As she pushed the door open, her surprise was evident. 'No Sarah?'

'Nope, just me. Thanks for arranging this today, Mona, it was a lovely thought.'

Twenty years in journalism had taught her when words were coming out someone's mouth despite the fact that their brain was thinking something very different. That was fine. She didn't need Tess to be enthusiastic about spending time with her. She wasn't particularly enthusiastic about this either. After all, she suspected that they were going to have a very major fall-out in the near future. Not that she would suffer a single sleepless night over it. In life, you had to go for what you wanted and if that meant stepping on the toes of someone's… she spotted Tess's flip flops before continuing the thought…. Primark shoes, then that was what she would do.

'Thank God for this coffee. I'm on my third cup and only barely recovering my motor skills,' Tess groaned.

'Well, you're doing better than my husband. He's in a semi-comatose state and I suspect he'll be that way for the rest of the day. What exactly did you all get up to yesterday?' she added with a joviality that definitely didn't reflect how she felt.

'It's patchy,' Tess admitted, 'but there was golf, then jet-skiing at the beach, then a piano bar and then… Like I said, it's patchy. I feel awful. In every way. Poor Drew had to work and there was me, drunk and irresponsible.' Mona could see that Tess tried to inject a bit of humour into that last bit but it fell flat. Well, well, well. So Piers had caused a rift between Drew and Tess. Maybe she had something to thank the old fart for after all.

'Don't feel bad about that,' Mona said soothingly. 'Really, don't. Drew was just saying yesterday that a few hours at the coal face with a big story breaking was so much more invigorating than spending a day relaxing or sightseeing. Honestly, don't worry about him. I've never seen him so happy.' Rub. Salt. Wound. It was cruel, but she couldn't help herself. The more oil she could pour on these troubled waters, the better.

Tess's face fell and Mona almost felt sorry for her. Almost. God, this girl didn't have a clue. Not a clue. She was like bloody Bambi, all big eyes and no idea that there was a ruddy great big shotgun just around the corner.

Mona took a wheatgrass juice from the chiller and sat back down on the gold chenille sofa, pulling her legs up underneath her. 'I hope you don't mind me saying that, do you?' She feigned concern. 'I just wanted to reassure you so that you could stop feeling bad about leaving him. It's your holiday, too, you're supposed to enjoy it. I'm sure he's thrilled that you had such a good time. I'm sure he was dying to hear all about it this morning.'

Ding ding, round two. Mona knew Drew well enough to

know with one hundred per cent certainty that he would have been furious that Tess had stayed out half the night with Piers and Max and then come home hopelessly drunk. As someone who never, ever drank to excess, he couldn't bear a drunk woman. She also knew him well enough to guarantee that he'd given Tess the sullen, disapproving treatment this morning. This was too much fun. It was blindingly clear to her that Drew was unhappy in his marriage, so the more unsettled she could make Tess, the easier it was going to be on all of them in the future. Tess didn't understand him. She didn't get who he was and what made him tick. She'd be far better off with someone who was more on her... level.

It was obvious that Tess's aura was now infused with fifty per cent alcohol and fifty per cent misery. Time to play with that balance just a little.

'You know, Tess, I really admire you. It takes a very special kind of woman to accept that she's second place to a man's job. I couldn't do it. I'm afraid I need to know that I come first. Terrible character flaw, isn't it?' Her laugh was laced with mock self-deprecation. Bambi's emotional pendulum just swayed sixty: forty to the side of misery. This was for her own good, Mona reminded herself yet again. The sooner Tess split up with Drew, the sooner she could find someone more suited to her. She was doing her a favour really.

Much as Mona was enjoying the emotional manipulation, she wanted to get on with the day. The clock on the wall ticked round to ten minutes past ten. There must have been a serious problem for Sarah to be this late. Any minute now, she would walk in, all flurries of apologies and self-conscious blushing.

At that very moment the door burst open and in she came, dressed, like the others, in a white towelling robe and slippers, with her hair pointing in so many different directions she looked like a barber shop floor. Mona braced herself for the gush of apologies...

'I just want you to know that I appreciate you doing this,' Sarah began. *Yep, right on cue.* 'But I feel rougher than a badger's bollocks, so I'll give it a go, but there's every chance I might have to bail out early and go track down a bacon roll and a hair of the dog.'

'I hear you, Sarah,' Tess concurred. 'And I'm right behind you – just give me the nod.'

Mona could hardly believe what she was seeing and hearing. These two were not only being chummy, but they were actively conspiring to spend more time together. Oh well, at least Tess would have an understanding shoulder when the inevitable came. After all, Sarah had been through exactly the same thing, so she would be able to dole out a side order of empathy with those vile cupcakes she insisted on bringing to every single occasion they ever celebrated.

'I could murder one of your cupcakes right now, Sarah.' Tess sighed.

Bloody hell, it was like she was reading her mind. Cancel that thought. If Tess really could read Mona's mind right now, she'd have more to worry about than the lack of cupcakes.

Sarah winked as she plonked herself down on one of the comfy armchairs.

'Sorry, luvly, but those aren't allowed when you're in *The A-Team*.'

Mona had no idea what she was talking about and frankly didn't much care. Today was all about gleaning information and improving her position. And if the price was spending the next few hours with women she had only one thing in common with, women from whom she felt absolutely no interest or respect, then it was a price she was willing to pay.

Sarah

Despite feeling tragically rough, Sarah's spirits were lifted by the expression on Tess's face.

'Oh no,' the younger woman groaned. 'I've had *The A-Team* theme tune in my head all morning. What did I do last night?'

'Played it on the piano in the bar and then announced to the whole world that you thought Bradley Cooper was a shag.'

Mona's wheatgrass must have caught in the back of her throat because she burst into a coughing fit.

Just at that, a very tall blonde man in his early twenties arrived and introduced himself as 'Sven'. Sarah noticed that his badge said he was from Sweden. No way. This took a Swedish massage to a whole new level of authenticity. Not that she actually knew what Swedish massage involved. Or a Glaswegian one for that matter.

Sven showed them through to a large treatment room that carried on the Balinese theme, with white satin walls, a dark wood floor, and she counted four Bhuddhas. Three white leather beds were waiting for them in the middle of the room, each one covered in thick cream paper, with a luxurious, fluffy beige towel on the end. It must take a whole load of fabric softener to keep them like that.

'Ladies, I'll give you a few minutes to prepare. Please lie on the bed and you can cover yourself with the towel we have provided. It's completely up to you whether you prefer to keep your underwear on or not. Your privacy will be maintained with the towel, and I promise I won't blush.'

Sarah felt a hot flush coming on. She hadn't had one of those since she hit the menopause at forty-five. But then, she hadn't been naked in front of a bloke since then either, massage therapist or not. Knickers or no knickers? What was the protocol here? She'd be damned if she'd add to Mona's smugness by asking her advice. Actually, she didn't have to. Mona dropped the robe, revealing a honey-coloured, perfectly toned, spectacular body that had… *do not look there!* But where the hell had her pubic hair gone to?

Sarah's toes literally curled as she realized she was staring and – *noooooo* – Mona had spotted her looking. Sarah smiled limply then climbed on the bed and performed something akin to a circus act – it took great skill to keep herself covered with the towel while trying to take off a robe underneath. There was no way she was revealing her humungous M&S cotton knickers to Mona and even less chance that she was going to reveal the foliage underneath. The hot flush now graduated to furnace level.

Over on the other side of Mona, she saw that Tess had very gingerly hung up the robe, then, with one arm covering her boobs, climbed on to the bed, wearing just a nude-coloured thong. Why hadn't she thought of that? Not a thong, obviously. She never wore them, fearing that they would disappear into her buttocks and require surgery to remove. But she should have gone for something a little more modern than huge white granny pants.

'Are you OK, Sarah? You look a little hot.' Mona asked with an edge of smugness.

'I'm fine. Absolutely fine.'

Mona was physically perfect. She had the limbs of a colt and the boobs of a woman who had never had children and who had halted the aging process at 21. But why, oh why, was she still standing there naked? *GET ON THE BED, WOMAN, AND COVER YOURSELF UP!*

Sarah felt a sudden tightening in her right thigh. Damn. The belt from her robe had somehow managed to get wound around her leg and it was stuck. The more she struggled, the more she got caught up. She was beginning to panic. There was no way she was now going to get up, remove the towel, disentangle herself from her robe, flash her large knickers to the world then lie down again, throwing her pendulous boobs over her shoulder to get into a comfy position. Nope, she was committed to this, even though she was fairly sure the overall image was one of two baby seals having a fight in a tent.

With one last tug, she somehow managed to extricate the robe, giving herself whiplash in the process. Weren't massages supposed to be relaxing?

Finally, FINALLY, Mona climbed on to the bed, the act

giving Sarah a gynaecological view that would live with her forever.

What the hell was she doing here? Lying in the scud next to her ex-husband's other two naked wives? The combination of the bizarre scenario and the alcohol that was still swirling around in her system gave her the giggles.

'What's so funny?' Tess asked, grinning.

It took Sarah a few moments to compose herself long enough to speak. 'Don't you just think this is the oddest situation? The three of us, all lying here, some more naked than others…' she looked pointedly at Mona, 'all brought together by the fact that we were married to the same man. It's like some weird wives club.'

The contagious giggles had now reached Tess and she nodded. 'We could be in a reality show – *The Real Housewives of Drew Gold.*'

'Just as well there are only three of us. They'd never fit four beds in this room.' Sarah added, setting them off again.

As she wiped a tear from her eye, she realized that the hilarity was coming in stereo from her and Tess, but there was a Mona-shaped void in the middle.

'Sarah, I've never seen you like this,' Mona said. 'You seem… I don't know, just different.'

Mona's tone was the same one Sarah had heard her use to describe things that utterly disgusted her. What had it been at Christmas? Oh that's right – harem pants. Apparently they were the biggest fashion crime since those eighties hairstyles that required so much hairspray they permanently damaged the ozone layer.

'I'm sorry, Mona, but the last few days have just been a bit overwhelming. I decided that I was going to take everything in my stride and open myself up to new experiences, but this all just seems a little surreal." She could see Mona was already losing interest in what she was saying so, against her better judgement she attempted to mollify her. "Anyway, it's been great so far. Piers was so much fun yesterday – he totally led us astray. You're a lucky woman.'

'Yes, I am,' Mona agreed.

But even while dealing with whiplash and the suffocating heat of a hot flush, Sarah got the sense that Mona wasn't being entirely sincere. Her haughty demeanour made the atmosphere in the room bristle, so it was a relief when the door opened again and this time Sven was accompanied by two women, one a petite, picture-perfect Japanese girl, confirmed by a badge that said 'Aoki, Japan', and a tall, catwalk-slender 'Valeria, Russia'.

Valeria headed for Tess, Sven moved to Mona's bed and, to Sarah's relief, little Aoki stayed with her. Thank goodness. She'd never been one for massages because on the one and only occasion she'd tried it before, a chunky female who – if she worked on this ship would have a badge that said 'Dinah, Dudley' – had just about put her in traction.

A few minutes later, she'd revised her opinion. Little Aoki might look like she'd have trouble peeling a banana, but she had all the gentleness of a shot putter on steroids.

Sarah wanted to swear. She wanted to stop this. She was actually close to wanting to cry.

Turning her head to the side, she noticed that Sven was caressing Mona with long, luxurious strokes along her spine. How did Mona get the equivalent of a good feel-up, while Sarah was at the hands of a masochist with Olympic-strength fingers?

It was almost as if Mona had planned this.

It was almost as if Mona had planned this.

It was almost… the thought was stuck in her head and even the physical torture didn't block it out. For the first time it crossed her mind to wonder why they were doing this. Why was Mona being so nice? Why did she want them all to be together today?

Let's face it, Mona had never been her bosom buddy. They tolerated each other. Played nice. Made civil conversation. But they *had* never – and she suspected *would* never – actually be friends. In fact, the only time Mona had truly been nice to her was when she was a young reporter and she used to pop around to the house to discuss work with Drew, and call him up at all times of the day and night with leads and queries. He was the deputy editor then, but Mona had looked up to him and always seemed to hang on his every word. At the same time, Mona would bring her cakes, offer to babysit the kids, act like Sarah was a true friend. Little did Sarah know that she was already sleeping with her husband.

She gasped as Aoki removed her spine without an anaesthetic. At least that's what it felt like. When her nerve endings eventually stopped screaming, Sarah found herself struck with a jumble of weird thoughts: Mona was only ever friendly when there was something in it for her. Mona had befriended her decades ago when she wanted to get closer to Drew. Now she was being extremely friendly to her and Tess. So what, exactly, did she want to get her hands on now?

9.

Alghero

Tess

'Fully recovered?' Drew asked Tess, as he handed her a plate with a pain au chocolat and a selection of beautifully arranged fresh fruit. The strawberries were the deepest red she had ever seen and the melon and kiwi fruit looked irresistible.

'Much better, thanks. The massage yesterday was lovely and so was the facial, the seaweed treatment, the manicure, the pedicure and the deep conditioning hair treatment. Mona is a serious spa bunny – she must spend a fortune on that kind of stuff.'

Drew grunted and pressed a couple of keys on his laptop. That thing was never bloody off. Tess was becoming more and more convinced that it was time for it to have an accident that ended with it dying on the seabed.

When she'd woken that morning they had already dropped anchor in the Bay of Alghero, on the north-west coat of Sardinia. According to the *Daily Vista*, Alghero was a beautiful medieval town with strong Catalan origins, leading to its nickname 'Little Barcelona'. It sounded like something worth seeing and Mona's smug assertions from yesterday about Drew enjoying work more than his wife's company had hit home. Time to shake things up and make him realise what he was missing.

'So what would you like to do today? The tenders to the shore are running every half hour. Shall we get dressed and go explore?'

He looked up, pondering the question. 'Do you particularly want to go ashore today? I'm happy to chill out here, if you are.'

She could feel the anxiety starting to build. 'Drew, this is supposed to be our holiday. We're supposed to be doing things together. Enjoying ourselves. Experiencing new things. Together. I'd have been just as bloody well coming on my own.' She didn't add, "Or with Sarah," but it was on the tip of her tongue. Actually, now that she'd got to know Sarah a bit better, she realised that she actually liked her a lot. Mona, not so much. Maybe she was being paranoid, but she always felt that Mona was like a viper, just waiting to pounce. 'I'm trying to be understanding as bloody always but you're pushing me too far'.

Wow, where did that come from? She cringed as she realized just how needy that sounded. God, he was going to think she was pathetic. But hang on, she had a right to her feelings and she had a right to damn well tell him. Didn't she? Oh, crap, she hated confrontation.

She braced herself for a furious objection, but to her surprise it didn't come.

'You're right. I'm sorry,' he said quietly.

What? That was weird. No indignant reply. No defensive attitude. Just silence now. This couldn't go on. She knew that she needed to face this, to get the air cleared and sort out what was going wrong in their marriage.

'Drew, I'm beginning to think we're not OK. At home I didn't really notice, to be honest. We were always so busy and you work such long hours. If you add up all the time we've spent together in the last year, it's probably less than most people spend together on a summer holiday. But here it seems that everything is magnified, including the fact that we don't seem to be connected anymore.'

Argue with me, she silently implored. *Argue. Tell me I'm wrong. Tell me you love me.*

'You're right.' He sat back with a loud, sad exhalation. For the first time, she noticed how tired he looked. Not just 'not enough sleep' tired, but the kind of sallow complexion, dog-tired appearance that comes with real stress. 'You're right,' he repeated wearily. 'I'm sorry Tess, but I don't know where we are any more.'

Her stomach felt like it was being ripped out through her windpipe. No. How could this be happening to her? And why bring her thousands of miles to the middle of the ocean to tell her?

'Do you still love me?'

'Yes!' he insisted. 'Of course I do. And I want this to work. I guess I just…' he paused to get his thoughts in order. 'I guess I just forget that you should be a priority too. Work is all about deadlines, and graft, and urgency and it's easy to get lost in that. Might be why I've been married three times.' He added a self-deprecating smile and a wave of love for him enveloped her. He leaned over and kissed her. 'I'm sorry. Running a newspaper is a young man's game and I'm fifty – takes a bit more energy to stay on top. But I'll try harder not to neglect you. I do love you.'

'I love you too,' she whispered as he leant over to kiss her, properly kiss her, the way he used to. Reluctant to break away, she curled her hands through his hair as he swept her up and took her inside to bed. Finally, he was saying what she wanted to hear.

Their lovemaking was tender at first, then, as their heartbeats quickened, erupted into a frenzy of grabs and thrusts that was over all too quickly.

He didn't seem to notice.

As they lay together afterwards, her head nestling in the space between his arm and his torso, Tess reassured herself that this was fixable. At least they'd started being honest with each other. All they needed was the time and effort to rediscover what had brought them together in the first place. Just the two of them, alone, without any…

The knock at the door disrupted her train of thought.

'Ignore it. It's probably housekeeping,' Drew told her. 'The Do Not Disturb Sign has probably fallen off.'

She would have complied if it wasn't for the niggling worry. Colita wouldn't bring any notes to the door, but what if she was off today? Or busy? What if someone else had got a message and decided to deliver it? What if they slipped it under the door? What if Drew picked it up and read it and…?

'It's OK, I'll just see who it is,' she announced chirpily, shooting out of bed like a rocket. She hastily threw on a robe and was still tying it when she swung the door open.

In hindsight, checking the spyhole first would have been a smarter move.

'Morning, darling,' Mona chirped, as she waltzed past her, not even bothering to wait for an invitation to enter. Tess's first reaction was relief that it wasn't a concierge bearing another communication from Cameron, her second was acute irritation that Mona was here again. Forget the viper comparison, she was like a bloody leech. Her third reaction was to feel bad for her second reaction. Hadn't Mona treated them to a blissful day of relaxation yesterday? The woman was going out of her way to be friendly and she shouldn't criticize her for that.

Mona stopped, a little stunned, when she saw Tess's bedhead hair, and then her vision swung up to the raised mezzanine to see Drew lying in bed with just a sheet covering him.

'Oh, I'm so sorry!' It was the first time Tess had ever seen her flustered. 'I didn't realize…'

'It's OK. Is something wrong?' Tess asked kindly – as opposed to what she really wanted to say, which was 'please bugger off, I've seen enough of you already these last few days'. Cue another pang of guilt for the thought.

'No, no!' Mona took a visible breath, then her smile immediately switched back to full beam. 'I just wanted to invite you to lunch. We thought we'd all go ashore on the one o'clock tender and have a long, luxurious *pranzo*.' She said the last word in a heavy Italian accent. 'That means lunch,' she added for Tess's benefit.

'I know that,' she replied cheerily. Actually, she did know that. But only because she had a thing for Gino D'Acampo and watched all his cookery shows.

This time Mona didn't falter. 'Great! The excursion team have recommended a fabulous little restaurant in the marina. John and Penny are even going to bring the twins, Drew.'

In other words, everyone is going and there is no way we could refuse, Tess thought. Oh well, at least it would get Drew off the ship and away from that bloody laptop.

'Sounds great,' Drew replied, without even a searching look to Tess to check it was OK with her. Bloody cheek. When she'd suggested a similar plan he'd told her he was happy to stay on the boat. Her irritation was interrupted as he continued to address Mona. 'We'll see you down there around twelve forty-five. Oh, and Mona…'

Tess braced herself. Drew was obviously going to dole out a gentle rebuke along the lines of 'Please don't barge in again.' Or 'Could you just call us in future.' Or even 'We won't be up for this every day because Tess and I want to spend some quality time together.'

'Yes?' Mona answered.

'Thanks for organizing this,' Drew said. 'Sometimes I don't know what I'd do without you.'

Furious, Tess realised she desperately wanted to find out the answer to that question.

Mona

'*Grazie.*' The waiter made a slight bowing motion as he thanked Mona for holding up her glass so he could refill it. She might be in an emotional flux, but she'd have to be blind, too, not to notice how gorgeous he was. And at least three of the other waiters must be related to him, because this was like going to sleep and having a dream featuring four insanely hot, beautifully built, Italian versions of David Gandy. Group sex wasn't normally her thing, but for this lot she'd make an exception.

'What are you thinking about? You're smiling away there,' Drew asked her.

Mona shook her head. 'Nothing special. Just how lovely this is, being here with everyone. It couldn't be a more perfect day.'

Of course that wasn't true. If this was a perfect day then she and Drew would be here alone, and she wouldn't have walked in this morning and caught Tess and Drew practically humping in front of her. Sweet little Tess, all tousled hair and pouty lips, not a shred of effort put into her appearance and yet she was utterly gorgeous. Urgh, that drove her nuts. It had also made her go change into something striking. White pencil skirt, (young, but incredibly chic), teamed with a white, off the shoulder, scoop-neck T-shirt that showed just a hint of cleavage. She looked like Audrey Hepburn on heat.

She might not have Tess's youth, but she had far more style. And anyway, that wasn't what really mattered. Drew was all about the cerebral stimulation. *He's not fulfilled by her. He's not fulfilled by her.* She repeated her new mantra. Tess might look all sweetness and fun, but Mona knew, just absolutely knew, that Drew was bored by her.

Who would he have talked to at this lunch if she hadn't been there? A bit of deft manoeuvring as they approached the table had ensured that she was in her favourite spot right next to him. Once again, Sarah and Piers were down at the other end of the table and spent the whole time chatting to John and Penny and entertaining the twins. Boredom central. Tess was on the other side of Drew, but she'd settled for speaking mostly to Max because as soon as they'd sat down Mona had engaged Drew in a conversation about the ramifications of the Brexit vote, a subject that he could talk about for hours. And they did, just the two of them, sitting in a beautiful marina, overlooking turquoise blue seas. If it wasn't for Pier's snorting, Sarah's incessant chat and the twins chuckling, she could almost believe it was just her and Drew there.

Down at the other end of the table, John and Penny stood up and announced that they were going to take the twins back to the ship for a nap. Thank God. The couple were almost unrecognizable as the two bedraggled, exhausted parents who had come aboard. The combination of sun, sea, and unlimited childcare had worked wonders. Further evidence that Mona had been absolutely right in her decision to avoid procreation at all cost.

'I'll come with you,' Eliza announced, blushing as she said it.

'Ooooooh,' her brother teased her, 'do I detect an ulterior motive? Could there be a boy involved in this?'

Both Drew and Sarah's heads snapped up at that one.

'You've met someone?' Sarah asked.

The teenager rolled her eyes. 'Would you all stop looking at me? You're all, like, soooo embarrassing.'

That invoked a chorus of 'ooooooh's from the whole table.

Eliza rolled her eyes again and made to leave. Great. One more unwanted lunch companion gone. And if Eliza had a boy in her sights it would keep her out of her Dad's way. Another bonus.

'Erm, just one minute, young lady. What's his name and who's he here with? And you're not leaving until you tell me, so you may as well cough up.'

Eliza looked fit to explode, but she knew her mother well enough to comply.

'Kai Latham. He's nineteen. From London. Here with his mum and dad. Cabin 12890.'

Drew smiled and said warmly, 'Same deck as us, but opposite end. Well, if I find out that you've ever seen the inside of cabin 12890, Kai Latham will be in trouble. Did you tell him

I have a gun in the garage?'

'OMG, you do not have a gun in the garage, Dad.' Eliza groaned.

'Yeah, well, he doesn't need to know that.'

Eliza tutted and tottered off on her six-inch platform wedges, muttering something about, 'lame' and 'well messed up' as she went.

'That went well,' Piers said, making everyone, including Drew, laugh again. Mona reflected that while her husband might now hold the attraction of a wet weekend in a tent to her, she couldn't deny that he was always good for an amusing quip.

Sarah stood up. 'I'm going to go for a wander around the town – if anyone fancies coming they're welcome to join me.'

'Actually, I'd really like that. Do you mind if Drew and I tag along?' Tess piped up, making Mona's teeth clench. There was no way on this earth that Drew Gold would go wandering around a Sardinian town. He hated sightseeing. And even if Tess had banged him into oblivion this morning, there was still no way he'd agree to it.

'Actually, I said I'd check in with the office at four, so I'll pass, honey.'

Mona almost punched the air as Tess's demeanour visibly deflated. 'Oh.' She attempted a bright recovery. 'Well, I guess it's just me then, Sarah. Is that OK?'

'Absolutely. I'd love the company.'

Max put his napkin on the table. The sun was clearly good for him, too. He already had a bit of colour and his white T-shirt and khaki combat shorts looked great on him. Mona knew from old photographs that Piers had looked exactly like that when he was in his thirties. She only wished he still did.

'I'm going to go for a wander, too. I feel like I should attempt to absorb some culture on this trip. Apparently there are incredible sea caves a little bit up the coast, so I thought I'd go do the sightseeing thing.'

'Sounds good, son,' Piers agreed. 'You up for it, Mona?'

Mona thrust one finely toned calf up in the air in reply, showing an eight-inch spiked heel on a beautiful stiletto. 'Piers, I'm wearing Yves Saint Laurent shoes. They're made for sitting and showing off, that's it.' Some men just did not get the fact that shoe wear did not multi-task. Not that she'd have gone even if she'd have been wearing her Prada flats.

'Come on then, ladies, we'll walk with you until we find a cab or a bar.' Piers joked to Sarah, who was quick to fire it back at him.

'Piers Delaney, you are not hijacking our day again. Some of my wounds from that jet ski will never heal. And besides, Tess and I have credit cards and we're not afraid to use them.'

A conspiratorial wink passed between the two women and Mona noticed again how friendly they were becoming. She was beginning to feel like she wasn't a part of their little gang. Fine by her. Girlfriends had never been her thing, although she'd make an exception for Donatella Versace and Stella McCartney.

When the others left, she felt a flash of triumph. Just her and Drew. Together. Alone. Drew asked for the bill, only to be told that Piers had already paid it. Typical of him. Flashing the cash once again.

Drew checked his watch. 'Three thirty. I'm going to head back now.'

'Yep, me, too. Actually if you don't mind, I'll nip over to your cabin later. I want to Skype the office and I've only got a tiny notebook with me, so the picture quality is awful.'

Drew shook his head. 'Nope, no problem at all. Pop over any time.'

She very definitely would.

Sarah

'Good move on the wedges.' Sarah gestured to the low-heeled espadrilles on Tess's feet. 'With these cobblestones, any kind of heels would be shredded in no time.'

'The *Daily Vista* warned about the cobbles,' Tess replied, then fell quiet.

Sarah knew what she was thinking: Shame the *Daily Vista* didn't warn about the husband who was going to be an arse.

Her heart had gone out to the younger woman at the table. Tess's disappointment had been so obvious. It was bizarre to her that Drew hadn't learned his bloody lesson. He was three marriages in – you'd think he'd have learned to compromise by now.

She kept her opinions on her ex-husband's behaviour to herself as they browsed around the old part of the town for a couple of hours. It was an eclectic assortment of quaint little trinket stores, the usual holiday souvenir shops, and a few designer boutiques with high ticket price tags.

Sarah bought postcards, a couple of T-shirts for the twins and a silver cuff bracelet for Eliza. She also tried on a beautiful silver ring with a turquoise stone four times, but she couldn't decide whether or not to buy it. In the end, she decided against it. Tess splashed out on two beautiful dip-dyed sarongs, but Sarah could see that her heart just wasn't in it.

'Shall we stop for a coffee? Or a cold drink, if you prefer?' Sarah suggested.

'As long as we don't end up in the same state as we did when we were in Palma,' Tess replied with a smile.

Sarah groaned. 'Don't even mention that. I can honestly say the last time I got pissed was decades ago. I've no idea what happened to us the other day.'

'Piers happened.'

'You're absolutely right,' Sarah said, laughing, as they stopped at a lovely little pavement cafe. "I bet he's got everyone in the sea caves singing by now." They chose a table under the awning, out of the glare of the sun. A waiter appeared almost immediately, and took their order for two coffees, and two large gelatos. 'Bit of a weird combination, but I'm feeling in need of both,' Sarah told him. The waiter nodded, obviously used to the strange requests of tourists. Coffee and ice cream. He'd probably been asked for worse.

'I like him though, don't you?' Tess said.

Sarah was confused. 'Who? The waiter?'

'No, Piers!'

The two of them thought this was hilarious. 'I mean, I'm sure the waiter is a very nice man, but I don't know him that well.' That set them off again.

'Oh, Sarah I needed a good laugh,' Tess told her.

'I know,' Sarah replied simply. As always, she didn't want to probe or interfere, so she thought it best to say nothing more.

'It's just that… well, things aren't great just now,' Tess continued hesitantly, before adding, 'Is this too weird, talking to you about Drew? It's just that, maybe it's just me, but I feel that you and I have become, sort of friends.'

Sarah nodded. 'We have. And I suppose it's a bit strange, but no stranger than going on holiday with your husband and his ex-wives,' she said with an amiable shrug. 'You know, I'm always here to listen if you need to talk. Not that I'm claiming to be a marriage expert, though. After all, I didn't exactly make a roaring success of being married to Mr Gold, did I?'

Tess smiled and they sat in easy silence for a few moments.

'Was he always like this, Sarah? Dedicated to work. Single-minded.'

Sarah nodded, her sadness palpable. 'I learned not to take it personally. John went all the way through school with one teacher who thought I was widowed.'

The waiter put their coffees in front of them, and then added large shell-shaped bowls of chocolate ice-cream.

Tess waited until he was out of earshot. 'The crazy thing is that I thought we were fine. You just fall into a routine and our routine consisted mostly of work and cancelled dinners. My friend Cameron calls himself Drew Gold's stunt double, because he's regularly called in to perform the duties my husband can't manage.' She suddenly yelped. 'Oh my God, I just realized how that sounded. I didn't mean *those* kind of

132

duties.'

'I know, I know! Don't worry.'

'You'd like Cameron. He's the funniest guy I know. Easy. Uncomplicated. The way a friend should be. The way a husband should be, too.'

They were both silent while they thought through where to go next with the conversation. Sarah was the first to speak. 'I suppose you just have to figure out if he's worth it. Is he worth the alone time? Is he worth hanging around waiting for?'

'Is he worth not having kids for?' Tess blurted, then immediately looked embarrassed. 'I'm sorry, I shouldn't have said that. I don't know why I did – it's not even as if it's on the table. We agreed that we wouldn't have children right at the start. I guess back then I definitely thought he was worth it.'

'And now?'

'I don't know. But lately I've wondered what will happen ten years down the line if things with Drew don't work out and it's too late to go back and make different decisions.'

'Sounds like you have a lot to think about.' Once again, Sarah felt a wave of sympathy. This poor girl. Drew was a bloody fool.

'I know. Oh, Sarah, I'm sorry, I've been totally hogging the conversation. What about you? Is it OK to ask if you're seeing someone?'

Sarah popped a large scoop of gelato in her mouth and sighed with pleasure as it gave an immediate cooling effect. 'It's fine to ask and no, I'm not. Although, I'm starting to think it might be nice to meet someone now. Eliza will leave home soon and it would be good to have company. How do you meet a man these days, though? I wouldn't know where to start.'

'Well, well, well, Max, it's those two women who follow us everywhere.' Piers' booming voice almost made Tess drop her coffee.

'Erm, I think you'll find that we were here first,' Sarah replied tartly.

The two men pulled out seats and joined them, asking the hovering waiter to bring them the same as the ladies.

'How were the sea caves?' Sarah asked, genuinely glad they were there – if anyone could cheer Tess up it was this bombastic creature and his son.

'Amazing.' Max replied. 'The one we went to is called

Neptune's Grotto and you go through it by boat. It was quite something.'

'It was a cave.' Piers snorted. 'A cave. All very lovely and all that, but not exactly one of the seven wonders of the world.'

'You can tell my dad's up on culture, can't you? If the cave had a fifty-four-inch plasma TV on the wall, he'd have been totally impressed.'

'Bloody right,' Piers agreed. 'Especially if they found somewhere to plug it in.'

It was impossible not to appreciate a man that could laugh at himself, Sarah decided. He was definitely one to grab life by the horns and live in the moment. Talking of which…

'I've decided,' she said to Tess, 'that I'm going to go back and get that ring.'

'Brilliant! So you should, it's beautiful. Shall I come with you?'

'No, you sit here. It's only around the corner. Five minutes and I'll be back.'

She was already on her feet when she realized that Piers was doing the same. 'I'll pop round with you. Wouldn't mind a nosy in the shops myself.'

They left Tess and Max ordering another round of coffees and headed to the shop. When the doorbell dinged to announce their arrival, the lady behind the counter opened her arms wide. 'Ah, you came back! And you bring your husband.'

She had no idea what she'd said to make the two customers laugh so hard.

10.

Shore Leave

Tess

'Your dad is a scream,' Tess told Max, as they watched Piers and Sarah turn the corner at the end of the street and disappear.

'He is now,' Max said affectionately.

'What do you mean?' Tess asked, her interest piqued.

Max shrugged off the question. 'Och, nothing. Sorry. Didn't mean to get all profound and heavy there.'

'It's the day for it. I've just been pouring my heart out to poor Sarah. She must be wishing she'd gone back to the boat with the others.'

'Why, is something wrong? Are you OK?' Max sat forward and gave a really good impression of being genuinely interested. This guy definitely got his people skills from his dad. He had a way of making you feel totally at ease and comfortable.

The waiter appeared yet again to deliver their coffees. 'Right,' Max told her, 'I've got caffeine, ice cream and I'm sitting in the shade. Shoot. Tell me everything.'

Tess might be comfortable, but she wasn't insanely indiscreet. 'Oh, it was nothing. Tell me about your dad.'

'OK, but then you have to tell me what's on your mind. Deal?'

She made an agreement she had no intention of keeping.

'He's a great guy,' Max said. 'But he wasn't always as much fun as this. When I was growing up he was always charismatic and a bit wild, but lately... I don't know. It's almost as if he's got a new lease of life. He's more into spending time with people now. I've seen more of him in the last year than I did in the ten years before that.'

'Do you regret the time you missed with him?'

Max shook his head. 'Nope, just delighted that we're closer now. There's no one like him. There have been times in the last few days when my jaws have actually been sore with laughing.'

'My mate Cameron has the same effect on me. Totally cracks me up.' The thought was out before she'd even considered it. It was true, though. No one else made her laugh the way that Cameron did. If he was here with them just now he'd be regaling them with ridiculous stories and him and Piers would be having a banter to the death. She missed him. At least she missed him before he went all bizarre and overstepped the line.

They could never work, her and Cameron because… because…

'Hey, you're away in another world again. What are you thinking now? Ah, here comes trouble.'

She turned around to see Piers and Sarah returning, Sarah sporting the very large, very beautiful, turquoise ring on her finger.

'You got it! Wow, it's beautiful.'

Sarah came over all bashful at the compliment. 'Right folks, are we ready to go? We're sailing at six tonight, so we don't have much time.' Tess was quick to agree – anything to avoid keeping the promise to share her woes.

There was a tender waiting when they got back to the marina and it whisked them to the boat in minutes. Security checked their passports, sea passes and bags at the top of the gangplank, then they headed for the lift before getting off at different floors to go their separate ways to their cabins, Tess surprised by the sense of dread at the prospect of yet another tense encounter with Drew.

As the doors pinged open on the twelfth deck, Tess saw that Colita was at her desk. Her heart immediately began to beat twice as fast as normal. She had to ask. Had to.

'Good afternoon, Mrs Gold. How are you today? Did you enjoy your time ashore?' Tess decided the Brazilian girl's porcelain white teeth really were the most beautiful she had ever seen.

'I did, thank you, Colita.' *OK, leave it. Walk away. It's better that you don't know. Don't ask. Do. Not. Ask…*

'Colita, are there any more notes for me?' The sensible person inside her was now slapping her forehead in despair.

'Yes, Mrs Gold, I have one right here.'

A manicured hand reached into a drawer and produced a white envelope with her name on it. Tess wanted to swear. Instead, she politely thanked Colita and took the letter with a shaking hand.

She turned the corner into her corridor and stopped, then gingerly pulled the paper out of the envelope.

> Tess, no pressure. I know this must be coming over as crazy. I'll totally understand if you don't show up and I promise we'll always be mates even if you don't come. I'm hoping you've discovered that you miss me. If you do, then please… Meet me in Monaco. In the square at noon. Cx

She slumped back against the wall, trying desperately to control her breathing. *Bugger. Bugger. Bugger.* This was ridiculous. And the most ridiculous thing of all was that he was right. She was missing him. If Cameron was here then his sheer exuberance would ensure that they made the most of every single moment of this cruise. They'd try out all the bars, they'd dance until dawn and they'd even be in with the oldies at the bingo. Cameron had been addicted since he won a Cabbage Patch doll on Blackpool pier when he was seven. The very thought of that made her laugh. See! Even when he wasn't bloody here he could make her smile. She missed him. She just wished that things were so fantastic with Drew that she didn't give anyone else a second thought.

OK, she couldn't stand here all day. She stuffed the letter into her handbag and sighed. She was married. Her husband was waiting for her.

She was so deep in thought that she didn't hear a cabin door opening up ahead of her. However she did see someone step out of the door, turn right, and speed away down the corridor in the other direction.

As if she didn't have enough uncertainty and worry in her life, now she had the most surprising question of all: Why was Mona Gold rushing out of Tess and Drew's suite?

Mona

Mona's first stop when they'd got back from lunch had been at her cabin for a quick shower to wash away the heat and the aroma of pasta. She opened her wardrobe, thought for a moment, then opted to go for something casual. Tiny denim shorts, a black boob tube and silver flip-flops. She pulled her hair back into a high ponytail and put on the chunky silver Tiffany double-heart toggle chain that Drew had bought her on their first trip to New York together. God, they'd been so in love then. They'd stayed at the Helmsley, overlooking Central Park, and they'd ate, slept, made love and watched CNN for three solid days without leaving the room. Only on the fourth day did they venture out and they'd gone dancing in the exclusive Rainbow Room at the top of the Rockefeller Center. Last time she was in New York a nostalgic notion had taken her back there, only to discover that the nightclub had shut down, consigned to history. A bit like their marriage. However, she'd since read that it had undergone a complete revamp and was back in business. All she needed was their relationship to follow suit.

She'd knocked twice on Drew's door before he opened it, and saw that he'd had exactly the same idea as her. Still wet from the shower, he had only a towel around his waist. A twenty-year-old Mona would have playfully snatched it away, confident of the response he would have been unable to resist. A thirty-something Mona didn't have the balls in case it led to rejection. That admission hurt her. Yep, the aging process was a cruel fucker.

'Just go ahead and use the laptop,' he told her. 'It's out on the balcony. I left it on after I spoke to Guy.'

'Thanks.' She grinned, hoping he was getting a whiff of her Chanel No5. It was his favourite. Classy. Simple. Sexy.

On the way to the balcony, she took two bottles of fresh orange out of the fridge and poured them into glasses, then added ice from the permanently stocked ice box. The service on this ship was every bit as magnificent as any five-star hotel she had ever been to.

Out on the balcony, she quickly Skyped the office and spoke to her assistant, Rupert. He was out and proud, with a core of steel – most of it accrued from years of self-defence caused by growing up in Glasgow with a name like Rupert.

She quickly ran through the following week's shoots – completely unnecessary as she'd left a list of notes that had the same level of detail as a NASA flight manual. 'Well done on the Cindy Trenchant spread,' she told him. It always helped to give praise where it was due.

Almost ten years ago, she'd plucked Rupert from a work placement stint, when he was sixteen and showed up in Gucci heels. From that moment, Rupert would take a Tiffany-designed bullet for her and she intended to ensure that level of commitment continued. 'Oh, it was so easy. The woman is a mess, so we had plenty of options to slate. What is it with political wives? Thank fuck he didn't shag Cherie Blair – we'd have had to dedicate a summer special to that one.'

There was only one person that could out-bitch Mona and she was looking right back at him. She had truly created a monster, but one she loved dearly.

'Right, my darling, got to go. Kisses.'

He air-kissed either side of the screen and signed off.

'Was that Rupert you were talking to?' Drew appeared from behind her.

'Yes. He's absolutely absurd but I do love him.'

'You know he flashed the mayor last week? They were at a function in One Devonshire Gardens. Apparently the mayor had to sit down with his inhaler afterwards but he decided not to take any action in case he offended the pink vote.'

Mona's expression combined incredulity and amusement. At least Rupert was never that hideous four-letter word: dull.

'I poured you an orange juice.' She slid it across the table to him. His bicep flexed when he picked it up. He was wearing black shorts now, but nothing else, and every single hour he put in at the gym showed. He might not be able to match a twenty-three-year-old male model, but he could give any forty-ish A-lister a run for his money. He still turned her on every bit as much as he had the first day she met him. She'd seen him almost every day of her life since then and the physical attraction had never waned. That had never been the problem. If only the other stuff hadn't got in the way, then they'd still be together and she wouldn't be sitting on a fucking ship with a family group that was dysfunctional with a capital bloody D.

'So, how are you enjoying this so far?' she asked him, stretching back on the chair and putting her feet up on table. He was quiet for a moment. That was Drew. No false platitudes and banal small talk. They were way too close for that.

'You know what, I'm not sure.' There was an unmistakable hint of sadness. 'It's great seeing John and Eliza and the kids, but…'

He left that one hanging in the air.

'Can I ask you something?' she said tentatively. Time to start gently picking at the seams in the hope of an imminent unravel of Drew and Tess's relationship.

'Sure.'

'Tell me if you want me to butt out, but I'm just concerned, and I mean this as a friend. Is everything OK with you and Tess? It's just that – and maybe I'm imagining it – but you seem a little… *disconnected*.'

Another pause. 'I don't know,' he admitted wearily.

She knew not to push it. For a guy who lived up to the typical 'emotionally closed off', West of Scotland stereotype, that small admission was the equivalent of three weeks of soul-baring in therapy.

'Tess is amazing. She's beautiful and sweet and funny and patient, and I've never known anyone like her.'

For the sake of her ego, Mona really hoped there was a 'but' coming soon.

'But…'

Hallelujah and praise be!

'Sometimes I wonder if I make her happy.'

'Of course you make her happy. How could you not?' The words just slipped out. The fact that they massaged his ego could only help her cause.

'Because she's given up a lot for me, Mona. She agreed to not having kids. She plays second fiddle to work. I don't give her enough time and, to be honest, I'm too damn knackered to make the kind of effort that I need to make. I don't want to get home at midnight and sit up until 2 a.m. catching up with her day. And if I'm supposed to meet her for dinner and a story breaks, then I'm not going anywhere. It's what I am. You understood that.'

'I did. I still do.'

'But it's impossible for anyone who's not in the industry to get that. Sometimes I think she deserves more.'

This was it. He was about to realise what he had to do. All she had to do was nudge him along.

'Maybe she does.'

The second she said that he flinched and his eyes locked with hers.

'I don't mean that badly, Drew, but come on, how long have we known each other?'

He thought for a moment. 'Twenty years?'

She nodded. 'And the one thing I know is that you need to be with someone who understands you and gets turned on by the same things. Tess is all those things you said she is, but I'm not sure that she's right for you. I hate seeing you this miserable.'

She thought about stopping there but how many more times this week would they get the opportunity to speak on their own like this? How many more chance would she get to apply subtle persuasion that it was time for Drew to rethink his current marital situation and opt for a new one. Or more accurately, an old one?

'I think you should be with someone you have more in common with, and trust me, you are more than enough to keep a woman happy.'

Drew smiled at that. 'I didn't keep you happy, did I?'

Shit, she walked right into that one.

'That was a different time and place, Drew.' There was no way she was getting into why they split up now. No way. This was supposed to be an attempt to get closer to him, not remind him of the very worst of times. 'Look, Drew, there's no point going over all that again. You have to deal with what's happening now. If Tess isn't right for you then you have to let her go. It's the decent thing to do, and in all the years I've known you, my darling, the one thing you have always been is decent.'

He looked so miserable, her heart almost ached for him. Decency was definitely overrated as far as she was concerned.

141

Much as she was tempted to stay and play the empathetic friend for a while longer, she was well enough educated in the ways of men, and Drew Gold in particular, to know that you should always be the one who chooses when to stay and go. Besides, now that she'd planted the seeds, she wanted to give him time to think about it. He was a smart guy. She was becoming more and more convinced that he would do the right thing.

Making a big play of checking her watch, she sighed loudly. 'Drew, I have to go. Piers will be back soon, and to be perfectly honest with you, I'm going through something similar.'

'Really? God, Mona, I'm so sorry to hear that. I had no idea.'

'It's OK, how would you? I'm beginning to think that Piers and I want completely different things. He's always on at me to slow down, stop working, take time out.'

'That's not you.'

'No, it's not,' she agreed. She leant over and kissed him on the cheek then squeezed him into a hug that he was more than happy to reciprocate. As she pulled away, she gave him her best parting shot. 'You know, Drew, sometimes I think the only two people that really get who we are is us.'

She didn't stop to see if his eyes followed her as she left and she didn't turn back at the door. Her job for today was done. Now she just wanted to get some time on her own before Piers returned to think about her next move.

Sarah

Sarah wandered along the port side of deck fourteen looking for a nice spot to sit down and relax. She had thought about taking the Tasmina Perry book she was reading out on the balcony, but the twins were wide awake and having supper in the cabin with John and Penny, so there was much shrieking going on. Not that she minded that in the least. When she'd returned from Alghero, she'd gone straight in to see the kids, then volunteered to take Lawrence and Lavinia swimming with John, so that Penny could have an hour to herself to get ready for dinner. They'd fallen into a routine that suited them perfectly. The nanny would take the children in the mornings to give them some 'couple time'. They'd all have lunch together, then John and Penny would put the little ones down for a sleep and chill out on the balcony. After their nap came a couple of hours of fun time, then supper, and some quiet play before bedtime.

Now it was almost six thirty and the ship had just begun to gently rock as it left the bay and headed into the horizon. They had no plans to meet for dinner tonight and Sarah was glad. She was enjoying getting to know everyone better, with one bitchy exception, and Piers, Tess and Max had been an absolute revelation, but it was nice to have some space, too.

The deck was virtually empty, most of her fellow cruisers either getting dressed for dinner, already at dinner or at the early show. There were now only a few stragglers left.

She wondered if she might bump into Eliza. The note on the coffee table saying, 'Out with Kai, be back later,' didn't exactly furnish her with many details about her daughter's day.

A couple on two adjacent sunbeds caught her eye, both of them entwined, kissing passionately. On second thoughts, perhaps it was better if she didn't stumble across her daughter. Although perhaps it was time for a gentle grilling as to the status of her friendship with this boy.

She carried on past the lovebirds and settled for a thick, padded wicker chair and footstool under a bright light. It was still daylight now, but she'd noticed that the night descended quickly, and earlier than at home.

As soon as she sat down, a barman appeared at her side. 'Can I get you a drink, madam?' asked Benji, Philippines.

'I'll have a gin and tonic, please. And a black coffee.' She didn't want to trouble him to do another journey in half an hour, so it was easier to order both now. At home a gin and tonic was normally her Friday night indulgence, but hey, she was on her holiday.

She opened up her book and began to read, stopping only to say thank you when Benji, Philippines delivered her drink. Bliss. Utter bliss. It still seemed strange to her that she'd been invited on this trip in the first place, but she was glad that she had been as it had been full of laughs. It was just a shame that there had also been a few not so funny surprises. When Tess had confided in her today she'd been both surprised and touched. She just hoped she'd handled it well.

'Is this seat taken, ma'am?'

She glanced up to see the cowboy she'd met on the first day on board and instinctively smiled. 'Well, good evening,' she replied. 'Please, be my guest.'

For a man who could pass as an extra at the Alamo, he was looking pretty good. He was wearing black jeans, beat-up cowboy boots and a steel-grey shirt with the top couple of buttons open.

'Your husband ain't up here with you?'

Oh bugger, she'd forgotten all about that whole debacle at their first meeting.

'I'm not married, Nate. That was my ex-husband. And his other ex-wife. And his current wife. And yes, I know that makes us sound like we belong on one of those shows with the lie detector and DNA tests.'

'Yup, that just about covers it, I reckon. Glad we got that straight. I was trying to work out if you gals were those polygamist sister wives.' He was obviously teasing her, so she gave him her very best stern look, the raised eyebrow of doom that had been the major force of discipline in her house since the children were tiny. He responded by grinning and winking at her, so she decided to stick to more neutral subjects.

'How have you been, Nate? Is Europe living up to your daughter's expectations?'

'Hey, you remembered. Yes ma'am, it sure is. We took the little ones to see Neptune's Grotto today. Kinda blew my mind how old it all is.'

'My friends went there, too. Said it was incredible.'

'That it was. So why are you sitting up here on your lonesome, then? Sick of everyone you're travelling with already?'

Sarah loved the mischievous glint in his eye. 'Absolutely.' She bought into the joke. 'Sick of the lot of them. Was just contemplating whether to jump and swim for shore. What about you?'

'Already cased out the lifeboats. Reckon I'm making a bid for freedom soon as night falls.'

'Yeah, well, give me a shout. You row one side and I'll row the other. We might just make land by daybreak. I'll bring cakes from the buffet so we don't starve.'

Nate was laughing now, a gorgeous, husky gurgle that came from the back of his throat. 'Sarah, I know this is a bit forward an' all, but would you like to have dinner with me tonight?'

Wow, she hadn't seen that coming. What to do? It didn't take much consideration. Back at home she'd have panicked, phoned Patsy, panicked some more, made a plan, shopped for an outfit, panicked and then cancelled with an hour to go. But that was the old Sarah. The new 'I'm on my holidays and I'm damn well going to enjoy it' Sarah made her mind up pretty quickly.

'Can we have it here? Over at that table there.' She pointed to a small wicker table for two at the edge of the deck overlooking the water.

'I reckon that looks just about perfect.'

When Benji next passed, they asked him for a couple of menus and he produced them from under his tray. They both ordered steak sandwiches and fries. It might not be the most exotic of romantic dinners, but it was just what Sarah was in the mood for. Perhaps this was where she had been going wrong all these years. Whipping dates up into a frenzy in her head when really she should just have chilled out and gone with the flow. And a steak-sandwich-eating cowboy.

'Now you know I'm gonna ask – why are you on vacation

with your ex-husband and all his other wives? Ain't that just a bit strange? I mean, I like my ex-wife fine, but I don't want to go to Disneyland with her.'

Her laughter even made the snogging couple stop and glance over. 'Do you know, I'm not entirely sure why. It's my ex-husband's fiftieth birthday celebration and I guess he just wanted everyone who'd been significant in his life to be here. I'm sure I was just invited in case the nanny service wasn't up to scratch.'

Benji arrived with two bottles of beer, prompting them to move to the table.

Over the next three hours they discussed family and jobs. They talked about their teenage years and their marriages. They shared stories that were normally reserved for friends. And they laughed. It was easy, uncomplicated and – Sarah decided – absolutely perfect.

Or at least, it was perfect until their peace was shattered by noise from the big screen further along the deck. It was used to show concerts and movies all day long to the guests who were lying by the pool.

Sarah checked her watch; 11 p.m. She'd noticed in the *Daily Vista* schedule that there was a late-night showing at this time every evening. Oh, crap. Their peace was about to be shattered by some bloody action movie and they'd have to shout to be heard over the racket of hand grenades and whatever weapons the invading Martians were using. 'Time for the movie,' she said, with a hint of sadness.

She was about to suggest that they call it a night when the sound of roaring applause came through the speakers, followed by a familiar voice.

'Thank you very much and I'm mighty thrilled to be here with you all tonight.'

More applause. Sarah was so dumbstruck her eyes actually filled up. She blinked away the tears. This was unbelievable. It wasn't a movie, it was a concert, but not just any concert.

'The first song I'd like to sing for you tonight is called "Just To See You Smile".'

It was only bloody Tim McGraw. Her very favourite singer of all time. The man who only married that tall, gorgeous, leggy, talented, blonde, multi-platinum selling artist Faith Hill because he didn't realize that she, Sarah Gold, was available.

Now he was here, serenading her under the stars while another cowboy reached his hand out to her.

'Would you like to dance, Sarah?'

She looked at Nate. Handsome, craggy, lovely Nate, and nodded her head. 'I'd love to.'

They stood up, came together, and by the time Tim McGraw was onto the second chorus, they were giving the snogging couple on the sunbeds a run for their money. Yes, Sarah Gold was kissing a virtual stranger.

And it felt great.

So great that half an hour later, as she was still slow-dancing in the moonlight, she didn't notice a jogger stop, turn, and stare at them for a long, long time.

And she didn't hear the sound of Drew's trainers hitting the deck as he jogged on into the night.

11.

Messina

Tess

'So the weather today is – let me see – yep, hot and sunny,' Tess announced in the voice of a breakfast television weather forecaster. Hot and sunny might have been an understatement. It was only 7 a.m. and already the heat coming through the open balcony door was stifling.

Today was a new day and she was determined to turn over a new page on her marriage and her holiday. Lying awake last night she'd decided that the answer was simple: she was going to ignore Cameron's notes, pay lots of attention to Drew, remind him why they fell in love, and all was going to be fine. Oh, and she was going to ignore Mona being a meddling, annoying pain in her slightly rotund arse who seemed to spend more time in their suite than her own. Optimism. It had always been one of her strongest characteristics and it was time to switch it back on. Yes, she might have made this same resolution before, but this time she was going to stick to it. She was going to fix her marriage. It was all going to be great. They'd work it out and get through this. Although, if she was being picky, so far this morning the start of the new chapter wasn't perfect.

They'd docked just a few minutes before and Tess had watched it from bed, with Drew lying next to her tapping away on his laptop. The laptop. In bed with them. If Cameron was here, he'd say that was Drew's version of a threesome. But she was turning over that new page so all thoughts of Cameron were banished.

'I've booked an excursion today,' she announced.

Drew stopped tapping and looked at her with an expression

that definitely wasn't optimism. He hated excursions. Hated trooping along in a guided pack, at the mercy of other people's schedules. But this one was different. She knew he'd love it, so she'd swallowed an assertive pill and booked it as a surprise.

'Where are we going?' he asked, his voice taking the Oscar for the least amount of enthusiasm in a single sentence.

Grinning, she started humming *The Godfather* theme tune.

'Tess, where are we going?' he said, switching from lack of enthusiasm to mild exasperation.

'That was your clue! It's called *The Godfather* tour. We're going to visit some of the locations used in *The Godfather* movies.'

'Really? Sounds interesting.' , OK, so he didn't pick her up and swing her around with glee, but the reaction was at least slightly encouraging. *The Godfather* movies were his favourite cinematic experiences of all time and even now his box set got dragged out every Christmas for a rerun.

At eight-thirty sharp, armed with water and sunscreen, and wearing comfortable shoes, they disembarked and headed for their designated coach, leaving the laptop back in the cabin and his second wife still on board. Tess had checked. Things were looking up.

The tour guide was a petite Italian woman called Paola, who began by insisting that everyone repeat '*buongiorno*' to her. Then again, but louder. Everyone else on the bus got into the spirit of it, but Drew stayed silent. He hated the panto stuff.

The coach set off, beginning the journey with a drive around Messina, which, Paola informed them, was the third biggest city in Sicily. They stopped briefly to take pictures at the beautiful Sacrario di Cristo Re, a stunning church that Paola informed them translated to The Shrine of Christ the King.

A Japanese tourist obliged by taking a picture of the two of them together, a beautiful, romantic gesture until the woman handed the camera back. 'Ah, lovely family photograph,' she told them in heavily accented English, before turning to Drew. 'You and daughter very handsome together.'

His lips tightened in irritation. Tess giggled and nudged him in the ribs. 'Oh, come on, it's not the first time. Lighten up, honey.'

He gave her a weak smile and headed back to the bus. She was about to follow him when she was stopped by an, 'Excuse me, would you mind taking a picture for us?' She turned to see a sixty-something woman wearing white slacks and a pink T-shirt, with a wide smile under a sun visor, and perfectly pink lipstick. The woman's accent placed her as being from the American south, and her hair was definitely the size of Texas. Tess loved her immediately. 'Of course!'

Tess snapped a shot of the woman with her husband, who looked like an aged version of an American astronaut from the sixties: tall, broad, with his side-parted, silver hair and eyes that still had a twinkle in them.

'It's our wedding anniversary,' she told Tess. 'Forty-five years.'

Looking through the lens, Tess watched as the woman turned to meet her husband's gaze and such a look of love passed between them that Tess's heart melted.

Forty-five years. What did it take to last that long, to spend that many years together and still love each other? There was obviously still such devotion between these two. When was the last time Drew had looked at her like that? She honestly couldn't remember. He hadn't even bothered staying with her while she stood outside the church, choosing instead to get back on the bus. When she joined him, he was deeply engrossed in his iPhone and didn't even bother to glance up. Bugger. He'd managed to bring the iPhone. She should have insisted he left that behind with the laptop and the annoying ex. Damn, he was infuriating, but she wasn't going to let this spoil the day. It would be fine. Stick with the optimism.

'The Dweezil story still running?' she asked, gesturing to the phone.

'Yeah, just checking out what the other papers are saying. We definitely scooped that one.'

'Great.'

Absolutely great.

The bus rolled on for an hour or so before climbing a twisting hillside road to the rustic village of Savoca. Paola herded them down cobblestone pavements to the Bar Vitelli, where Michael Corleone had asked Apollonia's father if he could court his daughter. It was one of Tess's favourite scenes in the movie. She'd first watched it with her dad when she was a teenager and then watched it time and time again with Drew.

They sat at a table outside and ordered granita, a semi-frozen flavoured drink that Paola told them was a speciality of the area.

Tess sighed happily and stretched in the sun. 'This is amazing. I can't believe I'm here. Seems so surreal.'

'It does,' Drew agreed. OK, now was the time for him to say he was glad they came. That he was enjoying himself. Perhaps even thank her for arranging it... 'Bloody hot, though. How long do we have to stay here before we can get back on the bus?'

Deep breathe. Optimism. 'Don't you want to explore? To go wandering around?'

'Why?' He seemed genuinely bemused. 'Tess, we can see it all from the bus, in the cool air conditioning with no bloody flies buzzing around.'

Right on cue, he swatted an insect from his face. Tess hoped it had time to bite him before meeting its doom.

So much for flipping positivity.

Irked, she ignored his repetitive checking of his watch and deliberately took her time with her strawberry granita, ensuring that they were the last people to reboard the bus. Drew wasn't pleased and yes, she realized that the sense of satisfaction this gave her was very immature and very petty, but it felt like a small victory.

Half an hour later, they stopped again, this time in Forza d'Agrò, a village on a mountainside that was overlooked by the ruins of a sixteenth-century castle on a higher peak.

They followed Paola again, through the narrow, winding streets, this time stopping when they came to an ancient church that she recognized immediately. Michael Corleone had stood exactly where she was standing and now Tess Gold was there too – with a disgruntled husband, a nice Japanese lady, and an American couple who'd been married for forty-five years.

Spine tingling, for a moment, Tess just wanted to stand and stare. It was so exquisite. So old. It took her breath away.

The anniversary celebrant interrupted her thoughts. 'Hon, will you take another photograph of me and Norm?'

'Of course I will.' Tess happily took the camera and snapped a gorgeous shot of the couple on the steps of the church.

When she was done, she handed the camera back over. 'Can you take one of my husband and me too, please?' This would be a beautiful memory. The two of them, outside this church, one that they could look back on after they'd made it to forty-five years married. She would be 69 and he would be 90 by then – hopefully his eyesight would be too shot to spend all day staring at his iPhone.

'Course I can,' Norm replied.

'Great. He's just…'

Tess glanced around, but Drew was nowhere in sight. He'd just taken off. Left. Done what he damn well pleased yet again without even telling her or suggesting that she come with him. His disappearance sparked a sudden realization: If things carried on like this, then after forty-five years together, all she would have to look back on was a lifetime of being alone.

Mona

Mona stretched out on the sunbed and sighed contentedly. This was bliss. Utter bliss. Of course, she was wearing factor fifty sun cream to protect against wrinkles and skin cancer, but the heat on her body was making her extremely happy. And extremely horny, she realized. It might even be worth tempting Piers back into the bedroom just for a quickie. She inevitably closed her eyes and pretended it was someone else anyway.

Taking a sip of her vodka tonic, she briefly wondered how Drew was getting on. The thought irritated her. What on earth had possessed Tess to arrange an excursion for them? And why had he agreed? Drew hated sightseeing. It made him miserable and grouchy and he always ended up wandering off on his own. The more she was around those two, the more she was certain that they had absolutely nothing in common.

All Drew wanted to do was drink good wine, eat good food, have in-depth, intelligent discussions and work out until he ached.

That thought sent a frisson of horniness coursing through her. It was incredibly crass, but she couldn't help thinking that she would give him a workout that was far more effective than an hour on a stationary bike.

But back to the point. Other than her obvious enjoyment of a large meal, Tess had no interest in any of the things Drew enjoyed.

Her inner monologue was interrupted when she felt herself chill, and realized that Piers was standing above her, shading her from the heat of both the sun and her filthy thoughts.

'Here you go, love, thought you might like a top-up.' He put another vodka tonic on the table beside her lounger. She shouldn't. She really shouldn't. But it was already two o'clock and she was on holiday – two drinks wouldn't kill her. She'd just work extra hard in the gym tomorrow morning to burn off the calories.

With a loud grunt of exertion, Piers plumped down on the sunbed next to her and playfully slapped her thigh. She fought the urge to return the gesture with a non-playful punch to his face.

'All right, pet? You look like one of those adverts for suntan lotion lying there.'

There was a compliment in there somewhere. Her leopard-print Dolce & Gabbana bikini would come up great in a publicity shot – especially if their poster boy, David Gandy, was removing it from her with his teeth. Two David Gandy fantasies in one week. Ah, if only Mr Gandy was here and if only her bloody husband wasn't sat there like a sweating whale, blocking her sun.

Right on cue, the second of those wishes came true, when the doorbell rang and Piers went off to investigate. Mona rolled on to her front and rejoiced once again that their suite came with its own terrace and sunbeds. It was definitely preferable to lying on the public decks with all those kids running around, and large men called Chad and Josh shouting at the tops of their voices while playing water polo in the pool.

'Good afternoon, stepmother, how are you today?'

As always, hearing Max say that caused a bristle of irritation to cut right through all the serenity.

'Max…' she said, her tone one of warning as she looked up to see Max grinning back at her.

He seemed to find this hilarious. 'Man, you're touchy. I was merely stating fact.' He continued to tease, pulling one of the other sunbeds out of the shade. Piers was laughing when he handed over a cold bottle of Bud from the not-so-mini minibar. The two of them settled next to each other, both of them bare-chested and wearing black swim shorts, the difference in their physiques making the scene look like a before and after shot for a fitness campaign.

'So, what do you reckon, Dad – who is the Old Firm going to sell in the off season?'

It was difficult to suppress the groan. The Old Firm – the collective name given to Glasgow's biggest football rivals, Celtic and Rangers. She immediately switched off, knowing that one question could spur a conversation that lasted for days. Really. Bloody days.

Her mind drifted back to her earlier 'Drew and Tess' train of thought, and an image of a highly pissed off Drew came into her head. Yesterday's conversation with him had thrilled her. There were clearly irredeemable cracks in his marriage to Tess and it was time they both realized that and called it a day. What was the point in flogging it to death? Far better to cut their losses and move on, to find (or re-find) someone that would make them happy.

They just needed to accept that they wanted different things. That was the key to this. What was taking them so long to see that? Let's speed it up, people, move it along.

An idea began to form in her head and she pondered it for the next few minutes, weighing it up and thinking through the logistics of it.

It could work, she decided. Or at least, help things along a little. And she was nothing if not helpful… especially when it came to getting what she badly wanted.

'Max, do you have any plans for tomorrow?'

Her stepson shook his head. 'Not yet. To be honest, I've lost track of where we're going to be.'

'Naples,' she replied.

'Cool.'

Oh bloody hell. Cool? Was that all he had to say? She'd been hoping he would at least pick that up and run with it a little.

'I once went to a stag night there. Helluva night. Lasted for a week.'

Mona chose to ignore her husband's contribution. 'I was reading the excursion planner for tomorrow and I noticed that they do boat trips to Sorrento, and there are all sorts of water sports involved. That's your kind of thing, isn't it?'

Max winced in jest. 'I don't know. Dad's jet ski nearly killed me.' He turned to his father. 'What happened to the jet ski after we left Palma?'

'Sent it back to the golf club and told them to sell it for the donkeys.'

For some reason this caused both men to collapse, hooting with laughter.

Suppressing an exasperated sigh, she nudged Max back on track, while trying to appear nonchalant. Any direct encouragement could arouse Pier's suspicions. 'It's up to you, but apparently there's the option to get a boat over to Sorrento, then drop anchor and spend the day trying out different sports.

I just thought you might like that.'

'If you fancy it, son, I'd definitely be up for tagging along,' Piers offered.

Bonus! Peace and quiet, thanks to having no Piers all day. This could work out even better than she planned. All she needed was for Max to say…

'Sounds great. I've never been snorkelling or windsurfing and always fancied trying it. You might want to notify the travel insurance company that a medevac situation could be imminent.'

That sent the two men off again. Honestly, she just didn't get their sense of humour at all.

She waited until they'd settled.

'In fact,' she declared as if she'd just thought of the idea, 'you should see if any of the rest of the group want to go with you. I'm sure some of them will be up for a bit of adventure.'

Sarah

'Guess where I am?' Sarah demanded, holding her mobile phone against her ear with her shoulder so that she could release her hands to sign the bill that Daisy, Hong Kong was holding out for her.

'In bed with a Russian body builder,' Patsy replied.

'Nope,' Sarah giggled.

'At a Mafia training camp in the Sicilian hills?'

'Nope.'

'OK, that was my two best shots. Where are you?'

'In a beautiful bar, on the top deck of a ship, overlooking the sea.'

'Oh. The Mafia training camp would have impressed me more.'

'I'm not done,' Sarah scolded her. 'I'm in a beautiful bar, on the top deck of a ship, overlooking the sea, waiting for a cowboy that I kissed the face off last night.'

Via the technology of the mobile phone, Daisy, Hong Kong was treated to a screech all the way from Glasgow. Sarah flushed red and giggled.

'You win. Tell me all,' Patsy said when she eventually calmed down.

Sarah settled back into her chair and pulled her legs up beneath her. Most people were heading back into their cabins after a day in the sun, so other than Daisy, who was now out of earshot, she was all alone in the bar, leaving her to be utterly indiscreet.

'OK, but first of all I have to tell you, Mona has no pubic hair.'

'I don't even want to contemplate how you know that, but eeew.'

'Thank you. I knew you would feel that way too. Anyway, the cowboy.'

'Does he do stripograms dressed as the Lone Ranger or

something?' Patsy asked, confused.

'No, he's an actual cowboy. Wears the boots and the hat and everything. Comes from Nashville. He's called Nate and he's the most charming man I've ever met. He reminds me of Tim McGraw.'

'Oh crap, I'll never see you again,' Patsy said.

'Last night we had dinner out on deck and then he asked me to dance, so I did. Not on an actual dancefloor, just out on the deck, under the stars, just the two of us. Then he walked me back to my cabin and kissed me again at the door like a total gentleman. Is this too sickly-sweet?'

'Absolutely. And I love it.'

'It was really nice, Pats. Really nice.'

'Well, I watched a double bill of *Law & Order*, so I want your life instead of mine. Seriously, Sarah, I'm so happy for you. It sounds completely blissful – apart from the bit where you viewed Mona's lack of a bush, obviously. That may crop up in future nightmares.'

Giggling, Sarah said, 'I miss you, Pats. I wish you were with me – we'd be having such a great time.'

'Sounds like you're doing just fine by yourself, my darling.'

Over to her right, Sarah spotted Nate coming through the heavy glass doors. 'Have to go, he's here.'

'Send me a picture.'

'I'll try. Huge hugs!'

She'd just snapped the phone shut when Nate reached her table and leant down to kiss her on the cheek. The cheek. He was so chivalrous.

'How's your day been?' he asked her, as he signalled to Daisy for a bottle of beer. Sarah had no idea how the staff remembered what everyone drank – they must all have photographic memories.

'Great. Really great. I sunbathed a bit this morning and then took the children swimming in the afternoon. I'm loving spending so much time with them. What about you?'

He went on to tell her how the whole family went to Mount Etna, something that his grandchildren thought was amazing.

They chatted easily for an hour or so, before he reached over and put his hand on hers. 'I hope you don't think I go around dancing with strange women on ships every day of the week. Last night was real good, Sarah.'

'It was,' she agreed, finding herself slightly tongue-tied. Urgh, she was rubbish at this. She felt like she was sixteen again, but without the flared hipsters and the really bad perm.

'If it's OK with you, I was thinking that maybe we could meet up again later.'

Flush. Tongue stuck. Inner beam of happiness. Eventually, she managed, 'Sure. Same place?'

'Same place,' he told her, then checked his watch. 'Darn, I have to go. I'm having dinner at eight.'

'Is it eight o'clock already? Oh, bollocks, I was supposed to meet the family fifteen minutes ago.'

She jumped to her feet and this time she took the initiative by leaning down and kissing him. On the mouth. Yes, the mouth. Patsy would be proud.

Walking swiftly, she made her way down to the Italian restaurant on deck ten, where everyone was already seated around a long, rustic wooden table. They burst into a round of applause as she sat down, turning her face the same colour as the red candles sticking out of Chianti bottles in the middle of the table. She sat down at the one free seat between Tess and Max. Excellent. The last thing she wanted was to be sitting next to Mona all night. She still had the strangest feeling that the other woman was up to something. She winked at Eliza who rolled her eyes in return. All normal there then. Last night when she got back to the cabin, Eliza was already asleep, so she still hadn't managed to have that chat about her daughter's newfound friendship with Kai. Not that she was exactly on the moral high ground these days, given her newfound tendency to spontaneously snog a man in cowboy boots.

'Where have you been, then?' Drew said with a smile. He looked tired, she noticed, and his smile didn't quite reach his eyes.

'Just… talking to a friend.'

'Mum's got a boyfriend,' Eliza interjected in a tone that suggested it was the grossest thing she could imagine. Sarah busied herself unfolding her napkin while simultaneously trying to kick her daughter under the table and change the subject. 'So what did I miss?' she asked, deflecting Drew's curious stare.

'Nothing much, we've not been here very long,' Tess replied, then leaned closer and whispered, 'but I'm dying to hear what you've been up to.' Sarah gave her a conspiratorial wink but said nothing. One of the best things about this trip so far was her newfound friendship with Tess – a real delight, despite the tangled family ties and the age difference.

The theme of the restaurant was traditional, family-style eating, so the waiters immediately began delivering large trays of antipasti and breads for them to share.

'What did you do to today?' Sarah threw the question out in the direction of Tess and Drew.

'We went on an excursion to the places where *The Godfather* movies were filmed,' Tess replied. Ah, that explained why Drew didn't look too chipper. He hated organized trips. He once threw a fit halfway round the Caves of Drach in Majorca because the tour guide kept screeching information at them. She was momentarily surprised that the younger woman didn't know to avoid excursions at all cost, even ones that were based on his favourite movie. But then, hadn't Tess said that she hadn't been away with Drew since their honeymoon?

'Speaking of excursions,' Max spoke up and everyone turned to look at him, 'Dad and I are heading to Sorrento tomorrow. Apparently there's a boat trip that includes some water sports, so we thought we'd give it a try. Anything but jet skis.'

Piers, Tess and Sarah automatically laughed at that, leaving the others bemused.

'You're all welcome if you fancy it. I'm sure there will be plenty of room on the boat.'

John was the first to answer. 'Sounds great, Max, but Penny and I will pass, thanks. We've got ourselves into a great routine on here. We're loving it. I can't thank you enough for this, Dad.'

Drew smiled at his son, and this time Sarah noticed that it reached his eyes. It gave her a little gush of pleasure to see her son and his family so happy.

'I'll pass too,' Mona said dryly. 'Not my thing.'

Of course it wasn't, Sarah mused. Mona's "things" were more designer clothes, snide comments and flashing her gynaecological anatomy to unsuspecting women with hangovers.

Sarah knew she was going to have to get over the fact that she found it difficult to look Mona in the eye these days.

'Not mine either, Max, sorry,' Drew said. 'I've got some calls to put in to the office, so I think tomorrow is aboard ship for me.'

Sarah sensed Tess tensing beside her and realized that she was biting her bottom lip. Oh dear, things were not good there at all.

'I'm up for it, Max.' It took a few seconds for her to realize that the voice was hers. Wow. One night with a cowboy and she'd turned into an impetuous adventurer. The thought sent another little gush of pleasure to her toes.

'Well, I'm in too, then,' Tess blurted, eliciting a raised eyebrow from Drew. Sarah just happened to be testing her ability to look straight at Mona at that point, when she saw a shadow of something that resembled smugness cross her face. Sarah's teeth clenched but she stayed silent, feeling distinctly uneasy

'What about you, Eliza? Will you come with us?' she heard Tess say. She really did appreciate how friendly Tess was to her daughter. It couldn't be easy taking on a sixteen-year-old part-time and, much as she loved her, she was under no illusion that Eliza was the easiest girl to deal with.

'Erm, if it's OK, I'll stay aboard, too.'

'Don't tell me! You're spending the day with Kai!'

Eliza nodded gleefully, setting off another round of applause, a raised eyebrow from Drew and another reminder that Sarah needed to have "a chat" with her daughter.

'You know, son, I'm just thinking – leave it to me to organize. I might have a couple of contacts.' Piers told Max.

'Oh God, not again,' Sarah roared. 'Tess, brace yourself, Piers is in charge.'

"I'll call my insurance company straight after dinner," the younger woman replied. Good on her for coming along and refusing to sit and wait for Drew to pay her some attention.

Her response drew a chorus of hilarity from the table that filled the whole restaurant.

Glancing at John, Penny and Eliza, Sarah sighed with contentment. Her whole family was happy. And as she reached over for a chunk of garlic bread, she realized that she could honestly say that she was, too.

12.

Naples

Tess

'Well, looks like it's going to be just the four of us again. Do you think the rest of them are trying to tell us something?' Tess asked, with a breezy grin that belied the way she was truly feeling. Drew had barely even spoken to her this morning and she knew it was because she had decided to desert him, without even discussing it with him. One half of her was feeling bolshie and defiant, the other was feeling guilty at leaving him on his birthday cruise. Bugger it, he would only spend half the day on the phone to the office anyway. She was here now so she may as well have a good time and deal with the fallout when she got back to the cabin It wasn't every day that she got to cruise the Med and while he might be content to sit on board, she wanted to make the most of it.

She hadn't been sure how to dress today, so she'd covered all bases by going with shorts and a vest top, with her swimming costume underneath. The cossie had cost a tenner in Primark and she wasn't sure that yellow was her colour, but hey, it wasn't as if she was trying to impress anyone and it sure beat the sheep from their previous excursion.

'Is that our boat?' she asked Piers as they walked along a jetty lined with an assortment of vessels, from fishing boats to the gleaming white yacht in front of them. About twenty feet long, it had a dark wood deck, white leather booth seats, and a large canopy structure on the front, surrounded by chrome railings. Tess was dumbstruck.

'Bloody hell, that looks like it's right out of *Miami Vice*,' Sarah whispered.

'What's *Miami Vice*?' Tess replied, causing Sarah to shake her head and mutter playfully, 'So young. What am I doing here with these toddlers?'

'Signore Piers!' A man on the boat waved to Piers, answering their question.

'Piers, how does he know you?' Tess asked, despite realizing that it was probably best that she didn't know the answer.

The older man laughed. 'Decided not to bother with the official excursions and got my secretary to track down Leo here. He's an old acquaintance. Once had a stag night here with an Italian mate and ended up ten miles out at sea on Leo's boat. It's a long story.'

'Were there donkeys involved in that, too?' Sarah asked, cracking them all up.

Piers and Max climbed on board and then helped the ladies in and introduced them to Leo, with much shaking of hands and salutations. 'Beer in the coolbox, Mr Piers.'

She had never had aspirations to excessive wealth, but she had to admit that after hanging out with Piers for a few days, she could see that it definitely had its advantages.

For the next half an hour, the boat whipped around the coastline, the breeze sending her hair flying behind her, leaving her breathless when they finally slowed down to approach the shore at Sorrento. Leo brought the boat to a standstill and then opened two cupboard doors right underneath where he was standing.

'We have snorkels, waterskis, and downstairs we also have a couple of windsurfing boards. You are welcome to everything. I will make lunch at one o'clock, but until then I will leave you to go for a sleep. My wife kept me up all night last night,' he added with a wink, before heading down into the galley.

Tess and Sarah looked at each other then shrugged gleefully. 'Swim?'

'Race you,' Max dared them and suddenly there was a flurry of clothes as they all stripped to their swimwear. Max hit the water, followed by Piers, then Tess, then Sarah.

'Not fair! I'm at a disadvantage,' Sarah hollered. 'At my age arthritis sets in and everything takes a bit longer.'

They spent the next couple of hours diving out of the boat, climbing back in, floating on lilos and just generally acting like they were fifteen again.

'Much as this is glorious, I'm going out to dry off,' Tess announced. 'My hands are turning to prunes.'

'Right, son, I'll race you to that buoy over there.'

'You're on!' The two men took off like torpedoes, remarkably keeping abreast of each other, despite the fact that Max's broad shoulders and lean physique should have left Piers' generous torso floundering in his wake.

'They're like big kids, those two,' Sarah said, as she grabbed a towel and handed one to Tess. 'I love it.'

'Me, too. I can't believe that this time last week I was trying to come up with a new and original way to market Doggie Doo Bags, and today I'm on a yacht in the middle of the Med.'

'I was making a tit cake,' Sarah replied, making them both burst into a fit of giggles.

Drying off as they walked, they moved to the front of the boat to lie on the bow.

'I'll never be able to go back to a normal two-week package holiday after this,' Sarah said, as they slapped on the sun cream and stretched out.

They passed a few minutes watching Piers and Max in the distance, keeping an equal pace with each other as they swam.

'Are you OK?' Sarah asked her eventually. 'Sorry, tell me if it's none of my business, but you seemed a bit upset again last night.'

Tess shook her head. Now wasn't the time to burden Sarah with her woes again – not when they were having such a fabulous time. 'I'm fine, Sarah, but thanks. And thanks for listening to me the other day. I'm sorry if I got a bit deep and melancholy.'

'No, not at all. Look, I know it's odd, but at least in a strange way I can understand what you're dealing with. I'm always here if you need some words of little wisdom.'

Tess returned the grin and tempting as it was to share and get Sarah's input, she chided herself. Nope, she wasn't going to do this now. Today was about fun, not rehashing her woes and bringing everyone down. Before she could share this thought, Max jumped back on board first, beating his father and celebrating by shaking water all over them both. Piers followed, declaring that he let his son win, to hoots of derision from the rest of them.

After an hour or so's rest, Max dug out the snorkels and they all took to the water again until Leo called them back for lunch.

They feasted on fresh crab salad, delicious slabs of lasagne and thick bread seasoned with garlic. They were picking at the most mouth-watering fresh fruit salad when Tess yawned. 'I could absolutely just go for a sleep now. All this doing nothing except enjoying myself is exhausting.'

She realised that the first part of that sentence was absolutely true. She was having fun. She wasn't worrying about Drew, there was no guilt about leaving him behind, and she hadn't thought about Cameron and his crazy notes all day. She was in the moment and planning on staying there.

'What happened to windsurfing and waterskiing?' Max teased her.

'I've realized that I'm clearly not an action woman. Angelina Jolie can rest easy, I'm no competition.'

'I'm with you there,' Sarah agreed. 'I've hurt muscles I didn't know I had this week. And there was me thinking I was coming for serious lounging and shopping. Talking of which – Piers, would you mind if I ask Leo to drop me ashore for an hour? I've been buying the twins T-shirts from all of the places we've docked and I'd love an excuse to wander around Sorrento for an hour. I've always wanted to go there.'

'Jesus, Sarah, you might not be an action chick, but if shopping was an Olympic event...' He winked and let the rest hang in the air. 'Tell you what, I'll take you in the dinghy.'

Sarah almost choked on a strawberry. 'You're going to row a dinghy?'

He squinted towards the shore. 'Doddle! What is it – two hundred yards?'

Leo nodded. 'Approximately, yes.'

'Right, that's my workout for the day then. Come on, love, and there had better be a cold beer at the other end for me. What about you son? Tess? Fancy coming along?'

'Not me, dad – wouldn't want to put extra weight in the dinghy and have to take over the rowing when your old man body gives out.'

Tess loved the banter between these two. 'And I'll pass too thanks. There's a spot on that sundeck with my name on it. This is wonderful, Piers. Thank you.'

'My pleasure, love. Right, Shopaholic Sarah, let's get going'

They both changed back into their street clothes and set off, with Sarah squealing as the dinghy rocked from side to side. 'If you drown me, Piers Delaney, I'll come back and haunt you.'

'Don't talk to the captain when he's concentrating on his seamanship,' Piers retorted.

Back on deck, Tess was in stitches. 'Can I say something totally inappropriate and borderline bitchy?'

'Absolutely,' Max said, as he rubbed sun cream on his reddening shoulders.

'Your dad seems much happier when he's not with Mona.'

He shook his head. 'I've noticed the same thing. There you go – I'm in the bitch club, too. Think I'll let Leo's ridiculously big lunch settle before I tackle the windsurfing and, at the risk of sounding less than macho, I might just top up my tan.'

They were both still laughing when they climbed up on to the sundeck and assumed chief sunbathing positions. As the sun beat down, competing with the glorious cooling breeze from the water, every single inch of Tess tingled with bliss.

That's when she realized that Piers and Mona weren't the only ones who were much happier when their partner wasn't around.

Mona

Sometimes, it was all just too easy, Mona decided as she pulled on a Chanel one-piece swimsuit, then draped a tiger-print Roberto Cavalli kaftan over the top of it. Bronze Gucci flip-flops and a long gold chain with a shark's tooth on the end of it completed the look.

She'd spent the morning at the spa having a deep-tissue massage and now her muscles throbbed in a delectable sensation that sat between pleasure and pain. Just the way she liked it.

Another hour or so and she'd go knock on Drew's door, but for now, what to do? She was bored in the cabin on her own. She didn't want to go mingle with a million tourists by the pool. And she definitely wasn't going to go swimming and destroy an ensemble that had taken hours to put together.

She flicked through the ship's brochure – how ridiculous that they'd been on this ship for six days now and she hadn't even got around to exploring it – and realized that there was an area of deck fourteen called Seclusion, which was billed as an 'adults-only haven of serenity'.

Right now, an adults-only haven of serenity sounded perfect. With copies of *Vogue, Marie Claire, Harper's Bazaar* and *Vanity Fair* accessorizing her look, she managed to find her way to the 'haven of serenity' with only one false turn on the way.

Tucked away at the back end of the ship (yes, she'd picked up that it was called the 'aft' area, but 'back end' just made so much more sense) was a minimalist paradise. The wood deck was punctuated by large bamboo plants that appeared so real she wondered if they actually were. Each one semi-obscured dark wicker loungers with thick cream upholstery and hooded cabanas that contained overstuffed double day beds for two. It was simply stunning, made all the more perfect by the lack of screaming brats, and she cursed the fact that she hadn't found it earlier.

Kicking off her flip-flops, she plumped for a double day bed, and sat back against a stack of pillows with her legs crossed and her pile of magazines in front of her. As always, a waiter immediately appeared at her side and she asked Anders, Norway for a sparkling water with ice and lemon. No alcohol yet. She wanted her head clear for later. Lying on the massage bed that morning she'd thought it all through, planned her strategy. She was going to go to Drew's suite around lunchtime, order something magnificent from room service, then act as confidante as she further explored the problems in his marriage. By putting the right slant on everything, she had no doubt that he would soon admit that he had made a huge mistake. She'd be there for him. Be his rock. Listen to him. Flatter him. Take care of him. And if he happened to fall into her arms and take it further physically, then that was even better. The important thing was not to push, or to make the first move, but to be there while he found his way back to her. Closeness. Opportunity. Result. That was her strategy.

'Excuse me, I really don't mean to be rude, but I think you'll find that bed was already taken.'

Shielding her eyes from the sun with her hand, she glanced up to see a dark-haired, incredibly buff, Mediterranean-looking guy, standing dripping wet in a pair of D&G shorts. She recognized them as this season's collection. If he hadn't just accused her of hijacking his sunlounger, she might actually be enjoying the spectacle.

'I don't think so,' she replied. How dare he? How bloody rude.

'Ah, but I do. If you look under that pillow you'll see a wallet, a watch and a room key, and if you look just behind your head there you'll see the towel I left on the bed, that has obviously been blown back into the cabana.

Something in his voice gave her the horrible feeling that he hadn't made a mistake after all. She gingerly put her hand under the pillow and pulled out a leather wallet, then a Tag Heuer watch, top of the range model. She craned her head right around… yep, there was a white towel nestling in the folds of the cabana.

Bugger.

'I'm sorry, I didn't realise. I'll move,' she said sharply.

'No, don't! I insist! I'll find another bed.'

He leaned over to collect his wallet and Mona was treated to a close-up of a rippling six-pack.

'There's really no need, I'll move,' she said, all antagonism blown away by the combination of his abdominal perfection and top class accessories. In fact she almost purred the words, giving the stranger cause to pause.

'I tell you what,' he suggested, as she knew he would. The voice always did it. Yes, she had far more important things to be focussing on today, but old habits die hard and what was a bit of harmless fun? God knows her ego could do with a boost. 'Why don't you take that end, and I'll take this end and maybe I could buy you a drink?'

'I have a drink,' she replied, holding up her glass. She watched as his face fell slightly before swooping in to make his day. 'But I'm happy to share my bed if you are.'

Grinning, he wrapped the towel around his waist and asked a passing Anders, Norway for a Jack Daniel's and Coke.

'I'm sorry, I didn't even introduce myself. I'm Blane Collins.'

'Blane Collins from New York,' she added. 'I'd say Connecticut.'

'Milford,' he nodded. 'You're good.'

'Yes, I am,' she concurred flirtatiously, enjoying this immensely. It had been a whole six days since she had a fine specimen to toy with.

'And I'd say you were in either sports or property.'

'Property,' he acknowledged, clearly even more impressed. 'How did you know that?'

'D&G shorts, this season, so you're up on fashion, suggesting a city dweller who cares about style and appearances. Tommy Hilfiger wallet – not too expensive, so I'm guessing you use this during the day when it could get battered around in some kind of manual environment. But you've got a Tag Heuer Grand Carrera Calibre 36 watch. Expensive. Slick. But incredibly sturdy, suggesting that you don't sit behind a desk all day and need a watch that can handle a few knocks.'

'Shit, you're brilliant. That's like the most impressive superpower ever.'

He sat down on the bed beside her, leaving a respectful distance. Friendly but not presumptuous – she liked that.

'At the risk of sounding really cheesy, why is a girl like you up here on your own?'

'I was bored in my suite,' she said, 'so I thought I'd come join the real world. What about you?'

'You mean you can't guess that?'

She laughed. 'Nope, there are limits to my superpowers.'

'I'm here with some buddies on a stag cruise. They've all gone into Naples, but man, I've had enough of the sightseeing stuff. Time for some sun and chilling. I'm more about taking it easy than taking in culture.'

He lost a couple of points for an answer that came straight out of the Little Book Of Naff Flirting. He got them back when he smiled at her and she realized just how gorgeous he was. Around thirty, she guessed. A little old for her toyboy phase, but good-looking enough for her to make an exception.

They indulged in seriously heavy, sexually suggestive flirting for the next hour. She was beginning to enjoy herself way too much, when her pragmatic side kicked in. Time to go. Things to do. Man to see. Reluctantly, she pushed herself up from the bed and announced that she had to leave. He was crestfallen.

'Sorry, prior engagement. But this has been fun.'

'It has,' he said, tracing a line down the inside of her forearm from the crevice of her elbow to her wrist, a motion that sent such a delectable tingle directly to every one of her erogenous zones that she was almost tempted to toy with him a little longer and take things to their natural, energetic conclusion.

'It was good meeting you Mona… and listen, any time you want to continue this discussion, I'm in suite 8210. Call by.' The implication and invitation couldn't have been clearer if he'd written them on his abs with suntan cream.

'I might just do that,' she told him – but not if things went her way in the next couple of hours.

Her nerve ending were still tingling as she strutted off, making sure she did her best catwalk sway to give him plenty to look at as she left.

Next stop, Drew's suite. She mentally worked out the best way to go. All the way along this deck, past the two adult pools and the kids' pool to the front of the ship, then down two floors. She decided to take the stairs instead of the elevator, because that would pump up the gluteus maximus and make her arse look even better.

'Mona! Mona, over here!' She was almost at the elevator bank when she heard the voice. Penny. And there was John and the kids too. Damn, she couldn't get away without speaking to them now. Her gluteus maximus would have to wait. 'Hi there!' she sang as she breezed over to them.

She was almost at the edge of the kids' pool where Lawrence and Lavinia were splashing furiously, when she realized who they were actually playing with. Drew burst up from under the water, making them shriek so loudly they could crack glass.

'Hi, Mona!' he greeted her. She just hoped the shock didn't show in her face. Or the disappointment. Didn't he realize she had a bloody game plan to adhere to? Obviously he didn't because here he was playing grandad of the bloody year.

'Want to join us?' Penny asked. 'We're going to hang out here for the rest of the afternoon.'

Only if the other choice was having her toenails removed by a great white shark.

'Thanks, Penny, but I was just on my way to do something. Got a couple of things I need to see to.'

She waved them all goodbye and didn't even care if they wondered why she headed back in exactly the direction she'd come from.

Back at Seclusion, Blane was still there, lying on the bed, his lazy smile suggesting he'd been half expecting her. She didn't mess around.

'Suite 8210, did you say? I was planning on trying out some of my other superpowers there today.'

Sarah

For years Sarah had been reading novels that featured glorious scenes of romance and passion set against the intoxicating backdrop of Sorrento, and now that she was here it was everything she had ever dreamt it would be. Cars and scooters whizzed around the winding streets, there were fruit trees branching out over cream walls that surrounded houses that looked like they'd been built hundreds of years ago. In the shopping streets, designer boutiques sat beside tiny cafes with elderly women dressed completely in black sitting outside them. She loved it. Absolutely loved it. And she loved the company, too. Piers had been a revelation, one of the main reasons that she'd had such a good time, and she'd grown incredibly fond of him. Now, they teased each other like an old married couple as they wandered in and out of shops. She found gorgeous little T-shirts for Lawrence and Lavinia and then couldn't resist the pull of a jewellery shop with a glass frontage and glistening white marble pillars outside.

In the window was a silver-coloured chain with a simple emerald teardrop falling from it. Before she could stop herself, she was pushing the door open. It wouldn't do any harm to have a wee look. Didn't Patsy always say that window shopping was good for the soul?

'Not another bloody shop,' Piers blustered good-naturedly.

'Oh, shut up and come on. You can buy something for Mona. It might straighten her face.'

Inside the cool, air-conditioned shop, a beautiful, graceful woman in her forties, with the most incredible bone structure Sarah had ever seen, greeted them and then nodded when Sarah asked to see the piece from the window. A few seconds later she was staring at her reflection in an oval mirror, admiring the simple, elegant beauty of the necklace. It was breathtaking. Utterly breathtaking. She was scared to ask the price and burst the bubble, because she knew for sure that she couldn't afford it.

'Can you tell me how much it is please?' *OK, get it over with. Go on. A girl can dream.*

'One thousand, three hundred euros. The chain is white gold and the stone is emerald.'

'One thousand, three hundred euros,' her brain repeated in a scandalized screech. That was a whole lot of tit cakes.

She gently removed it from her neck and handed it back, with a grateful, 'Thank you, I'll think about it.'

'Let me buy it for you,' Piers said quietly.

'What?'

'Let me buy it for you,' he repeated.

'No. You already bought me that ring in Alghero.' Back in that little shop, where the owner had mistaken Piers for her husband, she'd been rifling in her purse for the money when Piers beat her to it. "It's the least a man can do for his wife," he'd beamed, sending them both into hysterics.

'Sarah, that was five euros. It's made of tin.'

'I don't care, I love it,' she argued. 'You're not buying me this, that's ridiculous. Why would you do that?'

The shop assistant had very discreetly backed away to allow them to argue in privacy.

'Because I want to and because… because you deserve it, OK?' he told her, getting more adamant with every word.

'Why?'

'Because.'

'Oh, very mature,' she said bluntly.

'Because if it wasn't for you and Max on this cruise I'd have gone bloody crazy. I like you. You're amazing. I'm starting to miss you when you're not around and I'm having really strong feelings for you and I want to buy you the bloody necklace.'

The stunned silence lasted for what seemed like several minutes, before Sarah recovered her voice. 'Are you saying that you want us to be more than just friends, Piers?'

'Yes!' he blurted.

She recoiled like she'd been slapped. 'No,' she whispered, astonishment stealing her words again. Where the hell had this come from? It couldn't be happening. It couldn't. How dare he introduce this kind of drama into their lives? Did he think she was some kind of desperate tart he could just pick up with a few smooth words? A violent swirl of anger and shock consumed her and she fought to maintain some kind of balance.

'Thank you,' she repeated to the assistant, before calmly, with as much dignity as she could muster, walking out of the shop.

Piers followed her and as soon as they got outside, reverted to 'blurt mode'. 'Sarah, I'm sorry. I shouldn't have said anything.'

'No, you bloody shouldn't have,' she thundered. 'What in bollocks' name was that all about? You're married to Mona! And you're telling me that you miss me when I'm not around? What kind of crap is that?'

He grabbed the 'astonished' baton. 'Look, I said sorry! And I have to say that isn't the usual reaction I get when I say nice things to a lady. Is it my aftershave?'

It was supposed to be a self-deprecating joke to lighten the situation, but it had completely the opposite effect.

'ARE YOU INSANE!' she roared, not caring that two old women outside a nearby cafe had stopped speaking and were now watching them with open mouths.

'You are married to the woman who had an affair with my husband and then took him away from me and my children without a bloody care in the world. The whole world knew they were having an affair except me. THE WHOLE FUCKING WORLD! Don't you think that might have made me just a tad disgusted by people who think that adultery is just a peachy way to pass the time?'

With that she stormed off down the street, passing the two old women. One of them gave her a round of applause and the other shouted what sounded like some kind of rousing chorus of female solidarity.

Much later, she had no idea how long, he found her sitting in the square.

'Sarah, I'm sorry. I really am. I'm a total cock. I think I'm just so used to going for what I want in life that sometimes I overstep the mark. I meant what I said, though,' he finished softly.

She got up, not even looking in his direction. She wasn't sure what upset her the most. The fact that he'd spoiled what she thought was a wonderful new friendship, or the fact that he'd spoiled Sorrento.

Without even checking to see if he was behind her, she

retraced her steps back to the dinghy. She didn't care if he was there or not. She could row the bloody thing herself.

'I'll get those,' came his voice from behind her, before he passed her and picked up the oars.

Why would he do this? She'd had such an amazing time with him and now he'd completely spoiled everything. She just wanted to get back to the ship and think. One trip in a dinghy alone with him, that's all she had to get through.

They rowed in silence until they were about fifty yards away from the yacht and she saw Max and Tess burst into applause.

'We were about to give up on you two,' Max joked. 'Hurry it up, Dad – we've only got about half an hour to get back to the ship.'

Sarah's heart began to race and her stomach clenched with anxiety. Bugger! She'd lost all track of time. She checked her watch. Thirty-five minutes. Leo would have to put his foot down to get them there. The sooner the better. She wanted away from Piers before Tess and Max picked up on the incontrovertible fact that she wanted to kill him.

As soon as the two vessels touched, Sarah stood up and reached for Max's outstretched hand for support as she climbed the steps on to the boat.

Piers moved to the bottom step, and then with Max's help they hauled the dinghy up and clipped it to its moorings on the side.

'OK, let's rock and roll,' Leo announced jovially, clearly very proud of his English lingo. He ceremoniously prodded the button next to the wheel. Then he did it again. And again.

By the fifth time, Piers, Sarah, Tess and Max were watching him with expressions varying from astonished to horrified.

On each press of the button there was not a sound. The engine was silent. He tried it one more time, all of them holding their breath, willing it to work.

It didn't.

'Signore Piers,' he eventually conceded, shaking his head. 'I don't think we get you back to the ship on time.'

13.

Troubled Waters

Mona

Mona ignored the phone. Luxuriating in a bubble bath infused with coconut oils, it was much more fun to lie there contemplating the reasons that her muscles felt like they'd done a double session at a spin class. Blane had been a tad self-indulgent, but deft enough to make the afternoon she'd spent with him worthwhile. What the young ones didn't have in expertise, they made up for with energy.

Bless him, he'd been positively sullen when she had refused to give him her number or arrange another hook-up. What was the point? He had been a very nice distraction, but now it was time to focus one hundred per cent on the game plan.

The thought made her restless. Patience wasn't her strong point and it was time to start making progress. She pushed herself out of the water, dried off in front of the bathroom mirror, examining her reflection for flaws as she did so. Satisfied, that every bit of her was smooth and evenly coloured, she reached for her ivory silk robe. It had been bought during a huge blowout in Agent Provocateur after one of Piers' illicit little sojourns with Mistress Tart Emily of the Cheap Shoes. Despite the fact that she'd spent more than the cost of a small car, he didn't query the charge on his credit card. She almost wished that he had dared to, but... damn, why did that phone keep ringing? Irritated, she snatched up the handset that lay on the marble vanity unit.

'Hello?' she snapped.

'Darling, it's me.'

'Yes, I can hear that.' It struck her that the man could be

annoying even when he wasn't here.

'Oh. OK. Mona, we've got a bit of a situation here…'

He sounded odd. Very odd. If he was pissed again she'd kill him. They had a group dinner planned for the evening and she wasn't going to spend it trying to stop him from collapsing in his lobster bisque. It seemed like every time he was let loose with Tess and Sarah he ended up in a senseless state. No doubt he was bored rigid in their company and drinking to make it all more interesting. Or perhaps he was trying to show off to impress Max. Either way he had midlife bloody crisis written all over him.

'Piers, are you calling me from the bar? Because if you're pis… oh bloody hell, hang on – the cabin phone is ringing.'

She took her mobile away from her ear and picked up the phone on the bathroom wall.

'Yes?'

'Mrs Delaney, this is Richard Conrad, head of guest services. Sorry to bother you, but we have it on record that Mr Delaney left the ship this morning and according to our records he has not yet checked back in. Is that correct?'

'Erm, I'm not sure, let me…'

'Mrs Delaney.' He cut her off. 'I'm afraid we sail in ten minutes. If Mr Delaney is not back here in that time then I regret to inform you that sadly we must leave without him.'

It took a few moments to process this information. 'Mr Conrad, can you hold on please – I actually have my husband on the other line.'

As she switched phones, her mind whirled, evaluating the situation. 'Piers, where exactly are you?'

'Well, the thing is, that's why I'm calling you, darling. We've run into a bit of boat trouble and…'

'Just give me it in minutes, Piers. How far away are you?'

'At least an hour…'

'For the love of God…' she sighed, irritated by his failure to adhere to one simple task – return to ship on time. 'OK, hold on.'

She switched back to Richard Conrad. 'Mr Conrad, my husband won't make it back.'

'And you understand that we must sail on schedule?'

'Yes, I completely understand. Unfortunately my husband didn't seem to read the small print that said being an idiot wasn't allowed.'

Hanging up the cabin phone on a stunned guest services manager, she flicked back into calculation mode.

'Piers, are Max and the others with you?'

'Yes.'

She suddenly perked up. Oh, this just became a whole new ball game. Possibly literally.

'So what are you going to do?'

For a horrible moment she had visions of him hiring a helicopter and landing them all on the ship's helipad, like an invading Special Forces unit. There were many things in the world that she could live without seeing and Sarah's arse coming down a drop rope was one of them.

'I don't know, love. Leo has called his cousin and he's on his way – apparently he's a mechanic and will be able to get us going again. We'll just have to find a hotel for tonight and catch up with you tomorrow in Civitavecchia. I'll hire a car to get us there.'

It was difficult, but she managed to keep the laughter from her voice. There was no point in letting him know that he'd just done her the biggest favour. Far better to play both sides. This was definitely a situation to be exploited.

'Oh, Piers, that's terrible. I can't believe it. What am I supposed to do on here on my own?' And taking the award for the Best Performance in a Martyrdom Role…

'Look, I'm so sorry, Mona. It's been a bugger of a day.' He sounded utterly miserable. This would earn her at least another four-figure blowout in Agent Provocateur and this time he wouldn't be seeing any of her spoils. However, she sensed that it was time to throw him a bone of sympathy. No point in causing friction just yet. There would be plenty of that later.

'Don't worry,' she said, pitching it somewhere between concern and understanding. 'Just find somewhere nice to stay tonight and we'll see you tomorrow. Are the others OK? I hope you're taking care of them?'

'Yes, absolutely,' he replied, his voice thick with stress. No wonder. How uncomfortable must it be to be stranded with two virtual strangers? What would they talk about? Let's face it, Sarah and Tess weren't exactly stimulating conversationalists. Not that she cared. She was just happy that Tess was out of the picture for the night.

'OK, darling – call me in the morning and let me know what your plans are. I'll go organize things here and break the news to everyone. You take care and I hope it's not too awful.' The last line was said while sporting a veneer-flashing grin.

'Sorry again, Mona. Believe me, I wish this had never happened.'

But I'm so thrilled it did, Mona added in her head.

'It's fine, I'm sure we'll all muddle through. Talk to you in the morning darling. Big kiss.'

Yes, they'll muddle through somehow, she thought, excitement rising. Oh, Piers, the fool – he would never know that he just helped her move one huge step forward. Drew. Her. In the middle of the ocean. No partners. It was like all her wishes had just come true. Now all she had to do was motivate him to want the same thing.

She once read an interview in which Joan Collins claimed it took her twenty minutes to apply a perfect mask of make-up. Mona had it down to fifteen. Wardrobe choice took almost as long, but eventually she settled on one of her classic favourites - a red Roland Mouret wiggle dress, customised to fit her perfectly. Sleeveless, with a zip from neck to hemline at the back, it clung to every single curve. If a dress could represent emotions, this one was definitely lust. She teamed it with nude Louboutin heels and, as a contrast to the formality of the outfit, left her hair to fall in raven waves from a side parting. The illusion of a forties movie star had never been stronger.

Walking, or rather *strutting* to Drew's cabin, she mentally prepared herself. All week she'd been at his side, in work and in play, listening when he wanted to talk, proving that even now, years after their divorce, they still made an incredible team. It was time he realized it, too. Sure, it would be messy. They had two marriages to break and those other partners had to be considered. But they'd work it out. She would happily walk away from Piers with only what she'd taken into the marriage – her name, her own money and her career. Add those things to a new life with Drew, and she would have everything she wanted – the perfect picture.

It was time to get what she'd come on this trip for.

At his door, she inhaled deeply and then rang the bell, a heady mix of excitement and nerves making her hand tremble.

She heard the footsteps on the other side. Then the click of

the door handle. Then the swooshing noise as it swung open.
And there…

'Hi, Mona!'

'Eliza! Hi. How are you doing?' Bloody hell – what was it
with these kids today? The buggers were everywhere, wrecking
her intentions and foiling her plans.

'Yeah, fine.'

The teenager stood back to let her enter, but Mona stood
rooted to the spot. This wasn't exactly the scene she'd envisaged.
Damn. Her only hope was that the teenager was there on a
flying visit en route to resuming stalking Kai from London.

'Sweetheart, who is it?' Drew's voice got louder as he
appeared behind his daughter. 'Mona! Hi. Are you coming in?'

The thought of playing happy families all night was too
much to bear. Far better to suss out the situation first.

'Listen,' she began, 'I just wanted to let you know there's
been a bit of a problem. Eliza, darling, I don't want you to get
upset, but…'

'Are you about to tell me that my mum is stuck and she
missed the boat?'

Mona nodded. 'Yes, but darling, I don't want you to be
alarmed or worried.'

'I'm not. She'll be fine,' Eliza replied sullenly.

Behind her, Drew laughed. 'The treachery of youth. Sarah
called and told us what happened. She gave Eliza two choices –
come stay in this suite for the night or she was having the Italian
navy raid the boat and confine Eliza to her cabin.'

'So lame,' the teenager groaned. 'Like, as if I was going to get
up to anything.'

Drew let that one go.

'So housekeeping have made the sofa into a bed and I'm
going to have a movie night with my daughter. You can tell
she's thrilled,' he added, with a chuckle.

Mona's gaze switched back to a furious Eliza, clearly upset
that Kai had been removed from tonight's agenda. Mona could
empathise with that concept.

'You're welcome to join us – *The Break Up* and *The Proposal*
are on the viewing schedule.'

Oh the irony – if only that were a narrative of their future.
She quickly weighed up her options. A night sitting on the sofa
in the middle of a sullen teenager and a dad who is desperately

trying to placate aforementioned teenager. Or... Actually Drew or no Drew, anything would be better than that.

'Oh, thank you, but I'm just going to take the chance to have an early night,' she seethed through gritted teeth.

There was no way this dress, these shoes and this free evening were going to waste.

Now, what was Blane's cabin number again?

Tess

'Do you think it was something we said?' Max whispered to Tess, who shrugged in reply. She couldn't believe how hard Sarah and Piers were taking the whole 'missing the boat' thing. Since they'd sat down to dinner, the older two had barely said a word and now Sarah had gone off to bed citing a migraine, and Piers was sitting there looking like someone had just stolen his puppy.

'Dad, are you OK?' Max asked, out of what Tess could see was genuine puzzlement.

Piers got up from the table and gave an obviously forced smile. 'Course I am, son. Just knackered. Think maybe I got a bit too much sun today. Must have gone to my head as well.'

'Do you want me to see if there's a late night pharmacy – maybe they'll have something that can help?'

'No, no. Think I just need a good night's sleep. I'll turn in now if you don't mind. See you when you come up.'

The two of them watched him leave in stunned silence. Only when he was out of sight did Max shake his head. 'I've never seen him like that before. I hope he's not coming down with something.'

Tess took another sip of her coffee. 'That's so strange; I thought exactly the same thing about Sarah. She's been so subdued tonight.'

The waiter approached them with a jug of coffee and they both accepted refills. They'd just eaten a delicious meal of the best cannelloni Tess had ever tasted, and now they were having a break before ordering the gelato that she had been promising herself all day.

Remarkably, after the initial panic, she'd realized that she wasn't too frantic about missing the ship. What was the point? Drew probably didn't give two jots that she wasn't there. Sarah had called him to make arrangements for Eliza, but he hadn't even asked to speak to her.

Sod him. She was just going to enjoy this little addition to the adventure. They'd found a beautiful hotel just off Sorrento's busy Corso Italia, and their rooms had incredible views out to the Gulf of Naples and Mount Vesuvius.

It was beyond beautiful.

'You know, I'm wondering if they perhaps had a fight today.' Even as she was saying it out loud, Tess shook off the notion. Sarah just wasn't the confrontational type and she and Piers got on fantastically well – what could they possibly have to fight about?

'I can't see it. My dad thinks Sarah's great. They seem to have hit it off.'

'You're right,' she said, over the noise of her silver bangles jangling as she took another sip of her coffee. The jewellery had been a treat to herself to celebrate… well, nothing, actually. Just a treat.

'That dress really suits you.' The compliment came out of the blue and Tess felt her face reddening. Max noticed. 'Sorry, I didn't mean to embarrass you. That thought just came into my head and went right out through my mouth.'

'That's OK, and thank you. My credit card is still in shock, but I'm thinking it's worth it.'

They'd checked into the hotel with just the beachwear that they stood in, so they'd all ventured into the first clothing store they'd come across for vital supplies. Somehow, along with knickers, a bra and a nightdress, this dress had claimed her as its owner. She'd been unable to resist. Made of a white floaty georgette fabric, the slender shoulder straps merged into a simple A-line silhouette that ended just above the knee. The bangles and a pair of white jewelled flip-flops had finished the look – one that was in direct contrast to Max's black linen trousers and T-shirt. With both of them sporting the glow of a golden tan, they looked like any of the other couples enjoying the heavenly ambience in the restaurant. She was actually surprised at how relaxed and comfortable she felt, given that she'd only met Max a week before.

He clearly felt the same. 'So are you going to turn in too?" he asked, laughing. "Because I might just question my deodorant if you do.'

'Absolutely not – there's a gelato in the freezer that I'm planning on liberating.'

'Good. So. We can either talk trivial stuff about the holiday, or I can bore you with details of my every achievement going back to winning the prize for the best Victoria sponge in primary four, or you could keep the deal we made and tell me what's been bothering you for the last few days.'

Her smile faded a few degrees. She thought he'd have forgotten about that by now.

'I mean, just if you want to,' he added. 'I know it's none of my business. Honestly, I can talk about my Victoria sponge for hours.'

All the tension was immediately diffused. It was impossible to feel uncomfortable around him, Tess decided. He had that easy, warm manner that definitely came from his dad's genes.

She was about to reply when a guitarist started to play over by the door, some kind of intense, flamenco style piece. They watched for a few moments before turning back to the conversation.

'You remind me of my friend Cameron,' she told him, idly playing with a spoon on the table. It was surprisingly good to say his name. She'd tried to push the notes and his rendezvous plans to the back of her mind for the last couple of days, but talking about him again threw up so many mixed emotions. She missed him. She wanted to see him. But she was annoyed, pressured and utterly confused about her feelings for him. 'He's the easiest person to talk to. Makes me laugh. When he's around, everything just seems brighter, you know? Easy. He calls himself my husband's stunt double because he's always filling in for him.'

How come that had always seemed funny in the past, but now it gave her a sense of overwhelming sadness? Maybe it was because it came with the unequivocal realization that she was longing to talk to him. She pushed her coffee away and returned to the last few drops from the glass of red wine she'd had with dinner.

'Please don't say anything to anyone – especially your dad or Mona,' she continued, 'but I don't know… I think Drew and I have lost our way a bit. Everything seems to have got so…' She struggled to find the right words. 'So… complicated lately. And somehow I've gone from being a hundred per cent sure of everything to realizing that I know nothing at all. Does that make sense?'

'Sure. Marriage is hard,' Max said softly. 'I wish it came with a rule book and a CD instruction manual. Life would be easier.'

'And an express repair service if it's faulty. I want one of those,' she said. 'Anyway, enough about my woes. Poor Sarah has had to listen to me for the last couple of days and now you. You'll all be avoiding me or chipping in for a therapist. I wouldn't blame you.'

He topped up both their glasses from the carafe in the middle of the table and she nodded in thanks. It was impossible to be unhappy here. Really, what was the point? Enough of the maudlin stuff. Optimism. Positivity. It would all work out. She shook off the heaviness and flipped back to a happier note. 'One of the nicest things about being on this trip has been spending time with Sarah. We've met on loads of occasions over the last few years, but never spent any time together alone. I had no idea how funny she is, or how kind.'

'My dad and I were just saying last night how alike you two were.'

The statement surprised her. 'Really?'

'Yeah. I can't believe you don't see it. Obviously you're many years apart in age, but you actually kind of resemble each other and you've both got that same... I don't know how to put it.' He thought for a moment before deciding. 'You're both just easy to be around.'

'I like that. My ego just crawled off its knees for the first time this week.'

A couple at a nearby table gave them disapproving stares as their laughter disturbed the romantic ambiance. She felt like pointing out that there was a bloke making a bloody racket on a guitar in the corner – hardly the stuff of hearts and roses.

A conversation from a few days ago came back into her mind. 'Why didn't your wife come with you on the trip?'

'We're separated. Not my choice. I asked her to come back before I came here, but she didn't.'

'I take it that's why your dad isn't a fan?' she mused. 'I can't imagine that Piers would dislike her without reason.'

'It's a long story.' Max drank some more of his red wine. She decided that in the light of the table candle he looked incredibly handsome. Attractive and sweet – his wife must be crazy to walk away from him. It was difficult to imagine him ever being cruel, or dismissive or neglectful. She suddenly realized that she was comparing him to Drew. She mentally chided herself. This was ridiculous. She'd be sussing out the waiter's dedication to his job next. Wondering whether the chef had phoned his wife today to tell her that he loves her.

'God, what are we like?' she laughed, then gestured around the restaurant. 'This place is full of couples all staring into each other's eyes, and then there's us two saddos, without a decent relationship between us. No wonder we drink.' She raised her glass in a toast. 'To us. The romantically bloody hopeless.'

'The bloody hopeless,' he repeated with a clink. 'May we one day get the hang of it.'

Sarah

Sarah looked at the drop below the window and said a silent prayer that she wouldn't land on the ground with a splat. She'd paced back and forth across the room with her phone held up in the air, trying to get a signal, but no – the only place that one little bar appeared on her phone screen was on a corner of the balcony, and even then only if she stood on a chair. She just hoped no one down below spotted her and thought she was on the brink of ending it all. It had crossed her mind that she could use the room phone, but she'd heard that the charges were extortionate in hotels, and since Piers was insisting on paying for the rooms, there was no way she was going to take advantage. Wasn't that what he'd already done today?

She could feel the anger rise again. 'Come on Patsy, pick up,' she murmured into the phone as it rang. And rang. And...

'Hello!'

'Yay, you're there – I was beginning to think you were ignoring me,' Sarah said with a cheeriness that definitely didn't go all the way to her toes.

'I was in the bath, doll,' Patsy replied.

'Sorry. Anyway, too much of that relaxation stuff isn't good for you. Thank God I got you out of there,' she joked.

'I wasn't alone.'

'Oh my God, I'm so sorry. I'll call you back tomorrow.'

'It's fine!' Patsy cackled at her friend's embarrassment. 'To be honest, I was looking for an excuse to get out. I don't get the whole romantic bath thing. The water ends up freezing and there's no way I'm wobbling my bits about in a confined space. Could end up getting stuck in there for days. So tell me the latest. Has the cowboy line-danced you up the aisle?'

'Oh, bugger, the cowboy! I was supposed to meet him tonight. Shit! I'd forgotten all about that. He's going to think I stood him up.'

'Why?'

'Because we missed the boat. We got stranded in Sorrento – me, Tess, Max and Piers. And there's been a bit of a development.'

'Oooh, tell me.' Sarah could see Patsy in her mind right now. She was standing in the kitchen in her pink fluffy robe, she'd just poured a black coffee from the pot that was on morning and night, lit a cigarette, then sat down at her big old pine table, eager to hear the gossip.

'Got your coffee and cig?'

'Absolutely. Now shoot.'

'Piers told me he has feelings for me today. Says he misses me when I'm not around. Wanted to buy me jewellery.'

There was a choking noise on the other end of the line.

'Fuck me sideways, didn't see that coming,' Patsy eventually gasped.

'Me neither.'

'So what did you say?'

'I got completely furious, told him he was an idiot and stormed off. I haven't spoken to him since.'

'But did you take the jewellery? You should have. Never say no to anything that can be returned for cash.'

'Patsy, that is not the bloody point here,' Sarah demanded, exasperated.

'You're right, you're right! Sorry. Focus. So let me get this – your ex-husband's ex-wife's husband has hit on you. I love this. It's like a soap opera gone wrong.'

'Patsy…' The warning in Sarah's voice was as stern as she could possibly make it. It's just that it was difficult not to laugh when talking to Patsy, even when all around her was going to hell.

'I'm focussing! It was wrong of him to do that. Definitely. But then he's married to Mona – I'm surprised the poor bloke isn't clutching on to the ankle of every woman he meets, begging for some love and affection.'

'Patsy, you're not helping.'

'Sorry. Look, take the positives. He likes you. No wonder – you're fabulous. And it's not exactly the end of the world when a guy who you've been having a great time with decides to tell you how great you are. Just let it be. Stay friends. Don't get mad. And if Mona ever finds out and comes after you, don't worry – I reckon I can take her.'

As Sarah smiled with amused exasperation, she heard a knock at the door. The surprise almost made her topple off her chair. 'Patsy, there's someone at the door, I have to go. Bugger, my heart's racing. It had better be Tess, not Piers.'

'Keep me on the line, I want to listen!' Patsy screeched.

'No, my battery is about to…'

The phone went dead. Tess could just picture Patsy lighting up another cig while muttering in outrage at having her fun spoiled.

Crossing the room, her stomach was fizzing with anxiety. Please make it be Tess. Tess. Or maybe even Max. But no-one who came with drama or silly bloody notions.

This was exactly why she was better off happily pottering away in her kitchen with a bowl of cake mix, not having to deal with the complications of relationships.

When she swung open the door, deep down, she already knew who would be standing there.

'I'm sorry.'

She didn't know how to reply. He looked so thoroughly miserable that her first instinct was to give him a hug and make him a cup of tea.

'I shouldn't have said what I said earlier. I got carried away and blurted it out and it was stupid. Trust me, it wasn't something I planned.'

She sighed as she leaned against the doorway. 'And I probably overreacted,' she admitted. 'It's not the kind of thing that happens to me every day.'

'Well, it should,' he said simply.

'Piers, don't. This is so many different levels of wrong. Even if there was an attraction, I would never, ever go near anyone else's husband. It's just not in my makeup to do that.'

'And is there? An attraction?'

This was what it all came down to. It was up to her. Everything that Mona had ever done to her could be repaid with what happened next. She'd wondered about revenge so many times, contemplated whether it would make her feel better. It probably would – but only until her conscience kicked in and she had to answer to herself for what she'd done. The truth was that it didn't matter how she felt, the only thing she could do was what was right.

'No, Piers. I'm really sorry, but there isn't.'

14.

Catching Up

Sarah

Sarah was relieved that most of the journey to Civitavecchia passed in small talk and silence, and even then it was Tess and Max who were doing most of the chattering. It was good to see them getting along so well. Tess deserved some light relief from the problems that she was having with Drew. What a bloody fool he was. Speaking of fools... Piers had barely said a word other than to make idle chitchat with Leo, who had borrowed his cousin's jeep to drive them north. Sarah suspected that they were all spending their quiet time wondering if Italy had a reliable version of the AA, because there was a strange rattling sound coming from the engine. Wouldn't that just top it off? A breakdown on the way to the ship, causing them to miss it again.

It was a huge relief when they pulled into the port town. The literal translation of Civitavecchia was 'ancient town' and it looked like a wonderfully eclectic mix of the old and new. Normally Sarah would be dying to stop off and have a wander around, but for now it was probably best just to get back to the ship.

The security staff at the top of the gangplank processed their return and welcomed them back on board and, to her surprise, Sarah realized just how happy she was to be back. First priority was to see Eliza, then John, Penny and the twins, then she had a sinking feeling that an explanation to a cowboy was in order.

After friendly goodbyes in the elevator, she headed to her cabin only to find it exactly the way she'd left it yesterday. Good. Drew had obviously come through on his promise to keep Eliza in his suite overnight. She had no doubt whatsoever that her daughter had been hugely miffed not to have been allowed to stay on her own. Or more worryingly with Kai. Yes, it had been absolutely right to get Drew to step in.

Sliding the wardrobe open, she pulled out a pretty pale blue sundress and removed the tags. The more she thought about it, the more she realized she should keep all the new clothes she bought instead of returning them when she got home. Maybe her wardrobe did deserve to be updated once every decade.

She checked her watch. Two o'clock. John and Penny and the kids would probably be finishing off lunch. After a quick wash to freshen up, she headed up to Waterfalls, the self-service buffet restaurant on deck ten. On the way there, she made a decision – all she wanted to do was spend time with her family. That was it. No more exploits. No more flirtations. No more reckless adventures. Except maybe a wee line dance with a certain cowboy. But definitely no more time alone with Piers. Family. That's what this trip was all about.

It didn't take her long to find John, Penny and the twins, and, to her surprise, Eliza was with them too, looking predictably fed up, something that wasn't helped in any way by Sarah giving her a huge hug.

'Sorry about last night, darling. Did you have a good time with your dad?'

'Yeah, but now I'm on, like, lockdown or something.'

John and Penny found this highly amusing. 'Dad asked us to keep an eye on her today, but unfortunately my little sister doesn't seem to relish the thrill of spending time bonding with her big brother. Apparently we're depriving her of Kai time.'

Eliza just tutted and rolled her eyes, setting them all off again.

'I know, I know – we're, like, so lame,' John said, ruffling her hair.

Even a temperamental sixteen-year-old couldn't help but laugh. 'OK, Mum, so you're back now – can I get out of jail, please?'

'Oh, but honey, I thought we could have the day together, go for a wander in the port and do some sightseeing. Spend some time with just the two of us to make up for yesterday.'

Eliza's expression flipped straight back to horror.

Sarah was too amused to be hurt. 'Well, I suppose if you've

got a better offer…' she said with a smile.

Eliza was out of the chair like a speeding bullet, and this time the hug she gave Sarah had true feeling. 'Thanks, Mum, you're the best. See you later. Love you.'

She was gone, leaving Sarah shaking her head. 'You know, with that speed we should really have channelled her into athletics.'

'Only if there's an Olympic category in the one hundred metre chase of a boy,' John added.

'Penny, you're looking great,' Sarah told her daughter-in-law.

'I know,' Penny replied, bashfully. 'I'm never getting off this boat. Never. I thought it was going to be so stressful having two toddlers on holiday, but this is paradise. The twins are absolutely loving it and they're doing so many things that they're exhausted and sleeping through every night. I'm getting eight hours sleep, a nap in the afternoon, twenty-four-hour help if I need it, some sun, good food, and I even had a spa treatment yesterday. My body may still be in shock. You're going to have to bring in a task force to get me off when we dock.' Her eyes flicked quickly to her watch. 'John, we have to go. It's time for our pamper package.'

'Your what?' Sarah was beyond surprised. Her big tough West of Scotland son wouldn't normally have the word 'pamper' in his vocabulary.

'Don't ask, Mum. I had nothing to do with this. I've only agreed to go along on the condition that it becomes one of those family secrets that we all take to the grave.'

'I solemnly swear never to repeat it. Shall I take the twins? We could go swimming or down to the play area for the afternoon.'

'Thanks, Sarah," Penny replied, "but they've got yoga in ten minutes, then they're going to swim club and they really love both. You don't mind, do you?'

'No, not at all! I'm thrilled that they are having such a great time. Come here, you two, and give gran a huge hug.'

The twins were delighted to oblige, before John and Penny scooped them up and headed off in a flurry of excitement. Sarah's heart melted with another flashback to when John was small. Drew would lift him in those huge strong arms and sweep him off down to the sea to paddle or to the grass to play football and they'd laugh all day long. Watching John with Penny, she wondered if she should have worked harder at keeping her marriage together. Maybe she should have overlooked the affair, begged him not to leave for the sake of the children.

She hadn't.

She'd let Mona take him, determined that she wouldn't hang on to someone who no longer loved her. She and Drew should be sitting here now, with their children and grandchildren, planning what to do with their day. But he'd blown it and she knew she was right to cut him loose, even if it meant she was now left here on her own and her earlier resolution to focus all her time with the family now seemed redundant. The truth was that they didn't need her. Her first dip of the toe in the waters of independence hadn't gone particularly well. But maybe she was being too rash about deciding never to go back in the water. It was time to make a new life.

A figure over at the dessert stand stopped, turned, and caught her gaze, a flicker of uncertainty crossing his face.

Sarah stood up and made towards him. Perhaps it was time to put both feet in the pool and be damned.

Tess

Tess's lip was red raw by the time the elevator opened on deck twelve. With a chorus of goodbyes, Max and Piers got out and turned right while she turned to the left to see... did Colita ever go home? She seemed to be at that desk twenty-four hours a day.

'Ah, Mrs Gold, how are you? We were very worried about you yesterday. Glad to see that you made it back to us safely today.'

'Thank you, Colita.' *Please don't say anything else. Nothing. Just let me go in peace.*

'Mrs Gold, I also have another letter for you. Would you like to take it now?'

No. Absolutely not.

'Yes, of course, Colita, thank you.'

She took the white envelope and headed through into the corridor, letting it sear the inside of her hand. Why couldn't she just ignore it? She shouldn't even open it. She should just toss it away. This was all complicated enough. No doubt Drew was furious with her for missing the ship yesterday and she was going to have to do some serious making up. Maybe it would be good to have a row. Perhaps that would clear the air and they could find some way to hash out the problems and sort this out.

Or maybe she was kidding herself on. The last couple of days with Piers and Max had really given her some breathing space and she'd enjoyed it. In fact, it had been a real treat last night having dinner and not wondering if the man across from you would get a call any minute, then dash off into the night to chase some story, leaving you to nurse a glass of wine and pay the bill. It had been a real novelty sitting relaxing for hours, swaying from serious subjects to light-hearted nonsense. She'd almost told Max about the letters. Almost. But it hadn't felt right to tell him when her own husband knew nothing about them and she was still so undecided about how she felt about

194

them or the guy who was sending them.

Stuffing the letter in the bag, she decided that she'd read it later. The most important thing now was to check in with Drew and sort out the rest of the day. It was probably wishful thinking, but perhaps they could go lie by the pool or maybe even have a late lunch and go explore some of the areas of the ship that they hadn't been to yet.

The cabin door clicked as she slipped her key in the lock and she exhaled, then forced on a sunny expression.

'Darling, I'm home,' she shouted, to deafening silence. No doubt he was out on that balcony again, hunched over the laptop as usual. At this rate, the only way he'd have a souvenir from this trip that really meant something to him would be if he took home that chair from the balcony.

Nope, not there either. She searched upstairs, in the bathroom, nothing. He must have gone up for lunch with Eliza and John. Perhaps taken the twins swimming. Or, God forbid, maybe he was just lying out somewhere relaxing and switching off from the rest of the world.

A quick change and she'd go find him, but first she needed a drink.

The note was lying on top of the fridge. A scrawled few words on the ship's stationery. It took her a minute to decipher his scrawl and then she read it again, sure she must have been mistaken. But no.

> *Gone to Rome. Be back by nightfall... if we don't miss the boat. Drew x*

Her first thought was to wonder if the last part of the sentence was a gentle joke or a nasty dig. How sad was it that she really wasn't sure? Did she know her husband at all? Her second thought was one of surprise – it was now a well-established fact that he hated sightseeing. Thought number three was disappointment that he'd gone to Rome without her. It was only when she got to thought number four that her nerve endings began to bristle. He'd written 'we'.

She doubted very much that John and Penny would make the long trip into Rome with the twins, and they wouldn't leave them for a whole day. She couldn't see Eliza being prised away from the boy she was seeing. So that left… argh! Bloody Mona. That woman was everywhere. And meanwhile she and Drew were the proverbial ships passing in the day and night!

Furious, she swapped her bottle of water for a beer and then plumped down on the couch, where she spent the next ten minutes running through every insulting name she could think of for both of them. She was up to 'bastarding fucknuggets' when she remembered the letter in her bag.

Gingerly, she opened it and almost melted as she read…

> Missing you. No one to share my donuts with. Meet me in Monaco. I'll bring the ones with sprinkles. Cxx

Her conflicting emotions went to war, beating the crap out of each other – she missed him, he was pressurizing her, she loved her husband, she hated her husband, she would meet Cameron, she wouldn't meet him, she wanted off this boat, this was the most wonderful place on earth, she hated Mona – no, there was no opposition to that one – until she slumped into a torpor of numbness.

When the phone rang, she decided it was probably a bad idea to answer. If it was Drew, she couldn't trust herself not to blurt out 'fucketing traitors'. It would probably be a good idea to spend some time developing her swearing skills.

On the other hand, it might be Sarah looking for company and she could do with that right about now. She picked up the handset.

'Hey Tess, it's Piers. Can you believe those two have buggered off? I reckon we're definitely in the bad books, love.'

'Yep, I expect to see our faces on WANTED posters all over the ship,' she replied, trying not to sound bitter. So Mona was with Drew. She was right, but that thought gave her no satisfaction at all. An uncharacteristic wave of fury engulfed her, and it took every ounce of self-discipline not to blurt out a random profanity. Thankfully, Piers didn't notice, as he went on, 'Yeah, well, I suppose we deserve it after last night.'

Tess didn't comment. Quite frankly, she could have shagged Brad Pitt last night and she'd still be pissed off with Drew for spending the day sightseeing with Mona.

'So anyway, Max and I are going to go play a bit of basketball up on the sports deck. You're welcome to join us if you fancy a bit of exercise. Didn't want to leave you on your own.'

'Thanks for thinking about me, Piers, I really do appreciate it.' Oh the irony – Mona's husband was looking out for her a damn sight more than her own. But basketball? She had the sports co-ordination of a drunk baby deer, but the cabin suddenly seemed claustrophobic – the notes, the dilemma, the reminder that Drew had pissed off with Mona. 'I'll meet you up there – just give me ten minutes to change.'

'Great, love, see you then.'

'Oh, and Piers – shall I call Sarah and see if she's around? Not sure if she had anything planned for this afternoon.'

'Erm, sure. Up to you. I'll erm… see you later.'

When she put the phone down she had a niggling feeling that she was missing something about this whole situation. She just had no idea what it was.

Mona

'How's the calzone?' Mona tinkered with her spinach salad, wishing for a moment that her life was not one that was deprived of carbohydrates.

'It's great,' Drew replied, washing it down with a white wine that had come recommended by the very efficient head waiter. 'This was such a good idea.'

'Ah, but I thought you hated sightseeing,' Mona teased.

'There's sightseeing and then there's this. I'm not sure the two variations of tourism are in any way related.'

Mona kept a lid on her jubilation as she held her glass up in a toast. 'To doing Rome this way.' Drew's eyes crinkled as he returned the gesture. If this restaurant had rooms upstairs, she would, she realized, quite happily take him upstairs and show him a side to Rome that wasn't fit to be displayed in front of the masses of nuns that seemed to populate the city.

The day had gone exactly to plan, without a single hitch. She'd woken him with a phone call at seven, invited him to come along with her, and after an initial hesitation, she'd sealed the deal with four words. Lazio. Football. Press. Conference.

By an absolute stroke of luck, she'd noticed when she was checking the news online last night that the Lazio team were announcing the signing of a British player at the Stadio Olimpico that morning. A few phone calls back to the office, and a few favours called in, and their names were put on the press list. She arranged a limo to collect them at eight, which got them through the morning traffic and to the stadium six kilometres outside the city for the press conference starting at 10 a.m. She had no idea what was going on and could have cared even less. All that mattered was that Drew was absolutely in his element. Football. She sometimes wondered if anything even came close in importance to the majority of Glaswegian males. Men who were generally laid-back turned into passionate firebrands at the sight of a ball. Gruff guys who didn't cry when their children were born dissolved into tears when their team picked up a cup. She tried to compare it to the feeling she got when a new pair of Jimmy Choo's arrived, but how could twenty-two men chasing a ball even begin to compare to a structural work of art?

Anyway, it led to them spending a couple of hours in a room with fifty blokes, clamouring for answers to their questions. The admiring glances they threw her way didn't go unnoticed. But then, a body-skimming red dress teamed with black six-inch peep-toe shoes and a large floppy black sun hat were clearly not standard attire in a football ground.

Drew was so pumped up with enthusiasm when they got back in the car that she found herself swept up in the excitement of it all. Perhaps if she equated it to a pair of Manolos, a pair of Jimmy Choo's *and* the latest Louboutin's all arriving on the same day…

Working to her agenda, the limo then took them into Rome, where they drove around the Coliseum and then on to the Piazza Navarone, viewing the sights from the comfort of the air-conditioned car. Now, they were eating a late lunch off exquisite china at a table outside on the square, sheltered from the sun by a thick awning, being served by dashing waiters in smart uniforms.

It was perfect.

Almost perfect.

Time to move this up a gear.

She leaned forward and put her hand over his, noticing that he didn't flinch. Good start.

'I've missed this,' she said, pitching it halfway between wistful and friendly. 'I know we see each other every day in the office, but this is different. It's so good just to spend time together with no phones ringing.'

Easy does it. No big declarations. No emotional drama. Just an opening for him to take if he felt he wanted to. She congratulated herself on her restraint. 'Do you want to go upstairs and make love until I'm limp?' would have been her preferred option.

'I know,' Drew replied. That was it. No agreement. No further clarification. Just 'I know'.

She laughed, giving him the full benefit of fifteen thousand pounds worth of dental expertise. 'Wow, that was a bit of an enigmatic reply.'

He put down his knife and fork and flipped his hand over so it was now on top of hers. A combination of lust and anticipation caused her breathing to become just a little shallower.

'Mona, I've spent almost every day with you for the last twenty years and I know what's going on in your mind,' he told her. She crossed her legs as two men of the faith walked past, hoping that their divine powers couldn't tell them that she was sitting there so turned on she could orgasm with little or no effort. This was it. The moment of truth. *Father, forgive me, because I'm about to commit a whole load of sins...*

'Oh really,' she replied playfully. 'So tell me.'

'You want the truth?'

'Absolutely.'

He paused for a moment. Typical Drew, always considered, always careful to think things thorough before he spoke – unlike bloody Piers who had no edit function whatsoever on his gob.

Drew's stare drew her back to the moment. 'I think you're unhappy with Piers. I think you want to divorce him.'

Ding ding, two for two.

'Or at least you *think* you do, but for all the wrong reasons.'

Whoah, hold on. She wasn't sure what that last bit was about. 'You're right about wanting to divorce, but I'm not sure why you think my reasons are flawed.'

Surely it was obvious? She realized she'd made a terrible mistake in marrying Piers. This last week had proven without a doubt that she and Drew should never have divorced. Neither of them was truly happy unless they were with each other. And they should just get on with making that happen. Soon. Sometime in the next five minutes would be good.

'Because you're having an age crisis again. You're dreading that you're nearly forty and instead of embracing it and realizing how beautiful and talented you are, you're thinking that you need some change and excitement to make yourself feel alive again.'

'No! That's not it at all.' How could he have got her so wrong? How could he have her down as some sort of shallow, age-obsessed thrill addict, looking for the next fix? Actually, in truth his theory might have a modicum of truth, but still, he was missing the whole bloody point here. Time to hit a home run. She switched her demeanour from flirt to sad and tragic. 'Drew, Piers is having an affair. With his secretary. What a fucking cliché.'

His eyes widened with surprise. 'Oh, shit, Mona, I had no idea.'

Anyone else would have taken that at face value but she knew him too well. His brow went down in the middle and he glanced downwards for a split second – he always did that when he was lying. She wasn't sure how she felt about that.

'You knew.' It was a statement, not a question. It had never crossed her mind before, but of course he knew. There wasn't an illicit sexual activity going on within a hundred miles of his office that he didn't know about.

'I did. I decided it was none of my business.'

'But you didn't tell me?' Her eyes fired with anger.

'Come on, Mona, I was married to you and you're the smartest woman I've ever met – there's no way you wouldn't know about it. I didn't want to embarrass you by bringing it up. Like I said, it's none of my business. So what are you going to do?'

'Divorce him. And sure, those other things you said matter, too. I don't want to be forty-five and single. I want to be married. I want to grow old with someone. But it's got to be the right person and Piers isn't it.'

'I'm sorry this is happening to you, Mona. You know I'm here if you need me.'

I do. Every day. Every night. And if those priests would avert their eyes, then right here and now.

Instead of saying any of that she plumped for 'Thank you.' She'd done enough for today. Drew thought he knew her, but she knew him even better. Pushing him into a corner would be counterproductive. He had to take today's information, process it, think it over, marry it up with the fact that his marriage to Tess was terminal, and then come to the only conclusion that he could – they were supposed to be together.

It was only a matter of time.

15.

Livorno

Sarah

Sarah groaned as the daylight streamed in through the curtains. Why – despite her best efforts and daily wails of disappointment - had she been cursed with the habits of an early riser? She wanted to be one of those sexy, nocturnal beasts who lay in bed all morning and rose only to eat chocolate-dipped strawberries in bed at noon.

She lifted the mobile phone beside her and checked the time: 7 a.m. Probably just as well she was awake, because Eliza was due to meet the others at 8 a.m. for a quick breakfast, before they all set off in a hired minibus for Pisa. She'd been invited but had declined. She already had other plans, and besides, spending a day with Piers wasn't the best idea. Just thinking about him brought her annoyance flooding back. Shrugging it off, she focussed on bigger problems – like how to get Eliza out of bed.

'Eliza, Kai called and asked you to meet him in ten minutes at the Waterfall restaurant.'

It was a miracle on a par with Moses turning up, donning a pair of flippers and wandering right across the Med. Without Sarah even having to put a foot on the floor, her daughter was upright, in the bathroom, out of the bathroom with face washed and teeth brushed, fully dressed and clipping on earrings before she paused to look at her mother.

'Why are you smiling?' Eliza asked warily. 'You never smile at this time in the morning.'

Sarah said nothing; just let the realization slowly dawn.

'OMG, you were winding me up! You were actually

winding me up! Kai isn't waiting for me, is he? Mum, how could you?'

7 a.m. – sleeping teenager.

7.10 a.m. – incredulous teenager.

Suddenly, all five-foot-ten-inches of sixteen-year-old came flying in Sarah's direction, landed on top of her and began tickling her until they were both screaming with laughter.

Only a loud rap on the door stopped them in their tracks.

'If that's guest services coming to complain about the noise, you're in trouble, madam. I'm already on their hit list after missing the ship and that bloke Richard looks like a Bond villain. He could have me neutralized at any moment.'

Eliza responded by throwing a pillow that hit Sarah on the back of the head. Daughterly love was painful sometimes.

Fixing her expression to neutral, Sarah opened the door and was prepared to launch into a humble apology when she was confronted with Drew's concerned face.

'Are you two OK? I heard screaming.'

Sarah stood by to let him in, then lifted the room service tray that she'd requested to be left outside the door at 7 a.m. The aroma of hot croissant made her slightly giddy. 'Your daughter and I were wrestling. It's what we like to do in the morning. Beats t'ai chi.'

Bemused, he sat down on the sofa and accepted a cup of coffee from Sarah, who then took hers and crawled back under the duvet.

Drew turned to Eliza. 'Thought I'd better come check you were awake because we're leaving soon. I want it on record that I'm only going because I've never seen the Leaning Tower and I've been assured we're going straight there and straight back, only stopping for lunch. No trekking. No wandering. No dragging us off to other things.'

Eliza high-fived him. 'I hear you, Dad. I'm only coming because Kai and his parents are going there today too.'

'Not because you love your father and want to spend every moment you can with him?'

'That too,' she added with an impish wink. 'Back in a minute, just going to fix my make-up. It was done in a bit of a rush thanks to mommy dearest over there.'

With a pointed glare at Sarah, she headed back into the bathroom.

'Sure you don't want to come? There's plenty of room on the bus. Mona booked it, so it's probably one of those rock tour coaches.'

'Of course it is.' She tried to keep the bitchiness out of her tone but she wasn't sure she succeeded. 'Thanks, but I've got other plans for today.'

'Other plans?'

'A... friend. Someone I met on board. We thought we'd go for lunch and spend some time together.'

'A male friend?' he asked, his eyes narrowing slightly.

Her face flushed with embarrassment, which was clearly ridiculous. Drew was her very long ago ex-husband. He'd married twice since they split. He had no say in her life whatsoever. Yet, here she was, toes curling because she was telling him about meeting with another bloke. She gave her self-conscious gene a direct order to man up and stop being pathetic. Hadn't it taken a lot of nerve to apologize to Nate for standing him up, explain the situation and then, straight out, ask him for another date? Yes, she'd asked a man for a date. Tonight the moon would be blue and there would be flying pigs performing figures of eight in the skies.

'Yes. His name is Nate. He's a cowboy. Or a cowman, really.' Her blustering was becoming so embarrassing that her brain sent urgent signals to her mouth to close and desist. It wasn't listening. 'You met him the first day aboard, up at the bar. Remember? When I was doing the whole "vomit on my T-shirt" thing.' *Stop speaking. Just stop.* But still the stammering and stuttering continued. 'So, yeah. Erm... Nate. That's who I'm, erm, meeting.'

The whole time she was wittering away, Drew just stared at her with an expression she couldn't read.

It was a huge relief when Eliza finally came back out of the bathroom and rescued her. 'Ready, Dad?'

He put his coffee cup down and pushed himself up from the chair. 'Ready, sweetheart. See you later, Sarah. Maybe we could have a drink when we get back? There are a couple of things I've been meaning to chat to you about.'

'Erm, sure,' she replied.

For a long time after the door closed behind them, Sarah wondered what on earth he could possibly want to talk to her about.

Tess

'Anyone sitting here?' Max asked Tess as he got on to the minibus.

'No,' she said brightly. 'It's all yours.'

Cheery. Positive. That was going to be her mantra for today. Even if it bore no resemblance to how she was feeling inside. She glanced over at Drew, laughing at something Eliza said to him. It was great to see him having fun with his daughter, but she couldn't help thinking that he was slightly manipulating his 'superdad' status to cover up the fact that he was completely pissed off with her.

He'd returned from Rome with Mona only half an hour before they sailed last night – and yes, it did cross her mind that they might deliberately miss the boat as some kind of act of petty revenge – and then they'd endured a near silent meal for two in the steakhouse restaurant, before he went out for his late night run and she went to bed. She'd pretended to be asleep when he came back. What was the point of doing otherwise?

This morning he'd got on the bus and sat with Eliza, without even a glance in her direction. Dear Lord, he was treating her like some kind of delinquent kid. She got it. There were problems. She'd missed the boat. He had a lot on his mind. But he was taking this silent, brooding stuff way too far and – for once – instead of feeling terrible about it and wanting to fix it, she was happy just to sit there with the firm opinion that he was an arse. The minor act of mental rebellion made her feel a whole lot better about the situation.

There was a flurry of activity at the door as Mona got on the bus, making a big entrance as usual, in a forties-style mauve tea dress and huge white hat, before sitting down directly in front of Drew and Eliza and turning to talk to them. Tess decided she resembled a mushroom. One of the poisonous ones that can cause sudden death on contact.

Max leaned over and whispered in her ear. 'How are things?

Have diplomatic relations been resumed?' He motioned to the back of Drew's head.

'I think it's a temporary ceasefire, but I'm not holding out much hope of it lasting. He's really upset with me.'

'For what? You didn't do anything wrong.'

Not for the first time, she wondered what she would have done without Max on this trip. He'd gone from distant kind-of-relation to friend in such a short period of time.

Her answer was abandoned as John and Penny arrived with two fractious toddlers. 'Sorry, everyone,' John apologized, 'but these two are a bit grumpy this morning. We apologize in advance and recommend earplugs for the duration of the journey.'

John slid in behind Tess, then lifted Lavinia onto the seat next to him, with Penny taking the opposite seats for her and Lawrence. Tess automatically turned and made faces at her step-granddaughter, cajoling her out of her strop and making her giggle. Lawrence spotted this, joined in, and it somehow kept them amused all the way to Pisa, a welcome diversion from the tension in the atmosphere as the air positively crackled with negative vibes. Drew was annoyed with her. She wanted to pull Mona's hat down so she didn't have to see that smug face. Mona hadn't even looked at Piers, so there were obviously issues there. Sarah wasn't there for her to have a laugh with. And Piers was still being unusually quiet. A fun day out for all the family.

When they got off at the other end Lawrence and Lavinia demanded to hold her hands, unlike their grandfather who had charged off with Eliza and Mona. Just behind her, Max walked side by side with Piers.

Walking into the Piazza dei Miracoli was an unforgettable experience. The perimeter was walled, creating a courtyard in the middle. To her immediate left, on the other side of a grassy section, was the largest baptistery in Italy, a round, incredibly beautiful Romanesque building of cream stone with a stunning domed roof. Next to it was an eleventh-century cathedral, a work of architectural art in pale stone and marble, with huge bronze doors, its walls adorned with intricate carvings, majestic columns and arches. On the cathedral's right-hand side was the famous bell tower.

'Look at that!' She motioned to the tower that, yes, did

indeed lean to one side. The twins were completely disinterested, more focussed on chasing the birds that strutted around on the grass and she could see John and Penny really wanted to savour the experience. Perhaps they could do it in shifts. They could go now, and she'd have a wander around later.

'Why don't you guys go on ahead and do the sightseeing stuff? I'm happy to keep the kids amused here for a while,' she told John and Penny.

'Are you sure?' John replied.

'Positive. But I can't promise there won't be ice cream involved. I do believe in bribing children.'

Penny laughed and gave her a quick hug, before heading off to catch up with the others.

'Right, you two,' she told the twins. 'How about ice cream and then a play on the grass?'

She had them on ice cream.

Piers and Max caught up with her. 'Do you want us to stay and hang out with you?' Max asked.

'No, it's fine – if there's time later, I'll go inside the tower, but I'm happy just to stay here and potter around.'

And potter they did. With a twin holding each hand, she wandered along the long line of souvenir stalls on her right, picking up a miniature Leaning Tower for each of them. Tess threw in another one for her mum and dad – if they ever came back from their South American adventure, she knew her mum would love a Leaning Tower of Pisa doorstop.

Shopping done, they bought a couple of ice creams and lay in a shady spot on the grass. Or rather, Tess lay on the grass and the twins sat on top of her. They sang songs. They counted birds. They played tig. Then they all collapsed in a heap, while Tess shared at length – and with character voices and actions – her in-depth knowledge of how the tower used to be straight until a big giant leaned on it. Well, subsidence just wasn't that exciting. Let them take it up with a history teacher in later life.

Eventually, exhausted by the heat and the antics, Lawrence fell asleep with his head on her lap, while Lavinia watched, engrossed, as Tess made her a headband of daisy chains, feeling happier and more content than she'd done in days. This had been one of her favourite afternoons of the trip so far.

'You're good at that.'

She smiled up at the new arrival. 'Thank you.'

Drew sat down beside her. 'It's good of you to let John and Penny have some free time. I saw them over by the cathedral and they looked like they didn't have a care in the world.'

They sat in silence for a few moments. Tess decided that it was strange that they had so much to talk about, yet nothing to say.

'Are you upset with me?' he said eventually.

She nodded. 'I think things have gone wrong and I don't know how to fix them. We're like strangers this week. I'm not sure why.'

'You're chewing your lip again.'

She hadn't even realized she was doing it. 'Can't beat a bit of swelling – saves me getting collagen injections.'

Her attempt to lighten the mood had only a temporary effect, and they both lapsed into silence again, broken up only by Lavinia's demands for another story. This wasn't the time for a deep and meaningful discussion. So instead, Tess told Lavinia the one about Cinderella, and her evil stepmother. And she would forever swear that it was purely coincidence that when she described the root of all evil, the picture she painted was an exact match to the woman on the bus with a hat like a mushroom.

Mona

Mona watched them from a distance, her Yves Saint Laurent sunglasses covering her gaze. Tess was totally preoccupied with the children and Drew was lying staring into space beside them. It struck her how ridiculous they looked – like a grandfather, a daughter and her children, not a husband and wife caring for the grandkids. Much as it was tempting to barge right on over there, she decided to leave them to it. They looked miserable – better that she let that ferment for a little while.

Over to her right, she noticed Max going into the entrance of the tower, no doubt planning to climb the two hundred and ninety-four steps to the top. There was no way Piers would do that – too worried he'd have a coronary halfway up – so he must be around here somewhere.

She ducked around the back of the cathedral and spotted him, sitting alone on the steps with his back to her, partially obscured by a column, talking into his mobile phone. Of course he could be calling anyone at all, but she knew immediately that it was Emily the Frump. *Fucking typical.* He was here with the family and yet there he was, on the phone to a woman in bad shoes thousands of miles away. As much as she knew it was irrational, the thought irked her. How bloody dare he! That showed no respect whatsoever and it was time he was informed of that.

In fact, it was time he was informed of quite a few things and now was as good a time as any. They had an hour to kill.

She approached quietly, careful not to let her heels clatter against the stone stairs. She was almost at the pillar when she realized that, in typical Piers style, he was speaking so loudly that she could distinguish what he was saying.

'Love, I'm sorry, I really am. It just all got out of hand.'
Pause.
'You have every right to be upset. I'm a cock. I'm really, really sorry. But I wanted to tell you now because I know that

you've been offered that cracking job at Holyrood. You should take it, love.'

Pause.

'But Emily, come on. I was straight up with you from the start. You knew it was never going to lead anywhere.'

Mona almost yelped aloud. He was calling it off. He was actually giving that little tart the heave-ho. She wanted to punch the air. Sweet victory. Not that she was in the least bit interested in Piers now, but it showed she could still triumph over a woman half her age.

'No, it's not that, it's just… Look, you know I'm not one for being deep and profound, but I've realized a few things on this holiday and one of them is that I'm not the shagging-around kind of guy. It's time I grew up.'

Mona's eyes were like Royal Doulton saucers.

'I get it, doll. I just wanted you to know before the deadline for that job. I'm sorry, Em, I really am. But I guess I've finally realized what I want and I just hope it's not too late to get it.'

That bit almost took Mona's breath away. He'd finally seen sense and dumped that little tart.

But, in truth, it really didn't matter to her plans or feelings. He may have realized what he wanted, but it was too little, too late because she now knew, too. And a future with Piers wasn't on her wish list.

16.

Rocky Seas

Sarah

Sarah's hands were shaking and it wasn't just because pre-date nerves had left her unable to eat a thing all day. She'd arranged to meet Nate by the pool in the adults-only section and now she realized that was a big mistake. Massive. Meeting at poolside = revealing size of arse in swimsuit, not something she was entirely comfortable with, despite the fact that she'd been at the salon that morning for some much-needed maintenance. She'd had a layer of fake tan slapped on to enhance the honey-coloured sheen she'd acquired in the last few days. Next came eyelash extensions so long she now resembled a dairy cow. And finally a master session of hair removal, including what she referred to as a – she flushed at the very thought – a 'semi-Mona'. Her lady garden wasn't quite fully mowed, but it certainly wouldn't be requiring a Flymo any time soon.

Adjusting herself on the sunlounger, she pulled her sarong across her thighs, then moved the back rest down so that her stomach looked flatter. Another bad idea. She was now lying too flat to drink the gin and tonic by her side. Pushing herself up, she twisted around, causing the sarong to fall off and her stomach muscles to fail, allowing her spare tyre slump into evidence. *Buggery bugger.*

Now she was sweating, shaking and swearing.

'Well, hello there.'

Buggery bugger once again. Of course he would pick that moment to arrive. A thin layer of moisture broke out on her top lip, making the kiss he planted there extra moist. Was there no end to the indignity?

She tried not to watch as he peeled off his white linen shirt, revealing a set of shoulders and torso that could wrestle a bull in a rodeo. Actually, they probably did. Oh, dear God, he had a six-pack. No, make it an eight-pack. *Stop staring. Stop staring.* Why did she always have to bloody stare? She was like the Queen of Inappropriate Staringville. *OK, now stop thinking irrational thoughts. Be carefree. In control.* Oh, dear God, he was taking off his shorts and he was wearing Speedos. SPEEDOS! Did she have time to get to the medical bay before she died from hyperventilation?

Patsy would die laughing if she could see her now, lying with an expertly trimmed foliage next to a cowboy wearing Speedos.

'Can I get you a drink?' he drawled.

'Got one,' she replied, holding up her gin. She then took a sip from the straw that somehow lasted longer than anticipated and emptied the glass. 'On second thoughts, a gin and tonic would be lovely, thanks.'

The waitress, Oona, Belgium, delivered them with a smile and Nate signed them to his account.

'So, how did you manage to get out of going onshore today, then? Aren't you the family tour guide?' she jested, trying to dispel her nerves with a touch of light conversation.

Nate grinned. 'Yep, that about sums it up. But they've gone on an organized tour and I explained to my daughter that a very lovely lady had asked me to keep her company today.'

Very lovely. She liked that. She also liked the fact that his hand had flopped over on to her sunbed and was gently stroking her arm. Oh, that felt good. She just had to get over the Speedos and this would be close to bliss.

Another hour and another drink passed, and Sarah began to feel uncomfortable in the heat. She'd never been one for lying all day in the sun – a combination of a pale complexion and a Scottish predisposition to cold, wet weather. 'Nate, do you mind if we go inside for a little while? I'm getting way too hot here.'

He went up on one elbow and turned to face her, then leaned over and traced a finger down the side of her face. 'What do you say we go cool off in my cabin?'

People turned to stare as she choked on her gin and tonic until her eyes watered. At least they now matched her upper lip.

Somehow, through the indignity, she managed to nod. Why

not? He was gorgeous. And kind. And good company. And such a gentleman.

She ignored the other voice in her head that was saying, 'And he's wearing SPEEDOS!!! Do not look at the Speedos. Do not.'

They gathered up their things and travelled down to deck eight in silence, except from the thudding of her heart, which was so loud that teenagers were probably dancing to it up on deck fourteen.

Inside the cabin, the cool of the air conditioning made absolutely no difference whatsoever, especially when Nate dropped his things on a chair and then turned and gently put one hand on either side of her neck and kissed her.

They'd kissed before, outside on deck, smoochy snogs while they were dancing, but this was different. It was urgent, passionate. She wound her hands through his hair and returned the kiss, tasting a mixture of beer and salt on his breath. She could feel his pelvis pressed against hers, his hardness against her stomach. *Don't panic.* She was about to do filthy things with a man in Speedos. Yes she was. She could do this. *Don't panic. Focus on the positives.* It was intoxicating, delicious, horny and…

She pulled back. *Terrifying.* She panicked.

'Nate, can we slow down a bit? It's just that… oh, bugger, I don't know how to say this.'

He looked at her searchingly.

'It's just that… right, here it is. I haven't had sex for years. It might even be a decade. And I'm finding this mildly terrifying.'

In her head she saw an image of Patsy, fag in mouth, slapping a hand to her forehead in despair.

Nate checked his watch. 'Well, sure, honey, but the others are gonna be back real soon and I promised I'd go play soccer with the boys at six o'clock.'

Her laughter surprised her as much as it surprised him. She'd been a sexual vacuum for years and now a man in Speedos was telling her to get a shake on because he was due to play football at six. Her country and western cowboy couldn't have burst her romantic bubble more if he'd moon-walked across the cabin while farting out the tune to 'Islands In The Stream'.

What the hell was wrong with her? Why couldn't she just pucker up and get with it? She was an almost-fifty-year-old woman who could do whatever she damn well pleased and yet she was stuck somewhere in a bloody big pile of sexual repression. It was never like this with Drew. They'd met so young and were together so long that it was always great. Always right. Up until he met that tart, Mona…

A feeling of utter despondence crept up from her flip-flops to her moist upper lip. Regardless of the reasons, this – her, Nate, the fledgling fling – felt all wrong. Time to back out as gracefully as her sarong would allow. 'I'm sorry, Nate. I think maybe holiday romances are just not for me. I'm so sorry.'

With that she leant over, gave him an apologetic kiss on the lips, and then bolted out of the door, leaving a pair of rapidly deflating Speedos in her wake.

Tess

The cool breeze from the open doors to the balcony made the flames on the candles flutter. Up on the mezzanine, Tess swapped her shorts for a pair of skinny jeans and pulled a black jersey waterfall cardigan on over her white T-shirt. With her hair pulled up into a ponytail, she could have passed for a college student. Right now, she wished she still was. Being an adult was seriously over-rated.

Downstairs, Drew answered the knock at the door and then wheeled in a fully laden table from room service. The original intention had been for them all to have dinner together tonight, but the plans had been vetoed by just about everyone. Sarah called off with a headache. John and Penny wanted to have an early night with the kids. Eliza – gutted that she'd somehow missed Kai and his family in Pisa – was making up for it by meeting him at 7 p.m. Max had booked a circuit class in the gym. Piers claimed he had some urgent business to attend to and Mona... actually Mona was the only one who was disappointed that the dinner plans had crashed, but she'd been left with no option other than to make her own plans after everyone else did the same. Tess was grateful for small mercies. The thought of dinner with Mona held absolutely no appeal.

Drew pushed the table over to the window, then put the brake on and pulled over two chairs and placed them facing each other. He checked she was still upstairs. 'Dinner's here, honey.'

'I'm just coming down.'

He removed the cloches from the plates, unwrapped the linen cover on the bread basket and poured them both glasses of sparkling white wine. That had been a concession to Tess. He preferred red.

As Tess came down the stairs, it struck her how perfectly civil they were being to each other. Polite. Like good friends. Close neighbours. Old pals.

She pulled her cardigan around her and sat down, pulling one foot up on the chair, one hand wrapped around the knee that was now at her shoulder.

He smiled at her kindly and she responded in kind. She wanted to scream. Instead, she blurted, 'I want to have children.'

He sighed the weariest sigh she had ever heard. 'Tess, we agreed…'

'No, I agreed. Me. You told me that having children was non-negotiable and I loved you so much that I agreed. I agreed never to have children so that I could have you. That was the deal.'

He nodded. 'And that's changed?'

'That's changed,' she agreed. "I've known for ages really, but didn't want to admit it to myself. But this afternoon with the twins… it just confirmed it.'

Across the table, Drew took a bite of his steak, but Tess ignored her chicken supreme. She had no appetite for anything that wasn't one hundred per cent carbohydrate and in the food group labelled 'comfort eating'.

She waited until he'd finished chewing and was looking at her with piercing, sad eyes.

'Since the day we met, I've gone along with everything you wanted. This isn't a partnership. It's your marriage and I'm just in it.' There was no bitterness or accusation in her tone, just matter-of-fact calmness.

He didn't respond, probably – she thought – stunned into silence by her uncharacteristic assertiveness.

'I love you. But we're not making each other happy anymore and unless something changes I think we're going to end up resenting each other, Drew. In fact, I think I'm starting to resent you already.'

He put his glass down and stared at her for a moment. 'I don't think I've ever made you do anything you don't want to do.'

She shook her head sadly. 'The fact that you say that proves how disconnected we are.'

'Why?' his voice was getting agitated now. 'What have you ever done that you didn't want to?'

Refusing to let this escalate to a fight, she kept her voice calm. 'I've spent more nights alone than I could count. I've finished dinner by myself so often that I can't remember ever seeing you over dessert and coffee. I made myself believe that I could live happily without ever having children. And I'm here with you now. On a holiday I didn't want to take. I wanted to have a quiet, romantic trip, just you and me – but that wasn't enough.' She bit her lip to stop her eyes filling up. 'I was never enough.'

He seemed pained by that. 'You were.'

'No, I wasn't, Drew. And now I don't think you're enough for me. I want to have a family. You already have yours, but I want that, too.'

Say yes. The optimist inside her drummed up a whole scenario that took them straight to a happy ending. He would say yes. She would have a baby, maybe twins, since they obviously ran in the family. He would cut back on work, perhaps even take an early retirement and write the book he'd been talking about for years. Or even semi-retirement, taking a more consultative role at the paper.

Just say yes.

'Tess, I don't know what you want from me. I'm fifty years old. I'm too old to go back to changing nappies, and parents' nights.'

'Other guys do it. Ronnie Wood has just had twins and he's a hundred and six.'

Drew smiled, then reached over and took her hand, winding his fingers around hers like it was the first time they had ever touched.

'I don't know if I can do that, Tess.'

Their eyes locked again, a hundred different emotions and thoughts passing between them, layered with sadness and uncertainty.

'It's really simple, Drew. Think about it. I don't expect an answer right now. But if you love me enough, then you will.'

Mona

Bored. Mona was so bored she was close to calling her assistant, Rupert, for a gossip. How sad was that? Or perhaps she'd give that gorgeous model, Adrian, a call. God knows he'd left about twenty messages on her answering machine this week. Ah, the young. They were always so keen. And yet here she was, sitting in the Ocean View bar on her own, with not even a random stranger to flirt with for her own amusement. Blane would probably be an adequate distraction but she had no idea where he was.

They'd had dinner in the suite tonight, and then Mona had left Piers and Max watching some Italian football game on the television. It was an aversion tactic, really. She had to leave before Max headed to his circuit class, otherwise Piers might want to have sex and lavish her with love and affection. What was it he'd said to Emily? That was it – 'I've finally realized what I want and I just hope it's not too late to get it.'

Well, it was too late, but she wasn't going to tell him that until they were back on dry land and she'd made the preparations she needed to make to leave. A new home for her and Drew, and a lawyer to make sure that both break-ups were as painless as possible.

Two very tall, athletic guys came through the door and passed by where she was sitting with an appreciative glance. As they went on to the bar, she realized from their conversation that they were French. *Très bon.* She hadn't been with a French guy since Paris Fashion Week last year. Jean Baptiste had been both highly skilled and highly addicted to coke – a combination that made for long energetic nights and keeping as big a distance as possible during the days.

OK, enough of sitting here looking like an advert for (admittedly beautiful) desperation. She slipped her iPhone out of her silk Fendi clutch, then jumped as it rang in her hand. Caller ID informed her that it was the office. Rupert's claims of having psychic gifts he inherited from his granny might not be too off the mark after all.

'Darling, you read my mind. What are you still doing at the office so late?'

There was a momentary silence at the other end. 'Mona? It's Guy.'

'Oh, sorry, Guy! I thought it was Rupert. What can I do for you? Are you looking for Drew? I can get him to call you back in just a few minutes.'

Yes! A chance to go interrupt whatever cosy little tête-à-tête Drew and Tess were having, and remind him once again how indispensable his favourite ex-wife was to him.

'Actually, Mona, it's you I'm looking for. We've got a bit of a situation here.'

'Oh, God, what now? If Kate Moss has decided to sue because I said she looked like a haggard old bint last week, I swear I'll…'

'No, it's not Kate.'

'Oh.'

'You know a guy called Adrian Meadows.'

It was more of a statement than a question. 'Yes, he's one of my regular models.' If her brow wasn't Botoxed into an immovable state, it would have furrowed in confusion. 'Is he checking on last month's payments? I'm sure I passed them. If not, Rupert could sort it out in the morning.'

Bloody hell, what a farce. Calling her on holiday because some idiot in accounts had fucked up the payments again. They were probably too busy slashing her budgets to actually do the jobs they were supposed to be doing.

'Mona, it's nothing to do with payments.'

This time she registered the tone of Guy's voice. It sounded like the tone you would use to notify someone of a death.

'So what is it?'

'Adrian Meadows has gone to the *Sunday News*. Offered them a story and pictures. Said you were shagging him in return for jobs. He's accusing you of sexual harassment, blackmail, bribery – fuck, Mona, he's accusing you of everything short of being responsible for the breakdown of world peace. It's not good, I'm afraid.'

In an instant, her blood ran cold and she had to fight the urge to throw up on the table in front of her. That conniving, evil, blood-sucking, fame-hungry little bastard. A million thoughts collided in her head, before sorting themselves into a logical order:

This would ruin her.

There were enough people who would relish the opportunity to gloat about it and she would become a laughing stock.

Her career, everything she had worked for, would be over.

No one would employ her again with this kind of stigma attached to her name.

A lifetime of work, reputation and sheer talent destroyed because of that little fucker.

The humiliation. She could almost feel it searing her skin.

Drew. It would be over. There was no way in hell that they would have a future if this became public. Drew was Mr Clean, allergic to scandal, he deplored idiots who got themselves into messes like this. It didn't matter that the story was grossly exaggerated - she'd put herself in a position to incur national ignominy and Drew would avoid at all costs being associated with a public figure of ridicule.

But Drew was also the only one who could stop this.

He was powerful enough to kill this story dead, but she had never, ever known him to use that kind of influence. His philosophy had always been that as someone who exposed the lives of others, he'd be hypocritical to shelter a public figure from the consequences of their actions. Over the years he'd had the opportunity to act to protect several acquaintances and at least two close friends, but he'd refused. Publish and be damned for your actions. No, Drew wouldn't save a friend. But she would bet anything that he would act to preserve the reputation of his future wife.

'Guy, who knows about this?'

'Just Jay Lemming at the *Sunday News*, Adrian went directly to him. He called me out of professional courtesy and I've called you. That's it. Don't suppose you've got anything on Jay that will make this all go away?'

She racked her brain. 'Nothing, unfortunately. Guy, have you told Drew yet?'

'No.'

'Then don't.'

'Mona…'

'Guy, do not push me. You would be a foolish man to do so.'

They may have joked in the past about her knowing his secrets, but they both knew that Mona was well aware of many little escapades that his wife would probably rather not be aware of. 'Speak to Jay, and I don't care how you do it, but do not let them run the story in this week's paper. Tell him you'll get more details and he can run it next week. Pull in a favour. Hell, I don't care if you screw him over his desk, just buy me time.'

'I'll see what I can do.' Mona knew that he'd come through – for his own sake.

'And Guy, Drew had better not hear about this from anyone else but me.'

17.

Genoa

Sarah

Sarah clutched her morning coffee and watched as the ship slowly pulled into the dock at Genoa. Since she'd risen at 6 a.m. after a sleepless night, she'd gone for a walk, before eventually settling with a coffee on a thick padded reading chair at the front of deck fourteen to watch the sunrise and then the 7 a.m. arrival in Genoa. Glancing around now, her early morning companions were a few elderly gentlemen and a couple of young boys with binoculars who shouted, 'Wow, look at that!' every few seconds.

For the last half an hour she'd been deliberating whether to leave the ship today. The whole family was definitely going ashore in Monaco tomorrow for Drew's birthday dinner, and the following day they would be back in Barcelona. The thought of one last, lazy, solo day appealed to her. The only problem was that her options for lazy locations were limited. Staying in the cabin held no appeal – it felt slightly claustrophobic after a few daylight hours. Lying up in the adults-only area would be bliss… if it wasn't for the fact that there was every chance she would bump into Nate. On the other hand, she could find a sunlounger on one of the four relaxation decks, but she'd be on edge all day in case Piers walked by and spotted her.

Maybe going off the ship was a safer bet – less chance of male-induced anxiety. This was exactly the reason that it was better to stay in her kitchen making inappropriate sponge cakes for a living. No drama, and the only disaster was an incorrectly placed nipple.

'Can I join you?'

So much for avoiding Piers. God, he looked rough. Really, really rough. He was dressed casually in jeans and a pale blue polo shirt, but tiredness was etched into every line on his face. She couldn't help but feel a pang of sympathy for him.

'Are we going to have another argument that'll end up with me storming off? Only I've got coffee here that I don't want to spill,' she asked, unwilling to drag the animosity on any longer. She'd been thinking about him a lot in her restless hours. He was such a lovely man and there was no escaping the reality that most of her happiest, hilarious moments on this holiday had been spent with him. In fact, right up until the day in Sorrento, she really thought that she'd met a wonderful new friend. Maybe they could still salvage some of that.

He sat down beside her and said nothing for a few tense moments. Eventually, he turned to look at her.

'I just wanted to apologize to you. I'm really sorry I offended you and, trust me, that was the last thing I wanted to do.'

'It's OK. As I said, I think I probably overreacted a bit, too. This week has reinforced just exactly how crap I am at everything connected with male/female relationships. Honestly, if I was a horse, they'd shoot me.'

Piers laughed so loudly and with such relief that an old man nearby frowned and adjusted his hearing aid. 'Well, we'd have to go down together then, because I'm just as bad.'

There was a prolonged pause as both of them adjusted to their relationship coming out of the deep freeze. Sarah was surprised at just how much this pleased her.

'You know, I didn't want to come on this holiday – it was Mona who made it impossible to say no – but being here has made things so much clearer. I want you to know that I'm not the kind of guy who goes around chatting up every bird I meet and getting up to no good behind my wife's back. Actually that's not true.'

'You don't have to explain anything to me, Piers,' Sarah told him.

'But I want to. Not to try and win you over, but because I just want you to know that I wasn't pulling some cheap shot with what I said to you back there. Things between Mona and I haven't been right for a long time. She sees other guys. I was seeing someone else too. Shit, how bloody embarrassing is that? In truth, we should have called a halt to it a long time ago. I just wanted you to know that. I'm sorry for coming on to you. I've loved every minute of getting to know you, Sarah, and whatever bloke is smart enough to land you will be a lucky man. I'm going to sort things out at my end and start living a more uncomplicated life. Bloody ridiculous to be in this mess at my age. I won't bother you again, love.'

'Piers, you're not bothering me.' Now that she understood what was happening it was almost a relief. He and Mona were having a rough patch and he'd been confused and hit on her because he was miserable. It made sense now. Sort of. She was glad he wasn't just an old letch looking for a quick shag. 'Let's just forget Sorrento ever happened and move on. I'm sorry you've got problems with Mona. I'm sure you'll work it out.'

Her attention was caught by a figure in gym clothes running towards them from the right and she shook her head. 'Over three thousand folks on this ship and I keep bumping into the same people.'

Drew stopped in front of them, his running vest dark with sweat.

'Right, I'm off,' Piers announced, standing up and patting his slightly rotund abdominal area. 'Nothing personal, mate, but life can be shite enough without standing next to you in that Lycra get-up.'

Off he went, leaving Drew and Sarah laughing behind him.

'So what are you doing up here at this time in the morning?' Drew asked her, as he took the seat Piers had just vacated.

'Meeting everyone I know, apparently,' Sarah replied. He gave her that look – the one that she knew so well, the one that said OK, so now tell me what you're really thinking. He'd always been able to read her like that. She was sure it was why he'd got bored with her. Too predictable. Too easy. Too bland. Unlike the enigmatic and exciting Mona. Cow. 'I'm just… thinking,' she admitted. 'I've loved this week, Drew. But without coming over all Oprah on you, it's really made me re-evaluate what I'm doing and what I want out of life.'

'I know that feeling,' he concurred sadly. 'Do you sometimes wish you'd done things differently?'

'Sometimes,' she said. 'But there's no point in that, is there? It's not as if you can ever go back and change things.'

'I wish I could.'

He was staring so wistfully off into the middle distance that

Sarah wondered if he was actually talking to her or to himself. She also realized that she was waiting for him to leave, to jump up and say he had another appointment, to suddenly remember he had to make a call, to just be typically Drew – with no time for her or anyone else. If only his priorities had been different they might have made it. But they weren't and she realised now that she'd let him dent her self-confidence so much that for all these years she'd convinced herself she didn't want another relationship. No more. Time to start living again.

'What was it that you wanted to talk to me about?' she asked him, snapping him out of the weird stare thing he had going on.

'What?'

'The other day – you said you wanted to talk to me.'

'I did.'

Another silence. This was like pulling teeth. 'Well?'

'Good morning!'

Sarah didn't even have to turn to check the originator of the voice. For the love of Jesus, what was going on up here? Was there a team of guys at all the lifts, directing every member of their party along to this meeting point?

Typical Mona, Sarah decided as the other woman came around the seats and into full view – Gucci sunglasses at 7 a.m., before the sun had even had a chance to get its act together. Below the neck was typically glam, too – black spandex running tights and a boob tube that, should it ever find its way into Sarah's wardrobe, was so small it could be worn as an armband in time of bereavement.

'Tess said I would find you up here,' she told Drew.

'Is something wrong?' he replied.

'Nope, just thought I'd join you for a run. Sorry, am I interrupting anything important?'

Sarah and Drew looked at each other before both shaking their heads. 'No, not at all. Just gabbing,' Sarah said.

Mona nodded as if that was exactly the explanation she'd been expecting. Sarah racked her memory to see if she'd mentally called Mona any derogatory names so far this morning, but she couldn't be sure. *Mangled old boot.* There. That felt better.

'OK, then! I'm ready to go if you are,' she told Drew. He got up, but there was no hiding the fact that he looked weary.

As they jogged off, dodging elderly bystanders, Sarah felt a distinct sense of unease. It was absolutely none of her business, but perhaps it was time to have a word with Tess and give her a gentle hint. Whenever Mona was around her husband, Tess should really borrow a set of binoculars off those kids to keep an eye on her at all times.

Mona

The setting wasn't ideal, the timing wasn't great, but Mona had been pushed into a situation and the only thing she could do was go with the flow and aim for a win. Forty-eight hours. She had forty-eight hours to lock down a future with Drew and enlist his help with the Adrian situation. The very thought of that duplicitous prick made the hairs on the back of her neck stand up. When this situation was closed down, she'd make sure he was modelling jock straps in Siberia for the rest of his life.

They ran for another half an hour, side by side, keeping pace, before calling it a day and heading to the coffee bar for a couple of takeaway skinny lattes. Steaming cups in hand, they sat down at a wicker table near the back end of the ship. *Oh, OK, the aft.* But Mona still thought that was a bloody stupid thing to call it.

They'd only been there a few moments when she realized that they mirrored each other perfectly. They sat the same way, held their shoulders the same way, drank their coffee the same way, in perfect synchronicity. If ever there were two people who were meant to be together, it was them.

'Drew, do you ever wish you could go back in time and change the past?'

He laughed. Not the reaction she'd been expecting. 'That's so strange – I was just having exactly the same conversation with Sarah.'

That was a terrifying thought – being on the same wavelength as Sarah Gold was a milestone she did not ever want to reach in life.

'Oh really? How come?'

Drew shrugged. 'I don't know. Just getting a little melancholic, I guess.'

She processed and dismissed his explanation as being of no consequence. Sarah was no threat to this situation. The poor woman hadn't been in Drew's league since the seventies.

Mona pushed her sunglasses up on to her head, allowing Drew to see her eyes for the first time. He was visibly shocked.

'Mona, are you OK? You look like you've… have you been crying?'

His astonishment wasn't a surprise. He'd only seen her cry once in her life and that was that morning in 2004 when they called time on their marriage. Even thinking back to that day made her nauseous.

In fact, the red-rimmed eyes hadn't been caused by tears, but by a sleepless night, spent alternating between fretting about her situation and listening to Piers wandering around the cabin. It seemed like insomnia was the theme of the night.

However, the tears explanation worked just fine. Sympathy and concern were welcome if they helped her cause.

'Drew, I can't stand it. Honestly, I can't stand being married to him for another day.'

'I'm sorry, darling,' he said softly. Darling. He used to call her that all the time when they were married.

He fell silent again, waiting for her to open up some more.

'You know the other day, I said I wanted to divorce Piers and find someone new. I wasn't being strictly honest with you.'

He looked justifiably confused. 'So you don't want to divorce him now?'

'Yes, I do. But I don't want to be with someone new.'

It was a tad disconcerting that he sat back in his chair and laughed. 'Mona, you can't be single. You're not cut out that way. I've never met a sexier, smarter woman, and you like to be in a relationship so that you're reminded of those things every day. It's who you are.'

This was good. He'd just confirmed that she was the sexiest and smartest woman he knew. Excellent start. Nice bait. Now she just had to reel him in.

'I know that, but honestly, the thought of starting again horrifies me. I know what I want – the right man who fulfils me on every level, who gets me and buys into a future with us both blazing a trail.'

She checked to see that he was still hanging on her every word. Yep, engrossed. OK, here goes. Back straight, chest forward, jawline at highest position to flatter facial contours.

'Drew, the only man I want to be with is you. I don't want

anyone else. You're not happy with Tess and I'm not happy with Piers and I know it's because we should still be together. There is no better team than you and me. You know that. You do, Drew. Deep down, you know.'

Nothing happened. For what seemed like several hours, he sat there, blank. She was about to check him for vital signs when he finally leaned over, tenderly took her face in his hands and kissed her with joy and relief.

Actually, that last bit only happened in her head.

In reality, when he eventually snapped out of his full-function paralysis, he let out a prolonged, aching groan. 'Oh, Mona, this isn't good.'

It is good! It's great! she wanted to shout, but something stopped her.

Her stomach tightened with a horrible, unfathomable premonition of what he was about to say. No. He couldn't. If he rejected her now, her life was over. No Drew. No job. No credibility. No future.

'Mona, I love you…'

She could feel the weight of the 'but' that was about to come.

'But we don't belong together anywhere except in the boardroom. There is no other woman… forget that, no other *person* I would rather work with than you. But we want different things.'

'We don't,' she gasped, and immediately raged with herself. She would not argue for a man's love, not even Drew.

'We do,' he said, almost regretfully. 'Over the last few months I've realized that my work/life balance is completely messed up. I'm going to cut down my hours at the paper. Work less. Spend more time with family. And when I go home at night I don't want to discuss current affairs and be mentally stimulated. I want to relax. See the kids. Play with Lawrence and Lavinia. Read. Chill. I've made an absolute balls of things over the last while and I can see now that I need to fix it. We don't belong together, Mona. I want to work with you until the day I hang my jacket up, but that's where we're best together, not at home.' He ran his fingers through his hair, something he only did when he was ultra-stressed, then he leaned over and touched her face. 'I'll always love you, Mona. But I have to go.'

'Where?'

'To talk to my wife.'

Her eyes didn't even follow him as he left. Instead they closed, partly to stem the real tears that were threatening to flow, and partly because her brain was now going into frantic emergency disaster-recovery mode.

He didn't want her. And his professional ethics would prevent him from helping her by stopping the story. It was over. Her life and everything she'd ever worked for was over. No one would employ her, no one would be attracted to a joke, no one would take her on knowing that she was an object of derision for the whole nation.

She was done.

Unless…

There was only one other option.

Piers.

Sure, it would be tough when the story came out, but they'd weather the storm. It wasn't like she was the only one who'd been unfaithful. Anyway, hadn't he told Emily the Frump that it was over and said something about hoping it wasn't too late? Well, it wasn't. He was going to have to brace himself for the downside of that 'for better, for worse' stuff that they promised each other in front of five hundred illustrious guests and she was going to have to suck it up and stay married to him… at least for the time being.

No one would believe that Piers Delaney's wife would be capable of those things. No one would dare to labour the point for fear of incurring Piers' wrath. Hell, Piers would buy every edition of the *Sunday News* and make sure that the paper – not her reputation – was pulped.

It was her only option. In a couple of years, when this had all blown over, they could quietly divorce and they could both go find partners that would truly make them happy.

Pulling her sunglasses back down over her eyes, she got up and headed for the lifts. She hoped Piers was around somewhere, because this was about to become his lucky day.

Tess

Tess reread the note again.

One more day. Tomorrow. Monaco. In the square at noon. Please come.
Cxx

Her stomach was churning. Actually flipping over. One more day. How was she going to handle this? Tomorrow was Drew's birthday, a day they should both be excited about, and yet all other feelings were being squashed to death by the big fat ball of apprehension currently shuttling between her stomach and her throat. Thankfully, it was around the voice box area when Drew burst back into the room, stopping her from screaming as she swiftly thrust the letter under the mattress.

She got up from the bed and made her way downstairs from the mezzanine, stopping halfway when she saw his expression.

'What's wrong? What's happened?' she asked fearfully. He looked positively panicked.

'Nothing. Well, no, maybe something. I don't know. I need to talk to you.'

That ball of apprehension just got bigger. Drew was never like this. He was Mr Calm – middle names, Cool and Control.

He reached up for her hand and then guided her down and over to the dining table, before taking the seat across from her.

'What? What is it?' This was starting to get seriously troubling.

'Tess, I can't do it.'

'Do what?'

'Have more children. I'm so sorry. I wish that I could, but my time for that has passed. I don't want to start all that again. Not even for you.'

She absorbed what he was saying with a deep sadness. 'I know.'

'You do?'

She nodded. 'I've always known. And there's no point in me

screaming or shouting about it, because you were always up front about it. I didn't expect you to change your mind. Even when I was giving you the ultimatum last night, I knew you wouldn't change your mind, but I felt I had to try.'

He got up from his chair and took two bottles of fresh orange juice from the fridge, putting one down in front of her.

'So where does that leave us, Tess? I feel like we're two different people now, looking for two different things.'

'What do you want?' she asked him, trying to keep her voice calmer than she was feeling inside.

He pushed both hands through his hair, a gesture of exasperation that she'd never seen in him before. 'I don't know. I'm going to make changes. I'm going to work less, relax more, find some kind of healthy balance before it's too late.'

That should be great news, but somehow it didn't feel like a complete victory. 'Are you doing that for me or for you?'

That was it. That was the crunch of the whole situation. Was she a consideration in his life, or was she just a bystander to everything Drew Gold would ever decide to do?

The question took him by surprise and as always, he paused before answering. Tess knew he wouldn't lie – it wasn't in his DNA – even though they both suddenly realized that so much was riding on his answer.

'I'm doing it for me,' he said slowly, his voice thick with regret. 'But that doesn't mean I don't love you, Tess, because I do. I won't lie to you though, even if it's to say what I know you want to hear.'

She smiled sadly. 'Integrity really is overrated, you know.'

His fingers were coiling around hers now. 'I still think we can make this work,' he said. 'But I understand if it's not enough. So now it's my turn to ask you to think about our future. There will be more time for us. We'll be able to do things, go places, travel, experience new things, live good lives. But a family will never be part of the picture.'

She unravelled her fingers from his as conflicting thoughts crashed in her head. She loved this man and he was finally going to have time for her. The life he was describing sounded like the kind of existence that many people dreamed of. No financial worries. No stress. Lots of fun. With a partner who loved her.

A month ago she would have been jumping up and down

with happiness at this. Yet now, she wasn't sure. It wasn't just the barrier to having a family, because that had been there for a long time. It was more. A shift. A realization that she had never been top of the importance list for the man that she married. Hell, she wasn't even sure that she was in the top three.

She wanted this to work, she really did. There had never been a single doubt that she loved Drew Gold from the minute she met him. He was everything she'd ever wanted in a bloke... except there, present, by her side.

The question now, though, was no longer whether he loved her enough. It was whether she wanted the future that he described.

18.

Sunsets At Sea

Mona

If ever Piers had the requirement for one last meal before a life-ending moment, Mona was sure he would want to have it here. The Steak Grill restaurant was his idea of heaven, with traditional wooden panelling on the walls, beautiful table linens, expensive crockery and crystal glasses that sparkled. It was lush, indulgent without being too pretentious, and it served cold beer and hot T-bones.

It was perfect.

As they were shown to their table, she noticed that he actually looked quite dashing tonight. He'd decided to wear a suit, which was unlike him on holiday. His dress sense could definitely be hit or miss. He'd even come back from that day in Palma wearing swim shorts with bloody chickens on them! Oh, the mortification. It had taken her a while to get over that one – she was a respected fashionista and she was married to a man who had chickens covering his balls.

The thought made her shudder.

'All right, love?' he asked.

'Yes, just deciding I'm not having chicken tonight.'

'Good move – go for the steak. It's the speciality and I've heard it's out of this world. You look beautiful tonight, by the way.'

'Thank you.' It wasn't a surprise. She'd spent all day in the salon getting ready for this and she knew she had never looked better. They'd worked miracles with her eyes, which were now a smoky charcoal. Her complexion was flawless and her raven hair pulled back into a classic chignon. But it was her dress that stole the show – a white strapless sheath with a corset-style top that enhanced her curves, before clinging to every contour all the way down to her calves. It was so tight her steps were limited to ten-inch spans, but it was worth it. She'd been planning on wearing it tomorrow night to Drew's birthday party, but now that tonight had suddenly become the most important night of her life, she'd decided to deploy every weapon in her armoury.

This was it. The night she would either hold on to her life or lose everything – and losing wasn't an option she was prepared to consider.

Mona never came to a table without a game plan and tonight the strategy was clear: reconnect with Piers, reaffirm that their marriage was solid, warn him about the story. If he pulled the outraged, infidelity card, then she would bring up Emily. It was that simple. They would kiss, make up and agree to put the mistakes on both sides behind them. The end.

They stuck to small talk through the starters (salmon skewers for Mona, teriyaki chicken rolls for Piers) and main courses (Caesar salad and steak). It was all very amiable and pleasant. Not sparkling and fun, but then, it was Piers. He didn't do anything that remotely resembled fun to her. They passed on desserts in favour of Irish coffees in elaborate glass mugs, and it was only then that Mona felt the time was right to talk. To her surprise, she realized that she was uncharacteristically nervous, yet she had no idea why – surely this was a foregone conclusion?

'Piers, I need to talk to you.'

He put his coffee down and met her gaze with an unreadable expression. 'That sounds serious.'

'It probably is. Look, I know things haven't been great between us, but I want you to know that I'm happy being married to you and I want to make it better. I really do.'

His face went from unreadable to surprise to something darker that she couldn't quite pinpoint.

She reached over for his hand, but he slid it away as he sat back in his chair.

'Why?' he asked simply.

That was one question she hadn't prepared for and it threw her. 'What do you mean?'

'Why do you want to make it better? What's happened?'

'N… nothing. Why would you say that?' This was not going

according to plan at all.

Slowly, Piers removed his napkin from his lap and put it on the table with a gesture of resignation.

'Mona, I wasn't going to have this conversation until we got back home, but since you're bringing it up now, let's just get real. You don't want to be married to me. We both know it's over. What is puzzling me is why you seem to have had a change of heart.'

A frisson of fear crept around her neck and she suddenly found it hard to breathe. 'No. It's not over, Piers. It's not. Sure, we've had problems, but that's hardly unusual. Nothing we can't fix. I… I… love you.' She added a definite tone to the last two words, hoping that he didn't realize how hard it was for her to say. Bullshit had never been her strong point, but she had to try and make him believe it.

He stared at her for a long time, oblivious to the waiter who was floating around, desperate to be of service. Eventually Dimas, Greece went off and catered to another table.

After an interminable silence, her gut wrenching at the thought of her future hanging in the balance, he finally spoke. 'You don't love me, Mona.'

The panic was strangling her now. 'I do.'

'How many other men have you slept with since we married?'

A physical slap across the face couldn't have made her reel any further back. 'Wha… what?'

Piers was still deadly calm. 'How many? You can give it to me in dozens if that makes it easier.'

That was it. Desperate and needy didn't sit well with her and since he was clearly going on the attack there was no way she was just going to sit there and take it. Her temper flared white-hot, sending her as always into a state of deadly menace.

'Do not dare come over all sanctimonious on me,' she hissed. 'It's not like you haven't been banging your secretary for the last year. What did you do? Wow her with cash? You might at least have bought her a pair of decent shoes.'

She braced herself for the explosion but it never came. Now she knew why he was revered as one of the best negotiators in the corporate sector. This calm, icy demeanour obviously came from his business head. For a second she longed for the other, loud, rambunctious Piers.

'Now, now, Mona, play nice,' he replied coldly. 'Because if we're going to get really personal then I would have to point out that, A: you might want to stop shagging guys too close to home, because I hear you've been through half the twenty-five-year-olds in Glasgow, and B: you left your earrings in the cabin of that American bloke you've been screwing since we came aboard. He returned them yesterday. I offered him twenty quid as thanks for taking the time to bring them back. He took it.'

She froze, stunned, while he, completely nonplussed, signalled to Dimas, Greece for the bill.

'So I think this is what they call a stalemate, Mona. Neither of us gets the upper hand, neither comes out of this smelling of roses. The only thing I will say is that I didn't go near Emily until you were on your fourth or fifth little escapade. I think it was Danny, the twenty-two-year-old soap star.'

Oh. Holy. Fuck. How does he know all of this? And he was still speaking.

'The only thing puzzling me is why the change of heart? Why are you suddenly coming over all Mother Teresa and looking to patch things up? What happened? Between the American and the way you've been hitting on Drew all week, I'd have thought our marriage was the last thing on your mind. Did Drew knock you back?' He clearly meant the last comment as a parting dig, but immediately saw by her reaction that he'd got it absolutely right. 'My God, that's what happened. He did.'

In her head, Mona could hear the noise a slap would make when it hit his face. This couldn't be happening. She burned with fury and fear. It couldn't be. There was too much at stake. Too much to lose. She had to have one last try, even if it would shred every last piece of her dignity.

'Piers, I know I've been stupid. I know I have, and I'm so sorry. But you have to forgive me. I heard you on the phone the other day, calling it off with her, saying that you knew what you wanted and you just hoped it wasn't too late. It isn't too late for us, Piers.'

There. She'd said it. However, this just seemed to completely baffle him. It took a few seconds for comprehension to enter the picture, and then it quickly turned to weariness.

'You're right, Mona, I do know what I want now. But I wasn't talking about you.'

Sarah

Sarah lay awake, fully engrossed in the last few chapters of her book. She'd wandered around Genoa for a few hours in the morning, then had a panini and strong coffee for lunch in a quaint little street cafe. After returning to the ship, she had spent the afternoon in the peaceful surroundings of the library, where she'd finished her Tasmina Perry and then come across a Marian Keyes novel that she hadn't read. That solved the question of what to do for the rest of the day. It had been absolute bliss. No drama, no tension, just the quiet calm of Sarah, Marian and a sodding big comfy chair in a gorgeous room full of silent people.

Now, lying in bed, a niggle interrupted her thoughts and she checked her watch. Midnight. Eliza was supposed to have been back half an hour ago. Her daughter had loved every single minute of this holiday, and she was obviously trying to wangle a little more enjoyment time. Sixteen was a tough age. Old enough to marry. Mature enough to make most of her own decisions, yet still having to work within the parameters set by her parents. Sarah had hoped to spend more time with Eliza this week, but she'd been rejected on almost every request. She knew it was nothing personal. She and Patsy had spent hours staring at the telephone at that age waiting for the boys of the moment to call.

Back to the book; she read another couple of chapters and then checked her watch again. Twelve thirty. This wasn't good. Eliza occasionally wandered in five minutes late, but this was taking it too far. She tried her daughter's mobile phone – straight to answering machine. Trying not to panic, she ran through a list of plausible explanations, the first one being that the mobile phone was out of charge. Yep, that explained it. Eliza never wore a watch, so used her phone to check the time. If it was off, then she wouldn't realize it was so late and therefore wouldn't think to call. A perfectly logical explanation. Utterly reasonable. And while she was telling herself that, she was out of bed and throwing on clothes, while fighting to regain some semblance of calm.

Pulling on her Uggs, she listened for the sound of footsteps coming down the corridor. Nothing. OK, this wasn't the end of the world. It would be fine. Absolutely fine. She'd find Eliza and in an hour's time they'd be tucked up in bed laughing about this... after she'd murdered her for making her worry.

Grabbing her phone, she jotted down 'Gone to look for you – call me on mobile if you get in before I'm back' on a piece of paper and left it on her pillow.

Outside the cabin, she realized she had absolutely no idea which way to go. *Think logically. Where would she be?* And why hadn't she got one of those satnav chips put in her daughter when she got the Labradoodle done?

Think. Think. Nightclub! Eliza had been going to the teen nightclub every night. Sarah ran to the elevator bank and checked the ship map. Deck ten. Inside the lift, she banged on the number and then whispered 'Come on, come on,' as the lift rose at the slowest possible pace. Or maybe it just felt like that.

When the doors opened she was already in motion, sprinting out and down the corridor in the direction she'd memorized from the map. Finally the silver doors of the Venue were in sight and she checked herself. *Take a deep breath. Do not go running in there, or Eliza will never forgive you. Be calm. Act nonchalant. Threaten her with a lifetime locked in her bedroom only when you get her to a place of solitude and safety.*

Just as she was about to pull the door open, a huge man pushed out from the inside and Sarah realized what was missing. Music. 'Can I help you?' the Incredible Hulk asked her nicely.

'I'm looking for my daughter. Eliza.'

His brow furrowed in thought. 'Very tall, blonde, Scottish, usually comes in with a guy called Kai?'

'Yes!' *Oh, thank God. Thank God.*

'Sorry, but they weren't in tonight. We've just closed, so I don't expect they'll show up now. Can I help you search for her?'

Sweet guy, but the last thing she wanted to do was turn this into a full-scale ship drama. 'No, it's fine. Thank you. I'm sure she's just off enjoying herself and didn't notice the time.' Yes, that was it. For sure.

Turning on her heel, she realized that her brain was now completely ignoring the direct order not to freak out. *Breathe. Breathe. Right, start from the top.* Literally.

Not prepared to wait for the lift, she ran up to deck fifteen and checked the Ocean View. No Eliza. She scoured the rest of the deck. No sign of her. Deck fourteen. She checked the wave pool, all the loungers (interrupting a couple who definitely were not playing Scrabble under that blanket), the obstacle course, and even peeked in the church. No sign, but she did say a quick prayer for holy intervention while she dangled down to look under the pews.

No deck thirteen – unlucky for some. It would be bloody unlucky for Eliza when she found her. Her heart immediately wrestled control from the bravado section of her brain. *Please be OK. Please be OK.* The public areas on deck twelve were practically deserted, making the search quicker, but just as fruitless. On deck eleven, she popped her head into every restaurant, bar, and even the gym. Nothing.

Deck ten. Deck nine. Deck eight. Deck seven. Deck six. By deck five, she was close to passing out. Eliza was nowhere to be found. She must have gone to that boy's cabin, despite strict instructions not to. Surely his parents wouldn't allow that? What was his cabin number? Eliza had definitely said something about Deck twelve. Hadn't she?

Back in the lift, she counted to a hundred as it rose upwards, then darted out as soon as the doors opened. 'Good evening, madam, can I help you?' said a girl behind the desk whose name badge said she was called Colita, Brazil.

'Yes, I'm looking for my daughter, Eliza Gold.'

'Ah, Mr Gold's daughter.'

'You've seen her?' *Yes! Oh, yes! Yes!*

'Yes, ma'am, she stayed with Mr Gold a couple of nights ago. When we left Naples, I believe.'

Oh. Not the answer she was looking for, but it was a start. 'Have you seen her tonight? I believe her boyfriend, Kai, lives on this floor?'

'Yes. But I'm afraid they haven't been here tonight. Mr and Mrs Latham are in their suite, but Kai has not yet returned this evening. Shall I call Mr and Mrs Latham for you?'

Sarah weighed that up for a second, before shaking her head.

No point in worrying another set of parents just yet, but if she hadn't found Eliza in the next twenty minutes, she would.

But they had to find her. She'd be fine. She was here. She wasn't overboard. Or kidnapped. Or… Oh God, this was getting worse by the minute.

'No, thank you. I'm just going to pop along to see Mr Gold.'

'Of course. Please let me know if I can help you…..'

Sarah didn't even hear the rest of the sentence. She was already flying in the direction of Drew's room. She hammered on the door, forgetting that it was now 2 a.m. Eventually a very dishevelled Tess answered the door.

'Tess, have you seen Eliza? I've searched the ship and she's not here and she could be overboard. Oh shit, what if she fell over? What if…'

'Sarah, hey, hey, it's OK.' Tess's arms wrapped around her and gently pulled her inside. 'We'll find her, don't worry. Let me get some shoes. I'll help you. Drew!'

Her husband was already halfway down the stairs from the bedroom. 'What's up?'

'It's Eliza. She didn't come home. I've searched everywhere, Drew. The whole ship.' Tears were now flowing down Sarah's face. If anything happened to Eliza she'd never forgive herself. She shouldn't have let her go out alone. She should have stayed with her every minute of the holiday. She should definitely have got her bloody microchipped.

He was already pulling on his second shoe and a sweatshirt over his bare chest. His urgency panicked her even more.

'Hang on, I'll phone Max,' Tess said, picking up the handset. 'Max, it's Tess. Have you seen Eliza? No? OK, I'll buzz your dad. Oh. Well, can you ask him then? Thanks. Are you sure? That would be great. We're just about to start searching now.'

She placed the phone back in the cradle. 'Piers is staying the night in Max's room for some reason and neither of them have seen her. He's going to call Mona to check if she's seen her and then they're coming to help us look for her.' Sarah couldn't compute half of that statement but she didn't have time to ponder it.

By the time they got to Colita's reception desk, the other two men were there, worried and eager to help.

'Right, let's be organized about this,' Drew said. 'How long is it since you left your room, Sarah?'

'I don't know – about an hour? More?'

'OK, give me your key. Max and Piers, can you start at fifteen and work your way down. Tess, you go with Sarah to five and work your way up. I'll check the room and get John out to come help us search.'

'She won't be there, Drew. I left a note telling her to phone if she got back and she hasn't. Drew, where is she?'

'We'll find her. Trust me.'

It was so stupid, but just hearing him say that made her feel just a little bit better. They'd find her. Drew said so.

They all ran in their designated directions. All the way down the stairs, Tess held Sarah's hand, repeatedly reassuring her that this was going to end well. It had to. God, it had to.

At deck five, they ran along the so-called 'Main Street' between the shops. No sign. They were about to head up to six when Sarah's phone rang.

Drew.

'Sarah, I've got her. She's in the cabin.'

Relief, huge big bloody tsunamis of relief washed over her until her legs jellified and she slumped against the wall. 'But why didn't she…'

'I'll explain when you get here.'

'She's in the cabin. Drew's got her.'

Tess hugged her, both of them with faces flooded with tears.

'You go and I'll call off the others. Go, go!' Tess urged her.

She didn't need to be told twice.

She ran all the way, bursting in the door of the cabin to see a concerned Drew, standing over a horizontal Eliza, who was lying face down on Sarah's bed, sound asleep.

'But she didn't call…'

'Sarah, can you smell that?'

Sarah stopped. Sniffed. 'Booze.'

Drew nodded. 'I think our little darling has had her first boozy night out.'

Sarah rushed over and checked Eliza's vital signs, her pulse, her pupils. She was about to switch her panic from "missing teenager" to "alcohol-poisoned teenager" when Eliza smiled in her sleep, before adjusting herself into a comfier position.

'I don't think she's in too bad a state. She managed to get her pyjamas on.'

'Backwards,' Sarah noticed, a smile finding her lips for the

242

first time in hours. 'Drew, I was so scared.'

'I know,' he said, wrapping his arms around her. 'Do you remember when John did the same thing?'

'School disco. He was fifteen. Cider.'

He grinned. 'I'll phone Tess and tell her I'm staying here tonight. I'll take Eliza's bed. I've got a feeling we might have a sick girl at some point during the night.'

And as Sarah pulled a blanket over her daughter, she couldn't help but feel thankful that he was there. Just like he used to be.

Tess

Tess found Max and Piers at the entrance to the casino on deck ten.

'They found her,' she told them, grinning. 'Drew just called to say that she's asleep and they think she might have had one or two drinks.'

'Ouch,' Max replied. 'I'm thinking that's not going to seem like it was such a good idea in the morning.'

'I remember the first time you got pissed,' Piers interjected, before turning to Tess. 'Brought a team of pals up to my house, then drank my bar dry. I grounded him for a month.'

'I was twenty-two at the time,' Max joked.

They made their way down to deck twelve and suddenly going back to an empty cabin didn't hold much appeal. 'Do you two want to come in for a drink? Don't feel much like sleeping now – too much adrenalin. Drew's staying with Sarah and Eliza so it's going to be beer for one if you don't join me.'

'Was that a shameless attempt to guilt us into coming with you?' Piers said cheekily.

'Absolutely.'

'Then make mine a Budweiser. Purely to help you out, you understand.'

In the suite, the three of them lounged on the sofas, swapping stories about the week. Tess was dying to ask why Piers was staying with Max, but it was none of her business. She made a mental note to ask Drew in the morning – Mona didn't sneeze without him knowing about it.

'Right, you two, I'm off to make some phone calls. I've got a pal in New York I want to speak to, so I might as well take advantage of being up at this bloody time of night.'

How much her opinion of Piers had changed this week. She'd gone from being slightly intimidated by him to discovering that he was one of the loveliest, most generous, funniest men she'd ever met.

'I'll be along shortly, Dad. I'll just finish my beer and let you get your call over with.'

As the door closed softly behind Piers, Tess poured another drink, before curling back on to the sofa and pulling her feet up under her. 'I searched a ship in my pyjamas tonight,' she said, gesturing to her grey marl jersey trousers and white T-shirt. 'That's not a sentence I ever thought I'd say.'

Max's nose crinkled up when he smiled. She liked that about him.

'So how are things going with Drew? Did you work stuff out?'

She stared into her wine. 'Nope. It's not going great.' She tried to flavour her reply with a light-hearted tone, but it didn't work and she could see that Max didn't want to probe. 'I wanted him to work less, and he's agreed to that now. Should be a win, right? It's what I've been wanting for a long time. But now other things have come up that I didn't expect. When we met I knew he didn't want more children and I agreed to that, but now I'm not so sure. I thought I was happy, but I don't think I am. I thought we were perfect together, but...' That one hung in the air, a foregone conclusion that she couldn't quite bring herself to say out loud.

'What do your family and your friends think?'

'I haven't said anything to my mum and dad. I don't want them to worry and my mother would. She'd have Bolivian customs officers phoning me to check how I'm doing.'

'What about your friends?'

She shrugged. 'All my girlfriends love him because he's got that charm that just wins everyone over.'

Max nodded at that. Drew's charisma wasn't exactly a closely guarded secret.

'Only my friend Cameron has... reservations.'

'Why?'

'He thinks he doesn't treat me well enough. He thinks...' She stopped herself.

'Thinks what?' he asked. The pain as her teeth sunk into her bottom lip made her flinch. *Must stop doing that. Must stop doing that.* Suddenly she felt exhausted with the weight of the whole situation. If only her mum was here and she could discuss it with her. Or a girlfriend. Or Cameron, before he turned all secret-admirer-borderline-stalker on her. But they weren't here, Max was. She made a split-second decision, based on nothing but optimism that she knew him well enough to judge his character. He could keep a secret. She was sure of it. He was trustworthy and he was smart. And right now he was the only person who could make sense of all this before twelve noon tomorrow when a good-looking Scottish bloke would be standing in the middle of a square in Monte Carlo, waiting for her.

Decision made, she reached into her bag and pulled out the notes, then handed the first one over to Max and watched as his face shadowed with confusion.

'Cameron has been my best friend for years. We spend almost every day together. The day before we left to come here, he told me that he loved me. Wanted me to leave Drew, that we weren't right for each other, that he could make me happier than my husband.'

'What did you do?'

'Asked him to leave. Raged. Denied everything. But he was partially right. Then we came on board and I got that.' She gestured to the note.

> Tess, I'm sorry about that conversation but I meant every word I said. Require future discussion. I hope you agree. Am owed some time off so have decided to take a break. Checked the ship's itinerary and have an idea. Meet me in Monaco on the day you dock there. I'll be in the square at noon. Cx

'And then this one arrived a couple of days later.' She handed over the second note.

> Tess, I'm sorry to do this but I had to write again in case you thought I'd sent yesterday's note when I was confused. Or pished. I hope that you've had time to think about what I said. Meet me when you dock in Monaco. I'll be in the square at noon. Cx

'He sounds like a funny guy who loves you,' Max said.
'There's more,' she replied, handing over the next two notes.

> Tess, no pressure. I know this must be coming over as crazy. I'll totally understand if you don't show up and I promise we'll always be mates even if you don't come. I'm hoping you've discovered that you miss me. If you do, then please… Meet me in Monaco. In the square at noon. Cx

> Missing you. No one to share my donuts with. Meet me in Monaco. I'll bring the ones with sprinkles. Cxx

'And then finally today, this one came.'

One more day. Tomorrow. Monaco. In the square at noon. Please come.
Cxx

'Wow,' was all Max could muster. 'What are you going to do?'

'I don't know. I honestly don't. Please don't say anything about this, Max,' she pleaded.

'I won't, I promise.' He got up and rescued another beer from the fridge, topping up her wine glass in the process. 'Do you love him? Cameron, I mean.'

'Yes!' she blurted and then immediately clarified. 'I mean, I love him as a friend and we make each other so happy. Life's easy with Cameron. It's fun. Unpredictable. And we laugh all the time. But I've never thought of him as more than a friend, so do I *love* him? In that way?' she pondered the answer to her own question. 'I really don't know.'

There was a long, loaded pause, before Tess shook her head.

'You must think I'm a complete nightmare. I promise there's usually no drama in my life. I don't have men queuing at the door. Until a couple of weeks ago, I thought my future was all mapped out.'

'Life has a way of booting you in the arse the minute you think you've got it sussed,' Max said solemnly.

'Were those words of wisdom, Master Yoda?'

'Indeed,' he laughed, before a moment of contemplation descended. 'Do you want my advice or am I here just to listen?'

'Advice,' she said firmly. 'Definitely advice.'

'I think you need to sort things out with Drew before you even let Cameron into the picture.'

She let that one sit for a minute as she thought about it. He was right. She knew that. It was impossible to contemplate any kind of relationship with anyone else until she knew what was happening in her marriage.

'How'd you get so smart about these things?'

He did a mock bow. Tess thought he was just going to laugh it off. In the week they'd spent together, he'd never gone into any detail about what happened in his marriage.

'My wife left me. Met someone else. Said I worked too-long hours and I wasn't 'invested' in our marriage. Sound familiar?'

He said it without a trace of bitterness, just sad acceptance. 'That's why Dad hates her – because he saw me at my worst, when she'd just gone and I was devastated. The irony is she left me for my business partner and he always worked even longer hours than me. Not anymore.'

Tess pulled a cushion from the sofa into her chest and leaned her chin on it as she listened.

'I asked her to come back time after time, said I'd change, get it right, make her a priority, but she refused.'

'And how are you now?'

Max nodded. 'I'm doing OK. I can talk about it without anaesthetic. I actually think she did the right thing. We'd been together since we were in uni and I think if she hadn't left we'd have lived together forever in a kind of bland union that had settled into a rut about sixty years before its time.'

'What's her name?' Tess had no idea why that was important, but she wanted to know this woman, understand her, and a name would be a start.

'Belinda. Although according to Dad, that gets shortened to "cow".'

It was Tess's turn to top up the drinks this time, and she added in a couple of packets of crisps to the proceedings. She emptied them into a bowl, then moved over on to Max's sofa so that they could share them.

'Do you still want her back?' she asked, crunching a salt and vinegar Hula Hoop.

'No. But I just wish that she had given us a chance to resolve things before she moved on. Just a chance. I thought we deserved that.'

'You did.' It struck her. He did. And Drew deserved that chance, too. Except… The heat of Max's breath, only a few inches away from her face was having a strange effect on her. She must be drunk. Or giddy due to inhaling salt and vinegar fumes.

Suddenly, and totally unexpectedly, she had to fight the urge to kiss him. Blinking away the notion, she moved back to the other couch. What the hell was wrong with her? Were two complicated relationships not enough to be going on with? *Please tell me he didn't notice.* She searched his face for signs of discomfort, but there were none – just a chilled-out expression of care and contentment. She threw up a thanks to the Gods of

Oh-Crap-I-Nearly-Kissed-Someone-And-It-Would-Have-Been-Totally-Inappropriate.

'So what are you going to do tomorrow?' he asked.

Three Hula Hoops came between the question and the answer.

'I don't know. I honestly don't know.'

19.

Meet Me In Monaco

Sarah

Sarah pulled open the curtains and threw open the balcony doors, letting the warm morning air cut through the cool of the air-conditioning. She'd have burst into a chorus of 'The Sun Has Got His Hat On', if it weren't for the fact that she didn't want to risk waking the twins next door. On the bed, Eliza groaned and pulled a pillow over her head. Sarah immediately removed it and sang, 'Good morning darling,' in her highest, cheeriest voice. Eliza groaned again.

'You're going to make the most of this one, aren't you?' Drew mused, laughing. He'd slept on their sofa so he could help if Eliza was ill during the night. Thankfully, she hadn't been.

'Oh, yes. After the fright that I got last night, this girl will pay. Revenge will be merciless. It's the only way to ensure that she doesn't do it again.' The fact that she was giggling as she said it diluted the severity of her words down from ominous to teasing. 'Eli-za. Eliza darling,' she chirped. Loudly.

This time her daughter managed to get one eye open and recover some of her powers of speech. 'Don't. Feel. Well.'

'Yes, dear. I can understand that. I'm not a medical professional, but my official diagnosis is that this condition you are experiencing is a result of… what's the medical term, Drew? Oh yes, coming home pissed.'

The chilling revelation dawned on Eliza and she attempted to sit bolt upright, only to fall back down again. In the midst of the failed act, she absorbed the fact that Drew was there. 'Dad?'

'Yes, your father is here because you went missing last night. We had to call in the Italian police, and the coastguard only called off their search half an hour ago.' Behind her, she heard Drew swallow a chuckle.

'Honestly?' Eliza's voice was thick with fear.

'No. But you're in so much trouble you're going to wish that there was police protection involved.'

'I'm so sorry, Mum,' Eliza mumbled. 'And you too, Dad. Man, it's like, so weird seeing you both in the same room.'

'I'll leave you with that sunny thought while you go shower and brush your teeth. Twice,' Sarah remarked lightly. 'Right now, I'm going up to watch this ship sail into Monte Carlo. When I come back, we're going to discuss every form of punishment known to man, and then your dad and I will discuss which one we will use. Personally, I'm leaning towards putting a video of you throwing up during the night on to Facebook.'

'You didn't record that!' Eliza gasped.

'Shall we save that one for her wedding reception instead? What do you think, Drew?'

He could no longer even pretend not to be finding this hilarious. 'I think I'm glad I'm not on your bad side. Hang on and I'll come upstairs with you. In fact, why not come and watch the docking from our suite? We're right at the front so we've got a great view.'

Despite the fact that she'd much rather stick to her morning routine of watching the ship sail into port while sipping her morning coffee on deck fifteen, it was difficult to say no without hurting his feelings.

'Eliza, you and I are going to have a chat later on… I'll wait until after your mother has tortured you for a while longer.'

Eliza managed another long, pained grunt as her parents left, causing them to grin all the way to deck ten, where they picked up a pot of coffee before heading on up to Drew's suite on deck twelve. The lovely Colita, Brazil was still at the desk. Did she never go home?

'Ah, good morning,' she greeted them. 'Did you find your daughter?'

'We did, thank you, Colita,' Drew answered, then held open the door to their corridor.

When they reached the room, the first thing Sarah noticed was the empty glasses, beer bottles and crisp bowls. There was obviously a party here last night and for a moment she was sad she missed it.

The only light in the room came from a gap in the curtains, but it was enough to see that up on the mezzanine there was a large bump in the bed. Tess was still sleeping.

Sarah did a quick calculation. They hadn't got back to the cabin until well after 2 a.m., so if Tess had then had a bit of a party, she'd probably only been in bed for not much more than a couple of hours.

'Shall I go? I don't want to wake her. I can just take this upstairs,' she whispered, motioning to the coffee pot she was holding.

Drew shook his head. 'No, it's fine. Tess could sleep through an earthquake. We'll just go out on the balcony.'

Silently, he grabbed a couple of mugs from the table, then they slipped out into the sunlight, closing the door over behind them.

It was only when they were sitting watching the stunning panorama of Monte Carlo getting closer and closer, that Sarah remembered…

'Drew! Happy Birthday! I'm so sorry – with all the drama I completely forgot it was today.'

'Thank you. And don't worry – I'd be quite happy not to be reminded that I'm now fifty.'

'You're right. It's so old. Practically Jurassic. I'm absolutely sure you'll have arthritis and hair poking out of your ears by dinnertime.'

It was good to hear him laughing. Sarah hadn't spent much time with him on this trip, but when she saw him he always seemed to have the weight of the world on his shoulders.

'I miss this, Sarah.'

'What? Monte Carlo?'

'No – me and you, just talking. I miss you.'

Dumbstruck, she turned to face him. 'What? Drew we've been divorced for fifteen years. What is there to miss? Is this because you've turned fifty? Are you having a mid-life crisis and losing the plot?'

Humour was her only defence against a conversation that was making her just a tad uncomfortable.

'No. Over the last while I just realized that I made a mistake. All of it was a huge mistake. I should never have had the affair with Mona…'

'I'll give you that one – she's a torn-faced boot.'

It took a minute for him to recover from that. 'You're right. But she's a good person underneath all that hard stuff.'

'Drew, don't talk nonsense. It would be quicker to dig to the earth's core than to mine for Mona's hidden niceness.'

'True. But the fact remains, I shouldn't have gone there.'

This time there was no humour in her answer. 'No, you shouldn't. You broke up our family.'

'It was a mistake.'

'Yes.'

They were now about a hundred yards out from one of the most romantic cities in the world, yet Sarah was feeling anything but loving. Why open up old wounds? Why remind her of what she lost?

'I think that's why I married Tess.'

'What?' Sarah asked, astounded.

'It's taken me a while to realize it, but I think it was because she reminded me of you. You're alike in so many ways. I think I was trying to recreate what we had when we were twenty-five.'

'Did it work?' she asked doubtfully.

'No, because I'm fifty. I'm past that. I love Tess, but there's no denying that the age difference is a problem that becomes more prevalent every year. She's still wants to experience life – I just want to slow down a bit and savour it. In truth, I can see now that's why it was so important to me that you were here. I knew we'd appreciate this in the same way.'

Her chin would have hit the floor, if it wasn't engaged by the need to respond to what he'd just said. 'You're an idiot,' she said, calmly. 'You are so lucky to have her, Drew – she's special. She really is.'

'I know, but…'

Sarah's anger was rising now. 'Don't give me "but"!'

He matched her emotion, his normal cool, calm demeanour shed, a passionate argument in its place. 'Tell me you don't think it too! Tell me you never wonder whether we should have stayed together and tell me you don't think that if we were both single we could make a real go of it. We would be good together again, Sarah. I saw how you were last night – you wanted me there. If I let Tess go, then we could be happy.'

Sarah jumped up, sending her chair reeling backwards. 'No, we couldn't! Jesus, you are such a self-centred prick, Drew.

That poor girl… Argh, I want to bloody slap you. We. Could. Not. Be. Happy. Together. Yes, I was glad you were there last night because for once, ONCE, you were actively present when something was happening with the kids and it was good to have a bit of support. Believe me, it was a refreshing change. But do you know why we would never work? Because for the last fifteen years I've slowed down, savoured motherhood, let life go by me, but now? I'm ready to get out there and enjoy myself. In fact, if Tess has the good sense to send you packing I might see if she wants to bloody come with me. It's about time she started to live a bit instead of spending her whole life waiting for you!'

With the filthiest look she could muster, she turned, slid the door open and stormed back inside. At once, she realized that the room had changed, so she popped her head back out onto the balcony.

'Oh, and Romeo, your wife is no longer lying in bed. In fact, she's no longer here. So you'd better start praying she never heard any of your little speech there, otherwise you'll be needing a subscription to Match.com for your birthday. Arse.'

With that, Sarah walked out of Drew Gold's life. And it felt great.

Tess

The security guard at the top of the gangplank tried not to stare at the fact she was wearing pyjamas and her hair looked like an explosion in a straw bale. Tess didn't care. She really didn't care. *Bastard.* Drew, not the security guard, who was – she was sure – very lovely.

The moral of the morning was definitely 'Do not discuss your relationship when the door to where your wife is sleeping is very slightly ajar'. God, had this morning really happened? She'd heard Drew and Sarah come in, and stumbled out of bed to go say hello. She got to the doors just as he was getting to the good bit. So she was just a substitute for Sarah. Standing behind the curtain, she'd heard every word and it hurt like hell. Sod him. Sod Drew sodding Gold. She'd listened right up to where Sarah told him he was a prick and she wanted to slap him. That's the kind of attitude Tess needed. It was time for her to get a bit of fight about her and start sticking up for herself.

Everything made so much sense now. The disconnect in their relationship. The way he was never around. The fact that he didn't want children with her. He didn't want to spend the rest of his life with her – he was trying to convince himself as much as her that if they stayed together they'd have a great future. They'd both been kidding themselves on. It was all fake. All of it.

She showed her passport at the checkpoint and headed down the gangplank, then followed the crowd around the port on the Quai Antoine, veered right on to the Route de la Piscine, then immediately turned left, and ran up the pale stone steps. A sign at the top told her she was now on the Boulevard Albert 1er and she stopped to look around. It was exactly as she'd expected, only much, much busier. The road in front of her was already packed with gridlocked traffic, there were police everywhere, checking cars and trucks, but the views… It was spectacular. Up on the hills on the left-hand side she could see the cream walls

255

of the castle. To her right, high-rise buildings, most of them white, sitting side by side like a Lego village, rising up towards the hills that circled them like a protective cloak.

It was beautiful. Since she was a little girl, she'd imagined coming here. She just never anticipated that she'd be wearing pyjamas and white Converse trainers with no socks. They were the first things that came to hand when she'd dashed from the suite.

What a fool she'd been. No more. She pulled the map that had been left in their cabin last night from her bag, checked it, then walked briskly, following the promenade around towards the most built-up area. On her left were offices, shops, hotels – on her right, the sparkling blue waters of the seas, hundreds of gleaming white boats of all sizes in the Marina, and behind them the *Vistatoria*, sitting proudly in her dock.

The holdall on her shoulder dug into her skin, so when she saw an awning with the words 'Pizza, Pasta, Coffee' on it, she crossed the road and ducked inside. It was half-empty. An elderly man approached her with a smile.

'Mademoiselle?'

'*Un café, s'il vous plaît,*' she said, thrilled her high school French had left its mark.

While he went off to get it, she nipped in to the ladies and pulled everything out of her bag. She'd just snatched the first things that came to her in the wardrobe, so she could only hope there were the makings of a decent outfit. She surveyed the choices: one pink mini dress, one blue nightdress and a white jersey hoodie. Oh well, it was worth a try, but the pyjamas would have to stay on. At least it was sunny and adding the hoodie made it look more 'casual lounge wear' than 'off for a good eight hours' kip'.

Rummaging in the bottom of the bag she did, however, find a hairbrush and her make-up bag. She soaked her hair in the sink, then dried it into some kind of semblance of a style with the hand-dryer, then used some tinted moisturiser and Vaseline to tone down the stress-induced blotchy face.

It was only when she was back at the table that she noticed for the first time that all eyes were on a huge screen on the wall, watching a montage of clips of a man and a beautiful woman, waving at crowds. Of course! She'd read about this in *Hello!* magazine before she left, but hadn't registered the date.

One of the royal princes, she couldn't remember which one, was getting married this weekend.

'Monsieur,' she gestured to the friendly waiter. 'Le…le… wedding?' So much for her high school French.

He almost cheered his reply. '*Oui! Oui! Aujourd'hui. Hier a été la cérémonie civile. Aujourd'hui, ils auront la cérémonie religieuse au palais.*'

She got that. Yesterday was a civil ceremony and today was the religious ceremony at the palace. Mrs Catani, her ferocious French teacher, would be so proud.

The clips they were showing must be from yesterday's wedding, and now they were waiting for the next service to start. Oh, the irony. She was in the Principality of Monaco on one of the most special days in its history, the momentous occasion of a royal wedding, and she was sitting there in pyjamas, auditioning to be the poster girl for divorce. Or spousal homicide.

She checked her phone. Ten messages. Fifteen voicemails. Bugger it, she didn't care. She did however, notice the time. Ten o'clock. Two hours until Cameron said he'd meet her in the square. Going would be a bad idea. A really bad idea. Her life was a mess and meeting Cameron would only complicate it. He had no right to force her hand on this. She didn't ask him to come bloody galloping all the way from Glasgow to meet her there. She didn't need rescuing. This wasn't a flipping fairy tale.

No, she wasn't going. She would stay here until she'd calmed down and then go back aboard and request another room. Or stay with Max and Piers. Hell, she'd even stay with Mona if it meant she didn't have to see Drew's face again. Men were officially now a no-go area. All of them. She was done.

Three cups of coffee and a pain au chocolat later, she was still done.

She was.

Definitely.

And she was fed up of watching reruns of the same clips on that TV. The prince and new princess arriving for yesterday's civil ceremony. The prince and princess waving to crowds. The prince and princess going walkabout. Crowds streaming in to a seated area in front of the palace. Royals arriving. Superstars walking up red carpets. Prince Edward was there. Where was Victoria Beckham? Surely she'd be going.

Whatever. If there was any justice, the princess would be in a back room right now and her best pals would be telling her that there was a good bloody chance that whatever promises the prince made would turn out to be a sham and she'd end up sitting in inappropriate clothes crying her heart out into a bloody pain au chocolat.

That was it. Enough. She was going back to the ship. No Cameron, no Drew, no…

She sat back down. Cameron. He was here. He'd find this so funny.

'*Monsieur, où est la square?*' she said, hoping that she got the words right. Not that she was going. No. It was just curiosity.

'*La Place du Casino?*'

Cue blank look.

'The casino square?' he repeated in halting English.

'*Oui.*' It was the first thing that came to his mind, so surely that must be the place.

He picked up the map she'd left on her table and made a circle on it. Tess thanked him and paid the bill.

She wasn't going. No way. Definitely not.

She checked the time again. Eleven forty. It was too late anyway. She'd never get there on time. Back to the ship. *Turn right. Right! Turn right!*

Before she could stop herself she had turned left and started running. Bugger, why weren't there any taxis? They were all watching the royal bloody wedding. She clutched at the map and started running. She followed the Boulevard of Albert 1st until it merged into the Ave d'Ostende, then slipped over to her right and kept to the promenade. The *Vistatoria* was on her right now, the sun bouncing off its hull.

This place was like Disneyland but without the thousands of children. Every bush was perfectly manicured, every street spotless and every corner revealed another breathtaking building or view. Not that she had time to enjoy it, given that she was doing a Usain Bolt down the street. A sheen of sweat glistened on her face now, a perfect match for the attractiveness of her outfit. At every crossing, a galaxy of prestige cars went by: a red Lamborghini passed, a silver Bentley, a white Rolls Royce. She experienced a sudden pang of longing for her little yellow Ford Focus.

Eventually, after storming up an incline that stretched her

calves to breaking point, she was there. Fifteen minutes past twelve. Running to the middle of the road, she frantically looked around. The whole square was bedecked with white and red flags, flying from tall white poles, commemorating the day. The Hôtel de Paris was in front of her, the Casino de Monte Carlo to her left. Behind her a bloke in the flashiest car she'd ever seen was beeping his horn at her. She didn't care. Not a jot.

Because Cameron wasn't there.

Mona

'Where have you been?' Mona asked, as Piers wandered in at 10 a.m.

'I stayed with Max last night. I'll stay there tonight, too – just in case you want to invite the American over. It's fine. Don't mind me. And by the way, Eliza's fine. I know you were probably up all night fretting.'

His calm joviality and sarcasm had the perverse effect of sending her temper soaring. Damn him. If these weren't Jimmy Choo shoes one of them would be getting used as a missile.

'I want to know who it is.'

'Who what is?'

'Who you want to be with. Since it clearly isn't me, I want to know who it is. I think I have the right to know,' she demanded.

Her words were bolshier than she was feeling inside.

'Mona, you don't have any rights to know anything about me anymore. But I've got nothing to hide, so I'll tell you. Sarah.'

She wouldn't have been more surprised if he'd said it was the waiter who served his steak to him in the restaurant the other night.

'Sarah? Sarah Gold? Are you kidding me?'

He shook his head as he pulled a holdall up on to the table and started filling it with stuff from his drawer. 'No.'

'But you don't even know her! You only met her this fucking week. You've lost your mind, Piers, you really have. There is no way on this earth that you are passing *this* up,' she gestured to her body, 'for that fat bint, Sarah Gold.'

He paused, a rolled-up pair of socks in hand, and stared at her. 'You see, Mona, that just tells you why. Sarah would never say something like that. She has absolutely no idea of how bloody fabulous she is and that's the sexiest thing.'

'Aaargh,' she thrust her hands over her ears like they were being burned. Sexy? Sarah Gold? He'd lost his mind.

'And no, I haven't known her long, but that doesn't matter.

I'm old enough and I've been around long enough to know exactly what I want in life, and I knew it that first day in Palma.'

'Have you slept with her?' The notion made her want to gag.

'No.'

Mona snorted. The thought of being in love with someone without even having sex was ridiculous to her. What if they were incompatible? Let's face it – Piers was a pretty highly sexed guy, whereas Sarah didn't look like she'd had an orgasm since the eighties.

'Mona, I'm not going to get into this with you. I've told Sarah how I feel, she was having none of it. She's not interested. But that doesn't change anything between you and me. So you go ahead and do whatever you want to do. Let's try to keep it civil and we'll let the lawyers sort it out when we get home. No hard feelings, eh?'

Oh, she had plenty of hard feelings. Plenty.

The wall phone rang and she snatched it from the cradle.

'Mrs Gold, the car that you ordered is waiting at the dock for you.'

It was her last swansong. A day in Monte Carlo, shopping with Piers' credit card. She was determined to make it count. If she was going down in flames, she was going to go wearing Chanel, Yves St Laurent and Bulgari.

After picking up her favourite Chanel 2.55 bag, she clipped on large black pearl earrings and smoothed down her dress. It was vintage Balenciaga: a steel-coloured top with a Peter Pan collar and sleeves that finished at her elbows, with a row of tiny black buttons stretching from the neck down to the wide leather belt that pulled in her waist to impossibly small dimensions. The skirt was pencil tight to the knee, then flared into a fishtail at the back, stopping mid-calf. It was a statement piece – and the statement was, 'I'm expensive, stunning, and in this dress I'm fucking untouchable.'

By some power of osmosis, she sucked the attitude from the dress and without even bothering to say goodbye, strutted past Piers, giving him a back view of a body he would never touch again. *His loss.*

The chauffeur was waiting for her at the car, wearing a beautifully cut black suit and Versace shades. They knew how to do it in style here. Inside, he checked her out in his rear-view mirror as he introduced himself as Pascal and then, in perfect

English, asked her where she wanted to go. 'La Place Du Casino,' she replied in a flawless French accent. It was the hub of the best shops in the principality… and the most expensive.

The traffic was heavy as he cut up off the Avenue d'Ostende, on to the Avenue Princesse Alice, then turned right on to the Avenue des Beaux-Arts. Just as they came to a standstill behind a silver Bugatti Veyron, her mobile rang. The office. Guy.

She thought about ignoring it, but what was the point? She was going to have to face it and she might as well get it over with now and then block out the pain with some serious retail therapy.

'Hi,' she answered, trying not to sound like she was on the journalistic equivalent of death row.

'Mona, I'm sorry about this but the *News* has been on the phone again. They're not running the story this week because the lawyers haven't got everything signed off, but they're definitely leading with it next week.'

She didn't know if that was good news or bad. There was something to be said for it happening while she was out of the country. Maybe she just wouldn't go back. She could stay here until the money ran out and then get a job in Bulgari. At least her surroundings would be perfect.

'Right. Thanks for letting me know, Guy.'

'Are you going to defend it? We can't get it pulled, but we can run a counter story. Threaten to sue? Go the injunction route.'

She sighed wearily. She'd thought of all that, but really, what was the point? Hadn't all those super-injunction scandals featuring everyone from football players, to actors, to bank chiefs already proved that all that happens is the lawyers get very rich and the story eventually runs anyway?

Adrian was lying. She'd never used sex to blackmail him or harass him in anyway. But that wasn't the point. The story made her look pathetic – a woman approaching forty screwing a twenty-three-year-old in her lunch hour. The jokes would run forever.

'No, Guy, I don't want to add any more fuel to this. Leave it. Publish and be damned. I'll tell Drew tomorrow. I'm not going to say anything to him on his birthday.'

'Whatever you think. I'm sorry, Mona, I did what I could.'

She hung up, fairly sure that he hadn't done a damn thing.

Guy and at least a couple of dozen other aging hacks would love every minute of this. Mona didn't ever cry. Not ever. But suddenly, she could feel tears popping inside her lids, to accompany the excruciating twisting sensation in her stomach. Her life was over. When this ran, she would be left with nothing – and the first things to disappear would be her dignity and power.

One bold tear sprang free and ran down her right cheek. A pair of Tom Ford sunglasses were hastily put on to cover up her pain.

At that moment they came to a halt outside the Cartier store that sat on the corner beside the Hôtel de Paris. It was one of her favourite shops and the perfect place to start. A trinket from here and then she'd stroll the fifty yards or so along to Chanel. She had a few more days of being Mona Gold, the revered fashionista, and she might as well make the most of it. If this was death row, then she was about to have her last supper.

'Mrs Gold, can I ask where you are planning to visit?'

'I'll start in Cartier, Pascal.'

His gaze went immediately to the shop, then back to her. 'But Mrs Gold, I'm afraid that's not possible.'

'Why?'

'Because today is a public holiday. We have Royal wedding, Mrs Gold. The whole country is watching.'

Behind her Tom Fords, Mona closed her eyes and murmured an expletive under her breath. Death row sucked. This just could not get any worse. There was only one thing she could do.

'Drop me here, Pascal. I'll be in the bar of the Hôtel de Paris. And if you want to join me, that's absolutely fine by me.'

20.

What Happens In Monte Carlo...

Tess

He wasn't here. She'd missed him. Or maybe he hadn't come at all. Tess slumped down onto the edge of a huge plant pot next to the steps of the casino, fully expecting one of the nice security men in very smart hats to tell her to move. It didn't matter. Cameron wasn't here. Perhaps he'd realized how stupid the whole thing was and changed his mind. Or maybe it was a joke. Well, the joke was on her because he wasn't...

'Are you wearing your pyjamas?'

He was here.

She threw her head up and there he was, standing right in front of her, clutching two huge ice creams. 'I didn't think you were coming, so I went over there to get a cone and then I was just about to pay for it when I saw you. Thought you might want one too. It's chocolate chip. No donuts. What a pish place, eh?'

Tess had no idea whether she was laughing or crying, but there were tears and then his arms were around her and suddenly everything felt so, so much better. Even if she did drop her chocolate-chip ice-cream.

He held on to her tightly, burying his face in her hair, yet she still heard him whisper, 'I'm so glad you came. I so wanted you to be here.'

Pulling back, she realized that this was no place to say the things that needed to be said.

'Come on, let's go find somewhere to sit,' she told him, taking his hand and leading the way up to the Allée des Boulingrins, the beautiful garden area that swept up the hill in front of them. They found seats on the steps beside the fountain and for a moment they were both too stunned to speak. *Come on, this is Cameron. It shouldn't feel weird.*

'I don't know whether to hug you or… Oh, wow, this is so surreal. Those notes! Cameron, the notes – what the hell were you thinking?' she asked, her words hard, but her tone gentle.

'I just wanted to get you here. It worked, didn't it?' He grinned that incorrigible grin that won her over every time. This felt like it should be a movie moment, the big romantic ending that saw the heroine get swept off her feet by a man in a navy uniform or unfeasibly tight leather trousers.

'Cameron, this is crazy.'

'No, you wearing pyjamas is crazy. Is this a style trend that I missed?'

It was impossible not to laugh. 'It's a long story. Major drama with Drew this morning and I left before I could get dressed.'

Cameron's expression immediately flipped to the dark side. 'And how is Drew? Still going for an award for shite husbandry?'

'Cameron…' There was no mistaking the warning in her voice, but just as she said it her bottom lip wavered. Why was she defending him? Hadn't he stamped all over her loyalty this morning? 'He told his first wife that he should never have left her and that he only married me because I reminded him of her.'

The tears sprang right back up again and this time there was no stopping them.

'I mean, how could he do that? Was it all just a lie? Was I always just a poor replacement for Sarah?'

Cameron shook his head and tenderly pushed her hair back off her face. 'God, no! Tess, you could never be a poor replacement for anyone. Drew's an idiot. He always has been.'

Ignoring the intrigued stares of several other tourists who were milling around, she rubbed tears off her cheeks with the palm of her hand. She felt sorry for the German couple in front of her who would get home, look at their holiday snaps and realize that their most romantic photograph had a woman in the background wearing overly casual clothes and sporting a bright red blotchy face.

'Tess, forget him. Come back with me tonight. We'll go to Nice, fly home, you can stay at mine until… um, well, forever.'

It was a great idea. Walk away. Don't look back. Move along.

Nothing to see here.

Right now her admittedly cracked heart was overflowing with love for the man in front of her. She adored him. Absolutely adored him. Couldn't ever imagine life without him.

But…

'Cameron, I can't. I wish I could and then it would be this great big happy ending…'

'It could be,' he insisted.

'It couldn't, Cameron,' she said softly. 'Drew married me wishing that I was someone else and look where that got us. I could never do that to you. I love you so much – you're the best friend I could ever have – but it wouldn't be fair to tell you that we could make it as a couple because I don't think we could. I need you in my life, Cameron. Every day if possible. But I'm not *in* love with you and I'm so sorry – I really wish I was.' Gallons of tears accompanied the last crack as her heart broke in two.

It was so brutal, so harrowing to say these things to him, but it would be even more cruel to pretend that she felt something that she didn't.

His head went down and a few long, tense moments passed before he reacted. He lifted his eyes to meet hers and gave her the saddest smile.

'I knew. But I had to try. I think I've always known. If we were going to be together then it would have worked out before now. You would have woken up one morning, realized you couldn't live without me, dumped the tosser and come running after my body.'

The fact that he was still being funny made her love him even more.

'I'm sorry.'

'Don't be.'

'Please don't cut me out of your life, Cameron. I know it's selfish, but I don't ever want you to say goodbye.'

'I never could.'

There was a long pause as they stared at each other, sad smiles on both their faces.

'So what happens now?' Tess whispered.

'I go home. You leave Drew. You come to work. We pretend nothing has happened. I tell you stories about my Brazilian girlfriend. You tell me she's not good enough for me because I'm a one hundred per cent love god.'

She was laughing now, laughing so hard that the tears were back. 'Indeed you are. I thought you'd split with her anyway?'

'I did, but she wants me back.'

'Understandable.'

'I think so.'

Nothing would ever compare to the connection that she had with this man. If she felt a different kind of love for him then life would be perfect. But she'd rather risk losing him than pretend that they had something that wasn't there, because she knew exactly how much that hurt.

Cameron stretched as he got to his feet. 'I'm going to go now, before I do something very unmanly like cry and clutch on to your ankle, begging you to change your mind.'

'OK.' Tess didn't want him to go, but she understood. She stood up and pulled him in close to her. 'Cameron, I love you,' she whispered.

He leaned down and kissed her. 'I know you do.'

And then he was gone.

Sarah

Sarah spent the morning walking around the principality, marvelling at the grand houses, enjoying the serenity of the parks and gardens, and thinking about Tess. In the Cathedral of Saint Nicholas, she paused at the tombs of Princess Grace and her husband, Prince Rainier, then lit a candle, finding comfort in the silence and peace of the church. Then she thought about Tess again.

On she went, wandering up side streets, her gaze never still, always moving from one stunning spectacle to another, torn between treasuring every moment of this and worrying about Tess.

Soon she'd seen all the highlights mentioned in the guidebook she'd picked up at the excursion desk before leaving the ship.

This, however, she'd saved until last.

La Place du Casino. Casino Square. The sight of it filled her with such excitement that for a moment she was sad that she had no one there to share it with. However, giddy wonder soon pushed any sadness to one side. She strolled down past the shops and cafes on one side of the square, cut across in front of the steps up to the legendary casino, then completed the U-shape by staring in the windows of the fabled Hôtel de Paris as she walked past its majestic entrance. For a moment she toyed with the idea of going in, but of course she didn't. It was far too grand, too intimidating. Even in her navy Monsoon maxi dress (the most expensive of her Patsy-personal-shopper purchases), with layers of silver chains around her neck, she would feel out of place. Maybe next time. Perhaps one day she would come back here with the next love of her life and they'd drink champagne in the bar and revel in the electric atmosphere of it all.

Moving slowly through the throngs of people crowding the pavements, Sarah walked up the incline, past Cartier and

Celine, then crossed to the breathtaking gardens in the middle of the road.

That was where she encountered an image that must surely be a figment of her imagination.

'Tess? Tess, are you OK?' Sarah moved quickly over to the younger woman, who was sitting on the steps beside the fountain, in her pyjamas, staring at the water, locked in some kind of trance.

Sarah's arm stretching around her shoulder snapped her out of it and she turned to meet her eyes.

'Tess?' Sarah repeated, searching her friend's face for a hint of what she was feeling. 'I'm so sorry about this morning. I promise you I had no idea. I really didn't. If I'd known, I would have…'

'Sarah, I know that you didn't. I don't blame you for any of this.'

Sarah relaxed properly for the first time all day, every muscle in her body heavy with relief. That candle in the cathedral had somehow worked.

'I was so worried about you. The best thing that has come out of this holiday is getting to know you and I couldn't stand the thought that you might believe I'd done anything to hurt you.'

Tess flopped her head down on to Sarah's shoulder. 'I didn't, I promise. I heard him, though, Sarah. I heard what he said.'

'He's an arse,' Sarah replied.

'My friend Cameron just said the same thing.'

Sarah glanced around. Surely she didn't mean he was here? The phone. Must be the phone. 'You called him?'

'No, he just left.'

Oh, bugger, the poor girl was imagining things.

Tess pulled her head up, looked at her and smiled sadly. 'I'm not imagining things, I promise. He just left.'

Nothing to lose, she pulled the notes out of her bag and handed them over to Sarah, then told her the whole story.

'So what did you say?' Sarah could barely breathe as she waited for the answer.

'I said "no". I couldn't lie to him.'

'Do you want to work things out with Drew?'

Tess's shoulders slumped as she whispered, 'No.'

Sarah squeezed her a little tighter. 'Tess, Drew doesn't know what he's lost. He's a fool. A total fool.'

'I prefer "arse",' Tess added, with the closest thing to levity that she'd managed since she watched Cameron walk away.

'Yes, it does have a ring of authenticity to it,' Sarah agreed. 'So no Drew and no Cameron. You know my spare room is always free and there's a very nice single man who calls regularly on behalf of the local senior citizen charity.'

'Generous – but I think I'll pass.'

Every time Tess spoke or smiled, it reinforced to Sarah just what a mixed-up idiot her ex-husband had turned out to be.

'What about you? How did things turn out with Tim McGraw?'

Sarah sighed. 'I was about to do filthy things to him when I discovered he wore Speedos. It was a passion killer.'

The two of them were giggling now, so loudly that people were beginning to stare.

'Tess, can I ask you something?'

'I've never had sex with a man in Speedos. Was that the question?'

'No. Have you ever been in the Hôtel de Paris?'

'Sadly not.'

'Do you want to go?' Sarah's face was alive with excitement. It was a great idea. The best. Bloody brilliant.

'When?'

'Now?'

'No!'

Sarah groaned, 'Why not? I'm dying to go in and after the week we've both had we really should damn them all. Let's drink champagne in the Hôtel de Paris. Incidentally, if you feel a vibration that's my MasterCard cacking itself.'

'Sarah, I'm wearing pyjamas.'

'I know. I didn't like to say. Let's go buy something for you to wear.'

'All the shops are shut.'

Sarah just kept batting back every objection. 'But there's bound to be one in the hotel that's open. Those places never shut.'

Tess's mouth was opening and closing like a puffer fish, unable to come up with a worthwhile argument.

Sarah took that as permission to proceed, pulled her pal to her feet and they walked briskly down to the hotel, fortunately managing to duck in the door when the security guards were busy giving directions to a large group of golf-trouser-wearing Americans.

Inside, Sarah threw back her shoulders, adopted an air of confident entitlement, and strutted over to the concierge to ask directions to the shops.

They were in luck.

The instructions took them across the opulent lobby, under the most spectacular chandelier Sarah had ever seen. Her heart soared. This was such a great idea.

Barely ten minutes later, Tess was wearing a fine silk cream jersey T-shirt, black crepe trousers and simple black wedges. She was also refusing to let Sarah pay, insisting that she use her own credit card.

The shop assistant, a Slavic blonde with cheekbones that could balance spoons, rang up the purchases on what looked like a control centre for NASA.

'That will be…'

'Don't tell me!' Tess begged. 'Just put it on this card and leave me in denial. Sarah, have I just spent the cost of a car on an outfit?'

Sarah leaned over and checked the display on the till. 'Half a car. Maybe a small starter model. You're right, it's best that you don't know.'

'OK, where to now? I can't believe we're here. This is so irresponsible, yet it feels so absolutely right. Let's go.'

They followed directions to the American Bar and as they walked in the first thing they noticed was the grandeur of the room. The second thing they noticed was the piano player, filling the room with smoky, intoxicating jazz. The third?

'Sarah, do you see what I see?' Tess gasped.

Sarah nodded. Oh dear God, why? Why? What had she ever done to deserve this? A huge big fat seminal moment in her life and she could almost hear the Dyson sucking the joy out of it.

'Well, well, well – ladies! Isn't this a small world? Come! Pull up a chair!'

Sarah was absolutely crushed. 'Is she really here or am I just locked in some freakish nightmare?' she hissed.

'Nope, she's here,' Tess replied. 'And by the looks of it, she's been here for a long, long time.'

Mona

'It's Sarah! And Tess! Sarah and Tess! Helloooooooooo. Come sit down. Sit! Two of my least favourite people. Is Piers with you? That would make it truly the most shit party ever." Somewhere inside, pickled by alcohol, Mona had decided there was no point fighting it any more. Better to just embrace life's crapness and roll with it.

She thought about standing up to greet them, but wasn't entirely confident in her balance skills. Perhaps that last glass of Cristal had been a mistake. In fact, perhaps that last bottle of Cristal had been one too many.

'Sit! Sit!' she repeated, then was overcome by a fit of the giggles when she realized she sounded like a demented dog trainer barking out instructions. She'd be going for 'heel' and 'roll-over' next. Great commands when dealing with bitches.

The lovely waiter, Jean Paul, materialized as if out of thin air. Mona ordered another bottle of champagne and two more glasses. The two new arrivals didn't seem overly thrilled, but then they were hardly in their natural habitat. That would be… dunno… *Travel Inn? Holiday Inn Express? IKEA?* She had no idea where that last thought came from or why it was so funny, but it just was.

Her attention was suddenly taken by the images on the screen in the corner. A prince, dressed in his white ceremonial uniform, and his beautiful bride, standing in front of the priest, preparing to commit to spending the rest of their lives together.

'Don't do it, love!' Mona blurted, louder than she meant to, earning her furious stares from everyone within earshot.

She saw a look pass between Tess and Sarah. Those two were as thick as thieves these days. Thick. As. Thieves. Not far off the mark, really. Hadn't Tess stolen Drew from her? And now Sarah was stealing Piers. The bitches had so much in common.

'Mona, are you OK?' Sarah asked.

'Oh, yes, act all concerned, when we all know that you can't stand me. Well, go ahead and enjoy it, because you're going to love what happens over the next couple of weeks.'

'Why? What's going to happen?' Sarah asked.

Oh shit, had she said that last bit out loud? Oops.

Mona ignored the question, deciding it was time for some other home truths. What did she have to lose? She had nothing left. 'I don't know what he sees in you,' she slurred, looking at Tess. 'I mean, you're very nice. Very, very nice. And young. And pretty. But what do you have in common? Nothing. Sweet bugger all.' She finished her point with what she thought was a very elegant sweep of her glass. Her sleeve was now soaking.

She expected Tess's bottom bloody lip to start quivering like it usually did, but no, the other woman sat up a little straighter and stared right at her.

'Do you want to do this now Mona? Do you really want to?'

There was no mistaking the edge of challenge in Tess's voice. Well, who knew she had it in her?

'If you want Drew you can have him. I don't. Our marriage is over.'

'What? But he said…'

'It doesn't matter what he said. He doesn't want me. In fact, it's actually Sarah he wants.' Another look passed between them. 'But Sarah doesn't want him. And I don't blame her. So there we go. Feel free to give it your best shot.'

Mona was utterly gobsmacked and struggled until the words finally came. 'Sarah, have you got, like, paranormal knickers or something?'

This time it was Sarah who almost choked on her bubbles.

Mona wasn't done. 'I mean, Drew wants you, and apparently my husband is leaving me for you, too.'

Tess had to thump Sarah's back after that one.

Emergency intervention over, Tess was looking at Sarah expectantly now, too. 'Piers?'

Sarah shook her head wearily. 'That day in Sorrento. When Piers and I went ashore. He told me had feelings for me.'

'Wey-hey!' Mona cheered, knocking back another glug of champers.

'Oh my God, he didn't!' Tess gasped. 'I wondered what had happened when you two seemed weird with each other. What did you say?'

'I told him I wasn't interested.'

273

'Wey-hey!' Mona repeated, with another champagne chaser, then focussed on Sarah again. 'Sarah, you can have him. We're over. I appreciate that you knocked him back out of some moral… moral…' She got stuck on that. 'Some moral… thingy, but honestly don't hold back on my account. Poetic justice, eh? I took your husband and now my husband wants you. We're like a frigging soap opera.'

Sarah didn't reply, just waited as Jean Paul intervened to top up their glasses. He diplomatically skipped Mona's, but she just did it herself as soon as he was gone.

'I'm sorry I did that to you, Sarah, but I loved him. All's fair in love, eh?'

Sarah wasn't buying it. 'No,' she replied quietly. 'It's not.'

'Did I tell you he knocked me back, Tess?' Mona was getting confused now. *Note to self. Do not drink any more.* 'After everything, he knocked me back.'

'Yes, you told me,' Tess replied wearily. 'But what do you mean, "everything"?'

Bugger it, what did it matter if they knew?

'I wasn't even invited on this trip at first. Just you two. The two peas in a badly dressed pod.'

That required a short giggle before moving on. 'So I practically begged him. Told him Piers would love it. That Max had always wanted to cruise the Med. Then used Max as leverage to make Piers come. See! It takes skill to manipulate every side. But I thought that once we were here, I'd get him.'

Tess sat forward in her chair. 'Mona, if you wanted him so badly, why did you split up in the first place?'

'Ah, the big question!'

Sarah interjected. 'You don't know this?' she asked Tess. 'She slept with someone else. A football player, wasn't it?'

Mona nodded. 'Bit of a misjudgement. Thought Drew was losing a bit of interest and a tug of jealousy might nudge him back on course. I can still hear the sound of the backfire.' Ah, she might be pissed but she still had a way with words, she decided. Maybe she could be a poet after her life was destroyed next weekend. A poet. Mona the poet. 'Anyway, I know you both hate me.'

It still hurt just a twinge when neither of them objected. She handled it by sailing into fully-fledged martyr mode.

'You'll totally enjoy next weekend, then. I'm ruined. Done.

Going to be a laughing stock. So stick that in your... your... wellies and smoke it.'

'What are you talking about?' Tess asked, and Mona could see that she was clearly faking concern.

'Story coming out in the news about me shagging a young hot stud. All true. Dick the size of a small sausage, though. Don't think that will be in the story, will it? A kiss and tell. On me. I'm fucked. In all ways.'

Shit, those bloody tears were coming again. Sleep. Maybe she just needed to close her eyes. She felt herself swaying over to one side, then stopping as one of them caught her. She wasn't sure which one. They were both kind of blending into each other now.

'Want to go home. Just want to go home.'

She felt one of them on each side of her now. 'Come on, Mona,' she heard. The voice sounded nice. Kind. 'Let's get you to bed.'

21.

Barcelona

Sarah

'I thought I'd find you up here. Creature of habit.'

Sarah smiled, recognizing that Piers was using his ebullient banter to disguise the fact that he was nervous. He was right, though. She hadn't wanted to miss seeing the voyage end as they sailed into Barcelona.

'I just wanted to say thanks again for getting Mona home last night. She wasn't in the best of shape. Smelled like she'd spent the day lying on a pub floor.'

'Our surroundings were a bit more glamorous than that,' Sarah replied. 'In fact, I think you'll discover that when you get your next credit card bill.'

'I already checked it online. Just as well we're divorcing – I'd end up bankrupt if she goes on the drink.'

Sarah took another sip of her coffee, not sure what to say. She'd thought a lot about this. In fact, for third night in a row she'd had a restless, fitful sleep.

'Mona told me it was over. I'm sorry.'

Piers shrugged. 'Me too. But it's for the best. We're just weren't right for each other. Never were. She's looking for something that I don't know exists.'

'A twenty-five-year-old Drew?' Sarah suggested.

'You could be right,' he said with a smile.

There was an awkward silence, as Piers shuffled from one foot to the other. This was so out of character that Sarah almost felt sorry for him.

'So I'll go now,' he blustered. 'We're disembarking shortly. Thanks again. Er, take care, Sarah. And I'm sorry about... you know… about…'

'I'll go out with you.' Bugger. Had she actually said that? She had. And she meant it.

'About… what?' He whipped around to see her face, trying to gauge whether or not this was some crazy joke.

'I'll go out with you. I've thought about it all night and I've decided that if you still want to see me, then I'll go out with you. Mona approves. Although she was pissed at the time. Not that I give a toss what she thinks. But you'll have to be officially separated first because I'm not…'

She didn't finish because she was up off her feet being swung around the deck with a joy that Kate Winslet and Leonardo DiCaprio never managed to find on Titanic.

When he finally put her down, it was only to hold her even closer, before kissing her, really kissing her in a manner that was way too exuberant for a ship's deck at 6 a.m. Sarah loved every single second of it. The cowboy in Speedos felt so wrong, and now she realised why. This felt so, so right.

It was time. Time for her, time for Piers, and time to start living with some serious love in her life. Not that this was love. Not yet. Obviously. Well, maybe.

"But… She pulled back. 'There's just one thing, Piers.'

'Anything.' His eyes sparkled and his jaw was split from one side to the other in the widest grin. She'd made him smile like that and it felt great.

'I know that you have a lot of sway and a lot of power at home. So there's one thing I need you to do for me.'

Mona

Mona snapped the lock on her vanity case shut and had one last look around the room. The porters had taken their suitcases away half an hour ago, so all that remained was for her to carry off her hand luggage, then head home. The knot of anxiety in her throat sat heavily on the two painkillers she'd knocked back to attempt to quell the worst hangover in history. She didn't even want to think about that. She could clearly remember the things she'd said to the other women and it wasn't her proudest moment. Not that she cared. She'd never had female friends and that was unlikely to be something that would change any time soon, especially in any scenario featuring those two. In fact, this time next week, what friends she did have would be distancing themselves from her as quickly as they possibly could. She had one more week. Seven days, until the story came out that would ruin her.

With a deep, pained sigh, she brushed a few imaginary flecks of dust off her shoulders and adjusted the hemline of her jacket. She was wearing a deep aubergine suit with a short, peplum jacket and her customary pencil skirt. Black patent shoes with block heels and a Fendi shoulder bag completed the outfit. With her hair styled like a forties Wren, she looked nothing like a woman facing the worst experience of her life.

Bag on shoulder, vanity in hand, room checked, she headed for the door, only to jump back when Piers swung it open.

'Good morning,' he said in a friendly tone. 'How are you feeling?'

'Fine,' she replied. If he wanted to go the cordial route it was fine with her. They were both at fault in this. No point in finger-pointing and bearing grudges.

'What's your plan?' he asked her.

'I'll go back to our house, pack up, and find somewhere else to live. If you would stay in a hotel for a couple of days, I'll let you know when I'm done.'

'You can keep the house,' he said, causing her eyes to narrow with suspicion.

'What? But I never contributed to that house. It's yours.'

'Do you want it?' he asked her, like he was talking about a pint of milk or the last roll at breakfast.

'Of course!'

'Then have it.'

The delight had barely begun to bubble when reality came calling. What was the point? There was no way she could stay in Glasgow after the story ran.

'What is this – a guilt gift? For tossing me aside?'

'I think you'll find I wasn't the one doing the tossing,' he barbed.

She had no energy left to fight. Instead, she gathered her things again and took a step towards the door. 'Have it. After next week it won't matter anyway.'

'Are you talking about the story the *Sunday News* is planning to run?'

She stopped. Turned. Closed her eyes. 'How did you know?'

'Sarah told me.'

Of course she did. She probably loved it. They were probably counting the hours until it came out and…

'It's dead. The story is gone. Won't happen.'

'But… but… how?' Was this some kind of joke? Was he baiting her, lulling her into a false sense of security? First the house, and now this – it didn't make sense. He was up to something. Had to be.

'I spoke to Jay Lemming at the *News* and we came to an arrangement. He's been trying to get my advertising for years. Now he has it. The ads will be featuring a model called Adrian, who I believe is currently suffering from amnesia caused by the excitement of getting the gig.'

Mona reached to hold on to the table, as the intense gratitude and relief made her quite literally go weak at the knees. 'Thank you, Piers. Thank you,' she whispered.

'You're welcome,' he replied. 'I hope you find happiness, Mona – but I didn't do this for you, I did it because Sarah asked me to.'

Tess

Drew handed Tess her bag and then hugged her tightly. 'Are you sure you won't come back with us?'

She shook her head. 'No. Not yet,' she said, her voice thick with emotion. 'I'm sorry about your birthday dinner last night. I hope you had a good time.'

'I actually did. John and Penny and the kids were on great form, and Eliza brought Kai. He's a nice boy. I made sure they stuck to orange juice all night.'

Missing his celebration meal in Monte Carlo wasn't a deliberate act of spite or vengeance. By the time they'd got Mona back to her cabin, put her to bed, then watched her for a while to make sure she didn't fall out or throw up, it was too late to join the party. Instead, Tess had used the time to think. By the time Drew came back to the cabin, she had been ready to talk the situation through with him without feeling the urge to throw out insults and recriminations. It was time to move on. No point in looking back.

They headed down to the gangplank, and handed their passes in for the last time, before heading to the minibus Drew had hired to transport some of the group to the airport. She'd opted out of going with them and apparently, Mona had already left in a limo. Of course she had. Tess said goodbye to John, Penny, the twins, Eliza and Sarah, hugging them all tightly and promising to call Sarah soon. She meant it. Even when she was no longer a Gold, she knew Sarah would be in her life forever.

When everyone else was aboard the bus, Drew came back around to where she stood on the concourse and kissed her softly. 'I'm sorry, Tess.'

She knew that he meant it. 'Me, too.'

She waited until they were out of sight before turning to head back to the taxi rank. She was almost there when a black limo pulled up next to her and Max and Piers jumped out.

'Hey, congratulations,' she told Piers. 'I hear we have

something to celebrate.'

He bowed, his face flushing with happiness.

'I'm just going to nip back in to the loo. It's my age,' he said with a wink.

Max leaned back against the car. 'I know it wasn't exactly a peaceful trip, but I had a great time with you. I'm glad I came.'

'I am, too,' she told him truthfully. 'I hope everything works out for you.'

'So where are you off to?'

She shrugged. 'I'm not sure yet. My boss has agreed to give me a leave of absence for a month, so I'll stay in Barcelona for a few days and work out what I want to do.' It felt strange even saying that. For the first time in years, she was going to make her own plans. She wasn't sure whether sadness or excitement topped her emotional scale right now.

'You know, I was thinking about doing that myself.'

'Really?' she thought about it for a moment then made a spontaneous decision. Maybe it was time for her to take a few chances too. 'Company would be good. I'd like…'

'Holy fuck, tell me I'm not seeing that.' It was Piers. He'd reappeared beside them and was staring at a point over their shoulders. Both Max and Tess spun round, but Tess didn't see the problem. There was a line of taxis. A few people milling around. A very tall blonde female – hang on, she was walking towards them, her gaze unequivocally fixed on Max.

'Someone you know?' Tess asked, confused.

'Un-fucking-fortunately.' Piers whistled.

'Dad!' Max reprimanded him. 'Yes, I know her. That's my wife.'

Epilogue
One Year Later

'Sarah, you are stunning. Absolutely stunning.'

Tess gave her friend a huge hug. It wasn't a false compliment. Sarah's cream, one-shouldered Grecian dress fell in glorious waves to the floor, her hair, much longer now, piled up on her head with loose tendrils falling around her face. She was the most beautiful bride Tess had ever seen.

'Mona helped me pick it.' Sarah giggled. 'She made me promise not to spill anything on it, tear it, or accidentally tuck it into my knickers when I go to the loo. She still thinks I'm a hopeless fashion case.'

Tess spotted Mona, in stunning cerise with a hat the size of a tyre, working the room. 'How are things going with you two?'

'Good, actually. Can you believe it? She hasn't changed – still brittle with a twist of evil – but at least she's now civil. I think the winner was Piers giving her the house and moving in here. Oh, and Dweezil. Since she started shagging him she's had a much sunnier disposition. Listen, you know Drew's here. Are you OK with that? He's got his new girlfriend with him. I think she's twenty-two. They're going to Ibiza next week.'

'So much for slowing down! I'm fine with it, honestly. I'm happy for him, I promise. I just hope he doesn't pull a muscle on the dance floor.'

'Good,' Sarah said, unable to resist giving her another hug. 'Anyway, enough about us – tell me about you. You're looking great.'

'That's what eleven months touring South America in a camper van does for you. It was a riot. My mum and dad are still over there, but they're heading north. My mother reckons she's not too old to crack Hollywood.'

They were both still laughing when Piers joined them and cuddled Tess until she couldn't breathe.

'How are you doing, my love?'

'I'm great, you handsome big devil.'

He beamed. 'Can you believe we got married in our garden? I've wed the cheapest bride ever.'

'And you love it,' Sarah reminded him. Not that she had to.

'Yes, I do. I really do.' He kissed her tenderly, making Tess's heart melt, then took her by the hand. 'Can I borrow my wife, Tess? We've got a cake to cut.'

'Go ahead.'

They were only gone a second when another familiar face walked towards her.

'Hey, stranger.'

'Max! It's so good to see you!' He was beyond smart in his black suit, with his bow tie hanging undone around his neck.

'So, I hear you went travelling.'

She gave him the pamphlet edition of her travels through Columbia, Argentina, Bolivia, Peru and Brazil. It had been a wild, dangerous adventure – more because of her dad's driving than anything else.

'I just need to find a new job now,' she added. 'They couldn't keep it open for me for longer than a month, so I quit.' It wasn't worrying her. She was down to the last of her savings, but she had a few interviews lined up. And if all else failed, well, there was always Hollywood with her mother.

As a waiter passed, Max grabbed two glassed of fizzy stuff and handed one to her. 'What about Cameron?'

Tess chuckled. 'We actually met up with him and his girlfriend in Brazil. They're living there now and she's infatuated with him. He loves it. You should see her, Max – she looks like Gisele's more attractive sister. The last time I saw them they were dirty dancing on a rainforest float at the carnival. I think me turning him down was the best thing that ever happened to him.'

'I doubt that,' he said with a twinkle in his eye. 'I definitely doubt it.'

'Oh, really?' she toyed with him. It felt so good to be talking to him again. How many times had she thought about him over the last few months? Ah, if only…

She looked around, searching for the obvious missing person.

'Where's your wife? She couldn't make it?'

She'd forgotten how his eyes glistened when he smiled.

'I'm not married any more. Last time I saw her was that day at the port in Barcelona. As soon as I spoke to her I realised it wasn't what I wanted so I told her it wouldn't work. As far as I know she's back living with my ex-partner again.'

'Ex?'

'Yeah, I sold the business, moved up here to work with Dad.'

'Interesting,' she replied with mock seriousness.

'So I was wondering if, maybe some night you're not busy, or in, say, Peru, if we could maybe go out for dinner.'

She didn't even get the 'yes' out before he'd leant over, gently put his hand on the side of her face, and kissed her – a deep sensual kiss that she didn't ever want to stop.

'Hey, you two, that's enough. I'm the only one that's allowed to snog a hot chick here today.'

The entire crowd laughed at Piers' reprimand, and he held their attention. 'Ladies and gentlemen, my wife and I…'

Thunderous applause.

'Would like to cut our wedding cake.'

Sarah's friend Patsy wheeled out an enormous bosom, its modesty protected only by a huge white frilly marzipan bra.

The crowd went wild.

'That's so embarrassing!'

Tess heard the voice behind her and turned to give Eliza's hand a squeeze. She was with her new boyfriend, Josh, having decided that he was a much better option than having a long-distance relationship with a boy who lived hundreds of miles away.

The bride and groom kissed again, then made a speech thanking everyone for coming and announcing that they would shortly be leaving to go on honeymoon.

'Where are you going?' shouted a voice from the crowd.

Piers turned to his bride and kissed her again.

'I've no idea,' Sarah replied. 'Just as long as it's not a cruise.'

We hope you enjoyed this book!

Shari Low's next book is coming in spring 2017

For an exclusive preview of Shari's Low's *The Story of Our Life*, read on or click the image

More addictive fiction from Aria:

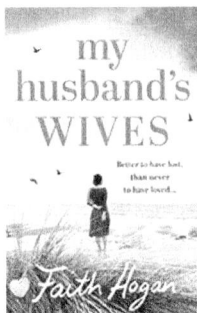
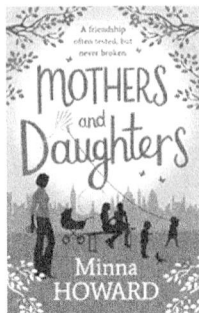

Find out more
http://headofzeus.com/books/isbn/9781784979560

Find out more
http://headofzeus.com/books/isbn/9781784977153

Find out more
http://headofzeus.com/books/isbn/9781784975852

Acknowledgements

To Caroline Ridding and the brilliant team at my wonderful
new home, Aria.

Thank you. xx

Preview

Read on for a preview of *The Story of Our Life:*

So what would you do if your husband slept with another woman?

Colm strolled into my life fifteen years ago. If there's ever such a thing as love at first sight, that was it for us both. A few weeks later we married, celebrating with those who cared, ignoring the raised eyebrows of the cynics. We knew better. This was going to be forever. The dream come true. The happy ever after.

Until it wasn't.

Because a couple of months ago everything changed. We discovered a devastating truth, one that blew away our future and forced us to revisit our past, to test the bonds that were perhaps more fragile than they seemed.

So now I ask you again, what would you do if your husband slept with another woman?

Because this is what I did. I'm Shauna. And this is the Story of Our Life…

Can't wait? Buy it here now!
http://headofzeus.com/books/isbn/9781784978242

When love at first sight
lasts forever.

The Story of
our
Life

Shari Low

1

Spring 2016

At the Church

Fifteen years ago, I walked up the same church aisle.

Back then, the first person I saw was Annie, my gloriously indomitable grand-mother, in dramatic purple and a hat that resembled a frisbee, disguising her tears because she was born of a stoic generation that was disdainful about crying in public.

Next to my grandmother were my parents. My father, resplendent in his best morning suit and golfing tan, no doubt keen to get the formalities over with so he could squeeze in nine holes in before dinner. Meanwhile, the woman who gave birth to me was preening, loving the attention being mother of the bride brought her, while breezily overlooking the fact that she'd shown no interest whatsoever in her daughter's wedding. When I called her to tell her we'd set a date, she'd said, 'Oh right, Shauna. Let me write that down so I don't forget it. I think we were planning to be in Spain that weekend. I'll check my diary.' Still, she'd made it. My gain was the Marbella Golf Club's loss.

In the rows behind the star attractions, a sea of smiles beamed at us as we walked down the aisle. Steps behind me, were my best friends, Lulu and Rose in matching pastel elegance. Was it okay to call them 'best friends' at our age? Did that belong back in the days of teenage territorialism? Okay, so my 'closest' friends, their grins masking hangovers that were crying out for a dark room and a box set of *Grey's Anatomy*.

Rosie, a hopeless romantic, had been on board with the wedding from the start, but Lulu had been resistant, listing all the reasons I should wait and keep my options open. I was only 24. My catering company was growing and would demand lots of attention. I was an independent woman with a flat, a job I loved, a bank account that was (just) in the black. And besides, a piece of paper didn't matter to a relationship. Marriage was an outdated institution. Married women inevitably dumped their friends in favour of nights in, pandering to their men while gaining five pounds a month and neglecting their roots – hair, not ancestry.

Not for the first time, I ignored her.

And the reason was there in front of me. Colm. My gorgeous Colm. Standing there at the altar, in a suit that fitted him to perfection, showing not a trace of nerves. His expression radiated enjoyment, like this was a party he'd been looking forward to for ages and now he was thrilled it was starting.

I was too.

I wanted to dance towards him, sashay and pirouette into his arms, skip straight to the kissing and cheering part.

I saw flowers, and light and love. I saw promise. Commitment. Belonging. Delight. Contentment. Lust. Excitement. The realization of dreams. An incredible future.

I saw happy ever after. Until forever.

But that was then. Before everything happened. Before time, like a well-worn yet inevitable cliché, took its toll. Before my heart was broken. Before one of those closest friends betrayed me. Before my husband slept with another woman.

Before death.

Fifteen years ago, I walked up the aisle in white.

This time, I'm wearing black.

2
2001

When Shauna Met Colm…

If he had been ten minutes later we'd never have met.

The bar was getting too crowded and too loud, with the sound of smug, boorish after-work suits trying to out-do each other.

'Nailed six million, mate. The yen played a fucking blinder for me this week.'

'Not bad. Keep it up and you'll get to play with us in the big boy pool. My margin on pharmaceuticals this week is buying me a Porsche,' his buddy gloated, his repetitive nose-rubbing suggesting he'd been celebrating with pharmaceuticals of a different kind.

Their chronic wankery didn't detract from the fact that I loved this bar. The classic white colonial frontage sat on the bank of the Thames, supporting the huge wooden deck that overlooked the water and Richmond Bridge, only yards away to the left. Even on a chilly October evening, as we stood outside, getting jostled by the masses, there was something of a fifties romance about it.

We'd come here for celebration drinks with Vincent, a mate from college, who had decided to start up a corporate catering service on the other side of the city. He was now deep in conversation with a five foot ten Cindy Crawford lookalike who was eyeing him with such lust I expected her to unhinge her jaw and swallow him whole at any moment. Vincent had that effect on women. Except me. The dark-haired, chiselled jaw, brooding hunk thing wasn't my type so I found it amusing to watch as he… yep, there it was. Cindy reached up and kissed him, then he gave me a wave, blew me a kiss and the two of them disappeared out the door.

Not a bad idea. It was time to go home.

It had been a long week. My feet hurt. I'd had three hours sleep thanks to a delightfully wealthy Battersea housewife who'd booked me to prepare a banquet breakfast for a fundraiser, ignoring the fact that if they'd just gone for bacon butties the recipients of the charity would have been a few hundred pounds better off. Not that I was complaining. The wealthy housewife market had been a fantastic source of income in the two years since I'd launched the company. When I say 'company' I mean me. And a van. My only other assets were boundless optimism, enthusiasm, and a small but growing customer base, so I was thankful for the work, even if it did mean that the aroma of eggs Benedict and smoked salmon blinis had followed me around all day like a sinister yet appetizing stalker.

The following morning, I had a children's party for thirty twelve-year-olds in Balham and those chicken goujons weren't going to prepare themselves.

My bed was calling me until Lulu, in typical fashion, changed my plans.

'Shauna, I'll be five minutes. Cover for me if Dan arrives,' Lulu hissed, before punctuating the request with a kiss on the cheek that definitely constituted coercion, possibly even conspiracy, with an added twist of emotional blackmail.

Every guy in the bar watched her as she wiggled her way past them. Captivating. Mesmerizing. I was probably the only one who noticed that she was actually following a tall, gym-formed Australian she'd been subtly flirting with across the bar all night.

A mental image of my bed faded. In Lulu's world, five minutes could mean thirty, or longer. She'd once left me holding her drink while she popped out of a bar for a cigarette with a ski instructor, and called me the next day from Gstaad.

'Bloody outrageous!' I added to the list of descriptive terms for the Jessica Rabbit redhead who was heading to the back of the restaurant.

'Who's outrageous?' Rosie asked, breaking off from the conversation she'd been having for the last fifteen minutes with Paul, the mature student. This was the third time she'd invited him to join us for a drink, and there was a spark there, but he was a very measured, analytical academic who was studying geology, or psychology, or zoology, or one of the ologies, so the spark was taking a long time to ignite into anything more than deep discussions about… actually, I had no idea what they were talking about.

'Our friend,' I whispered, smiling as I gestured to the departing wiggle. 'Remind me to kill her at some point. I promise I'll make it painless.'

'I'd help dispose of the body but I'm a bit preoccupied,' she replied, making sure Paul was out of earshot. I hoped he was good enough for her.

If ever there was an illustration of how there was no equality or fairness in the distribution of confidence and self-assurance, my friends were it. Lulu killed at life, at fun, at demanding attention and getting it. She took risks, and she grabbed what she wanted. Rosie, on the other hand, the eternal people-pleaser, quirky, with a huge heart, lived in hope of love and adoration finding her .

The restaurant was filling up now, the noise level increasing as Toploader finished 'Dancing In The Moonlight' and handed over to Kylie who was, for some inexplicable reason, 'Spinning Around'.

'Bugger, there's Dan,' Rose whispered, urgently.

Of course it was. Because, hey, the Gods of Reckless Friends loved this kind of shit. I should have left already, made the escape sooner, before the devastatingly handsome boyfriend of my darling friend was strolling towards me, while aforementioned darling friend was outside, undoubtedly doing something immoral, possibly illegal, definitely wild, with a tattooed Australian. Instead, I was about to give a performance that would win me an Oscar for "Best Liar In A Friendship Situation."

'Hey girls,' he greeted us, with a kiss on each cheek. I'd always thought that Dan Channing was one of those enigmas, people who looked like they were something other than what they actually were. He looked like a square-jawed, impossibly handsome male model or an actor. Or at the very least, one of those firemen who strips naked with a strategically positioned hose in a Christmas calendar. But no, he was in sales of something I wasn't exactly sure about. Car parts? Mechanical supplies? Anyway, he managed a sales team that travelled around garages flogging some vital component of a vehicular nature.

'Where's Lulu?' was of course his first question.

'In the ladies,' I replied. 'She might be a while. Think the cystitis is playing up.'

A mischievous lie but I couldn't resist laying the seeds for a discussion that would make Lulu squirm. It was less than she deserved for putting me on the spot. My grin was quickly accompanied by a scarlet flush of the face, as he stepped to the side to reveal the curious gaze of green eyes of a tall, cute guy standing right behind him. 'Guys, this is Colm. Colm, meet Rosie, Paul, and the one that's talking about cystitis is Shauna.'

Ah, a resounding moment of dignity, one which Colm took in his stride by reaching out to shake my hand, saying, 'Please to meet you. And just to get it out of the way, I have never suffered from cystitis.'

Yes, those were the first words the love of my life ever spoke to me. It wasn't exactly Mills & Boon, but that didn't matter. I've no idea whether it was the soft Irish accent, the rapid humour, or the way he smiled the most open smile I'd ever seen, but right there and then I decided he was mine.

3
2015

Shauna and life before everything changed…

We were a few minutes away from Lulu and Dan's house and he still hadn't asked me. Maybe he wouldn't. I'd noticed that lately it was sometimes just taken for granted, a raised eyebrow of question in my direction when he opened the first beer. Invariably, I'd nod, almost imperceptibly, using fourteen-years-married coupledom telepathy to convey my agreement. Okay, you drink, and I'll drive home. I didn't mind, but sometimes it would be nice to be asked.

'You okay?' Colm asked, taking one hand off the wheel to put it on mine.

'I'm fine, just tired. Been a long week.'

A definite understatement, yet I bit my tongue, determined not to do that thing where I listed all the tasks I'd carried out that week and pointed out that he was probably oblivious to them all. You know the one… 'I worked six ten-hour days, took our daughter to school every day, ferried her to five after-school clubs, did two lots of baking for school functions, cleaned the house, organized flowers for your mother's birthday, booked the car in for a service, spent hours researching a holiday that meets the needs of everyone in the family, cleaned the house from top to bottom, organized a sitter for tonight, cooked a meal in advance and left it ready for the sitter and our daughter to eat later, then rushed upstairs and got ready in five minutes, throwing on the first decent thing I could find, and slapping on a quick make-up job in the car so YES, IT'S SUNDAY NIGHT

AND I AM BLOODY KNACKERED.'

Instead I just turned my attention back to staying awake while letting his touch soothe me out of 'harassed working mother and wife mode' and into me mode. Just Shauna. If I really tried, I might even summon up sociable Shauna, and enjoy our first night out in ages.

I felt myself responding to him, stroking my thumb against his palm, as I glanced at him and realized he looked tired too.

'I think it's time to have the chat again,' I told him amiably, as I leaned my head back against the cream leather headrest, a motion that took my ponytail to a whole new level of messiness. With a bit of luck it would at least camouflage the fact that highlights for my dark blonde hair were long overdue.

Colm nodded. 'The one where we say we have a crap work/life balance and we need to redress it?'

'Yep, that's the one.'

How often? Once a month? More? Probably as often as work allowed – and that was the problem. We'd slipped into 'work to live' instead of 'live to work'. We had to sort it out. Definitely. And we would. When we had a spare five minutes to breathe. I mentally added it to the To-Do list. Defrost fridge. Arrange new school uniforms. Address roots. Have life-defining conversation with husband.

We pulled into the drive and I grabbed the bottle of Prosecco and huge tub of eighties retro sweets – Lulu and Dan's respective favourites – then headed up the path. Lulu and Dan's home had a façade that belonged on a Christmas card. Left to them by Dan's grandparents, the four storey, redbrick Georgian house overlooking Richmond Green had the beautiful white panelled windows that were typical of the era. The stairs up to the front door were bordered by wrought iron, and ivy wound its way around the red gloss door. Lulu and Dan lived on the ground floor and basement, with the upper levels split into two more apartments, which they rented out to give them a healthy monthly income. Dan had been meticulous in retaining as many of the original features as possible, so it still had the original tile floors, high ceilings and ornate cornicing. It was gorgeous, which made Lulu's ongoing mission to persuade Dan to sell up and move to a modern, eye-wateringly expensive, high-tech shoebox down at the river so much more perplexing.

Exhaling, I slapped on a smile and shook off my fugue just

as the door was answered by a giggling Lulu.

'Come in, come in! Hey gorgeous, how are you?' That was directed at Colm, not me, but it did make me laugh. Lulu, the irrepressible flirt, had barely changed in personality or looks in the two decades I'd known her. Eternally wild and reckless, she still had the long flowing red hair, the ridiculously curvy shape, the wide eyes that were designed for mischief and her alabaster skin was almost unlined despite the fact that, let's face it, forty was on the horizon, ready to ambush us.

'I suppose you're not bad either,' she offered, when she prised herself away and hugged me next.

'I could kill you with one squeeze,' I told her in my best serial killer tone.

'Please do, it'll save me from Dan,' she countered. I was probably the only person who would pick it up, but it was there, the undertone of truth under the jocular barb. Oh God, not again.

'Hey, we're matching!' she observed, pointing to my black jumpsuit, with the crossover front, cinched waist, and mildly protruding shoulder pads, a style match to her red version of the same look. Gotta love cyclical fashion trends. If the eighties were wrong, I didn't want to be right.

'Jesus, we look like a Nolans tribute act,' I told her truthfully. 'If either of us could hold a tune, there could be a new career option here.'

'Fuck it, I need a new job. Make it happen and I'll mime,' she retorted. There it was again. Lulu had worked with Dan for the last six years, ever since he and Colm had gone out on their own and set up their management and training consultancy. In the early days, Lulu did the books, typed up the invoices and generally took care of everything that needed to happen to let Dan and Colm go out there and earn. That was then. Now the business was a bit more established, with a steady income, she'd taken the first opportunity to reduce her workload. With no mortgage and no kids, and a firm belief that there was more to life than slogging in an office during her prime years (her words, not mine), she cut back to a couple of days a week doing the paperwork and spent the others in a function she called 'networking and raising the company profile'. Others would call it 'shopping and doing lunch'. The reality was that it left Lulu with far too much time on her hands – a dangerous situation for someone with the attention span of a fairground fish. When it came to Lulu, too much time led to boredom, which led to a need for excitement, which led to trouble, usually for her either her bank balance or her marriage. Or both.

We headed through to the open-plan kitchen and dining area at the back of the house, which had been extended to add a lounge area too. It was the only room that was thoroughly modern, with its white walls, cream travertine floor and glass doors that spanned the whole of the back wall, letting the solar lights of the garden create little spheres of gold that looked like floating stars.

The others were already sitting round the dining table. Rosie was the first to welcome us. 'Hello lovelies,' she said, her beaming smile as wide as the large goblet of red wine she held aloft in greeting. I'd always thought Rosie was the personification of a Betty Boop cartoon, with her short black pixie cut, her huge blue eyes, and eyelashes that could sweep floors. Not much over five feet, she celebrated her curviness in fifties-style clothes that made her stand out for all the right reasons. Tonight she was in a white low-cut top, with red polka dots that matched the scarlet of her lips, with a coordinating scarf tied around her neck.

In my standard colour palate of funereal black, I suddenly felt resoundingly bland compared to my Technicolor friends. More stuff for my to-do list. Must wear colour. Must take longer than five minutes to apply make-up.

I did the rounds of hello's – Rosie first, then her boyfriend, Jack, a life coach who sat somewhere between hipster trendy and those guys who wore man buns and carried yoga mats. They'd met in Rosie's café and despite the fact that he could be a little studious and earnest, we were all hoping for Rosie's sake that this one was a keeper. Six months in, the easy vibe that flicked between them suggested that he could be. However, we'd been here before so we weren't buying hats just yet.

After hugging Dan, I slid into the empty seat next to him. Over at the marble island, Colm flipped open a bottle of beer. Ah, there it was, as predicted – the raised eyebrow of enquiry.

'Honey, what would you like to drink?' Colm asked.

'Vodka, straight.' I answered, and watched as a momentary flicker of surprise was replaced by a grin.

'Or maybe I'll just stick with water,' I said, smiling. In truth, I didn't really mind. Beth had ballet in the morning and a crowd of five-year-olds wasn't something I wanted to negotiate with a hangover.

Next to me, Dan immediately lifted a large jug from the centre of the table and poured iced water into the wine glass in front of me.

'You didn't bring Beth?' Rosie asked, with a hint of disappointment.

There were many things I adored about my friends, and one of them was that they treated Beth as a communal child, not a hindrance or an irritant to spoil their sophisticated chat. (Not that we ever actually had any sophisticated chat, but that was beside the point.) So many of these dinners ended with Rosie on the floor with Beth, doing a jigsaw or channelling Little Mix on the karaoke, the two of them laughing helplessly. Jack, whose sole experience with children extended to informing Kensington mothers that their family life was encroaching on their opportunities for meditation and growth, didn't ever give a hint that he minded his evening being interrupted by an impromptu game of rounders in the garden. Even Lulu and Dan, who had no plans to add to their family, loved having Beth around, mostly, I suspect, because they got all the fun but didn't have to deal with the responsibilities.

'Cinema and sleepover with one of her classmates,' I answered, before the bang of the oven door diverted our attention to Lulu. 'Something smells great,' I told her.

'Lasagne, garlic bread, salad,' she replied. 'I'm not winning any prizes for originality over here.'

I loved the fact that it clearly didn't bother her in the least. Tonight, like all our gatherings, was about chat and catching up. The food was way down the priority list, and given that I'd spent a long week cooking for other people, I was just happy that it wasn't me over there using a cheese grater to slice cucumber into a bowl of leaves.

Colm joined us at the table and immediately turned to Dan. 'How'd you get on with the Bracal Tech pitch prep today?'

'Hey, hey, hey! No work talk at the table please!' I interjected. It was the one overriding rule, set down about a year after the guys first went into business together. 'Lulu has salad tongs and she's not afraid to use them,' I added, gesturing to Lu, who stood one hand on hip, raised tongs in the other.

Whilst the others were laughing, it took me a moment to realize that, beside me, Dan was uncharacteristically straight faced.

His demeanour didn't change too much throughout dinner. On the surface, the conversations were as convivial as ever but I sensed an undertone. I decided not to question it. Nothing good could come of probing.

Instead, I had a couple of chunks of garlic bread and let the company of my closest friends shake off the lethargy that had been seeping into my bones earlier.

Colm looked like it was having the same effect on him. The dark shadows under his sea-green eyes were still there, but his crooked grin and the remains of a garden tan saved the day. Right now he was telling some story about a buff, Lycra-clad guy in the gym who'd hit on him the week before, and the others found it hugely amusing that he'd been so concerned about hurting the guy's feelings that he'd let him down gently then taken him for a coffee. That was Colm. The dark brown hair might now be flecked with grey, and there may be a few grooves on his face that weren't there fourteen years ago, but he was still the loveliest, funniest guy I'd ever known.

Next to me, it was obvious that Dan still wasn't feeling the same happy effects of the gathering. In my peripheral vision, I could see his jaw was clenched now, his knuckles pale as they squeezed his glass. A quick glance from Rosie told me she'd noticed too. It wasn't like him. Sure, he could be impatient and was sometimes easily riled, but in this environment, surrounded by friends, he would usually be chilled out and regaling us with stories of his week.

Rosie had obviously decided to steer the conversation to a topic that would cheer him up. 'So, guys,' she said breezily, directing the conversation at Lulu and Dan, "I was thinking, we should do something for your wedding anniversary next month.'

In a perfectly executed act of dark comic timing, Lulu, who was clearing the table, picked that moment to drop the salad bowl, laying a carpet of withered, leftover rocket across the floor tiles.

'Fuck,' she blurted.

I jumped up to help her clear it up, but ended up doing it

myself as she'd already moved back to the centre island and was decanting several inches of red wine into her glass, her sociable joviality suddenly replaced by a silence and barely supressed irritation.

'Let's wait and see if we make it that long, shall we?' Dan replied tersely, removing any semblance of forced joviality from the group.

Oh God. I suddenly wished Beth was here to divert us all with an innocent game. I spy with my little eye, something beginning with an excruciating silence and a murderous glare-off between Lu and Dan.

Eventually, Lulu was the first to blink.

'You really want to do this now?' she asked, her exasperation tempered with something that sounded like defiance. It was classic Lulu. When under attack, go on the offensive. When irritated, scared or just bloody fed up, steam right through those feelings with a forceful blend of rebellion and boldness, then hope for the best.

'Might as well,' Dan shrugged, meeting her gaze. 'Do you want to go phone your boyfriend first and ask his permission?'

Suddenly my weariness had returned and I could see it settling on Colm and Rosie too. Jack was too new to the group to understand the dynamics and history of this situation.

Actually, I was a founding member and struggled to understand it too. Throughout their entire relationship Lulu and Dan had adhered to their own set of rules and they were written in a language that no one else understood. However, even when they were in one of their frequent rocky patches, they generally kept things convivial when we were together as a group, so whatever was going on now was obviously serious. One thing I absolutely did know for sure, was that the worst thing we could do was intervene. I really wished I wasn't driving. A cocktail would have been much appreciated right about now.

Lulu took a gulp of wine then set it down on the worktop with the slow, definite movement of someone who was trying desperately to stay in control.

She barely skipped a beat before she spoke. 'I'm not sure of the number. Perhaps your girlfriend might look it up for me?'

'If it salves your conscience to think that, you go ahead,' Dan retorted, his voice low with anger. 'But we both know this one is on you. Why don't you tell our friends about the afternoons at the Richmond Hotel?'

'You bastard,' Lulu hissed. 'You had me followed?'

'Didn't need to. You used your credit card.'

'For personal training sessions! And I can't believe you checked my card. How low can you go?' Lulu retorted.

'Not as low as you it would seem. I checked. You're not a client there. So go on, come up with as many excuses and explanations as you want… or you could save us all the trouble and be honest. Admit it. You did it again. Who is it this time? The guy who works in the gym? The local estate agent? Or are you going for a variety and spreading it around?'

My previous resolve to stay out of it crumbled in the face of Dan's fury and the sure knowledge that I had to try to cut this off before it got out of control.

'Dan, don't,' I cautioned gently. I wasn't taking sides, but I couldn't let this escalate because I instinctively knew it wasn't heading to any kind of happy place. I had no clue as to Dan's culpability in whatever battle they were having, but I recognized Lulu's expression. It was the same combination of guilt and determination not to cry that she'd shown in every sticky moment in her life, especially when the problem was of her own doing.

Rosie was watching it all, mouth agape. Colm was rubbing his temples with his fingers. And Jack was studying the empty plate in front of him with intent fascination.

'Look, we should go,' Colm said. 'It's getting late and my head is banging.' He didn't add, 'And I can't do this again,' but I knew that was what he was thinking. How many times had we been through this? Three? Four?

Lulu and Dan had the most tempestuous relationship I'd ever known. Her relentless need to flirt and hedonistic tendencies had been a constant source of discord in the early days, but it was her need for thrills that would surely break them. There had been two affairs that I knew of on her side, one on Dan's. They were a couple who needed constant drama, constant excitement to survive. I couldn't comprehend it when they were dating and I couldn't comprehend it now, but I knew the best way to deal with it was to bail out until they'd sorted it out themselves. Taking sides would be a fatal friendship mistake, because when they made up – which they had done on every previous occasion – you didn't want to be the one who'd bad-mouthed the other.

Rosie was already on her feet. She was no pushover, but she hated confrontation, avoided disharmony at all costs and, like me, knew that this was all going to get messy and the best thing to do when Lulu was escalating to battle stations was to evacuate the area. 'I think so too. Jack?' She didn't need to ask twice. Jack was on his feet and already heading for the door, waving as he went. 'Er, thanks for dinner. It was lovely.'

I winced in pity for him. Clearly he was in the 99.9 per cent of the population who would find this deeply uncomfortable.

Dan sat staring morosely at the table, while Lulu followed us out, handing over our coats from the vintage stand at the door.

I slipped mine on. 'You okay? Why don't you come stay at our house tonight?' Guilty or innocent, at fault or not, I wanted to give her a way out of tonight's shitstorm.

She shook her head. 'Not tonight, but I might take you up on it tomorrow night. I'm leaving him, Shauna. I can't do this any more.'

Droplets of tears gathered on her lower lids and she blinked them away. To be honest, I didn't take her vow particularly seriously. The number of times she'd threatened to leave him over the last fifteen years stretched to double figures.

I gave her a hug. 'Let's talk about it tomorrow. If you change your mind about staying, come over any time during the night. Just use your key and crash in the spare room.'

Her squeeze was cutting off oxygen to my windpipe.

'Thanks babe.'

Beside me, Colm still hadn't said anything, and he remained silent as he headed out the door and back to the car. Only when I'd switched on the engine did he finally speak. I wished he hadn't.

'I don't know how you can stand by her when she does this. Come on, Shauna, she's a nightmare.'

'Hey, Dan did it too.'

'Only after he'd put up with her humiliating him for years. Not the same.'

'How isn't it? You can't judge her, Colm. You don't know the dynamics of their marriage and what makes it work. Or not,' I finished ruefully.

'Maybe not, but I know enough to be bloody sick of the way

she treats him. Dan works damn hard to give her a great life. Why can't that be enough for her?'

I sighed and leaned back against the headrest as I steered on to George Street, heading towards Richmond Bridge. Brilliant. My friend was allegedly having an affair, yet it was Colm and I who were now fighting.

It didn't help that Lu was the one person who could press his easy-going, live and let live buttons. In the years since that first night at the bar in Richmond Bridge, they'd developed a relationship that had almost a sibling dynamic. They loved each other, but Colm didn't shy away from calling her out or standing his ground with her. When she was wrong, he was direct and honest with her, even when she didn't want to hear it. When she was right, he'd be the first person to step in to help or back her up. She drove him crazy, yet two minutes later they'd be buckled in mutual hilarity at some inside joke.

But hilarity was in short supply tonight.

In my peripheral vision I could see that he had his eyes squeezed shut, and he was rubbing the bridge of his nose.

'Are you okay?' I asked, more to break the atmosphere of conflict than anything else. I wasn't big on confrontation avoidance, but tonight I was so damn tired I was making an exception.

'Thumping head,' he said, surprising me. I'd thought it was just an excuse to leave when he'd mentioned it earlier.

'I've got some paracetamol in my bag,' I told him, gesturing to the handbag in his footwell.

I thought he was leaning down towards it, but then realized that his hand had veered over towards the radio and was twisting the volume dial. It wasn't on, so his actions had no effect.

'What are you doing?' I asked, puzzled.

'Trying to switch this damn thing off.'

'Colm, it's not on.'

'So what's the noise?'

Was this a joke that I wasn't getting?

'What noise?'

He sat back in the seat. 'You can't hear that?'

'What?'

'It's like… I don't know. Radio interference. Like a crackling sound.'

I'd have blamed the alcohol, but I knew he'd only had a

couple of beers. And not only was the radio off, but there was no other noise to be heard. Had to be a joke.

'Okay, skip to the punchline.' I told him lightly, grateful that he wanted to add a bit of levity and salvage the mood of the night.

'Shauna, I swear I'm not kidding around. You honestly can't hear anything?'

'No.' I pulled up at a set of traffic lights on red, and turned to him to see a mask of confusion and uncertainty. This no longer felt like much of a joke.

'This is so weird,' he said quietly.

'Has it happened before?' I asked.

'Couple of times. Think it used to happen to my mum, though. Migraines.'

'Yeah, migraines can have all kinds of weird symptoms,' I said. 'Couple of pain killers and a good night's sleep and you'll be fine.'

The lights turned to green and I pulled away, trying to ignore the creeping unease that was infiltrating my nerve endings.

I should have paid attention.

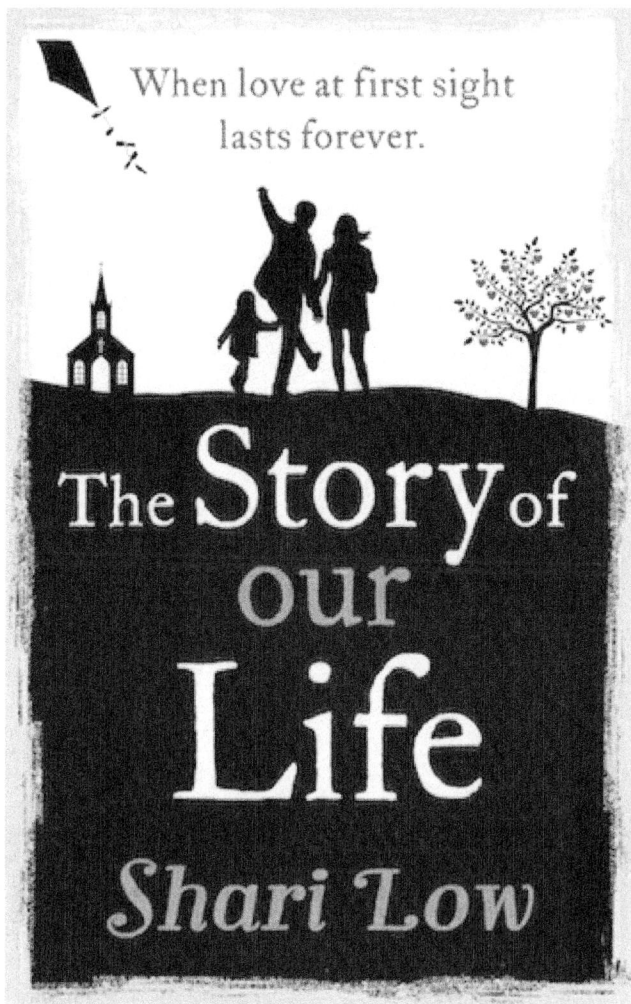

When love at first sight
lasts forever.

The Story of our Life

Shari Low

About Shari Low

SHARI LOWS lives in Glasgow and writes a weekly opinion column and Book Club page for a well known newspaper. She is married to a very laid-back guy and has two athletic teenage sons, who think she's fairly embarrassing, except when they need a lift.

Find me on Twitter
https://twitter.com/sharilow?lang=en-gb

Find me on Facebook
https://www.facebook.com/shari.low?fref=ts

Visit my website
http://www.sharilow.com

Also by Shari Low

When love at first sight
lasts forever.

The Story of
our
Life

Shari Low

Find out more
http://headofzeus.com/books/isbn/9781784978242

Visit Aria now
http://www.ariafiction.com

Become an Aria Addict

Aria is the new digital-first fiction imprint from Head of Zeus.

It's Aria's ambition to discover and publish tomorrow's superstars, targeting fiction addicts and readers keen to discover new and exciting authors.

Aria will publish a variety of genres under the commercial fiction umbrella such as women's fiction, crime, thrillers, historical fiction, saga and erotica.

So, whether you're a budding writer looking for a publisher or an avid reader looking for something to escape with – Aria will have something for you.

Get in touch: aria@headofzeus.com

Become an Aria Addict
http://www.ariafiction.com

Find us on Twitter
https://twitter.com/Aria_Fiction

Find us on Facebook
http://www.facebook.com/ariafiction

Find us on BookGrail
http://www.bookgrail.com/store/aria/

Addictive Fiction

First published in the UK in 2015 by Shari Low

This eBook edition first published in the UK in 2016 by Aria, an imprint of Head of Zeus
Ltd

9 7 5 3 1 2 4 6 8

A CIP catalogue record for this book is available from the British Library.

ISBN (E) 9781786692009

Aria
Clerkenwell House
45-47 Clerkenwell Green
London EC1R 0HT

www.ariafiction.com

One husband, one wife and two ex-wives
on the voyage of a lifetime

The Other Wives Club

Shari Low

Printed in Great Britain
by Amazon